P9-DHE-515

A0004500200035 9

SHAMROCK PUBLIC LIBRARY

7·16·12
8·16·12
9-7·12
4·16·16
7·16·16

Black Dawn

THE MORGANVILLE VAMPIRES NOVELS

Glass Houses

The Dead Girls' Dance

Midnight Alley

Feast of Fools

Lord of Misrule

Carpe Corpus

Fade Out

Kiss of Death

Ghost Town

Bite Club

Last Breath

Black Dawn

THE
MORGANVILLE
VAMPIRES

Black Dawn

Rachel Caine

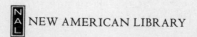
NEW AMERICAN LIBRARY

New American Library
Published by New American Library, a division of
Penguin Group (USA) Inc., 375 Hudson Street,
New York, New York 10014, USA
Penguin Group (Canada), 90 Eglinton Avenue East, Suite 700, Toronto,
Ontario M4P 2Y3, Canada (a division of Pearson Penguin Canada Inc.)
Penguin Books Ltd., 80 Strand, London WC2R 0RL, England
Penguin Ireland, 25 St. Stephen's Green, Dublin 2,
Ireland (a division of Penguin Books Ltd.)
Penguin Group (Australia), 250 Camberwell Road, Camberwell, Victoria 3124,
Australia (a division of Pearson Australia Group Pty. Ltd.)
Penguin Books India Pvt. Ltd., 11 Community Centre, Panchsheel Park,
New Delhi - 110 017, India
Penguin Group (NZ), 67 Apollo Drive, Rosedale, Auckland 0632,
New Zealand (a division of Pearson New Zealand Ltd.)
Penguin Books (South Africa) (Pty.) Ltd., 24 Sturdee Avenue,
Rosebank, Johannesburg 2196, South Africa

Penguin Books Ltd., Registered Offices:
80 Strand, London WC2R 0RL, England

First published by New American Library,
a division of Penguin Group (USA) Inc.

First Printing, May 2012
10 9 8 7 6 5 4 3 2 1

Copyright © Roxanne Longstreet Conrad, 2012
All rights reserved. No part of this book may be reproduced, scanned, or distributed in any printed or electronic form without permission. Please do not participate in or encourage piracy of copyrighted materials in
violation of the author's rights. Purchase only authorized editions.

 REGISTERED TRADEMARK—MARCA REGISTRADA

LIBRARY OF CONGRESS CATALOGING-IN-PUBLICATION DATA:

Caine, Rachel.
    Black dawn: the Morganville vampires/Rachel Caine.
    p. cm.
    ISBN 978-0-451-23671-5
    1. Vampires—Fiction. I. Title.
    PS3603.O557B53 2012
    813'.6—dc23   2011052660

Set in Centaur MT

Printed in the United States of America

PUBLISHER'S NOTE
This is a work of fiction. Names, characters, places, and incidents either are the product of the author's imagination or are used fictitiously, and any resemblance to actual persons, living or dead, business establish-
ments, events, or locales is entirely coincidental.
    The publisher does not have any control over and does not assume any responsibility for author or third-
party Web sites or their content.

This book is dedicated to my friend and writing mentor Patricia Anthony. Without her steady guidance, fantastic advice, and brilliant example, I would never have reached the place I am today. Thank you for pushing me, Pat. I hope you keep doing it for years and years to come.

It's also dedicated to the Bexter, and Ronan.
Welcome to the world, little man! Congrats, Mom!

ACKNOWLEDGMENTS

To my friends at the Tucson Marriott University Park, especially Kat, Sandy, and Echoe, who made the last part of my writing task so much easier with their enthusiastic support and cheering-on.

To the semi-official support group of the Smart Chicks, especially Kelley and Melissa. It's so nice to be part of such an amazing group of women, never mind amazing writers. Rock on, Smart Chicks.

To Joe Bonamassa, because, always.

And to Cat, who puts up with the endless long days and deadlines and crises, and does it so gracefully. Love you, sweetie. I promise someday there will be a day without word count. But not today.

AUTHOR'S NOTE

In previous books up through *Bite Club*, we've seen events in Morganville through the eyes of Claire Danvers; since then, we've been visiting other points of view, especially in *Last Breath*, the book immediately prior to this one.

We'll continue to see events this way in *Black Dawn* . . . so be sure to note who is narrating the scene for you at the beginning of each chapter. Because everyone has secrets . . .

. . . And some of them will be deadly.

Black Dawn

INTRODUCTION

Morganville, Texas, isn't like other towns. Oh, it's small, dusty, and ordinary in most ways, but the thing is, there are these . . . vampires. They own the town. They run it. And until now they've been the unquestioned ruling class.

But now this dry, landlocked town has been flooded by unnatural rains, and the rains have brought something else . . . the predators who've hunted the vampires almost to extinction.

The draug.

They hide in the water. They feed on vampires by preference, humans by necessity, and even in a desert town, there's no place safe now that they've arrived. Not for the vampires or for those few humans still standing beside them.

So hold on tight. Because Morganville's changed.

And it's a very dark new day.

CHAPTER ONE

CLAIRE

☽

It would have been better if he'd screamed.

Michael Glass didn't scream. Instead, he made a terrible keening noise in the back of his throat, arched his back, and began to flail violently inside his zipped-up sleeping bag. Fabric shredded under vampire strength, and insulation bulged out of the tears as he fought his way free, but even once the weight was off him he just kept . . . flailing.

Across the room, Claire Danvers bolted straight to her feet, tripped over her own sleeping bag, and managed to catch herself against a wall just before she hit the floor face-first. Her heart was slamming too fast against her ribs, and she had the sour, helpless taste of panic in her mouth.

They're here was the only coherent thought in her head. She had to be ready to fight, to run, to react, but all she could think of was how utterly scared she was just now. And how helpless.

There were things out there in the world, things that *vampires* feared, and now those things were here. She was only seconds out of a very light, fitful sleep, but she knew that the nightmares had followed her effortlessly right into the real world. *The draug.* They weren't vampires; they were something else, something that moved through water, formed out of it, dragged vampires down to a slow and awful death.

A week ago, she'd have laughed something like that off as a bad joke, but then she'd seen them come for Morganville, Texas. Come with the rains that rarely fell in this desert-locked, sunbaked town where the vampires had, finally, made their last stand.

Today she woke up with the blind and panicked knowledge that no matter how bad the world was with vampires in it, a world that held the draug was *vastly* worse. They'd come to Morganville, infiltrated stealthily, built their numbers until they were ready to fight . . . until they could sing their awful song that somehow, impossibly, was also beautiful and irresistible. To humans as well as to vamps.

The strongest of Morganville's vampires had gone up against it, and scored a few hits . . . but not without cost. Amelie, the ice-queen ruler of the town, had been bitten; without her, it was all going to get worse, fast.

Michael was still thrashing and making that terrible *sound*, and it came to Claire gradually that instead of cowering here while her brain caught up, she should go to him. Help him.

And then the lights brightened from dim to dazzling in the big carpeted room, and she saw her boyfriend, Shane Collins, standing in the doorway, looking first at her, then over at Michael, who was still desperately struggling against . . . nothing.

Against his nightmare.

Claire pulled in a deep breath, shut her eyes for a second, then made the OK sign to Shane; he nodded back and went to their friend's side. Michael was tangled up in the shredded remains of his sleeping bag, still flailing and, as far as Claire could tell, still dead asleep. Shane crouched down and, after a brief hesitation, reached out and put his hand on Michael's shoulder.

Michael came awake instantly—vampire speed. In one blurred second he was sitting up, one hand wrapped around Shane's wrist, eyes open and blazing red, fangs down and catching the light on razor-sharp points and edges.

Shane didn't move, though he might have rocked back on his heels just a little. That was better than Claire could have done; she'd have fallen backward at the very least, and Michael would probably have broken her wrist—not intentionally, but *sorry* didn't matter much when it came to shattered bones.

"Easy," Shane said in a low, calm voice. "Easy, man—you're safe. You're safe now. It's over. Nobody's going to hurt you here."

Michael froze. The red died down to embers in his eyes, and when he blinked it was gone, replaced by cool blue. He looked pale, but that was normal for him now. Claire saw his throat work as he swallowed, and then he shakily pulled in a breath and let go of Shane's wrist. "God," he whispered, and shook his head. "Sorry, man."

"No drama," Shane said. "Bad one, right?"

Michael didn't respond to that immediately. He was staring off in the middle distance. She didn't need to wonder what his nightmare had been about. . . . It would have been about being trapped in the Morganville Civic Pool, anchored to the bottom under that murky, poisoned water . . . being fed upon by the draug. Drained slowly, and alive, by creatures that found vampires as delicious as candy. Creatures that were, right now, invading and taking everything they could. Including every juicy vampire snack, straight to the bottom of whatever pool of filthy water they were hiding in.

There were, Claire realized, still tiny red marks all over Michael's skin, like pinpricks . . . fading, but not quite gone. He was healing slower than usual—or he'd been hurt far more seriously than it had seemed. "Yeah," he finally said. "I was dreaming I was still in the pool, and . . ." He didn't go on, but he didn't need to; Claire had been there, seen it. Shane had not only seen but *felt* it— he'd dived in to save lives. Vampire lives, but lives all the same. The draug had attacked him, too, and his skin had the reddish tint of broken capillaries to prove it.

Claire had a vivid, flashback-quality vision of the pool . . . that insanely creepy underwater garden of trapped vampires, tied down, stunned and helpless as the draug sucked away their strength and life. It had been one of the worst, most horrifying things she'd ever seen, and it had also outraged her on a very deep, primal level. *Nobody* deserved that. *Nobody.*

"It was real bad." Shane nodded in agreement with Michael. "And I wasn't in there nearly as long. You hang in there, Mikey." He reached out again and squeezed Michael's shoulder briefly, then rose to a standing position. "You feel the need to scream like a girl, let it out, dude. No judging."

Michael groaned and rubbed his hand over his face. "Screw you, Shane. Why do I keep you around, anyway?"

"Hey, you need somebody to keep you humble, rock star. Always have."

Claire smiled then, because Michael was starting to sound like his old self again. Shane could always do that, to any of them—a flip remark, a casual insult, and it was all okay again. Normal life.

Even when nothing at all was normal. Nothing.

Now that her panic was receding, she wondered what time it was—the room gave no real hint of whether it was day or night. They had evacuated to the Elders' Council building, which—like most vampire buildings—didn't much favor windows. What it *did* have was plenty of sleeping bags, a few rollaway beds, and lots of empty space; the vampires, apparently, were all about disaster planning, which didn't surprise her at all, really. They'd had thousands of years in which to learn how to anticipate trouble and what to have together to meet (or avoid) it.

Right now, she, Michael, and Shane were the only ones sleeping in the room, which could have held at least thirty without feeling crowded.

There was no sign of their fourth housemate, Michael's girlfriend, Eve. Her sleeping bag, which had been near Michael's, was kicked off to the side.

"Shane," Claire said, her fear getting another kick start. "Eve's missing."

"Yeah, I know. She's up," he said, "organizing coffee, believe it or not. You can take the barista out of the shop, but . . ."

That was, again, a tremendous feeling of relief. Shane made a profession of taking care of himself (and everybody else). Michael was a vampire, with all the fun advantages that came along with that in terms of self-defense. Claire was small, and not exactly a bodybuilder, but she defended herself pretty well . . . at least in being smart, careful, and having all the friends she could manage on her side.

Eve was . . . Well, Eve liked to live on the edge, but she wasn't exactly Buffy reincarnated. And in some ways her hard edges made her the most fragile of all of them. So Claire tended to worry at times like these. A lot.

"Coffee?" Michael asked, still rubbing his head. His hair should have looked crazy, but he was one of those people who had a natural immunity to bed-head; his blond hair just fell exactly the way it should, in careless surfer-style curls. Claire averted her eyes when he threw the sleeping bag back and reached for his shirt, because although he was always good to look at, he was seriously spoken for, and besides, Shane was standing right there.

Shane.

It came back to her in a dizzy rush, how he'd stopped her on the way into this place, in the faint dawn light. *"I want you to promise me one thing. Promise me you'll marry me. Not now. Someday."*

And she had promised, even if it was just their private little secret. She felt that shivery, fragile, butterfly-flutter feeling in her chest again. It was a fierce ball of light, a tangle of joy and terror and excitement and, most of all, love.

Shane looked back at her with an intense, warm focus that made her suddenly feel like the only person in the world. She watched him walk toward her with a diffuse glow of pleasure. Michael was hot, no denying that, but Shane just . . . melted her. It was everything about him—his strength, his intensity, the off-center smile, the hunger in his eyes. There was something rare and fragile at the center of all that armor, and she felt lucky and privileged that he allowed her to see it.

"You doing all right?" Shane asked her, and she looked up at him. His dark gaze had turned serious, and it saw . . . too much. She couldn't hide how scared she was, not from him, but he was the last one to think it was a sign of weakness. He smiled a little and rested his forehead against hers for a second. "Yeah. You're doing just fine, tough girl."

She shoved the fear back, took a deep breath, and nodded. "Damn right." She ran her fingers through her tangled shoulder-length auburn hair—unlike Michael's, hers had suffered from a night on the hard pillows—and looked down at her T-shirt and jeans. At least they didn't wrinkle much . . . or if they did, it didn't much matter. They were clean, even if they weren't her own. It turned out there was a storehouse of clothing in the Elders' Council building basement, neatly packed in boxes, labeled with sizes. Some of it dated back to the Victorian age . . . hoop skirts and corsets and hats stowed carefully away in scented paper and cedar chests.

Claire wasn't sure she really wanted to know where all that clothing had come from, but she had her sinking suspicions. Sure, the older clothes looked like things the vampires themselves might have saved, but there were a lot of newer, more current styles that didn't seem to fit that explanation. Claire couldn't see Amelie, for instance, wearing a Train concert shirt, so she was trying hard not to think about whether they'd been scavenged from . . . other sources. Victim-y sources.

"Did you have nightmares, too?" she asked Shane. His arm tightened around her, just for a moment.

"Nothing I can't handle. I'm kind of an expert at this whole bad dreams thing, anyway," he said. And oh God, he really was. Claire knew only a little of how many bad things he'd seen, but even that was enough to spark a lifetime's worth of therapy. "Still, yesterday was dire, and that's not a word I bust out, generally. Maybe it'll look better this morning."

"Is it morning?" Claire peered at her watch.

"That depends on your definition. It's after noon, so I guess technically not really. We slept for about five hours, I suppose. Or you did. Eve bounced about an hour ago, and I got up because . . ." He shook his head. "Hell. This place creeps me out. I can't sleep too well here."

"It creeps you out more than what's happening out *there?*"

"Valid point," he said. Because the world out there—Morganville, anyway—was no longer the semi-safe place it had been just a few days ago. Sure, there had been vampires in charge of the town. Sure, they'd been predatory and kind of evil—a cross between old-school royalty and the Mafia—but at least they'd lived by rules. It hadn't been so much about ethics and morals as about practicality. . . . If they wanted to have a thriving blood supply, they couldn't just randomly kill people *all* the time.

Though the hunting licenses were alarming.

But now . . . now the vampires were in the food chain. They'd always been careful about human threats, but that wasn't the issue, not anymore. The *real* vampire enemy had finally shown its incredibly disturbing face: the draug. All that Claire knew about them was that they lived in water and they could call vampires (and humans) with their singing, right to their deaths. For humans, it was fairly quick . . . but not for vampires. Vampires trapped at the bottom of that cold pool could live and live and live until the draug had drained every bit of energy from them.

Live, and *know* it was happening. Eaten alive.

The draug were the one thing vampires feared, really and truly. Humans they treated with casual contempt, but their response to the draug had been immediate mass evacuation, except for the few who'd chosen to stay and try to save the vampires already being consumed.

They'd *all* tried—vampires and humans, working together. Even the rebellious human townies, who *hated* vamps, had taken a drive-by run at the draug. It had been a heart-stopping military operation of a battle, the most intense experience of Claire's life, and she still couldn't quite believe she'd survived it . . . or that *anyone* had.

Even with all that effort, they'd saved only three vampires from the mildewed, abandoned pool—Michael, the elegant (and probably deadly) Naomi, and the very *definitely* deadly Oliver. Then things had gone from terrible to awful, and they'd had to leave everyone else.

Except Amelie. They'd saved Amelie, the Founder of Morganville . . . sort of. And Claire was trying not to think about that, either.

"Hey," Shane said, and nudged her. "Coffee, remember? Eve'll be all sad, emo Goth face if you don't drink some."

Again, Shane was the practical one, and Claire had to smile because he was completely right. No one needed sad, emo Goth Eve today. Especially Eve. "I could kill for a cup of coffee. If there's, you know, cream. And sugar."

"Yes and yes."

"And chocolate?"

"Don't push it."

Michael had, by this time, gotten up and joined them. He still looked pale—paler than usual—and there was something a little wild in his eyes, as if he was afraid that he was still in the pool. Drowning.

Claire took his hand. As always, it felt a little cooler than room temperature, but not *cold* . . . living flesh, but running on a much lower setting. Almost as tall as Shane, he looked down at her and smiled the rock-star smile that made all the girls melt in their shoes. She, however, was immune. Almost. She only melted a little, secretly. "What?" he asked her, and she shook her head.

"Nothing," she said. "You're not alone, Michael. We won't let that happen again. I promise."

The smile disappeared, and he studied her with a strange kind of intensity, almost as if he was seeing her for the first time. Or seeing something new in her. "I know," he said. "Hey, remember when I almost didn't let you into the house that first day you came?"

She'd shown up on his doorstep desperate, bruised, scared, and way too young to be facing Morganville. He'd been right to have his doubts. "Yep."

"Well, I was dead wrong," he said. "Maybe I never said that out loud before, but I mean it, Claire. All that's happened since . . . We wouldn't have made it. Not me, not Shane, not Eve. Not without you."

"It's not me," Claire said, startled. "It's not! It's *us*, that's all. We're just better together. We . . . take care of each other."

He nodded again, but didn't have a chance to reply because Shane reached in, took Claire's hand from Michael's, and said—not seriously, thank God—"Stop vamping up my girl, man. She needs coffee."

"Don't we all," Michael said, and smacked Shane on the shoulder hard enough to make him stagger. "*Vamping up your girl?* Dude. That's low."

"Digging for China," Shane agreed, straight-faced. "Come on."

Claire could follow the smell of brewing caffeine all the way to Eve like a trail of dropped coffee beans. It gave the sterile, funereal, windowless Elders' Council building a weirdly homey feel, despite the chilly marble walls and the thick, muffling carpets.

The hallway opened into a wider circular area—the hub in the wheel—that held a huge round table in the center, which was normally adorned by an equally large fresh floral arrangement . . . adding to the funeral home vibe. But that had been pushed to the side, and a giant, shiny coffee dispenser had been put in its place, along with neat little bowls of sugar, spoons, napkins, cups, and saucers. Even cream and milk pitchers.

It was surreal to Claire, as if she'd stepped out of a nightmare and into a fancy hotel without any transition. And there, emerging from another door that must have led to some sort of kitchen, came Eve, with a tray in her hands, which she slid onto the other side of the big table.

Claire stared, because although it was Eve, it didn't really *look* like her. No Goth makeup. Her hair was down, loose around her face and falling in soft black waves; even without her rice-powder coverage, her skin was creamy pale, but it looked movie-star beautiful. Natural-look Eve was *stunning*, even wearing borrowed clothes . . . though she'd found a retro fifties black pouf-skirted dress that really suited her perfectly.

She had a red scarf tied jauntily around her neck to hide the bites and bruises that Michael—starving and crazy from being dragged out of the pool—had inflicted on her.

She, and this setup, all looked a little *too* perfect. Shane and Michael exchanged a look, and Claire knew they were communicating the same thought.

Eve gave them a bright smile and said, "Good morning, campers! Coffee?"

"Hey," Michael said, in such a soft and tentative voice that Claire felt her stomach clench. "You should be resting." He reached for her, and Eve flinched. *Flinched*. Like he'd tried to hit her. His hand dropped to his side, and Claire couldn't look at his face. "Eve—"

She spoke in a rush, running right over the moment. "We have hot coffee, all the good stuff—sorry I couldn't get mocha up and running, but this place has a serious espresso deficiency . . . oh, and the croissants are hot out of the oven, have one."

"You baked?" Shane's eyebrows threatened to levitate right off his face.

"They were in one of those pop-open rolls, moron. Even I can bake those." Eve's smile wasn't so much bright, Claire thought, as it was totally breakable. "I don't think anybody ever used the kitchen in here, but at least it was stocked up. There's even fresh butter and milk. Wonder who thought of that?"

"Eve," Michael said again, and finally she looked directly at him. She didn't say anything at all, only picked up a cup, filled it with hot, dark coffee, and handed it to him. He took it as he stared at her, then sipped—not as if he really wanted it, but as if it was something he was doing to please her. "Eve, can we just—"

"No, we can't," she said. "Not right now." And then she turned and walked back to the kitchen, stiff-armed the door, and let it swing shut behind her.

The three of them stood there, only the sound of the door creaking on its hinges breaking the silence, until Shane cleared his throat, reached for a cup, and poured. "So," he said. "Aside from the five-hundred-pound gorilla in the room that we're not going to talk about, does anyone around here have half a plan on how we're going to live through the day?"

"Don't ask me," Michael said. "I just got up." The words sounded normal, but not the tone. It was as odd as Eve's had been, and just as strained. He put his coffee back down on the table, hesitated, then took a croissant and walked away, back toward the room where they'd been. Shane started to follow, but Claire grabbed his arm.

"Don't," she said. "Nothing we can do about this, is there? Let him alone to think."

"It wasn't his fault."

"I know. So does she. But she got hurt, and he did it, and that's going to take time, all right?" She held Shane's gaze this time, and he was the first one to look away. He'd hurt her before—more emotionally than anything else. And *he* hadn't been in his right head-place, either. But sometimes explanations just didn't matter as much as time. It was a hard lesson to learn, for both of them; it was going to be even harder for Michael and Eve.

God, sometimes growing up *sucked.*

"Okay, so it's down to us, then. We still need a plan," he said. He drank coffee, and she fixed hers up and gulped down a hot, bitter, wonderful mouthful. Next was the croissant, still steaming inside from the oven, and it was heaven in bread form, melting in her mouth. "No, strike that. We need SEAL Team Six, but I'll settle for a half-ass plan right now."

She swallowed. "Don't talk with your mouth full."

He did exactly what any boy—no, *man*—his age would do: he showed her a mouthful of mashed croissant, which was gross, then drank more coffee and showed her again. Gone.

"That is disgusting, and I will never kiss you again."

"Yes, you will," he said, and proved it by pressing his lips to hers. She wanted to squirm away, just to prove the point, but *God,* she loved kissing him, loved that his mouth was so warm and sweet and bitter with coffee . . . loved being so close to him now, teetering on the edge of the end of . . . everything. "See?"

"It wasn't bad," she said, and kissed him again. "But you really need to work on your technique."

"Liar. My technique is awesome. Want me to prove it?" Before she could protest, his lips touched hers, and he was right about the proof. She slipped her hands under the loose hem of his shirt, fingers gliding lightly over the tensing muscles of his stomach, up to the hard, flat planes of his chest. His skin was like warm velvet, but underneath, he was iron, and it took her breath away.

Or so she thought. But when he skinned her Train T-shirt up and fitted his strong hands around her waist, pulling her to him even closer, she gasped against his mouth, moaned a little, and just . . . melted.

The hot, golden moment was sliced cleanly by a cold voice saying, "I can bear a great many things, but *this* is not one of them. Not now."

Claire jumped back from Shane, guilty as a shoplifter. It was, unmistakably, Oliver's voice, and it was coming from behind her. She hated round rooms. Too many ways people could come at you, especially sneaky, cranky vampires. She turned and faced him as he stalked toward them—no, toward the coffee, since he brushed them aside and filled a cup. She'd never seen him drinking it, but of course, he would; he owned the local coffee shop, Common Grounds. Or at least he had when there was still a Morganville that was alive and kicking.

Common Grounds, like everything else in town, was closed.

Oliver had always taken pains to present himself as human . . . maybe because he, of all the vampires, seemed the furthest from it. He was cold, unfeeling, acerbic, and sarcastic, and that was on a *good* day. It clashed with his friendly-aging-hippie vibe of tie-dyed shirts and jeans that he wore at the coffee shop, but he'd dispensed with all that now. He'd donned clothing that suited him, in a sinister and scary way—black pants, a black coat that must have been about a hundred years old, and a white shirt with a ruby pin where a tie would usually have gone. Except for a top hat, he could have stepped out of the turn of the last century. These, Claire felt, were his *own* clothes. No hand-me-downs for Oliver.

"I guess it's pretty useless to say good morning," Shane said.

"Especially as it's neither morning nor good, yes," Oliver replied, just shy of a snap. "Don't try to banter with me, Collins. I am far from in the mood." Claire could make out the red mottling on his pale skin, like Michael's, a souvenir of his time spent in that drowning pool. She wondered how he'd slept, *if* he'd slept. "As to plans, yes, I have one, and yes, it is under way."

"Mind if we ask——?"

"Yes, of course I *mind*," Oliver said, and this time it *was* a snap. There was a gleam of red in his eyes. He looked tired, Claire thought, and there was a flicker of something almost human in him. "If you wish to be of use, go find Theo Goldman and bring him to me. Now."

"Theo?" Claire was startled, because she'd heard that Theo had gone missing, like many other vampires in Morganville ... and she'd assumed he'd been in the pool. A casualty, when Amelie had resorted to throwing silver into it to kill the draug and their trapped victims with them. "Is he here?"

"If he was *here*, I wouldn't ask you to *find* him, would I?"

Shane was doing that thing now, his posture getting stiff with challenge; he didn't like it when Oliver treated her—or any of them—like idiots. But especially her. The last thing any of them needed today was to fight each other. They were working together—more or less—and that was how it had to be to survive this. So Claire put a hand on Shane's arm to hold him back and said, in a very reasonable tone, "Do you have any idea where to look for him?"

Oliver's hand trembled, just slightly, but enough to make the cup rattle lightly on the saucer. He, like Michael, still felt weak. That should have made Claire feel reassured, because he was usually so intimidating, but instead it made her feel extra vulnerable. "No," he said. "I do not. But I require his presence, so you will find him." He let a second pass and then added, without looking at either of them, "For the sake of the Founder."

For Amelie. And there was a very slight change in his tone when he said it, something that almost seemed . . . softer.

"She's worse," Claire said. Oliver turned and walked away without responding, so she looked at Shane. "She's getting worse, right?"

"Probably. Who knows with him?" But Shane had the same thought she did; she knew it. If Amelie died, they were at Oliver's mercy. Not a good thing at all. He was a general, and when he fought wars, he liked them bloody—on both sides. "Maybe we should have left town when we had the chance. Just picked up and run for it."

"And left Michael behind? And Eve? She wouldn't have left him. You know that."

He didn't answer. She knew that Shane wasn't someone who ran away, but he couldn't help thinking about it—Morganville's version of living a rich fantasy life. After a moment, he shrugged and said, "Too late now anyway. Where do you think we should start, if we're supposed to track down Goldman?"

"No use looking at the hospital. It's closed," Claire said. "They moved all the patients out in ambulances and buses. And there are way too many places he *could* be. It's not that big a town, but big enough to hide one vampire. He sent his family away, you know." Theo, unlike most vamps Claire knew, actually *had* a family, and cared about them; it was very like him to be sure they were clear of the trouble, then stay behind himself.

"Can't go close to the hospital anyway," Shane said. "The whole area's a no-go zone; the singing starts when you come anywhere close."

The singing of the draug was not just eerie; it was deeply dangerous. It got hold of you, made you forget . . . and made you vulnerable to them. Claire nodded. "We'd better stay away from any water, too."

"Toilets? Please say you don't mean toilets, because this is rapidly turning into no fun at all. I mean, I like peeing on a wall as much as the next drunken redneck, but——"

"Chemical toilets," she said. "Amelie had them brought over from some construction company. And *please* tell me you don't pee on walls."

"*Moi?*" He put his hand over his heart and did his best wounded-innocent look. "You must be thinking of some other uncouth jackass. Which makes me jealous, by the way."

She would have played along with that, but the idea of the tap water made her suddenly realize that she was drinking the coffee in the cup in her hand, and she resisted a sudden violent urge to gag. "Uh, the coffee . . . ?"

"Made with the finest bottled water," Eve said. She was back, and she'd brought cookies this time. "And these are sliced off a roll, so don't think I've gone all Martha Stewart, Shane. The vamps stocked up on bottled water some time ago. I'm guessing it's their version of survivalist training, if they've been worried about the draug for so long. All those plastic containers may be bad for the environment, but they're really good for us right now. So . . . you're looking for Theo?"

"So says Oliver," Shane said, and stuffed a whole cookie in his mouth.

"Trust me, I work for Mr. Scary Guy in Charge, and you do *not* want to disappoint the man, even if you're just pulling espresso shots. Especially not now. Besides, having Theo here would be a nice antidote to all this"——Eve gestured at the marble, carpet, dim lighting——"gloom. Theo's cheerful, at least."

He was, mostly. Although Claire thought that like all vampires she'd ever met——except Michael, and his grandfather Sam——Theo was essentially concerned about his own survival first. Once you accepted that was how vamps saw the world, it was a whole lot easier to understand what they would do, and why. Morganville, for instance. It was pragmatic, having this isolated town, which they controlled for their own safety. They were cruel sometimes, but they saw it as self-defense. . . . Let the humans get the upper hand, and the vampires feared they'd be killed, sooner or later. Claire didn't agree with it, but she understood it.

Theo was . . . less pragmatic about that than most. Thankfully. And Eve was right. He would have a calming effect here, *if* he wasn't floating somewhere in a pool of water, being eaten alive.

Claire shuddered.

"Want to come with?" Shane asked, licking melted chocolate from his lips. Which was a little bit mesmerizing, actually. Claire had a dizzying impulse to help him with that, but she shook it off. *Time and place, Claire, time and place . . .*

"She can't come with us," Claire said, as Eve opened her mouth to agree. "Come on, Eve, you lost about two pints of blood last night. You're not strong enough yet and you know it. You need rest."

Eve's mouth closed without making a comment, but she gave Claire a steady, cool look, as if she'd let her down by even mentioning what had happened. Although it was pretty clear that Eve, and Michael, were thinking a lot about it.

"Right," Shane said in the silence. "That was awkward. Eve, you stay and . . . bake or something."

"The hell I will," she snapped back, way too tense. "If you don't want me with you, maybe I'll just grab a couple of Amelie's boys and take them shopping for more weapons. We need to arm up, and we need to do it fast. That okay with you, or should I change into my pearls and an apron and die like a good girl?"

Shane held up his hands in surrender and took a step back.

"I—have nothing to say." *Smart boy*, Claire thought. "But *if* you go out, you take more than a couple of vampires with you, Eve. I mean it. Take Michael."

"Well, you know what they say: less is more," Eve said. She didn't even comment on the Michael issue, but there was a stubborn, wounded look to her, and she didn't meet Shane's eyes.

"Right now, more is more, and much more is much better. You can't dick around with these . . . things. You know that, right?"

"Oh, I know," Eve said. Her dark eyes were filled with shadows, windows in a haunted house. "I was just thinking that it would be a good idea to start making weapons stockpiles around town. If we start a running fight, we need to be able to get to weapons when we need them."

That was . . . a very good idea, Claire realized, and she nodded without speaking. Shane even looked respectfully impressed, which was an odd look for him; he wasn't impressed by much. "Get silver," he said. "If you can, knock over a jewelry store and get all the silver chains. We can break them up into pieces. Makes a good grenade." Silver hurt, or killed, both vampires and draug. Shane sounded practical about it, but then, he'd spent his high school years being dragged around with his vampire-hating father. He probably knew more about killing vampires than anyone else in town . . . except the vampires themselves, of course. "It's about the only thing that *does* work on these bastards. Talk to Myrnin about making more shotgun shells, too."

Myrnin being Claire's vampire boss—if a relationship that crazy could be called employer-employee, anyway. She was Igor to his Frankenstein. He had an underground lab and everything, which she'd managed to make a whole lot less creepy during her tenure with him . . . but not less chaotic. Myrnin was walking chaos, and a lot of the time that was fun.

Sometimes, not so much.

Eve rolled her eyes, now almost back to the old carefree girl Claire knew. "Yeah, Collins, I wouldn't have thought of Myrnin *ever*. Of course I'll talk to him. He's the only one who had his crap together before we went out the first time."

"Hey!"

"Present company excepted, supposedly."

"Better," Shane said, and surprised her by suddenly enfolding her in a fierce hug. "Stay safe, all right?"

"Safe." Eve agreed, and then held him at arm's length, studying him with thoughtful intensity. "Huh. You don't hug, you know. Unless you get hugged first."

"I don't?"

"Nope. Never ever."

Shane shrugged. "Guess everybody changes once in a while."

All of a sudden Claire was struck by how different they *all* were now. Eve had grown steadier, more thoughtful. Shane had taken his aggression in hand and was starting to understand it, channel it. Even open up a little more than he had.

Michael . . . Michael's changes were more unsettling, less easy to appreciate, but he'd *definitely* changed. He was struggling not to change even more—not to drift further away from his lost human life.

As for Claire herself, she couldn't say. She couldn't tell, really. . . . She supposed she had more confidence, more courage, more insight, but it was hard to imagine herself from the outside like that. She just . . . was. More or less, she was still Claire.

Eve waved good-bye, hugged Claire hard—*that* was a typical Eve gesture—and headed toward the room where they'd left their stuff. Michael was in there. Claire hoped they could work out their . . . *Problems* didn't seem a strong enough word, and *issues* sounded too mundane. There wasn't really a word for what was going on between her best friends, other than *complicated*.

Claire grabbed coffee to go, wolfed down a couple of cookies— premixed or not, they were hot, melty, and delicious—and followed Shane down another hallway. It might be, she thought, the one Oliver had used, but this place was confusing. If there were signs, they were visible only to vampires. But Shane took a right down an identical hallway, then a left, and then they were in another round room, this one with a massive barred door at one spoke of the wheel. The door also had guards . . . lots of them. *Amelie's personal detail*, Claire thought as she recognized some of them. They didn't look as spotlessly turned out as she was used to seeing. The dark tailored suits were gone, and so were the sunglasses. Instead, they wore clothing from the same archival stores that she and her friends had scavenged . . . and she supposed that what they'd chosen at least indicated what period in history they were most comfortable with.

The two guards at the door, for instance. The taller, thinner one with the light hazel eyes and close-cut blond hair . . . he was wearing a chunky black leather jacket with spikes and buckles, and skinny jeans. Very eighties. His friend with the sharply drawn cheekbones and narrow eyes had on the tightest polyester pants Claire had ever seen, and a square-cut jacket to match, with a tight buttoned shirt in a loud earth-toned pattern.

"It's like disco inferno up in here," Shane muttered, and she smothered a laugh. Not that it mattered; vampires could hear that, and if they wanted to take offense, they would. But the seventies addict just smiled a little, showing the tips of his fangs, and the eighties dude couldn't be bothered with that much response. There were more guards standing around the walls, still as statues. Most had chosen clothing that wasn't so . . . retro, but one was wearing what looked like a gangster suit from the Prohibition era. Claire half expected him to be toting a violin case with a machine gun in it, just like in the movies.

"No one goes into the armory," Disco Inferno said. He was apparently the spokesman for the door. "Go back, please."

"Order from Oliver," Claire said. "We're to find Theo Goldman."

"Yesterday," Shane put in helpfully. "And we'd like to not die. So. Armory it is."

"No one goes into the armory," the vampire repeated, sounding bored now and staring over the top of Shane's head, which was quite a trick even for a tall guy. "Not without authorization."

"Which they have," said a voice from behind the two of them. Claire turned quickly, which she tended to do now, when vampires talked behind her, and found that Amelie's pretty blond vampire "sister"—not by family but by vampire blood, although she didn't exactly get all of that relationship detail—Naomi was standing three feet behind them, having arrived in eerie silence. She smiled and bowed her head, just a little. She was still very formal, used to the manners beaten into her hundreds of years ago, but she at least was trying; it wasn't a full curtsy or anything, not that such would have been practical with the khaki cargo pants and work shirt she was wearing. "I myself have spoken with Oliver. I am to accompany these two and help them locate Dr. Goldman."

That held some weight. Disco Inferno and his eighties counterpart—Billy Idol?—did some heavy lifting on what looked like solid steel bars, plus a complicated lock, and finally swung the doors open for them. Naomi passed the two of them and looked over her shoulder with that same charming, though slightly awkward smile. "I hope that you do not mind me accompanying you," she said. She had a bit of an accent, antique and French, and Claire could see that it had an effect on men in general, even Shane, who was more than a little anti-vampire in any form.

"Nah," he said, "I'm good. Claire?"

"Fine," she said. She liked Naomi. She liked that the ancient vampire was trying so hard to be . . . modern. And she liked that Naomi wasn't, after all, attracted to Michael, as they'd all thought at first. "Uh, Naomi, do you know how to actually . . . fight?"

"But of course," she said, and led the way inside. They entered a big square room, which was—and this, Claire thought, was no real surprise—stacked floor to ceiling with racks of boxes. Vampire paranoia really *did* have no limits. Naomi stopped at the first one and opened the hinged top of it. There were shotguns inside. She removed one, broke it open, and snapped it shut again with a practiced flick of her wrist as she smiled. "All vampires can fight," she said. "I am less familiar with modern weapons, but blades do not work so well on the draug, as we found to our horror long ago."

"What else did you use, the last time you fought them?" Claire asked. Naomi was opening another box. This one contained swords, and she shook her head sadly and let the lid fall shut.

"Courage," she said. "Desperation. And a good deal of luck. Silver is the best charm we have, but it burns us as well. We've found nothing else that will hurt them but fire, which is dangerous enough for us, too. . . . Ah." She flipped back the lid on yet another box and lifted out something that looked big, clumsy, and complicated, with tanks and a hose. Definitely a Myrnin invention, judging by the brass ornamentation on it, but beneath that it looked sleek and industrial. "As you see."

"What is it?" Claire asked, frowning. It looked a little like one of those rocket jet packs that the science fiction movies loved so much.

"That," Shane said, taking it from Naomi's delicate hands, "is freaking *awesome*."

"Yeah, but what is it exactly?" Claire asked.

"Flamethrower," he said, and huffed with effort as he lifted it to his shoulders like a giant backpack. It had quick-release buckles that he did up around his chest and over his shoulders. "So this will work on the draug?"

"Yes," Naomi said. "But be very careful. The draug are not only hiding in water, they *are* liquid—and when you touch liquid with fire it becomes steam. *They* can survive in the steam, for a short time. If you breathe it in, they will kill you very quickly from within. Even the touch of them on skin in any form is dangerous, to humans or vampires."

Shane's enthusiasm for the flamethrower dimmed, but he didn't take it off. That, Claire thought, was because there was something incredibly macho about walking around with flammable weapons that she would never quite understand. If she'd tried it, it would have just made her totally aware of how non-flame-retardant she was. "Right," Shane said. "Keep it at a distance."

"And watch where you aim it, please," Naomi responded coolly. "I believe I speak also for young Claire in that. Fire is no great friend to humans in battle, either."

Claire rejected the crossbows that she found in the next container—silver-tipped, but they wouldn't do nearly enough damage. They'd just punch right through the draug, which had a body consistency somewhere between Jell-O and mud, except for the master draug, Magnus. *He* was plenty strong. Strong enough to snap necks, say—something Claire was horribly familiar with and tried hard not to think about. At all.

"What about fire arrows?" Claire asked. "Would they work?"

"Not very well. The draug's nature will douse small fires. Only something on the order of what Shane is carrying will truly damage them. Even, say, bottles of gasoline and fire—"

"We call those Molotov cocktails," Shane said helpfully. Mr. Mayhem.

Naomi gave him a blank look and continued. "These would not do much to slow them down. It would be as if you threw the bottle into water; most likely the flame would simply be extinguished. Perhaps there might be some effect, but I doubt this is a time when you would prefer to experiment. There's going to be little time to refine your techniques and tools in the heat of battle."

"Well, I liked Myrnin's shotgun shells," Claire offered. "Has he made—"

"More? Yeah. Found it," Shane called, leaning over another open crate. He fished out a handful of shells and held them up.

"Are you sure those aren't just regular . . ."

Shane silently flipped one to her. On the casing was drawn, in black marker, the alchemical symbol for silver. Definitely Myrnin, because only he would think to write a warning that nobody but the two of them could possibly read. "How do *you* know what this means?"

Shane looked faintly injured. "I make it my business to know everything about silver. And I saw your notes. I study up on everything when it comes to your boss, anyway." There was a flicker of jealousy about that, but she didn't have time, or energy, to consider it very much. Not even whether she liked it.

"There must be hundreds of shells in there," Claire said wonderingly, as she leaned over the crate. Her hair, growing longer now, brushed over her face, and she impatiently pushed it back. It needed a wash, and that made her yearn for a shower, but cold bottled-water rinses were all she could look forward to for a while. "I thought he used everything he had during the battle last night."

"He's worked straight through," Naomi said. "Shut away in a room down the hall. He summoned guards to bring these here only an hour ago. I understand he has commandeered others to make these cartridges as well."

When Myrnin worked that feverishly, it meant one of two things: he was desperately afraid, or he was in a severely manic phase. Or both. Neither was good. When he was afraid, Myrnin was very unpredictable. When he was manic, he was inevitably going to crash, hard, and there was no time for that now.

As if she'd read Claire's thoughts, Naomi said, "He does need looking after, but it can wait until we find Theo."

"Amelie's that bad?" Shane asked.

"Yes. She is that bad, I'm afraid. If I still had a heart, it would ache for her, my brave and foolish sister. She should never have come after us. The law is the law. Those caught by draug are already dead. Rescuing us put all others at risk."

Claire stopped loading shotgun shells into her messenger bag to stare. "She saved *you*. And Michael. And Oliver."

"It doesn't matter who she saved. The point is that she allowed herself, our *queen*, to be put at risk for others, and that is foolish, and emotional. The time of Elizabeth in armor is long over. Queens have ever ruled far from the battles."

"News flash, lady. There are no queens anymore," Shane said. He loaded shells in a shotgun and snapped it shut, then searched for a place to strap it on that didn't interfere with the flame-thrower. "No queens, no kings, no emperors. Not in America. Only CEOs. Same thing, but not so many crowns."

"Vampires will always have rulers," Naomi said. "It is the order of things." She said it like the sky was blue, a plain and obvious fact. Shane shrugged and gave Claire a look; she shrugged back. Vamp politics were *so* not their business. "Come. We must find the doctor."

Shane shook his head. "He's the only one you have?"

"No," Naomi said, "but he is the best, and the only one we have who has moved somewhat beyond medieval techniques of bleeding and cupping." She handed Claire a shotgun and gave her a doubtful look. "You can shoot?"

Claire nodded as she loaded the cartridges. "Shane taught me." Not that it was easy for someone her size; a shotgun packed a hard kick to the shoulder, and she'd always come away from practice bruised and aching. Naomi was even more frail, but Claire was willing to bet that it would be nothing for her.

Shane settled his flamethrower more comfortably on his shoulders. "Ladies? After you."

"Rude," Claire said.

"I was being polite!"

"Not when you have a flamethrower."

CHAPTER TWO

MICHAEL

I miss my guitar.
That sounded stupid in my head, and it probably *was* stupid, but my fingers ached to be holding the weight of it. Music always stilled the noise inside me, made everything seem orderly, logical, not so out of control and terrifying. From the first time I'd picked up an instrument I'd realized that those sounds that other people made, *famous* people . . . those could be mine, mine to control, mine to use to speak without words. And that had been more than magic.

It had been survival.

Now, without my guitar, I felt naked, alone, out of control. But it would be deeply risky to go back to the house to retrieve anything, much less something everybody would see as nonessential. Maybe I could get to the music store where I taught lessons; that was farther uptown, away from where the draug were holed up. Didn't matter if it was closed. A vampire didn't have to seriously worry about things like locked doors and steel screens over windows, and entry restrictions didn't apply to stores.

I still couldn't quite reconcile that. I was a *vampire.*

I know, it wasn't a revelation, exactly. . . . I had been a vampire for a while now, and before that, I'd been half vampire, half ghost, trapped in my house, put on hold between life and death. But until today, I hadn't felt so . . . wrong. So alien.

So not myself.

Naomi, who had taken more interest in me than the others, had warned me this would happen, that I'd start to feel distance between me and the humanity I'd once had; she'd warned me that living as I did, trying to still *be* what I'd been, would start to hurt me, and hurt the people I cared about.

And she'd been right. I'd proven that, hadn't I? I'd lost control. I'd *bitten Eve.*

I'd almost killed her.

The shirt they'd given me to wear, to replace the one soaked with foul water and wet with Eve's blood . . . the shirt itched. It felt wrong. I ripped it off over my head and threw it on the floor as I paced. When I looked down, my skin was too white, the veins too blue. I looked like living marble, and I felt as cold as that, too.

And inside, I was shaking. My whole world was shaking. It wasn't just the draug, though we all were afraid of them. . . . I was afraid of *me*, of what I was, what I was capable of doing to the people I supposedly loved.

Love. Did I even really know what that meant now? Had I ever really known? What the hell was I doing? What was I thinking, risking her life every time I was around her? I'd thought I had it all under control, handled, *fixed*, and then . . . then all my illusions of being in charge of the monster broke.

I paced, and tried not to think about how *good* that had felt. I hadn't realized how on guard, how tense, how desperately tight my control had been until I'd been forced to let go.

Something went very still inside me, and I paused in my rambling, because Eve was coming.

I heard her walking toward me in the hall, despite the thick carpets; I could smell Eve's skin, the individual and soft perfume of her.

The door opened and closed behind me. Now I could smell the peach-scented shampoo she'd used, and the soap, and the salty hot blood beneath all of that.

I didn't turn around.

"Where's your shirt?" she asked me.

"It itches," I said. "Doesn't matter. I'm not cold." But I was. Room temperature, except when her skin warmed me up. Cold as the dead. "I'm going to go look for something else."

I turned then, but Eve was blocking my path to the door. My heart didn't beat anymore—not often, anyway—but it still felt like a stab straight into it when I looked at her directly. She was standing there, fearless, chin up, with a white bandage on her neck and a scarf trying to disguise the damage I'd done. That was Eve, all over—hurt, and hiding it. The Goth look had always been armor against her terror of the vampires. The retro polka-dot dress, the shoes, all of it was just another form of armor now. Some kind of shield to hold between the real girl and the world.

And me.

"That's it?" she asked me. "Your shirt itches, and you're going to get another one? That's what you're going with in this conversation, here."

I couldn't look her in the eye. Instead, I sat down on a camp bed and sleeping bag—not mine; mine was a shredded pile of fluff. I fiddled with the shirt in my hands, and pulled it over my head again. It wasn't the clothing that was the problem, anyway. It was me that itched all over, remembering . . . remembering what it had felt like to utterly surrender myself to hunger. I hadn't stopped myself. I *wouldn't* have stopped myself. Drinking her blood had been . . . bliss. Heaven. As close as I would ever come to it, now.

I'd thought I understood what being a vampire was all about, until that moment of sheer, red pleasure when I'd grabbed Eve and mindlessly *fed*. It felt like the floor had broken open under me and all my assumptions, and now I was in free fall, grabbing for a life that was moving away from me at light speed.

If it hadn't been for Claire somehow—using the strength of desperation, I guessed—pulling me off just long enough for some sanity to return, I'd have killed the woman I loved.

The woman standing in front of me right now, waiting for my answer.

"I can't do this," I said. The words felt dull gray in my mouth, like a mouthful of lead, and they landed just as heavily on her. I wasn't watching her face—I couldn't—but I had a vivid mental picture of the suffering in her eyes. And the anger. "Let it alone, Eve."

"You mean, let *you* alone," she said, and crouched down, perfectly balanced on those ridiculous prim retro heels, to stare me in the face. Her eyes were big and dark and, yes, they were haunted and full of pain, pain I had caused, was causing her now. "Michael, it wasn't your fault, but you hurt me, and we have to talk about this before it gets . . . inside us. You know what I mean, don't you?"

I did. And it was already inside us. Inside me, anyway, eating away like acid, burning and sizzling and toxic. "Talk about it," I repeated. "You want to *talk* about it."

She nodded.

"You want to talk about how I grabbed you and threw you down and took something very personal from you while you screamed and tried to fight me off," I said. "How someone else had to stop me, because I was acting like an animal."

She wasn't a fool, my Eve; she knew what I was saying, and she paled almost to the same color she would have had in her Goth makeup. "Michael, you didn't *rape* me."

"That's exactly what I did," I said. "You know what Shane calls it? Fang rape."

"Shane's got no idea what he's talking about." The words lacked some force, though, and Eve sounded more than a little shaken. "You just—you weren't in control, Michael."

"So that's a valid excuse now for me, when it isn't for any other guy out there who hurts someone?" I wanted to touch her, but I honestly didn't dare. She opened her mouth, but nothing came out, and finally she just closed it. Her eyes filmed over with tears, but she blinked them away. "It's not an excuse and you know it. It can't be, if we're supposed to be together."

"You were hurt. You weren't in your right mind. That matters, Michael."

I reached out and put my hand on her shoulder—vampire speed, not trying to slow it down. We both felt the wrench as she tried to pull away, before she got control of her instinctive reaction.

It proved my point, and she knew it.

"Eve, you flinch when I touch you," I said. "You pull back. You remember what it was like to have me hurting you, holding you down, not knowing if I was ever going to stop or if I was going to kill you when I was done. Of *course* it matters. It matters to us both."

"I——" The words died in her mouth before she could speak them and she just stared at me. Because of course I was right. I'd seen it, and she knew that.

"Doesn't matter whether it was my fault or not, whether I was in my right mind or just a sick bastard who got off on it," I said. "I'm a vampire, Eve. And this is what we do. We take people's blood. Sometimes they offer it up, and that's nice, that's really convenient, but sometimes we just take what we want. The fact that it's instinct doesn't excuse it. It all comes out the same in the end: with you getting hurt, maybe killed, even though I love you. Just like they tried to tell us from the beginning. We're a tragedy waiting to happen."

"No!" She lunged forward and tried to put her arms around my neck, but I'm a vampire; grabbing me isn't that easy when I don't want to be grabbed. I moved back just enough and before she could register the fact that I'd done it, I was holding her forearms in my hands. Tightly. She flinched and I felt it shiver all the way through her body, but she didn't try to pull away. "Michael, *no*, don't do this. I just need time, that's all. It just happened *last night*. Give me a little space to deal with it and I'll be . . ."

"Fine?" I let my eyes go slowly red. I let my fangs come down. "Really. You're going to be fine with me, like this."

Now she *did* pull back. Hard. And I didn't let her go. Her strength was nothing compared to mine, not here, where I had leverage. "You're trying to scare me, and it's *not going to work!*"

I let go of one of her arms and used a fingernail to cut the scarf away from her neck. The spots of blood on the pale square of bandage made something in me growl, deep inside, and even though I loathed that beast I also knew I couldn't keep it caged up forever.

That was why Morganville had hunting licenses, and allowed vampires to hunt on a carefully regulated basis. The beast was why Amelie allowed some measure of violence in Morganville—because without it, we turned toxic. As I'd turned toxic on Eve.

"Stop," she said. Her voice didn't sound so strong now. "Damn it, you jackass, *stop it!*"

"Isn't that what you told me last night?" I asked her, and I shook her, hard. "Isn't it? Did I stop, Eve? Did I?"

She twisted free and slapped me across the face. It didn't hurt, but the explosion of sudden warmth on my skin from hers made me blink. I let go of her other arm. She rocked back and then, all of a sudden, something stabbed me. Not in the heart, but off to the side, and the sensation of it sliding in was cold and horrible and yet also burning.

Silver.

I looked down. There was a small silver knife buried in my right side to the hilt. The skin was starting to smolder and burn around it.

Eve was breathing hard now, and there were tears rolling down her face, but she looked tough all the same. Unyielding.

"I *can* stop you," she said. "I can *always* stop you if I have to, Michael, damn you. I could have put that in your heart because you weren't ready for it, because you'll always be vulnerable to me even if you don't want to be. So we're even. Because I'll always be that way to you, too. That's called *trust*. It's called *love*." She grabbed the knife and pulled it swiftly out, and I choked and collapsed sideways on the sleeping bag. *God*, it hurt. Badly. I shuddered and writhed as the silver's influence continued to punish me, but it wasn't a fatal wound—not even close. She'd picked her spot, and the duration of the blow, very well. And in a weird way, I loved the pain. I needed it.

I deserved it.

"You hear me, Michael? Don't even try to think you're the only badass in this room. I will *not* let you do that to me again, ever, so you can stop obsessing about how damn powerful you are and how weak I am. *I am not weak.* Screw you for even thinking it. Get over yourself, your vampire angst, and your power trip."

She pushed up to her feet, staring at me for a moment, then walked away with the silver knife glinting in her hand.

I pulled in just enough breath to gasp, in genuine surprise, "Is it crazy right now to say I love you?"

She didn't even pause. "Given that I just stabbed you? Seems a little weird, yeah."

"I do," I said, and put my head down again. "God, Eve. I do so much it's killing me. I just don't want it to kill you, too."

I watched her walk away, slow and steady steps, a woman totally in control of herself and what she was feeling.

I just didn't know what that was, but I was afraid . . . afraid that it wasn't love anymore.

I collapsed on my back and closed my eyes, and tried to heal.

CHAPTER THREE

CLAIRE

☽

The unfamiliar weight of the shotgun made Claire feel awkward. She'd fired guns, but she'd never *carried* them around, not like they were a normal, everyday kind of thing. Like a book bag, for instance. She deeply missed her book bag. It had symbolized everything important in her life, and suddenly being a poster child for the National Rifle Association ... didn't.

Around her waist she had added a belt Shane had dug up in the back of the armory—it held small sealed bottles on hooks that she could pull free easily. Silver nitrate. Very dangerous to vampires, and draug. She was now about as loaded down with advantages as she could be.

And she felt incredibly clumsy and awkward, but that fell away as the big, scary vampire guards manning the main entry door of the Elders' Council building slid it open and she, Shane, and Naomi stepped outside.

It was midafternoon, but it was gray and raining. That had felt wrong enough when all this had started, with overcast skies and rain, because it almost never rained in Morganville, and when it did it was a violent burst that cleared the same afternoon. This had gone on for days . . . and it had brought the draug with it. Until they were gone, Claire thought, Morganville would never see the sun again.

Naomi glowed in the wan light like some kind of angel—the wrong kind, but still beautiful. She nodded to Claire and Shane and surveyed the world that they could see from the steps.

It looked . . . quiet. So terribly quiet. Stretching out in front of the Elders' Council building—a big, Romanesque temple of a place, with stairs like Niagara Falls of marble—was the green of Founder's Square, with its trees and ponds and footpaths and antique lighting that had come on to fight the gloom. Genuine gas lighting, the kind that hissed very softly, like snakes in the garden. In the center of the green was a wide, clear space with a raised platform. That was where they held town meetings, and where—not so very long ago—there had been a cage to hold humans who dared to attempt to kill vampires. Sometimes they were punished just by being caged. Sometimes, if the vampire actually died, the punishment was a whole lot worse.

But the cage was gone now. That was one thing Claire could be proud of, at least. . . . She'd gotten Amelie to get rid of it. Managed to secure some basic rights for the human population, but those were not exactly popular, or consistently honored.

She tore her gaze away from Founder's Square and its bad memories, and looked over Morganville itself. Not a huge place. From this vantage point she could see the gates of Texas Prairie

University, her school. It blazed with lights, still, like a beacon; when she squinted, she thought she could see that the gates were all closed. "They shouldn't still be here," she said to Naomi. "The students."

"They aren't," Naomi said. "They've been evacuated, every one of them. Amelie could ill afford to explain a disaster of this magnitude; they are hard-pressed to cover the normal attrition rates."

Attrition. That was what vampires called it. Claire called it murder. "What did she tell them?"

"Nothing. The dean made an address and said that deep cuts in the state budget required them to cut the semester short. All students have been granted excellent marks and will receive free admission to all courses at the beginning of next term. Then they announced an emergency evacuation based upon a chemical spill to drive off the faculty and the workers."

"That's going to bring a lot of attention to this place," Shane said, scanning the horizon. "Last thing Morganville wants."

Naomi shrugged. "It is the best we can manage now. Not that it will matter, when this is done; the university will never reopen, and of course we will leave this town. We must. Amelie will see the sense of it soon, or Oliver will. Morganville is dead to us."

She said it as if it was vampire religion or something—that running was the only option. And Claire guessed that given the long and terrible experience the vamps had with the draug, maybe that wasn't so unreasonable. But Amelie had decided to fight. Oliver would fight, too; he'd made it clear that he'd rather do that.

What scared Claire was that he might now be the only one, other than Myrnin, who really felt that way. The vampires weren't heartless, exactly, but they were extremely *focused.* If they stood a better chance of survival by sacrificing the humans who were supposedly under their Protection, well, they'd send flowers to the funerals and feel a little bit sad. *You can't trust them,* Claire reminded herself. *Not when it comes to something like the draug, something that can kill them. They'll always put themselves first.*

But how did that really match with how Myrnin acted? Or Amelie, or even Oliver, for that matter? Vampires were different, just like people were different. Some ran. Some didn't. Some fought. And some, a very few, actually cared.

"I can see our house," Shane said, and pointed. There it was, barely visible in the gloom—a white house no larger than a toy from this distance, distinguished from its neighbors by the Victorian shape. No lights burning there. No one to need them now. And there weren't many lamps burning out there anyway. A few candles or fireplaces flickered in windows, but the steady glow of electric power was out now, except here in the very heart of the city. Most people had left town already, when the vampires were distracted; Claire suspected Myrnin had lifted the barriers to allow them to do it undetected. The ones who remained were, like Shane, fighters. People who just didn't go when they got pushed. "I told you that the outside needed paint. Truth is, this whole town needs a damn makeover."

He was right. Morganville, soggy and dripping in the rain, did look horrible. The fierce desert sun wasn't much kinder to it, but at least it had looked . . . clean. Not like this, so utterly washed of life, muddy and disheartened.

"First on my list," Claire said, "after we try not to die. Paint the house."

"It's good to have goals," he said, and held out his hand. "Watch your step."

Naomi gave them a curious look, but jogged down the stairs, moving as lightly as a cat, and with the alien, fluid grace of one, too. Claire and Shane followed more carefully, since the rain had left the marble slippery. "How can we tell if the draug are here?" Shane called to Naomi as his boot splashed into a puddle on the first landing. She was also wearing boots, big ones that laced up to her knees.

"I expect you will know when you feel their bite," she said. "In small, isolated puddles they are not so dangerous, but the rain keeps coming. Avoid any running streams and large bodies of still water. We're lucky the ground soaks up so much, so fast. An advantage of the desert."

"That's why she built here," Claire said. The rain was already soaking through the warm hoodie she'd thrown on over the T-shirt. She was, she thought, going to spend a lot of the day feeling cold and damp. Naomi had worn a full raincoat, with hood, though Claire felt it was less protection against the cold than against the idea of the draug drizzling down on her bare skin. "Very little rain, and people leave you alone way out here. She could control things."

"It's an illusion, control," Naomi said. "You ought to understand that by now, young Claire. We are never in control of our destinies, even the strongest of us. All we can hope to do is not be too badly damaged by events."

God, she *did* sound like Amelie. Depressing. Maybe they really were related after all. Shane shrugged; he wasn't big on the concept of destiny anyway, and even less so when it was being preached by vampires.

At the bottom of the stairs, Shane said, "Which way?"

"We must keep to high ground," Naomi said. She stood where she was for a moment, looking out over the town, and then shook her head. She pulled a device from the pocket of her raincoat; it was, Claire realized, one of Myrnin's, with all the crazy hallmarks of something he'd cobbled together—gears, wires, tubes with strangely colored liquids. One was bubbling. Naomi adjusted a dial on the side and nodded as she returned it to her pocket. "The magic is working, at any rate."

"Magic?"

"It wipes away the call of the draug," she said.

"It's not magic; it's noise cancellation," Claire said. "It's just physics. You build one wave to cancel another, the way you build one to amplify another."

Naomi just looked at her with polite, empty interest, and then said, "As you say. It appears to be working, which is fortunate, or this would be a very short venture for me. And for you." That last was added as an afterthought.

"You said you had a way to find Theo," Shane said. "Time to bust it out, lady. I don't want to be out here when it gets dark. Well, darker."

Naomi reached in the other pocket of her raincoat and took out a sealed vial. It was half full of a red powder, and she popped the cap and added a dash of water from a flask before she recorked it and shook it to mix. The liquid turned the dark red of blood. She uncapped the vial again, put it to her lips, and drank.

"The hell?" Shane stared. "Seriously, you brought a snack?"

"It's Theo's bloodline," Naomi said. She grimaced and dropped the vial, then crushed it into tiny shards beneath her foot. "All the bloodlines have trace records in our libraries. It is so we can find them as we need. I could likely find him easily were he of Bishop's bloodline, but he is not, so I must rely on this. It tastes foul, dried so . . ." She stopped talking, stood in silence for a few seconds and then suddenly bent over and retched violently. Then she sat down on the lowest step, as if she couldn't find the strength to stand.

"This plan doesn't exactly fill me with confidence," Shane said to Claire. "Even with the cool flamethrower."

Naomi held up a shaking hand, palm out, to signal them to wait, but then the hand curled into a fist before it finally relaxed. She sat back and raised her face to the cold rain, looking . . . well, not *pale*, but almost *blue*. Her lips had taken on a light tint of cyan. She looked like she'd been carved out of cloudy ice.

"Different bloodlines," she whispered. "It is like different blood types to you."

"It makes you sick," Claire said, and got an erratic nod.

"How sick?" Shane asked. "Can you walk?"

"A moment," Naomi said. She sounded stronger already. "We must go before my bloodline destroys his within me, but the battle between them is . . . challenging. He comes of strong stock." She gave them a faded smile, and pushed to her feet; Claire was prepared to prop her up, but she didn't need it. "He is in that direction."

"That's . . . not so good," Shane said, because the way Naomi was pointing was toward the interdicted end of Morganville, the one the draug had slowly claimed as their stronghold. "Why would he be staying in there? Why not get out?"

"It's possible they have him," Naomi said, but then shook her head to correct herself. "No, I would feel that, through this link. He is alive, and in hiding. But it won't be easy to get to him, even now."

"Less talking," Claire said. "More walking. I mean it, we're not out here after dark, no matter what happens."

Naomi's eyebrows climbed higher. "Even if one of us must be left behind?"

"If one of us is," Shane said, hefting the flamethrower higher on his shoulders like a heavy backpack, "it's going to be you. No offense."

Naomi smiled, very prettily. "Oh, but it is very much taken."

Claire wasn't actually sure, looking at her, whether she meant it or not, but it was better to be safe with a vampire than really, really sorry. She nudged Shane sharply in ribs that weren't protected by the flamethrower straps.

"Sorry," Shane muttered. "I mean, we'll all come back or none of us. Of course. I'm sure you're thinking the same thing."

"Assuredly." That same sweet, impartial smile, and again, there was just no figuring out if she meant it or not. But it didn't matter, because they were in it now, together, and they needed to move.

Fast.

Leaving Founder's Square, with its safe little circle of lights still burning and its cordon of police and vampire guards . . . That was difficult. Not just because, deep down, Claire didn't want to go, but also because the guards wouldn't *let* them go. As in the Elders' Council building, everyone had been given strict orders, and Claire imagined they'd been along the lines of *Whatever you do, don't let those bastards in here, or let anybody else go out.* Naomi, though, wasn't taking no for an answer, and there were few human cops who were willing to stand up to a vampire with an attitude, and a gun.

"Nice," Shane said under his breath as she led them out into the street. The wreckage of cars and dropped weapons had been mostly cleared from that area—residue of the not-so-successful riot that humans had staged the night before against the vamps; it hadn't been effective, but it had definitely been enthusiastic. "Any idea of how far we have to go?"

"No," Naomi said, and furrowed her brow. "Why?"

"Just thinking that it might be better to go in a vehicle than on foot. For safety."

"You," Naomi said, "have a flamethrower, which is not of much use in the enclosed space of an automobile. Perhaps you might have considered that in your choice of weapons."

"Not a car. A pickup," he said without hesitation. "I get the back. Ladies in the front. Maximum speed, minimum exposure, plus a good firing platform for me and Claire, with the shotgun. Or you. Whichever."

Naomi cocked her head and looked at him in silence for a few seconds, then nodded. "Very well," she said. "Obtain one, if you please."

"I always knew hot-wiring skills would come in handy, other than getting me more frequent-flier jail points," Shane said. "Stay here." He jogged away, light and lithe even under the weight of the heavy equipment he was carrying, and Claire watched him go with a hungry little stab of anxiety. For all his easy comebacks, Shane was as vulnerable as any of them. Even Naomi, who was *also* watching her boyfriend with a thoughtful frown grooved between her brows.

"I was told Shane Collins was unreliable," she said, "but I see little sign of it now. I was also told he loathed my kind and would see us dead if he could. Yet he came with you to rescue us. Odd."

"People change," Claire said.

Naomi shrugged, and made it look like some exotic foreign gesture. "Assuredly," she said. "But mostly I find they change for the worse, not the better. In fact, some who once liked me have changed so much that they tried to burn me as a monster."

"Well, then you're even," Claire shot back, "because Amelie had Shane in a cage and was going to burn *him* for something he didn't even do. He's changed. For the better. And he didn't have to."

"Perhaps he has changed for you."

For some reason the whole idea of that just made Claire . . . angry. "No. *Not* for me. He's a good guy, deep down, and he wants to make things better. Same as me. So just—shut up about it." She was, she realized, short of sleep, tired, anxious, and scared, and Naomi's cool analysis of someone she loved made her unreasonably irritated.

Naomi said nothing, just gazed at her with placid, polite interest. There was a lot of frost inside her. She'd been nicer when there hadn't been lives at stake, Claire thought; now survival was a big and increasing concern for her, and it was testing the limits of her willingness to put up with disrespectful humans.

But she didn't snarl, glow red eyes, flash fangs, or otherwise try to make a vampiric comeback, so Claire had to be satisfied with that. They waited in silence for a few uncomfortable moments before the growing throb of an engine and a splash of headlights across the pavement signaled the arrival of a massive pickup truck that pulled to a stop neatly ahead of them. It idled slow and deep, and the bed of the thing was approximately the size of a blue whale. The interior of the cab could hold a soccer team. It even had a handy—though empty—gun rack in the back window.

The bumper sticker read: YOU CAN HAVE MY GUNS WHEN YOU PRY THEM FROM MY COLD, DEAD HANDS. Some joker—possibly the owner of the truck—had added UN before DEAD with a black marker. Claire cast a glance at Naomi, who was focused on the same words. There was an odd, vaguely amused smile on her lips that was not just a little creepy.

Shane leaned out the window of the truck and said, "God, I love rednecks. Who wants to drive this bad boy?"

"Not me," Claire immediately said, at the same time that Naomi said, "I do not know how."

Shane jumped down from the cab, paused, and stared at the

two of them with a blank expression. "Don't want to?" he asked Claire, and then swung his attention to Naomi, looking even more stunned. "Can't? Seriously, there's something wrong with the two of you."

"If by *wrong* you mean *sane*," Claire said. "That thing is like a tank, only a tank gets better gas mileage."

"This is your biggest concern right now? Gas mileage?"

"No, I don't think I can actually see over the dash! Who drives this thing? Bigfoot?"

"Rad," Shane said. "You know, Rad, who owns the mechanic shop and sells bikes? That guy. C'mon. I'll buy you a booster seat."

Claire gave him a doubtful look, but he pointed to the pale gray sky, at the brightest point. A silent reminder that the day wasn't getting any younger and their chances of finding Theo were dimming with the afternoon sun.

"Fine," she said. Shane had to boost her up to the chrome step, and then she climbed into the cab of the truck itself. There were eighteen wheelers that were lower to the ground, she was convinced. Naomi had no such issues; she made her entrance to the passenger side look graceful. Claire slotted her shotgun into the rack behind them, but Naomi kept hold of hers, eyes distant and watchful.

It turned out she could see over the dash, after all, though she had to pull the seat all the way forward to reach the pedals. Shane vaulted up into the open bed of the truck and slapped the side of the truck in a signal to go.

"Well," Claire muttered, "here goes nothing."

Literally.

She stalled the truck immediately, then leaned out the window to yell at Shane, "Who drives a *standard* transmission these days?"

"Manly men," he called back. "C'mon, Claire, you can do it!"

She could, but she just hated shifting. Too much to think

about, especially in their current, extremely complicated situation. No help for it, though; she gritted her teeth, adjusted the seat even closer, and got familiar, again, with the clutch. It was painful and humiliatingly awkward, but she managed. The truck leaped forward with a low, rumbling growl, and she thought, *We could probably pull down a building with this thing.* Worth noting, anyway.

Leaving the false circle of safety—false, because Claire knew it was just an illusion, sponsored by all those lights—still felt like a Very Bad Idea. She flipped on the headlights, on bright, even though it was still murky afternoon, and after a moment reached out and turned on the truck's heater as well. The hot, dry blast of air made her shiver in relief. She felt chilled to the bone, and slimy, even though she knew there *probably* hadn't been any draug in the raindrops that had soaked through her clothes.

What if there had been? How many of those contaminated raindrops does it take to make a whole draug? They knew next to nothing about these things, and lack of knowledge always bugged her. She glanced over at Naomi—or, actually, at the back of Naomi's head, because the vampire was turned to hold her shotgun out of the passenger window, watching for any sign of attack.

"Left," Naomi said in a flat voice. "Then straight ahead." She didn't sound like she was much better than she had been, back on the steps . . . coping, but not happy about it. Claire wondered how long it would take for her antibodies—if vampires had such things—to destroy the invading blood . . . and what would happen if a lot of foreign vampire blood was introduced, all at once. Her skin prickled, and it wasn't from the chill. *It might kill them. It would certainly go a long way toward knocking them down, fast.* She wondered how many humans knew that. It was good information, but it made her shudder to have it in her head. They didn't like having their vulnerabilities known.

Claire turned left at the dead stoplight, after a brief pause. Kind of stupid, really, because there wasn't any traffic to worry about. As far as she could tell, they were the only headlights moving in town. The rain had slacked off to a dully falling mist, and she kept the wipers working to clear the windshield. The steady *thump-thump-thump* had a soothing, normal kind of rhythm.

And then she heard something singing along with it.

At first she thought it was Naomi, unlikely as that was; it was a low hum of sound, elegant and just at the edge of her hearing. Then she thought it was the truck's radio, or maybe a CD playing, but turning the dial didn't bring up the sound.

She should have known it was the draug, but something kept her from remembering that. Instead, she found herself gradually turning the wheel toward the sound, hunting for it, trying to understand what that song was, a song she knew and loved and could *almost remember*. . . .

As she was gliding into a slow right-hand drift toward the infected part of town, a drift that would take them on a wide turn into a main street, Naomi suddenly reached out and grabbed the wheel in a bone white hand, wrenching it back the other way. Holding it there.

Claire stomped on the brakes, suddenly and violently aware, and glared at her. From the back of the pickup she heard a metallic clang as Shane's back hit the cab of the truck, and then an outraged, "Hey! *Flamethrower!*"

"I must adjust frequencies," Naomi said, and twisted knobs on the device she'd taken out of her pocket again; suddenly the faint singing faded into a blessed white-noise silence. "You need to be careful, Claire. If you hear them, then they hear you—sense you, at any rate. Magnus has a taste of you now. He's curious about your return. You don't want to be in his hands again."

Magnus. The head of the draug—their master, as Claire understood it. They all looked identical, but there was something about Magnus that was just more . . . there. A kind of density that pulled everyone around him into the dark.

In his hands again. She couldn't help but remember the cold, damp feeling of his hands around her neck, and a violent shiver seized her, as if her whole body wanted to throw off that memory. Deep, calming breaths, and then she nodded at Naomi. "I'm okay," she said. "I know what to listen for now."

"The point is *not* to listen," Naomi said, but she let go of the wheel. "I assume you may have read a classical text or two, in your education, or is that no longer done?"

Claire was a little bit ashamed to think that it wasn't, but she only said, "One or two."

"You remember Odysseus, lashed to the mast of his ship, screaming to be released while his men rowed on, with wax blocking their ears?"

She did. It had been one of the stories her dad liked, one he'd read to her and they'd discussed when she was still just a girl. All of the great Greek myths, especially the ones about Odysseus. She'd always liked him. He was clever and dangerous, and he didn't have any special godlike powers, either. Just his mind, and his will.

Listening to the sirens' singing had been his own test.

"Odysseus was rarely a fool," Naomi said, "but he was a fool then. That was the draug, singing to him, though the Greeks had a different name for them. He wanted to hear their song, and he did; he was lucky to avoid madness."

Shane slid the back window open and stuck his head in. "Ladies, I'm sure this a fascinating conversation about shoes or whatever, but could we maybe not sit out here like a big old piece of bait? And by *we* I mean mainly *me*."

He was right; this probably wasn't the best time to be holding a review of the classics. Claire cleared her throat and put the truck back into gear to ease it straight down the road, in the direction Naomi pointed.

It was odd to realize, looking at her, that Naomi wasn't much older than Claire herself; she must have been frozen at the age of eighteen or nineteen. Of course, at the time *she'd* been alive, eighteen or nineteen was old enough to rule kingdoms and have multiple children, so Naomi had been considered an adult long before she'd become a vampire. It all felt very new to Claire, still.

Naomi suddenly pointed to the right. The street name sign flashed briefly in the truck's headlights but Claire didn't really see it; everything in Morganville looked strange to her, shrouded by the falling rain and the lack of lights, and life. This was a residential street, and it looked completely deserted. Not even a candle flickering in a window, much less anyone in view outside.

Naomi's hand clenched into a fist, and Claire drifted the truck to the curb and stopped—gently this time, careful of throwing Shane around in the back. He opened the back window again and watched as the vampire pointed straight at one of the houses in the middle of the block. It was just like a hundred other houses in Morganville—plain wooden frame, built probably in the 1940s, small by modern standards. Its pale paint (no telling what color it had originally been, since the sun faded everything to a uniform gray) peeled liberally from the boards, and some of the trim was rotted and falling off. There was a rusted bicycle lying in the weed-tangled yard and a metal swing set that listed so far to the right any child that sat on it would probably be killed in the collapse.

Typical.

The name on the mailbox, written in messy black paint, was

SUMMERS, but there was nothing in the box itself when Shane snapped it open. He shrugged and closed it, then unshipped the flexible hose of the flamethrower from behind him.

Claire mouthed, *It's a wooden house!* She had to try three times before comprehension dawned on him. He looked disappointed, but he put the flammable fun away and got out his silver-loaded shotgun instead. Claire had hers hanging heavy in the crook of her arm, pointed so that if anything happened it would fire into the ground (and probably her foot, but that was better than the alternatives). *Hunters would be so disappointed in me,* she thought. She didn't even really know how to carry the thing safely.

The front door—plain wood, warped from wind and weather—was tightly closed. Naomi studied it for a moment, then kicked, and the entire door *and* the frame slammed inside to lie flat on the narrow hallway floor.

Even Shane looked respectfully impressed . . . until she stopped at the threshold. She made a sign shooing them inside, and Claire finally understood that there was still some kind of barrier in place on the house itself. Someone—someone human—was still in residence here, and without an invitation Naomi was barred from entry. The rules of ownership were complicated in Morganville— ancestral houses and bloodlines, current occupants, whether vampires lived inside, all factored in, but clearly this was a human house, with a human barrier that kept vampires out, period.

Great. Well, at least she'd opened the door.

Shane must have figured it out, too, because he nodded to Claire, winked, and stepped through the doorway, walking on the unsteady fallen door itself. There was a faint dust of plaster in the air, and Claire sneezed, but she didn't figure they were being particularly stealthy, what with the door blowing in and all. Shane was holding his shotgun easily, pointed at an angle toward the floor, so she imitated him. The wisdom of that became apparent when she tripped; she realized, with a cold start, that if she'd had the shotgun pointed up, near her face, she might have killed herself if she'd hit the trigger.

Shane checked the open room on the left, and she took the room on the right. Whoever had lived here, they hadn't been more concerned with the inside of the house than the outside; it needed work, badly. The ceiling was sagging as if there'd been a bad leak that was dissolving the plaster. In fact, she could see water drops running down the wall from the light fixture, which wouldn't have been safe if the power had been on. Even on its best days, though, this house would have earned a failing score on any of those how-clean-is-your-home reality shows; it smelled of mold and rotten food, and it felt icy cold. The furniture had the off-kilter look of a nightmare, and where there were children's toys, they too had the look of something a serial-killing tot would drag around.

This did not look like a place where one would find Theo Goldman. Not at all.

She and Shane searched the whole house, even the attic, which revealed a bucket-sized hole in the roof through which water continued to drip. No wonder the place was falling apart. But no sign of anyone, human or vampire.

"This place needs housekeeping," Shane said. "With my flamethrower." It was a sign of just how bad things were that *Shane* thought that.

She looked up to smile at him, and although she heard nothing, she saw the sudden dawning of shock and alarm in his face, and had just enough time to gasp and try to turn around before a heavy, sweaty, muscular arm went around her neck and jerked her off balance. Shane instantly put the shotgun up to a firing position, but then realized what he was doing and put it down again. He set it carefully on the table and held up both hands in an *I surrender* kind of position.

Claire squeaked for air, went up on her toes, and tried to ease the strain on her throat. She was having a terrifying, white-out flashback of the moment that Magnus had seized her, had twisted until she'd felt and heard the crackle-snap of bones. Her heart was as loud as a jackhammer in her chest, and her pulse was roaring so loudly it sounded like a hurricane in her ears. She couldn't see who held her, but it was a man's body, a man's hairy arm. She clawed at it, but her blunt nails weren't going to do much. *Think, Claire.* Shane had taught her some basic things to do. *Everyone is going to be bigger and stronger than you,* he'd said, without being critical about it. *You have to learn how to hit them in the weak spots.*

The first thing he'd taught her to do was *not* to do what she was doing now . . . standing on her tiptoes, cooperating with her captor. It was terrifying, but it was Shane's calm voice in her head now, telling her exactly what to do. *Turn your head toward his elbow. Tuck in your chin. Grab his left wrist in your right hand. Punch down and behind you with your left as you turn and pull. Then don't stop when he lets go, move in, go for his eyes and punch his throat. Never run. Never let him get his momentum again.*

She did it, calmly, turning and tucking and punching, and suddenly she was free, and she was facing her attacker. She registered him only as a foot taller than she was, and only for geometry's sake; faces and names didn't matter right now. Her right fist blurred as she went for a fast, hard punch to his exposed throat . . .

But she stopped, because Theo Goldman stepped in like a shadow and grabbed her fist before it landed.

Her attacker stumbled back, white-faced with shock; he clearly hadn't expected the little girl to come at him like that, and Claire felt a savage sense of victory before sanity kicked in again.

"Theo? What the *hell*?" He really hadn't changed, but then, vampires didn't, did they? He just looked . . . kind, with warm dark eyes and hair dusted with gray, and lines on his face that most vampires didn't have. Smile lines.

He did, however, look tired.

Shane hadn't moved, except to pick up the shotgun. His eyes were steady and cold on the man with Theo who'd grabbed her, and Claire sensed that he was waiting for the guy to make a second attempt.

The guy didn't move, though Claire, still trembling and adrenaline fueled, was almost sorry.

Theo shook his head, then walked to the table and picked up a curling piece of paper. He turned the sheet over and wrote swiftly, then held it up so they both could see through the dim light of the kitchen window. HAROLD IS A FRIEND. HE WAS TRYING TO PROTECT ME. APOLOGIES.

"Great," Claire muttered, but her fury was rapidly fading as she looked at Harold. He looked . . . wrong, a little. He seemed awkward, and fidgeted uncomfortably like a schoolkid caught cheating on a test. He also seemed scared.

In fact, despite his large size, he was acting *exactly* like a kid. Even down to the body language. There was something developmentally off about him, and he looked at Theo with miserable distress, as if he knew he'd done wrong but didn't know why.

Claire backed up next to Shane and pushed down on the barrel of his shotgun. He was getting the same impression, she saw, and he nodded and dropped his guard. Slightly.

Shane said, "We're here to get you," but Theo shook his head and pointed to his ears. There was something weird about the way they looked, but Claire honestly couldn't make out the details in the shadows. Shane claimed the pencil again and wrote, WE NEED TO GET OUT OF HERE. HAVE TRUCK. WILL TAKE YOU.

Theo read it, considered, and shook his head. He marked through it and responded, MUST TAKE HAROLD, TOO.

Shane shrugged, marked through it, and wrote (in smaller letters, since the paper was running out), BIG EFFING TRUCK.

Theo circled the word EFFING and raised his eyebrows. Claire made a frustrated noise in her throat, grabbed the pencil, and marked it out.

Ah, Theo mouthed, and smiled. *Good.*

The paper was scribbled over, thoroughly, so Claire hunted around in the wreckage of the kitchen, avoiding the piles of trash and *really* avoiding the sink full of dried, filthy dishes, until she found a balled-up flyer in the corner of the room. It was, she realized, the gym flyer, the one that had caused them so much trouble when Shane had taken up self-defense classes there a few months back. Another aftershock, but less terrifying.

She turned it over and wrote, AMELIE NEEDS YOU. URGENT. VERY SICK.

Theo's face went blank, and then tight with alarm. He scribbled back, WHAT HAPPENED?

DRAUG, she replied. BIT HER.

He mouthed something that she didn't understand, and covered his mouth in a gesture of real distress. Then he nodded decisively and turned to Harold. He made a series of fluid hand signs, and Harold brightened up and nodded.

It was right about then that Claire realized what was so weird about Theo's ears. There was something sticking out of them, sideways. Like . . .

Like *needles*. Really long needles. Knitting needles.

It was so shocking that she took a step back, eyes wide, and finally recovered enough to point to Theo and then gesture at his ears, urgently.

He smiled, but there was something dark in it. He took the paper back and wrote, MUST KEEP MY EARDRUMS PIERCED. OTHERWISE CANNOT RESIST THE CALL.

The vampire version of earplugs, she realized . . . literally disabling his ears. But it must have hurt horribly, keeping those needles in place to block healing. She felt faint imagining it.

Harold fell in docilely enough behind Theo, heading for the door; Claire, at Shane's hand wave, darted on ahead to make sure Harold didn't do anything crazy when he saw Naomi.

But Naomi was gone, and for a second Claire was terrified that something had happened to her. Then she heard the rumble of the truck's engine and saw that Naomi had started it up. She might not have driving experience, but she'd learned how to turn an ignition key, at least.

It all looked safe.

Claire put the gun at a ready position and stepped outside . . . just as a sudden gush of liquid rushed out of a rusty drainpipe at the corner of the porch, sending a thick wave across her path. At the same time, rain started falling faster, and harder, pounding like ball bearings on the fabric of her jacket and stinging her exposed skin.

She had just enough time to bring the shotgun up as the draug rose up out of the pool of water in front of her, clawed hands outstretched.

Still, even now, she couldn't say what it actually looked like . . . because the human brain tried and tried to fit it into some sense, some pattern, but failed utterly. There were eyes, horrible gelatinous eyes that somehow weren't eyes at all; there was a body that was not a body. What she registered as *clawed hands* was probably something else again, something worse, but it was the biggest warning her uncomprehending brain could screech at her, and she reacted instantly.

She pulled the trigger.

The impact slammed the stock of the shotgun against her shoulder so hard that she felt something crack—bone, probably— and a white snap of pain sizzled through her from neck to heels. At the same time, the roar of the shot hit her like a physical slap.

But that was nothing compared to what the silver did to the draug.

The pellets didn't have time to spread far, but tore a neat circular hole four inches across straight through the draug's—well, *head*, she supposed, was the nearest equivalent. There was a shriek of high-pitched agony, and then the draug collapsed in a wet *slap* as it lost all consistency and shape. Claire yelped as she leaped out of the way of the wave of its . . . corpse? If it was dead, which she couldn't assume. But it wasn't coming for her, and that was what was important.

There were more of them, rising out of hidden pools in the muddy yard, out of the drain in the street, condensing out of the rain itself.

Oh God. There were so *many*.

The sound of Shane firing as he pushed forward shocked her into pumping her shotgun, raising it, and firing again. It hurt, but she kept it up, racking and firing again and again. Shane was clearing a path to the truck, so she concentrated on keeping the draug away from the sides. She fell back behind Theo and Harold, keeping them as safe as she could.

The draug didn't really care about humans; too little gain for them, so it was Theo she really had to worry about. They'd kill to get to him, of course, but unless Harold got in the way he'd be all right . . . for now. She killed, or at least discorporated, at least five draug before they reached the truck.

Theo didn't get in. He stood aside, calm as ice water, as Harold scrambled up first. Claire and Shane took up positions on either side of him, firing to keep the draug away, and even though her ears were ringing and her heart racing, Claire could hear another shotgun going off. Naomi was keeping them away from her side of the truck as she waited.

Finally Theo jumped up and into the bed of the truck, and Shane followed last.

Now he tossed the shotgun to Theo, unhooked the nozzle of the flamethrower, and hit the ignition button.

Claire gasped and dived for the driver's side of the truck. Naomi let fly with one last blast at a draug ten feet away, then slid over, and Claire climbed in. Had she thought the truck was too tall before? She didn't even remember jumping up this time.

The dim afternoon suddenly exploded in orange light behind them, and Claire looked in the rearview mirror to see her boyfriend spraying the entire street with an intense stream of pure, concentrated flame. Where it touched the draug, they evaporated. She could hear the grating, metallic screaming even through the hearing protection of Naomi's noise cancellation. They sure weren't singing anymore.

As she put the truck in gear and popped the clutch, Shane lurched forward and nearly fell out of the open bed of the truck— right into the draug.

But Theo grabbed him by the shoulder and held him in place as Harold crouched in the corner of the truck's bed, looking scared out of his mind.

Claire sighed in relief, and hit the gas pedal hard. In less than thirty seconds, the rain had lessened again to a gentle patter on the roof, and Shane shut off the flamethrower's little ignition burner.

Naomi kept watch out her window, shotgun ready, all the way back to the warm, welcoming lights of Founder's Square.

CHAPTER FOUR

CLAIRE

E ve's coffee and breakfast and cookies were still out on the table when Claire, Theo, and Harold passed through the big round hall. Well, some of it was still there; it looked as if her cooking had been popular this morning. Claire didn't see Eve, which was odd; she would have expected her to still be working off her nervous caffeinated high. Probably still baking. Or, more worrying, maybe she really had gone out with vampires to put together caches of weapons around town.

Please be made up, she thought to both Michael and Eve. *I don't like it when things are bad.*

But she had a sinking feeling that things were going to get worse before they got better between those two.

"Harold," Theo said, and opened up a door. "You'll be safe here. I will be back soon."

Harold made urgent signs to him—deaf, which was probably the only reason he'd survived out there in draug-held Morganville. Theo smiled and shook his head.

"No," he said. "No one will bother you here. You have my word."

Harold didn't seem convinced, but he went into the room and Theo shut the door behind him.

"So . . . is he a friend of yours?" Claire asked.

"A patient," Theo said. "And now we must go to another of my patients: Amelie."

All the doors leading out of this room looked alike to Claire, and she hesitated, wondering which one led to the Founder of Morganville, but Theo didn't. He made straight for one of them, opened it, and hurried through; she sped to catch up before the door closed again.

They were in one of the building's endless, identical carpeted hallways, with the tasteful (and probably outrageously expensive) art on the walls. At the end of the hall was a set of double doors, guarded by two vampires. Amelie's bodyguards.

"Theo Goldman," Theo said as he approached. "I'm expected."

"Doctor." One of them nodded, and reached to open the door for him. "First room on the left."

Claire followed him in. The guards eyed her, but neither moved to stop her. They just closed the door quietly behind her.

It was odd, but the smell struck her first. Vampires generally didn't smell of anything . . . maybe a faint rusty whiff of blood if they'd just fed, or faded flowers at the worst, but nothing like the cloying, damp, sickroom aroma that had sunk deep into the room's thick carpet and velvet drapes. The place looked beautiful, but it smelled . . . rotten.

Oliver stepped out of the first room on the left and closed the door behind him. He had his sleeves rolled up to expose pale, muscular forearms. There was a fading bite mark on his right wrist, and a bright smear of blood. He looked . . . tired, Claire thought. Not the Oliver she was used to seeing.

When he saw them, he straightened to his usual stick-up-his-butt posture and nodded to Theo. His gaze passed over her, but he didn't say anything. *It's like I'm not even really here*, she thought, and felt a surge of anger. *We just risked our lives for you, jerk. The least you could do is say thanks.*

"How much did they tell you?" Oliver asked Theo, who shrugged.

"Not much," he said. "She has been bitten, yes?"

"By the master draug. Magnus."

Theo paused and went utterly still, his gaze locked on Oliver's face. Then he glanced down at the bitten skin, and the faint blood-stain. "That won't work," he said. "You know that. You only en-danger and weaken yourself."

Oliver said nothing. He just stepped aside and let Theo pro-ceed into the room.

When Claire would have followed him, just like the shadow she appeared to have become, Oliver's hand flashed out and grabbed hold of her shoulder. "Not you," he said. "She is too ill for human visitors."

What that meant, Claire thought, was that Amelie was beyond distinguishing between friends and, say, food. She shuddered. She'd seen Amelie go savage, but even then it had been Amelie in control, just in full vampire mode.

This would be different. Very different, and very dangerous.

Oliver was not looking at her, though he still held her shoulder in a tight grip. He said, in a distant voice, "I suppose I should thank you for finding him."

"I suppose," she said, and pulled loose from him. He let her do it, of course. Vampires could smash bone with their kung fu grip if they wanted to hold on to something badly enough. "Is she that bad, really?"

"No," Oliver said in that same quiet, remote tone. "She's much worse, as he'll presently see." He looked at her then, and Claire saw just how . . . empty he looked. "She will die soon."

"Die—but I brought Dr. Goldman . . ."

"For easing her pain," he said. "Not for saving her. There is no saving one of us from the bite of a master draug, save by measures that are . . . fatal themselves."

Claire waited, but she didn't feel any shock or surprise. She'd known, she supposed, known from the moment that Amelie had fallen to the ground outside the Morganville Civic Pool. But the town wouldn't be the same without the Founder. There was something distantly kind about Amelie that was missing in the other vampires. Not kind the way humans were, and not emo about it even when she was, but it was hard not to feel some kind of loss at the thought of her being . . . gone.

Even if it was just fear of the unknown who would step up and take her place.

"I'm sorry," she said softly. Oliver snapped back to himself, then—or, at least, the himself she expected him to be.

"So you should be," he said. "I promise you, Amelie tolerated much more than I ever will from you and your kind. She let herself believe that we can live as equals, but I know better. There is an order to all things in the world, and in that order, humans are lower than vampires. They always will be."

"And vampires are lower than the draug," Claire said. "Right?"

He slapped her. It happened so fast that she registered only a faint blur of motion, and then a sharp, hot sting on her cheek. She rocked back, caught off guard, and was then furious because of it.

"Know your place," he said. She could barely hear it over the angry rush of blood pounding in her ears. "Amelie tolerated your sarcasm. I will not."

She was, to her surprise, not afraid of him at all. And he must have seen it. Claire lowered her chin and stared at him with unblinking eyes, the way she'd seen Shane do when he was ready to deliver serious mayhem. "Let's get it straight: you need us. Not just for our blood and our tax money and whatever stupid buzz you get from ordering us around. You need us to protect you from the draug, because they are coming for you right now, and you haven't got enough vamps to fight them off, do you? So we're not your minions, and we're not your servants. If you don't want us to be equals, fine. We can get out of this town anytime we want."

"Not if I order Myrnin to keep you here. We still control the borders of this town."

She laughed, and it sounded as bright and bitter as tinfoil. "I'd like to see you order Myrnin to do anything. He likes Amelie. It's the only reason he came here in the first place. He doesn't like you."

Oliver was . . . well, speechless was the only way she could really think of it. She'd never actually seen that happen before.

"I know you're angry and you're scared," Claire continued, "but don't take it out on your friends. And if you hit me again, I'll hit you back with a pair of silver-coated brass knuckles Shane made me. And it'll hurt. Promise."

"Friends," Oliver repeated, and the sound he made was almost a laugh. "Really."

"Well, in principle. Not if you ever hit me again."

She held the gaze until he finally leaned back against the wall and crossed his arms. His head tilted a little to the left, and she saw the gray-threaded brown hair of his ponytail tied back behind his shoulder. The lines on his face seemed to smooth out, just a bit.

"How long have you been here, Claire?" he asked, in a very different tone. "Almost two years, yes?"

"Almost." Her eighteenth birthday was approaching fast. Once, she'd have been so focused on that milestone that nothing else would have mattered, but it almost seemed meaningless now. In every way that could possibly count, she was already adult. In Morganville, you really did grow up fast.

"I've only been here a bit longer than you," he said. "Did you realize that?"

She hadn't really. Oh, she supposed she knew intellectually that Oliver had drifted into town about six months before she'd made it to Texas Prairie University, but he'd seemed such a long-time fixture by then that imagining Morganville without him had been impossible. "What's your point?"

"I am as ill-equipped to lead here as you," he said. "Most vampires came with Amelie, or soon after; a few entered gradually over the long years. But I came to conquer. I came to take my rightful place as the leader of the last of our kind. I came to kill Amelie and destroy this place. And they all know it. It makes my situation somewhat . . . difficult."

She knew it, too—at least she'd always suspected it; by the time she'd arrived there had been a cautious truce between Amelie and Oliver, but they were pretty much equally matched in power and ruthlessness, and Claire had always figured that Oliver had made an attempt to take over at least once before she'd come to town.

And Amelie, weirdly, had let him live to try again.

"She's so very intelligent, and so very cold," Oliver said. He was no longer exactly talking to Claire, more just . . . talking. "She knew that forcing me to act as her second-in-command would seem a worse punishment than outright death, and Amelie, above all others, dislikes to do her own violence; queens never dirty their own hands. I was . . . suited, and after a short time it ceased to be such a shackle dragging on me. She had—has—no reason to trust me. None. But she did, and I was forced to . . . respect that. And her." He paused then, and said, "I find myself in the curious position of saving humans. Saving this town. Saving her. These are not instincts that come to me naturally."

That was, she supposed, some kind of roundabout apology. She didn't think she accepted it, mostly, but she did see his point, a little: Oliver wasn't built, like Amelie, to be a calm, ice-cold ruler. He was a warlord, impatient and brutal, and he had no long-term interest in the little people.

"So you are right," he finished, even more quietly. "In order to accomplish these things, I will need the help of humans, and of you and your friends. It galls me, but there is no possibility of success without mortal assistance. Vampires have battled the draug, fled from the draug, and died. But the draug are not used to fighting mortals. You are . . . unpredictable. And as a general, I will use whatever weapons come to hand to win my battles. Do you understand me?"

She gave him a small, thin smile. It felt like a cut in her lips. "You're saying that we're expendable."

"All soldiers are expendable, young or old, vampire or human, and ever have been." He turned his head a little, as if he'd heard something, and a moment later the door to Amelie's room opened and Theo Goldman stepped out. They exchanged a look, and Theo shook his head.

"It won't go well," he said. "Her transformation is . . . under way. She can hold to herself for a while longer, but within another day, two at most, she won't be the Amelie we know. I can't stop the poison inside her without destroying her as well. Nothing can. We have to take action before she becomes . . . what he intends her to be."

"But not yet," Oliver said.

"Soon. Would you like me to do it? An injection of silver nitrate would be . . ."

"A cruel death," Oliver finished. "And not one due a queen. I'll care for her when the time comes, you may mark me on it, with a straight, sharp blow."

Theo shook his head. He seemed very sad now, Claire thought, but in a grave, distant way . . . the way doctors were sad about terminal patients. "Be sure you don't wait too long, Oliver. Now—I must see to Naomi. She took a great risk to find me, and she's paid a price for ingesting the blood. I shall need a donor of Bishop's line to help her."

"Naomi." Oliver's voice was a little too flat. "Save her, then. I care not. Make Amelie comfortable first. That is all I ask of you."

Theo nodded, frowning a little. "You're going to fight the draug, I gather."

"It is what she wanted. And in truth, what I want as well." Oliver's eyes gleamed a little with red sparks. "Not many good fights left in this sad, pallid world, with its frail, sensitive people. The draug at least do not mewl and whine about a few bruises."

"You've always been insane," Theo said. "Insane for your beliefs, insane for power, insane for blood. I suppose that may be what we require now. More insanity."

"That may be the kindest thing you've ever said about me, Doctor."

"I didn't mean it kindly. Come, Claire. I don't like leaving you in the company of such a—" Theo stopped, looking at her, and his eyes widened, just a little. She didn't know why, and then realized that there must have been a mark on her cheek. Maybe not quite a bruise.

Theo turned back to Oliver. "You struck her."

"She was impertinent."

"Hit one of them again, and you will answer to me."

Oliver smiled. "You terrify me."

"I should," Theo said softly. His eyes glowed with hellfire, just for a moment. "There is nothing more frightening than a medical man willing to inflict pain, Oliver. And I will, should you abuse the power you've been given. Or taken." He took Claire by the arm. "Come. There's nothing here for you, and we should see to Naomi as quickly as possible."

When she and Theo left Amelie's rooms, Myrnin was standing in the round area with the coffee station, staring at the remaining bits of breakfast on the trays and frowning as if he couldn't quite work out what to do with the cup and saucer in his hand.

I'm in vampire central, Claire thought. She wasn't used to being *constantly* surrounded by the nonbreathing sort of people; most of the time it was just her, Shane, Eve . . . and she never really thought of Michael as a vampire, much. Myrnin was familiar, but she never forgot how sharp his fangs were, either. She was with Theo, had just come from Oliver, and now there was Myrnin, and she was starting to feel a little like a hamburger at a dieters' convention. Nobody was likely to snack on her, but absolutely everybody noticed she was edible.

Myrnin was, not surprisingly, dressed weirdly. Well, not

weirdly for *him*, but Theo's old-fashioned suit jacket and pants were positively wallpaper by comparison. Myrnin had dragged out the Hawaiian shirts again; today's was neon yellow, with palm trees and surfboards. He was also wearing baggy knee-length shorts, which left his legs looking . . . pale. Very, very pale.

He'd actually matched the whole thing with sandals this time, instead of bunny slippers, which indicated a certain razor-sharp focus in his thinking, the coffee confusion notwithstanding. He set the cup and saucer down empty with a rattle as his gaze focused on Claire.

"How is Amelie?" he asked, moving from her to Theo. "Oh, and hello, glad you're not dead, Doctor."

"Likewise," Theo said pleasantly. "But she is not well, my friend. As you no doubt already know."

"You were up all night," Claire said. "I saw the weapons room. How long did all that take you?"

Myrnin flipped a hand impatiently, pushing the whole question, and her concern, aside. "Weapons are simple," he said. "I've set up a workshop for them, and I've put Amelie's bully boys to work, as well as a few human . . . volunteers, from the prisons. We have more important concerns than that, if we are to save ourselves. Defense alone won't work. We need to launch an offensive operation."

Myrnin was talking like a soldier. *Myrnin.* Claire looked at him doubtfully. "Have you, ah, talked to Oliver?"

"Yes," Myrnin said. "He thinks I am insane."

That did not bode well, not at all. "Ah . . . okay. Let me . . . get back to you."

He put his hand on her arm and said very seriously, "I am not exaggerating when I tell you that if we do not take a more aggressive and scientific approach to this problem, we lose the rest of the town, and we will all die. Do you understand me? We cannot hold here unless we plan our moves now, in detail."

"And Oliver's not giving you help, if things are that bad?"

"Oliver has his own concerns, and just now those revolve around Amelie. While I have no such constraints, dear as she may be to me. Gather your friends and I will show you why I have such concerns. Please." He turned to Theo then. "And you, good doctor, could be quite the asset as well."

But Theo was already shaking his head. "Quite impossible," he said. "Naomi is very ill, and I must see to her immediately. Dragoon someone else, Myrnin." He walked to one of the guards who had just entered the room—it was Billy Idol—and they exchanged words. Billy Idol pointed a spike-braceleted arm down one of the spoke hallways, and Theo left without a backward glance.

"Claire? *Please.*"

When Myrnin asked like that, with those dark, puppy-dog eyes pleading his case, she couldn't really do much except nod. "I'll find them," she said, "and then you're going to explain this. In detail. And you'd better not be wasting our time."

"True, there is no time to waste," he agreed, and picked up his cup and saucer again. "There is a shocking lack of tea in this array of choices, do you realize that? Also, the carafe of type O is quite empty."

Claire gave him a wordless stare and headed for the door.

"But the AB is still warm. Lovely."

Claire shuddered and reached for the knob of the door, but it twisted before she touched it, and opened to admit Shane. "Hey," he said, and the warmth she felt at his brief smile was out of all proportion to the moment. "Where's Theo? Naomi's looking pretty bad."

"He just headed that way," she said.

His dark gaze stayed on hers. "And Amelie?"

"They wouldn't let me see her," Claire said. "Which I think we both know means she's not doing all that well."

He nodded slowly, his face settling into grim, hard-edged lines. "Oliver takes over, we're long-term screwed, you know that. Maybe we win against the draug, but what happens then? He's old-school vamp, with old-school ideas about how humans ought to behave."

She couldn't really dispute that, not at all, and it gave her a sick, rolling feeling in her stomach. She hoped that Shane couldn't see where Oliver had hit her, because if he did, the human/vampire war wouldn't even be *that* far off. But luckily, he didn't see it—or if he did, he must have assumed it was due to all their running, jumping, and fighting the night before. Not unreasonably.

"Where are your friends?" Myrnin asked, as he sipped on whatever blood type was in his coffee cup. "Michael and Shreve."

"Eve."

"Yes, yes, that one." He flipped a hand impatiently. "Get them."

"Eve's not here," Shane said. When Claire sent him a startled look, he shrugged. "I asked. She took about a dozen vampires, got Oliver's approval, and went out to set up weapons caches at different places around town. She's not back yet."

"Did Michael go with her?"

He didn't say anything, but she knew all too well what that meant—even before Michael came walking in, looking rumpled, tired, and about as depressed as she'd ever seen him. He didn't meet anyone's eyes as he walked over to the center table and tested the carafes.

"That's AB," Myrnin said helpfully. "It's still warm. Oh, and there's a hint of sweetness in it. High triglycerides. I think the donor needed a bit of medication."

"Are you high?" Michael asked him, in a totally colorless voice.

Myrnin blinked, and looked at Claire for help. "He means, are you on drugs."

"Well, *obviously*."

"More than usual?"

"Oh. No, no, just the usual doses. And where is Shreve?"

"Eve," they all said in unison, and exchanged a look. Well, Shane and Claire did, and Michael made a fast-aborted effort at it. Shane licked his lips and continued, "She's out."

"Of the building?" Michael asked, still in that same nothing voice.

"Yeah. She's got escorts, though." That sounded weak, even from Shane, and he clearly didn't know where to take it from there. "I mean, I'm sure she's okay and everything."

Michael just nodded. He looked tight and grim, and he sipped his cup of blood as if he really didn't want it at all. Myrnin looked from him to the others, eyebrows going up and down as if he was about to blurt out a question that none of them wanted to answer, and then shrugged. "Very well," he said, "evidently there is some difficulty that I really don't care about, and is no doubt quite dramatic. Does anyone else care for coffee?"

Claire glanced at the red-stained cups he and Theo had left, and shuddered. "No, thanks."

Shane clearly decided a change of subject was in order. He turned his most harassed expression on Michael. "Bro," he said, in an injured tone, "I had to go out with a *flamethrower*, and you weren't there to see it."

"Pics or it didn't happen."

"Dude, little *busy* for pics. You know, *throwing flame*."

That earned a glance up, and a brief grin, and some of the tension leaked out of Michael's body language . . . but not all. And the grin didn't last. "Wish I'd been there," he said, with a clear implication of *anywhere but here*. Which did not, again, bode well for the whole deal with Eve.

Myrnin rolled his eyes. "Oh, enough of this. Follow me." He immediately set off at a rapid, though not vampire-quick, walk down yet another hallway, identical to all the others; Claire fell in with Shane, behind Michael.

"What the hell are we into now?" Shane asked her.

"Nothing good," she replied. "But then, that kind of describes our day, right?"

"Speak for yourself. It describes my whole *life*." He reached out and took her in his arms, a sudden and unexpected crush that drove her breath right away. "Except for you." He kissed her, and despite everything, despite the hurry and the vampires and the draug and the doom hanging over them, it felt like sunlight shining right through her skin, melting her bones into soft, pliable gold. It couldn't have lasted long, that kiss, but it felt eternal to her, as if it might echo forever. "I can handle anything now."

"Well," she whispered with their lips still touching, "as long as you have a flamethrower."

He laughed, and let go . . . but kept hold of her hand.

Myrnin led them into a room that had obviously started life as another ballroom . . . but in the course of what could have been only hours, or at most a day, he had managed to transform it into a chaotic mess that reminded Claire strongly of his original laboratory. Books were stacked, scattered, and dropped everywhere, some open to a possibly important reference, or maybe just opened at random. He'd dragged furniture in to improvise work space, with limited success, and he'd taken the shades off the elegant lamps to let the bright incandescent bulbs glare freely. The room smelled strongly of oil and metal, and . . . burned hair?

Myrnin strode across the deep maroon carpet (now liberally smudged with spots of dirt, oil, and who knew what else) to what had once been a giant sideboard, except that he'd ripped it away from the wall and shoved it into the middle of the room. It held about a dozen books, scraps of metal, bars of silver, and nails; he swept the whole thing clean with one dramatic gesture and then unfurled a set of blueprints across the lavish marble top—already stained from at least one chemical spill.

It was a map of Morganville. A standard-issue civilian kind of map, but there was a clear plastic overlay on it, marked with careful, precise handwriting and colored dots—Myrnin's writing, though far more controlled than Claire had ever seen it. The entire side of town from the border up to the TPU gates had been colored in flat black, simply marking it out.

Draug territory.

"Now," he said, and set random pieces of junk at the four corners of the map to hold it open. "Obviously, we're here." He pointed to a red dot overlay on the building at Founder's Square. "This is the police perimeter around us." A solid red line, as precisely drawn as with a compass. "This is the outer ring of our defenses." Another ring, but this one of individual red dots, spread evenly. It reached as far as Lot Street, where the Glass House—their home—sat empty. "There is nothing within this circle that has not been drained of standing water, or salted with silver if we couldn't drain it, so the draug cannot get here easily."

"The rain—," Shane began, but Myrnin cut him off.

"They can use the rain only when it is heavy and constant, and even then it's a risk; by spreading themselves so thin, they lose many parts into the dry soil. It's a bit of a kamikaze attack, to put it in human terms, and they dare not employ that method to attack us here, in our stronghold; there's no catch basin for them to use that hasn't been treated and prepared against them. But our problem is outside of this circle." He tapped the other two-thirds of the town, where black dots and puddles of dark ink marred the surface. "I've tracked all the reports I could find. Claire, you said the draug came after you just now, correct?"

She nodded. "Came after Theo and Naomi, probably. But there were a lot of them."

"Not so many now," Shane said, and yeah, that was smug. "Flamethrower."

"Still, worrisome," Myrnin said, and marked the map where Shane pointed. "That is far out of the area that Oliver predicted they would occupy. Could you hear the singing?"

"Naomi had that noise cancellation device, but Theo—" Claire's throat closed up on the words, but she forced them out anyway. "Theo had needles in his ears. To keep himself from hearing."

Myrnin's eyebrows climbed again, and he tapped the marker against his lips. "An interesting tactic. Perhaps one we should think about as emergency equipment to be issued to all personnel."

"Ugh. No. *Human* eardrums don't grow back, Myrnin."

"Oh, right. Well, just the vampires, then." He scribbled a note on a random piece of paper—actually, over the printing in a book—and went on. "Oliver believes the draug are consolidating their position here, in the occupied areas, but I think he is very wrong. Look at the blue marks."

For a few seconds they didn't seem to make any sense; it was Michael who said quietly, "Bodies of water."

"Fountains," Myrnin said, and tapped a couple of spots. "I've sent operatives to shut off any flow to or from them, and poison them; Oliver discounts them strategically, and he's likely correct. But our biggest issue is obviously here."

That was a *large* blue dot. Very large.

"What the hell is that?" Shane asked, frowning. "Morganville High?"

"No, that's taken care of," Myrnin said, and tapped another dot. "The pool there has been drained and filled in. No, this is a far different sort of problem altogether."

"That's the water treatment plant," Michael said. "Out on the edge of town."

"There are exposed pools of water there, and inflow and out-flow controls for the pipes in the city. If I were Magnus, I would move my headquarters immediately to *that* as the most strategic point. No doubt he has already done so, or is in the process."

"You're kidding. He's hiding in sewage?" Shane asked.

"Not sewage, no, though that gets treated through this operation as well. What is in those exposed pools is commonly known as gray water—the water from baths, showers, sinks, washing machines, and such. It needs treatment to be clean for drinking again, but it doesn't contain sewage. By preference, this is where we will find the draug. Not in the sewage tanks. Even the draug have *some* standards." Myrnin shook his head slowly. "The difficulty is that there are two necessary tasks to be performed. First, of course, we must attack the draug directly in those pools, *if* they exist there— and Oliver does not believe they do. He says he has sent operatives and they have reported it clear."

"But you don't believe that."

"I think the draug are more than capable of strategy," Myrnin said, "and strategically, they are in a defensive mode at this point. We've hurt them; they have not overwhelmed us as quickly as they'd hoped, and they can't attack us directly at Founder's Square. So they're hiding until they regain their numbers, and I believe they will conceal themselves here, at the treatment plant. It is a natural stronghold for them—they can infest this maze of iron and water like a horde of starving cockroaches, and they'll be just as hard to anticipate and to kill in such close quarters."

"Wow," Shane said. "You really know how to drum up team spirit. Did you print up Team Total Fail jerseys, too?"

Myrnin gave him an entirely crazy smile. "Would you be surprised if I had?" He threw another large sheet of paper out over the map. It was a blueprint. "There are two phases to this operation, if there is to be one. The pools are a direct attack, but there is something else that is entirely necessary before that can occur: we must stop them from easily traveling through the pipes in Morganville. Right now, they have easy access through those pipes into homes, businesses, all of the abandoned structures. The university. We cannot allow them to have such easy mobility."

"Okay, it isn't manly to admit it, but I don't speak blueprint," Shane said. "So what are we talking about exactly?"

"We need to shut off the water system," Myrnin said. "There are emergency cutoff valves that will stop the flow of water in the pipes throughout Morganville, trapping the draug where they are if they've infested them, and stranding those at the treatment plant there, unable to retreat."

"It's still raining," Shane pointed out.

"True, but in this desert it can't last forever. The only reason they attempted it was that it was the only way they could reach Morganville at all. Amelie chose this town specifically for its isolation, dry climate, and lack of standing water. It's served us well, until now."

Myrnin, Claire thought, was sounding remarkably together,

but he also looked tired. She could see the bruised skin under his eyes, and the slight tremor in his hands. Even bipolar vampires needed sleep from time to time, and he was well past his recommended safe dosage of stress.

Michael was staring at the blueprints as if he really understood what he was seeing. He was even nodding. "Right," he said. "So it looks like there's a main control room here"—he tapped the plans, then traced a line—"and physical shutoffs here, for emergencies. What are our chances that the draug haven't already figured out this is a point of danger for them?"

"Zero," Myrnin said cheerfully, "since Magnus is remarkably intelligent about such things. The draug in general are poor and limited in their reasoning skills, but their master is another matter altogether."

"Why can't we go after him?" Michael said. "What happens if we kill Magnus?"

"That would, of course, be ideal, *if* we could find him. However, Magnus in particular has developed excellent chameleon skills, *and* fashioned his draug to exactly resemble himself, so it is a fool's game to target him. He can hide himself in plain sight, and if that fails, he can surround himself with copies. It would take someone with the ability to see through his . . ." He blinked, and turned toward Claire. "See through his glamour."

She felt suddenly exposed and uncomfortable, as if he'd turned a spotlight on her and asked her to dance. "Why are you looking at me?"

"You're the only one who noticed him originally," Myrnin said. "When no one else took note of his presence at all. Even vampires. Now, the question is, can you distinguish him from his vassals?"

"I don't . . ." She thought back on it, on the draug in the Civic

Pool building. There had been a lot of them, but when she'd seen Magnus she'd known, deep down, that it was him. He had more . . . well, just more *density*, she supposed. "Maybe. I don't know if I can do it all the time or anything. He might not know—" Wait, he *did* know. There had been a reason for Magnus to follow her home in the rain from the store, to invade their home, the Glass House, to *kill* her. He must have been tracking down and dealing with what he perceived to be a genuine threat.

She was a threat to him. Somehow.

"An interesting question," Myrnin said, "and one we will have to explore as we go along, I suppose." His gaze lingered on her for a moment, cool and assessing, and then he went back to the blueprints. Claire gave up quickly; the maze of lines made about as much sense as trying to read a bowl of spaghetti. Michael and Shane, though, were much more interested, and Myrnin was happy to be chattering away.

Her attention wandered to the idea of water . . . flowing through pipes, carrying the draug into every house, every business. The vision of a draug emerging from a toilet bowl made every kind of nightmare she'd ever had about the bathroom pale in comparison. And *showers.* It was bad enough being out in the rain, knowing what was out there, but being naked and vulnerable, with the draug building themselves out of drops around you in the shower . . . yeah, that was *Psycho* times ten. And forget about baths. She'd never be taking a bath again. Horror movie time.

"You're going to need Oliver's permission for any of this," Michael said. "You know that, right?"

"In fact, I do not. He specifically told me I was not allowed to initiate any *battles*," Myrnin said. "This is not a battle. I need you to go into the building and turn the cutoff wheels. Nothing more.

It's a simple enough operation, and quite obviously necessary. Oliver will be happy with the results."

Michael shot Shane a look. "Translation: what Oliver doesn't know won't hurt us, theoretically," he said. "So we're doing it on our own."

"How exactly is that any different from any other day?" Shane asked. "We got this, man. And if he's right, it needs to happen or we have no shot at all at controlling these things. They'll take the town away from us until there's no place left to hide except right here in Founder's Square, surrounded. Food and water will run out, sooner or later, even if they can't break through."

"And vampires must also feed. They will begin to take blood where they can get it," Myrnin said softly. "It's something I very much wish not to happen, Shane. But at this point it is inevitable if we don't act *now*. This is as much to save your lives as ours. Oliver refuses to see that just now, and we cannot wait. Will you do it?"

"I only need to know one thing. Am I going to need the flame-thrower?" Shane asked.

Myrnin smiled, with fangs. "Absolutely."

CHAPTER FIVE

EVE

So, I was running around Morganville in what was just about twilight with a bunch of vampires, none of whom were Michael. Or even Myrnin. Or even *Oliver*.

This was not comforting.

I know, my idea, and it was a good one, but being surrounded by fangs when my body was still shuddering off the effects of . . . what had happened . . . wasn't a personal best time ever. I'd briskly introduced myself to the female vamp who seemed to be in charge; she'd said her name was Adele, but not in any way that encouraged me to use it. The other vamps didn't volunteer so much as a nod. I was invisible.

And maybe, thinking about it, that was kind of a good thing. I mean, I'd rather be invisible than a walking snack-pack. But at least worrying about my veins kept me from thinking about the dangers of running around in a town where the draug could pop up at any time.

Oh, and the vamps were wearing what looked like headphones, with some kind of bubbling copper attachments on the sides— Myrninwear, apparently, to cancel out the draug's siren song. I hoped they were efficient noise cancellation. Me, I stuck to foamy earplugs.

Of course, we were in a vamp sedan, which meant I couldn't even look out at scenery, such as it was in Morganville, since the window tinting was on the extreme side. I could only admire the pale skin of my co-riders, and think about the many, many awful ways this could go wrong.

And miss Michael, in a traitorously angry kind of way. I couldn't believe that I'd *stabbed him*, but then, he'd not only hurt me, he'd tried to scare me. Seriously tried. And I wasn't going to let that kind of bad boyfriend behavior go on without some kind of response, though in retrospect, escalating the domestic violence might not have been the most positive choice.

Got the point across, though, and I wasn't sure that when you were dealing with a vampire, counseling really worked. *God, Michael. Why did this happen to us?* I wanted to ask him that, not that he'd have any kind of an answer. I wanted to be in his arms, snuggled together under layers of warm blankets, safe from the world.

But I wasn't sure anymore—or at least, my *body* wasn't sure— that I was safe with *him*. Which was exactly what Michael had been afraid of this whole time. What all the vamps, including Amelie, had warned us about.

What I'd totally refused to believe, until that moment when his eyes had opened bloodred, and his teeth had slid down sharp as steel, and his hands had grabbed my shoulders so hard they left blue-black bruises, and for an instant I shivered at the touch of his hot breath on my neck and then, and then . . .

I squeezed my eyes tight shut because I did *not* want to remember him that way. Or me that way. Or *us* that way, out of control, careening toward the darkness. That wasn't Michael, my sweet golden Michael with his music and his strength and his gentle touch; that wasn't me, with my confidence and quips.

That was a killer and a victim, and there was nothing romantic about it, nothing sexy, nothing but pain and blood and darkness coming on fast. I believed in Michael enough to know that if he'd actually done it, if he'd drained me dry, when he'd come to his senses he would never have been able to live with what he'd done. Shane would have killed him, but it wouldn't have mattered to him because he'd have been dead inside already. Walk-into-the-sunlight dead inside.

Toxic love.

Maybe he's right, some part of me kept whispering. *Maybe you should give it up. Move on. Let him find some nice vampire girl he doesn't have to be afraid to be around.*

I hated that part of me so much I wanted to kill it with fire. But I was also afraid it was the smartest part.

I was crammed in the backseat between two motionless vamps, both male, who had been staring out the darkened windows; now, as the car pulled to a halt, they opened their doors and got out. By the time I'd scrambled out, they were taking up positions facing away from the car, and Adele, the driver, had popped the trunk open. She pointed to me, then to the trunk, then to a house.

I was still getting my bearings, which wasn't easy to do; the rain had stopped for the moment, but the clouds were thick and dark, and with no lights on, this was a totally anonymous street . . . until I caught sight of the sagging white picket fence and the bleached-white bulk of our house, the Glass House, rising up in menacing Victorian angles toward the sky. No lights on. It totally looked haunted, even though just now it actually *wasn't* for a change.

She gestured to the other vamp, who reached in the trunk and handed me a thick canvas bag. I staggered under the weight, but grabbed it in both hands and lugged it up the steps and onto the porch. I had the front door key in my pocket, where it always was, and as I unlocked the door I felt a sense of relief, of coming home.

But stepping over the threshold didn't bring any rush of warmth, or welcome, or anything that I expected to feel. The Glass House felt . . . dead. Abandoned.

I leaned the canvas bag full of weapons and ammo in the corner by the front door and flipped the light switch. No response. The power was out in this part of town, but I hadn't come unprepared; I took a mini flashlight out of my cargo pants pocket and dragged the bag into the parlor room. It was as dusty as ever. Shane had left a jacket thrown over the wing chair. I unpacked the weapons and ammunition and laid everything out carefully on the coffee table and sofa, easy to grab if we needed it . . . and then considered the empty canvas bag.

I *was* here, and having our own clothes would feel a whole lot more comfortable in exile. So despite the vamps waiting impatiently outside, I ran upstairs, rummaged in each of our rooms as fast as possible, and shoved shirts, pants, underwear into the bag.

I wanted to take *everything*, but there wasn't time. On the way out, though, I hesitated, then put Michael's guitar into its case and clicked it shut.

The vamps could just stuff their objections.

I came out on the porch and locked the door—habit, I suppose—and turned to see . . .

. . . Nobody.

The vamps had all vanished.

The sedan was sitting at the curb idling. All the doors were shut. The trunk was still open.

I didn't like the feeling of the earplugs, suddenly; they felt oppressive, magnified my fast breathing, made me feel oddly suffocated. I wanted to take them out, and I actually reached up for the left one before I realized what I was doing. I could make out, very faintly, a high-pitched sound.

Singing.

Dammit.

I ran for the car, threw the bag and guitar into the trunk, and grabbed a shotgun pre-loaded with silver shot, plus a couple of the vials of silver nitrate. Then I pulled open the door of the sedan.

I wasn't exactly shocked to find it empty. The impulse to get in and drive away—even if I'd be driving blind, given the opaque tinting—was almost irresistible, but though the vamps hadn't even wanted to give me their names, I was the one who'd gotten them out into this. The noise cancellation headsets clearly hadn't worked . . . or else something else had drawn them off. Either way, I owed it to them to find them.

So I went looking.

I mean, it was my own neighborhood. *I lived here.* That was the Farnhams' house right there; I didn't like them, because they were a mean, bitter old couple of the get-off-my-lawn variety, but they were familiar. Across the street was Mrs. Grather, who'd been a librarian since books were carved on stone or something. She was always out puttering around with dying flowers. I knew each and every person who lived on this block, or at least *had* lived here, before the events of the past few days. Maybe they were still locked up inside, hiding. Maybe they'd left Morganville for good.

Maybe they were dead and gone.

But it was my neighborhood, and we didn't allow bad things to happen here. Not *here*.

Not even to vampires who wouldn't give me their names.

I found the first one walking along half a block down; it was one of the two who'd been in the backseat with me. His headphones were gone, and he looked . . . vacant. *Dammit.* I didn't know how to stop him, short of killing him; he was shambling along with a purpose, drawn by the eerie song of the draug toward a watery grave.

I ran back toward the car, looking, and found signs of a struggle. Smashed fence at Mrs. Grather's house, some bloodstains, and a broken headset. I tried it, and it still lit up, even though the headband had snapped in half. I ditched the shotgun and dashed back to the vamp, who was still walking along, and sneaked up behind him to slap the two halves of the headphones in place over his ears.

He took another couple of steps, with me awkwardly duck-walking with him as I held the pieces in place, then stopped and reached up to hold the headphones himself as I pulled back. Then he turned and faced me, and instead of seeing just another vampire, I saw . . . a young man, maybe twenty-five or so. He had thick brown wavy hair, cut into a vaguely old style, and he had dark eyes, or at least they looked that way in the gloomy afternoon.

Kinda cute, in a bookish sort of way. He nodded to me and said, "Thank you." At least, that was how I read his lips. He gave me an awkward, shallow bow, too.

I wished I knew his name, suddenly, but there wasn't much point in conversing, seeing as how he had his headphones on and I had squishy earplugs. I gestured for him to follow me, and ran back toward where I'd dropped the shotgun. No sign of draug, at least here; my new friend kept up with me easily. He nodded in a way that I interpreted to mean *wait here*, and dashed in a blur back to the car, where he dropped his broken headphones and, in almost the same gesture, grabbed a new pair from the dashboard and snugged them in place. I saw his body language relax as they kicked in.

Okay, that explained *him*. It didn't explain the lack of Adele and the others. We made awkward sign language Q&A for a bit, and I got that there had been a draug popping up, and his headphones had gotten snapped, and Adele and the others had chased the draug. No props to Adele for tactical smarts, obviously, but before he'd succumbed to the singing, my new buddy had seen which way they'd gone.

So we followed, both now armed with shotguns.

We rounded the corner into the middle of a micro-rainstorm.

I mean, one second it was clear, the next there was a blinding curtain of rain that smashed down from the sky in a thick silver flood, and it was as cold as ice and took my breath away as it hit me. I couldn't see a thing, but I could feel a burning creeping over my exposed skin.

Draug, in the rain. They were concentrating on this one spot, flooding down to add their bulk to what looked like a flooded low spot in the road.

I could see them moving like shadows through the rain, surrounding Adele and the other vampires, who were shoulder to shoulder in a circle-the-wagons formation. Even through the earplugs I could hear the muffled blasts of the shotguns.

My fanged friend grabbed my shoulder and pulled me to a halt. He was right—we couldn't get closer; with three vampires firing in there, and taking a toll on the draug, we could get hit by friendly fire just as easily. He pointed to the silver nitrate glass jars that I'd clipped to my belt carabiner, and then to the thick, squirming puddle in the depression of the road.

I gave him a thumbs-up, passed him my gun, and unclipped the jars. My hands were cold and wet, and I had to concentrate to make sure I didn't slip and drop them. And then it occurred to me that my brilliant plan was to run right into the middle of the draug.

It was suddenly not so brilliant.

The vampire bumped my shoulder and gave me an encouraging nod. He had a shotgun in each hand, like something out of a badass Old West movie; all he really needed was a big hat and bandoliers over his chest to complete the picture. And maybe a poncho. Ponchos are cool.

I got the message. He'd be right behind me, firing on the draug coming from the sides. Plus, they wouldn't be nearly as interested in me if there was hot, tasty vampire within reach.

I gave him a firm, calm nod (and didn't feel that way at all) and ran forward.

Adele must have spotted us, because her gunfire in our direction stopped, but behind me I heard the close percussive booms of my new friend's shotguns going off as draug lurched out of the rain from the left and the right. *Don't stop, don't stop, no matter what, don't stop . . .*

I ran directly into a draug.

Literally.

It was just forming itself out of the rain, and behind that human form was something vile and monstrous and formless, twitching and oozing.

I didn't have the time to stop, even if I'd wanted to. I don't know which of us was more surprised, actually.

I ran right into it, and *through* it.

It felt like half-congealed gelatin, or the thickest possible slimy mud. I retched at the feel of it on my skin, and it burned hard and fast, like an acid bath . . . but then I was out of it, and the rain, even draug-infested, was cleaner, and sluicing the ick away.

And then I was at the edges of the puddle.

A draug crawled up out of it, but passed me, heading for the vampire behind me. He shot it in half. I was *really* glad for excellent vampire aim, because my hands were trembling hard now, and I was scared to death, horribly and miserably terrified, and I felt like I was screaming and I probably was, but I managed to bring my hands up and smash the two jars together, hard enough to pop the glass.

Silver rained down into the water, and where it touched, the water turned black, rotten and foul with dead draug.

The singing must have changed pitch, because even through the earplugs I could hear the screaming.

A hand shoved me down flat, and a shotgun clattered to the pavement next to me. My new vamp friend was still upright, standing over me now, firing steadily as draug tried to escape from the pond's poisonous waters.

I got up to my knees and fired, too, choking on the stench of gunpowder and the moldy flavor of the draug.

Finally, the rain eased, then puttered to a stop, and Adele fired the last shot into the pulpy mass of a draug, blasting it into slime . . .

. . . And it was over.

Me, and the vampires.

Victorious.

My new friend reached down and offered me a hand up. I took it, breathless and shaking, and the help turned into a handshake.

Adele gave me a cool assessment, raised an eyebrow, and mouthed, *Not bad.*

Just like that, I was part of the team.

Lucky for us, the rest of the trip wasn't quite so eventful.

CHAPTER SIX

CLAIRE

☾

"She should be back by now," Michael said, checking his cell phone as they followed Myrnin out of the lab and into yet another maze of hallways. "Claire. You text her."

"Her cell won't work," Claire said. "The human network's still down, except for police and emergency workers." The vampire network was, of course, fully operational . . . at least for now. "Maybe one of the guys with her . . . ?"

"I don't know who they are," Michael said, and frowned at the screen. "She ought to be back."

What he really meant was that he ought to be with her, Claire thought, but she didn't say that out loud. "She's okay," she assured him. "Eve knows her way around town, just like you do. Just like Shane." It was true, but she knew it wasn't particularly comforting. The draug represented an entirely new dimension of danger that not even Morganville natives were fully equipped to handle. "She's got loads of vamp firepower."

"Yeah," he said softly, and for a moment she saw a flash of red in his blue eyes. "Look how that turned out before."

Ouch. She had a sudden vivid vision of him crouched over Eve's motionless body, his fangs in her neck. The look on his face, the desperate and unholy *joy* of it ... it haunted her. She couldn't imagine what it was like to be in his head right now, or for that matter, in Eve's. That moment had destroyed all the expectations they might have had about themselves.

"She'll be okay," Shane said. "Let's worry about us, bro. Because no matter how much of a little operation Myrnin wants to tell us this is, it ain't."

Michael nodded. He still looked pale and miserable, and he wasn't going to get much better until Eve got back ... and maybe not even then, if things were as bad as she feared.

Maybe mortal danger *was* the best thing for him right now.

It was still grudgingly daylight outside, but they didn't go out in it ... not at first. Myrnin said it wasn't necessary. Instead, he led them down a maze of corridors into a storeroom, small and dark, that stank of chemicals. Claire remembered it. It seemed a whole lot smaller with the five of them packed inside, but Myrnin squirmed past her, shut the door, and flipped on the overhead bulb, which swung in true horror-movie fashion back and forth above their heads. Just barely above Shane's, in fact; he hunched to avoid it.

"Great," Shane said. "Look, I'd rather not be on janitorial duty. I have allergies to cleaners."

"And to cleaning," Michael said.

"Look who's talking. Didn't they do one of those Animal Planet documentaries about the roaches in your room?"

Myrnin gave a frustrated growl and crossed to the other side of the room, next to the industrial shelving that held bleach, gloves, scrub brushes, and other things that Claire didn't think were going to be of much use against the draug. There was one un-cluttered wall, and he faced it, took a shallow breath, and closed his eyes.

The wall wavered, as if a heat wave had passed over it, but then it solidified again into just . . . a wall, plain white, with the usual scuffs and dings any wall got over time. Claire poked it experi-mentally. Paint over drywall over boards. "I don't think that's working," she said. "Isn't Frank still, you know, on duty?"

"On and off," Myrnin said. He tried again, with the same results—a flicker that might have signaled the establishment of a portal to another location, but too brief and unstable to step through. *If* it went where it was supposed to go, which might not have been the case. "Frank has been unreliable of late, to be per-fectly honest."

Frank was the town's computer nerve center—literally. He was a brain wired into Myrnin's computer in his lab, a sinister mixture of steampunkish brilliance and vampiric blood. Frank had started out a Morganville native, then left town, then came back at the head of a motorcycle gang to try to take it over. That hadn't gone well, and he'd ended up a vampire himself . . . the last thing he'd ever wanted to be. From there, he'd become a brain in a jar, mainly because Myrnin had needed one and Frank's had been not quite dead enough.

Oh, and Frank Collins was—had been? still was?—Shane's father, a fact that had haunted Claire for a long time since she'd discovered what Myrnin had done, since Shane had thought his father was completely dead and gone. The discovery hadn't gone over well, and even now, at the mention of his dad's name, Shane's face went stiff and blank, as if he'd reached for a mask. Self-defense. Frank hadn't exactly been Father of the Year even before he'd taken up running with bikers and hunting vampires, much less become one.

"What's wrong with Frank?" Shane asked. "Too much vodka in his blood smoothies? Or is he just being his usual bastard self?"

"Shane," Claire murmured, half in reproof and half in sympathy. There really had never been all that much about his dad that she could find to like, and she tried to find something good in everyone. Frank had been drunk, abusive, and angry when he was a human; as a vampire, he'd been mostly suicidal from rage over his conversion. He'd hurt Shane, a lot, but a son never stopped loving a father, she supposed. Even if he didn't want to.

"He's been having trouble adapting," Myrnin said. "I fear Frank won't be able to bear the strain of disembodiment for too much longer. I'll have to disconnect him and look for a new subject unless he stabilizes soon." He must have thought about that for a second, because he said, not as if he really meant it, "Sorry."

Even though he wasn't glancing her way, Claire felt a kind of pressure settle on her; Myrnin's original plan, which she very well knew, was that *she* would be the one to end up in the center of his machine, the eyes and ears and nervous system of Morganville. It wasn't a role she ever wanted to play, and he knew that.

It didn't mean he'd really given up his dream, though.

Though he *might* have been halfheartedly apologizing to Shane, too. Who knew?

After another try, Myrnin sighed and shook his head. "The portals aren't working," he said. "We will have to go in vehicles. It's not my preference, but it's the best option we have. Going on foot is a ridiculous risk. We will certainly need a fast escape route."

"Lucky for you I have a bitchin' pickup downstairs," Shane said. "Which provides an excellent fire platform for a flame-thrower, by the way."

"I was thinking more along the lines of a tank," Myrnin said. "Pity we don't have one."

"Actually," Michael said slowly, his forehead creased in thought, "we just might. Follow me."

Anything was better, Claire thought, than the smelly, chemical-heavy cleaner's closet, and she sucked down a deep, clean breath of air once they were back in the hall. It made her cough. She could almost imagine her breath puffing out the sickly gold color of Pine-Sol. Her clothes reeked of the stuff. She didn't know if it was bothering any of the others, but it definitely wasn't her favorite smell in the world, especially in that intense burst.

Michael led them down to the elevators and pressed the button for the parking garage. He looked . . . well, smug. Definitely smug.

"Spill it," Shane said. "You look like you won a year's shopping spree at the blood bank or something."

"You'll see," he said, and then the elevator doors dinged and rolled open . . .

. . . And Eve was standing there. She was wet and muddy, and there were four other vampires with her. She actually took a surprised step back when she saw Michael.

And he took the same step back when he saw her.

Oh, *so* not good. Claire's heart practically ripped in half at the expression on Eve's face—a fast-changing mixture of longing, anger, fear, love, and finally, sadness. She reached up and pulled her earplugs out and said, "Sorry—I was just surprised."

Michael didn't answer. He was looking . . . well, *sick* was probably the only word for it. Myrnin ignored the whole thing and pushed past him, out of the elevator. Shane, after a hesitation, followed, with Claire. Michael stepped out last, and only because the doors started to shut on him.

In the sudden and uncomfortable silence, the brown-haired vamp standing next to Eve took his headphones off and said, "Is there some problem?" He was talking to Michael, but he was looking at Eve.

"No," she said, and smiled brightly. "Thanks, Stephen. It's all good. You guys go on."

"Good work," said the tall, dark-haired vampire woman, and opened the elevator doors again for the four of them to step inside while Eve lingered behind. "Call on us anytime, Eve."

She nodded without taking her gaze off Michael, her dark eyes large and unreadable now.

"Making new friends?" he asked her. No mistaking the jealousy in that tone. "*Stephen?* I thought you were off vampires."

"Lighten up," Eve said. "I saved his life. It's not like we're going out."

Even Shane winced at that one. Michael didn't. He remained stone-faced, staring at his girl, and then he shrugged and said, "Well, you can go with your new friends or come with us. Your choice, I guess."

"Where are we going?" Eve asked, like it wasn't even a real question. Which it probably wasn't.

"The water treatment plant," Myrnin said. "I'll catch you up if you'd like."

"That's—okay," Eve said, and held up a hand when he would have kept talking. "I'm so not in the mood, Chatty Batty. Just hand me something to do."

"Oh," he said, and rubbed his hands together, "I think I can do that. Yes, absolutely. Michael? If you would lead on, please?"

Michael was no longer smug, but he led them toward the far

end of the garage. It felt oppressive and damp down here, and smelled of wet concrete and mold—smells that reminded Claire vividly of the draug, the pool, the horrific fight to survive.

The fear.

She took hold of Shane's hand, which was strategically stupid but emotionally smart; his warm, steady grip anchored her and made her feel less out of control. She couldn't tell what he was thinking, but he didn't let go.

A boxy gray shape loomed up in the dark, and Myrnin said, "Ahhhhh," in the way people do when they finally understand something. Claire squinted, but couldn't see much until Eve flicked on her flashlight and cast a harsh white glare over the gunmetal gray surface.

It was an armored cash truck, with some logo on it that was too sun-faded to read. It had a thick metal hide and a very intimidating door on the back.

"Nice. Gun ports," Shane said, flicking a fingernail at a round metal covering on the side of the truck. "Heavy steel. Run-flat tires. Bullet-resistant glass. Me likey, Mikey."

"It's a tank," Michael said. "Or at least as close as we're likely to get around here."

"Pop quiz," Eve said, and held up her black-fingernailed hand like a kid in school. "Does this thing actually, y'know, run?"

"Oh, yes," Myrnin said. He was walking around the truck, tapping a finger on his bottom lip. His expression was elated but thoughtful. "It's the Founder's personal security vehicle, for her protection in emergencies. Used for her personal evacuation only."

"Where are the keys?" Shane asked. He'd tried the driver's side door, but it was, of course, locked.

"No one but Amelie and her assistant would know, and her assistant was evacuated with the others, I'm afraid. Don't bother trying to force the lock, Michael. It's hardened against vampires as well as humans. Without the proper keys, we're not getting in. And yet . . . it *is* a good idea. Very good indeed." Myrnin turned suddenly and focused directly on Claire. "I will go ask Amelie for the keys."

"Excuse me?" Claire blinked. "That's . . . really not a good idea. Oliver wouldn't let me anywhere close to her. He said she was . . ."

"Unpredictable," Myrnin said briskly. "Well, if anyone can handle unpredictable, I should think it would be me. Don't worry. Oh, all right, then do worry, if that pleases you, but we need the key, and Amelie's got it. There's no choice."

"Pickup truck," Shane said. "That's a choice."

"Not a good one where we're going," Myrnin said. He held out a finger toward Michael, then Shane, then Eve, and said, "Stay."

"Excuse me, we're not your pets," Eve said. "You don't get to order us around . . ." But she was talking to empty air. Myrnin had already vanished, vampire-speed. The only one who might have caught him was Michael, but Michael wasn't moving.

When Claire started after him, Michael grabbed her by the shoulder. "No," he said. "He's right. Nobody's better qualified to handle unpredictable vampires than he is. Certainly not you. You are *way* too vulnerable."

"I'm not staying here," she said. "Are you coming or not? Because I don't think you want to have to tie me up to make me stay."

Shane heaved a sigh. "Nobody's tying her up," he said. "Sorry, Mike. It's not that I don't think you're right, it's that I know my girl. She's going. We can either watch her back or stay here. And I'm not staying here, mostly because I don't take orders from— what did you call him?"

"Chatty Batty," Eve said. "Hey, it fits."

"I like it."

Claire shook off Michael's hand. He let her. "Then let's go, before he gets himself killed."

Shane *probably* didn't mean it when he said, "Wait, that was an option? Because I could still stay."

Myrnin was already well ahead of them, of course, and they had the guards to deal with, but since Claire had already been admitted once today, with Theo, they let her in.

But *only* her.

"We're with the band," Shane said, and tried to push his way past. That got him an iron-hard vampire grip on his arm that made him wince and stopped him cold. "Claire, don't. Stay with me. He'll be okay."

But in her bones Claire didn't really think he would be. She looked at the guard holding Shane's arm and asked, "Is Oliver still in there, too?"

"He's gone to find the doctor," the guard said. "Myrnin just went in."

"So he's alone?" She felt a surge of anxiety. "Well, he wants us with him."

"Us?" The vampire wasn't buying that one. "You, maybe. The others stay here. They're not on the list."

"There's a list? And I'm not on it?" Eve said. "I'm deeply hurt. I'm *always* on the list."

"It's not a club," Michael said.

"Still."

Claire backed away, down the hall, mouthed, *Sorry*, to Shane, and hurried on. From the look on his face, she knew they'd be having a serious conversation about this later, but she couldn't wait to try to talk it out now.

Myrnin was in trouble. She could just feel it.

Inside the room, Claire shut the heavy door but didn't lock it behind her; the anteroom was a sitting area, hushed and airless. It reeked of the damp and sickness, and it also seemed a little like a museum . . . as if someone had created it for show, not for use. *This is how vampires lived in the twenty-first century*, the exhibit card would read. *Pretending that everything was normal.*

Claire took in a slow, calm breath and opened the bedroom door. She half expected to find it empty, but Myrnin was there, standing stock-still a few feet from the bed.

Looking at Amelie.

She looked like her own statue—immobile and white, lying exactly in the center of the bed with her hands folded over her stomach. The sheets were drawn up and folded back just below her arms. It looked as if she was wearing some kind of thick white nightgown, with incredibly delicate lace at the collar and cuffs. Her hair was loose, and it spilled over the pillow in a pale silk fan.

There was a thick bandage on her throat, but it was soaked through with dark, wet blood.

Seeing her like this was . . . strange. She looked very young, and vulnerable, and somehow very sad. Claire remembered seeing pictures of the tombs of queens, of the marble images carved to top them that were replicas of the bodies below. Amelie looked just like that . . . an eternal monument to her own mortality.

Myrnin raised his head and saw Claire standing there, and his expression turned from blank to tormented. "Get out," he said. "Get out *now*, while you still can!"

He sounded absolutely serious, and Claire took a step backward, intending to follow his instructions.

And then Amelie opened her eyes.

It was sudden, a flash of movement that made Claire's heart

skip a beat. Amelie's eyes were a paler gray than they'd always been, more like dirty ice.

"Someone's here," she whispered. "Someone . . ."

"Claire, get *out*," Myrnin said, and took a step closer to the bed. "I'm here, Amelie. Myrnin. Right here."

"You shouldn't be here," she whispered. Her voice was thin as silk, and just as soft. "Where is Oliver?"

"Gone, for the moment," Myrnin said. "Oh, my dearest. You are far too pale. Let me get something for you to eat." He meant blood, Claire thought. Amelie had *no* color under her skin. She looked almost translucent.

"Don't you mean some*one*?" Amelie asked. It was nearly a joke, but it wasn't funny. "I asked Oliver to end my suffering. I didn't mean to make him so angry, but he really must face facts, soon. Will you do it for me, Myrnin? As my friend?"

"Not yet," he said, and took her hand in his. "I am not quite ready to let you go. None of us are."

"All things die, even vampires." That same distant tone, as if none of it mattered any longer. "If it was only death I faced, I would go gladly. But I can feel it now, inside me. The pull of the sea. The tides. The hunger." Amelie's eyes focused on Myrnin again, and there was a strangely luminous glow to them. "The seas came first. All life flowed from them and must in the end return there. As I'm returning. As you will. I was a fool to believe the draug could be defeated. They are the tide. The sea. The beginning and end of us." The glow intensified, and Claire found herself oddly . . . calmed by it. Amelie seemed so peaceful, lying there. And being around her seemed so safe. Myrnin must have felt the same; he sank to a sitting position on the edge of her bed. "There's no escaping the tides, don't you see? Not for me, or you, or Morganville. Because the tide always comes."

Myrnin pulled in a sharp gasp, and looked down at his hand, held in hers. He tried to pull free, but couldn't. "Stop," he said, in a voice only half as strong as it should have been. "Amelie, *stop*. You must not do this."

"I'm not," she said, sounding very sad. "There's so much inside that isn't me any longer. You shouldn't have come. Either of you."

Her ice-pale gaze captured Claire's, and Claire knew she was walking forward, drawn by forces she didn't understand and couldn't control. She couldn't stop herself. Didn't really *want* to stop herself.

And then she stretched out her hand and Amelie's pale, strong fingers locked over hers.

She felt the tingle, and then the burning, like a million needles piercing her skin.

She watched the bitter cold of Amelie's skin change, take on warmth.

Blood.

Blood drawn out of *Claire*. By a *touch*.

The same was happening to Myrnin, Claire realized. He was panting now, mumbling frantic pleas, trying to pry her hand free from his but failing.

Amelie no longer needed fangs to feed. Like the draug, she fed at a touch.

And it was happening so *fast*. Claire felt light-headed, pleasantly tired, even though somewhere deep inside she was shrieking in protest.

Just close your eyes, Amelie's voice was saying gently, far away. *Just close your eyes and sleep now.*

And then something hit her and knocked her away, halfway across the room and into a heavy wooden table with a gigantic bowl of dried flowers. It all crashed to the carpet, spilling shattered glass and broken petals, and Claire was lying on her side, staring up at the wall. There was a painting there, something famous, with dark paint and bright bursts of color all done in furious layers and peaks. She blinked slowly, not quite comprehending what had just happened, and saw a bright spot of red closer to her than the painting.

Blood. Blood on her hand—no, on her fingers, welling out as if she'd been stabbed with a hundred pins.

It hurt in a sudden, blazing ignition of feeling, and she realized what had just happened. It crashed in on her fast and hard, and she felt terror rip through her. She squirmed back and up, sitting against the corner, holding her injured hand close to her chest.

Oliver was helping Myrnin unwrap Amelie's fingers from his wrist. As soon as it was done, Myrnin fell to the floor and half crawled, half slid into another corner, cradling his wrist just as Claire was holding her own injured fingers. He looked . . . appalled. And scared.

Oliver was standing between the two of them and the bed. Amelie hadn't moved. Not at all. Oliver looked as furious as Claire had ever seen him, face as sharp and pale as bone, eyes like coals smoldering red beneath the black. "You *idiots*," he snapped, and came toward Claire. When she flinched, he looked even angrier. "I'm not set to hurt you, stupid girl. Let me see your hand."

She was all too aware of the red pooling in her palm, but he didn't wait for her consent; he snatched her arm, vamp fast, and stretched it out to inspect the wound. If the blood itself affected him at all, he showed no signs of it. He took a moment, then let her go, strode away, and came back with a small white towel, which he pitched into her lap. "Clean yourself," he said. "I told you very clearly you were not to enter this room. I never took you for this much of a fool. And you, Myrnin. What the devil were you thinking?"

"We need the key," Claire said. Her teeth were inexplicably chattering, and she felt ice-cold inside, as if she'd lost a lot of blood, not just a little. Maybe it was shock. "The k-k-key to the armored truck, downstairs. W-we need to use it to g-get to the water plant. Myrnin said she had it."

"The key?" Oliver almost laughed. "Don't be ridiculous. It wasn't only the key, was it?"

Myrnin raised his head then. "I needed to find out just how much you've been lying to me about her condition. A considerable amount, it seems to me."

Claire never saw Oliver hit him; she just inferred that it happened from the blur, and Myrnin's head snapping back. He wiped blood from his mouth with the back of one hand, never looking away from Oliver, and said, "You said that she was holding her own. She just asked me to *kill her*."

"She fights," Oliver said. "And she fights it better without these ridiculous distractions. Take the girl and get out. You risked yourself, and her, for nothing. I thought you liked the child better than that."

"I like both of them better than that. But I came for a reason, and the reason still holds."

"Your curiosity is an addiction that will kill you one of these days. I'm not Amelie. I'll not put up with your whims. Consider this fair warning, Myrnin: when I tell you to stay away, *stay away*, and keep your pets on leashes."

Myrnin looked past him at Claire. "Are you all right?" He still seemed shaken, but he was pulling himself together fast. He stood up and helped her rise as well. She didn't think she was all right, exactly, but she nodded anyway. Bruises, for sure, but nothing broken. Her hand was the worst of it, and the towel Oliver had thrown at her was soaking up the blood. "Oliver. We still need those keys."

"Keys?" Oliver interrupted, and barked out a laugh. "Keys to *what?*"

"The Founder's transport car. The armored one. I require them," Myrnin said.

"Be off with you. I don't have them."

"No, the *Founder* has them." Myrnin stressed the noun a bit more than necessary, and it seemed to make Oliver angrier still, if that was even possible. "And the *Founder* will give them to me, if she's still herself at all. She knows that I wouldn't ask for no reason."

"Myrnin." Amelie's quiet, gray voice hardly broke the surface of the silence, but both of them turned toward her instantly. There was a flash of something in Oliver's face, something like—fear, Claire thought. It was gone too fast for her to be certain.

"I am sorry, but I cannot control this," Amelie said. "It's best that you leave now. All of you. Leave me to this. I fight it as I can." Her eyes slowly closed, then opened again. "Keys. Keys are in the black box in my desk. Take them." It hurt her to do whatever she was doing—even Claire could see it—but she even *smiled*, just a little, through the pain. "I don't want to hurt my friends. Oliver has been trying to protect you, you should know that."

"Oh, my dear," Myrnin said, and blinked back tears. "Amelie, hold. You must *hold*. I'll be back and we will find a way to stop this."

"No," she said. "Don't come back. *Never* come back, Myrnin. Or I'll have you." She suddenly looked toward Claire, and the impact of it made Claire take in a sharp, painful breath. "I'll remember the taste of you. Don't let me get so close again."

It was a naked, chilling warning, and Claire took it seriously. So, she saw, did Myrnin.

But Oliver had to drive it home. "If you do come back," he said, "I'll kill you before she gets you. It would be a kindness."

Myrnin shook his head. "She'll get you first, you know that."

"I'm not as easy as all that." Oliver held the door for them, and his eyes brushed over Claire, then came to rest on Myrnin. "You of all people should know."

Then he let the door slam shut behind them.

"Let me see," Myrnin said, in the sudden silence of the anteroom, and she realized he was asking about her hand. She unwrapped it and held it out, and flinched as his cool fingers touched her hot, bloodied ones. "They've swollen a bit, but that's good. Your body is fighting the infection. You'll be all right." His hand came away with a smear of blood on it, and he looked at it, then sighed and wiped it on the towel. "That is a great waste."

"What, the blood?"

"Of course not." He sighed. "Amelie, of course. We shall not see her like again in these weak times."

He set a wicked fast pace down the hall; Claire grimly trudged along for her enforced aerobic workout and wondered if her hand might feel better if she just *hit him*. He was so far ahead she almost missed which turns he'd taken; this building always got her turned around, as she suspected it was supposed to do. There were no signs, no names on doors, just those expensively generic paintings. She supposed that if she could tell one old masters landscape from another, she'd know her way around, but her brain wasn't really wired that way.

"Slow down!" she finally yelled, as Myrnin disappeared around a distant corner. She was tired, shaky, and irritable, and the bruises she'd collected were making themselves felt, definitely.

She also had a hot pinpoint headache forming in the center of her forehead.

Myrnin popped his head—just his head—back around the corner at a very weird angle to say, "Oh, just *hurry up!*" and then he vanished. If Claire had been in the habit of cursing like, say, Shane, she'd have scorched the carpet with it. Instead, she just set her teeth together, hard, and moved faster.

Amelie's office, without its usual complement of guards, was halfway down the next hall, or at least that was the door that Myrnin was in the act of kicking open. It took several attempts, which must have meant that Amelie had built her security against vampires, not humans—sensible, really. Before Claire reached him, Myrnin had beaten the locks, and the heavy wooden door splintered open with a crash. "Faster would be better," he said, "given that her guards are not *fully* off duty, and they may not appreciate that I took dire measures, even with permission. They have to fix the doors eventually, you know."

He zipped inside, kicked open Amelie's inner sanctum door with a few *more* violent blows, and by the time Claire got there he was at the desk, ripping open another (locked) drawer and removing a black box.

He hissed and dropped it on the desktop in surprise. His fingers looked burned—in fact, there was a faint wisp of smoke coming from them. But it was a *black* box, not . . .

Claire picked it up, or tried to. It was very heavy. When she scratched it with her thumbnail, the paint peeled off and bright metal was revealed.

Silver.

"Locked," she said. "Do you have the key?"

"Cherub, do I look like I have *any* keys to *anything* in this room? The doors I just knocked down would argue against that, I'd

think. Here." He snatched up a letter opener—steel, not silver—
and set it against the lock. "Hold the box still."

She did, and he hit the letter opener sharply on the end with
the heel of his hand, and it drove into the lock and snapped it.
Claire folded back the hinged top and said, "Oh, no."

Because there were literally dozens of keys in the box, and not
a one of them was labeled. They had colored tags, but that didn't
mean anything to her or, she could tell, to Myrnin. He shook his
head and said, "Bring the box. Damnation, I believe her security is
coming." He glared at her injured right hand, then took hold of a
heavy velvet curtain over the window and ripped it down. It didn't
make the room that much lighter, since darkness was falling fast.
Myrnin smothered the box in the thick velvet and scooped it up.
"Well? What are you waiting for? *Run!*"

She didn't know what they were really running *from*, and wasn't
in any mood to find out. She'd memorized turns this time—right
out the door, down the hall, left, then another left—and then she
spotted the vampire guards at the end of the long stretch of corridor.

And her friends, waiting.

"Why is there a bloody towel on your hand?" Shane demanded, and then he spotted Myrnin behind her. "Maybe that
question's for you, asshole. What happened?"

"She touched something she shouldn't have, and we don't have
time for this. Here." Myrnin shoved the curtain-swaddled box at
Eve, who yelped at how heavy it was. Michael took it from her.
"It's full of keys. Find the ones we need. Careful of the silver,
there's a good lad." He didn't pause, just hurried on with Michael
and Eve in his wake. "To the garage!"

That left Shane still holding Claire. He didn't let go. "What
happened to your hand?" he asked. "Because if it was him—"

"It wasn't." Well, that was debatable, but she wasn't about to tell Shane; there was enough tension between him and Myrnin already. "It was Amelie. She's turning into . . . one of them. The draug." She stripped off the towel and showed him her hand, and the red pinpricks of bite—or stings—that covered her fingers. He winced. "We don't have much time to save her."

"If we can," he said, and lifted her injured hand to his lips. His kiss felt so good that it washed relief all the way through her. "I know you. You're going to try like hell to make everything right again."

"Hell's what's coming," she said. "I'm just trying to avoid it. Come on."

As soon as the elevator doors opened, they heard the sound of an engine coughing, catching, and taking up a heavy thrumming idle. Shane cocked his head in that direction. "That's our cue," he said. "You ready?"

"No." She laughed a little, and he kissed her, and she just wanted *that*, more of *that* and less of the blood and terror. Morganville had always been bad, but this had to get better. *It had to.*

But first, she strongly suspected, it was going to get worse.

Driving inside an armored truck was boring, Claire found. She'd gotten the shotgun seat, which was useless even though she actually *had* a shotgun, because the windows were vampire tinted and she couldn't see a thing. Michael drove in silence, with an occasional muttered "Sorry" when the heavy truck hit a bump. It wasn't made for bumps. At all. The three in the back were getting bounced around like mad—no, *two* of them, Eve and Shane. Myrnin had taken the only seat, the one as plush as a throne, with a safety harness. It had obviously been built for Amelie. There were hanging straps for, well, hangers-on, and Shane and Eve were clinging to them, not that it helped much.

"I think I may puke," Shane called up, which was met by a chorus that he'd better not. He wasn't serious, at least. Or Claire *hoped* he wasn't. "You could fill this thing up with water and detergent and spin clothes in it. Does it even have shocks?"

"Stop complaining," Myrnin said, sitting perfectly comfortably in his velvet-covered seat. "It is the most protected vehicle you could possibly wish to be inside. It is bulletproof, lightproof, and most important, *waterproof*, although if you could please not put that to the test by driving it into any deep ponds I would appreciate it."

Michael looked sideways at Claire and said, "Could you please see if you can get him to shut up before Shane punches him, or I do?"

"Myrnin," she said wearily, "just shut up."

"You wound me."

"Not yet, but keep it up."

Myrnin didn't answer that, but his smirk, which Claire glimpsed over her shoulder, was enough to make her want to smack him anyway. He was clearly feeling better.

The bouncing slowed to a crawl, finally, and Michael said, "I can see the treatment plant up ahead. The gates are shut. Do you want me to run it?"

"Yes. The less time we spend on foot, the better," Myrnin said. "Run the gate by all means, and take us as near as you can to the main entrance. No discussion once we arrive, we simply *move*, and everyone must know their jobs. Michael, you and Eve will stay behind to lock the vehicle; we don't want any unpleasantly moist surprises waiting for us when we get back. Once it's locked, you go in and to the second floor on the north side. There are clearly marked manual valve control panels at the end of the hall; shut them all down and evacuate back to the vehicle immediately. Yours is the shortest distance, so you should get back to the truck the fastest. That is why you will have the keys."

"What if something happens? Are these the only keys?"

"Yes," Myrnin said, "so don't let anything happen, by all means. I should deeply prefer not to have to rescue anyone on this particular outing. Shane, you and Claire will take the manual valve controls on the second floor, on the south side. You have a greater distance to go, so you should do the same as Michael and Eve—shut down the valves and run back for the van."

"And what about you?" Claire asked.

"I will be in the center of the first floor, main control room at the far east end of the building. I will be there to disable the start-up panels and program the system to reverse the flow of the pipes. That process is going to take the longest."

Shane raised his hand. "Uh, question?"

"Yes?"

"You didn't design this plant, did you? It's not made out of—I don't know, cow entrails and flywheels or anything?"

Myrnin gave him a cool, blank look and said, "In fact this was built by an engineering firm from Houston, I believe. In the 1950s. There is a sad lack of entrails, cow or otherwise. Are you finished?"

"Suppose so." Shane shrugged. "Hey, is it okay if I wear the flamethrower this time?"

"Can anybody stop you?" Myrnin asked. "By all means."

Shane grinned and put the straps on, lifting the contraption onto his back and checking the ignition flame to be sure it turned on. "Good to go."

"Hold on," Michael said, and pressed the accelerator. Shane

and Eve yelped and clung to their panic straps with both hands. Claire felt that they were hurtling through space blindly, and she fought an urge to yell at him to slow down because she couldn't see, but he could, and then there was a shudder, the truck thumped hard, and he *did* hit the brakes to bring them to a skidding stop.

The sudden silence lasted only an instant before Myrnin bellowed, "Move, *now!*" and lunged with vampiric speed, throwing open the back doors. Shane scrambled out after him and swung Eve down just as Michael stepped out of the driver's side and Claire got out on the passenger's side. Michael locked up the doors from the electronic key fob and handed it to Eve.

"You hang on to the keys," he said. "Insurance."

She gave him a curious look, but at least it wasn't angry anymore. Just . . . conflicted. Then the two of them ran after Myrnin, who had already disappeared inside.

Shane took Claire's hand in his. The water treatment plant was a sprawling mass of concrete, pipes, and shadows, and nothing was moving.

Overhead, thunder rumbled, and it seemed that the clouds were growing thicker. No rain yet, but it was coming. Could the draug actually *push* the clouds? Make them go where they wanted? That seemed impossible, but then, the thought of something able to break itself apart into individual drops and reform was impossible in itself.

"Stay with me," Shane said, and she nodded. The weight of her shotgun was heavy in her right hand, but it didn't slow her down any as they ran after their friends, into the dark.

The water treatment plant had a horrible smell to it, rotten eggs mixed with vomit, and Claire hadn't expected that. Her eyes teared up, and she coughed and choked and made a completely useless fanning motion in front of her nose, as if the stench was something she could wave off. Shane seemed wretched, too, but stoic about it. "Burst pipe, probably," he said. "Raw sewage. Try not to breathe too deep, but keep breathing. You'll get used to it."

"The not-breathing-deep part is easy," she said. "This is *really* gross."

"Did I ever tell you I worked trash and dead animal pickup? One of the many glamorous jobs I've held in Morganville. Not everybody can be a rock star or a mad scientist vampire assistant. Somebody has to clean up the crap. In my case, literally."

The lights were on in the plant, but they seemed dim and discolored somehow, and they flickered from time to time. The electrical grid wasn't too stable, Claire guessed, or else the place was running on emergency power. She felt for the small LED flash that she'd clipped to the belt loop of her jeans—still there. It wasn't super bright, but it would help. Eve had brought some monster aluminum-cased thing that could double for a baseball bat, of course; she'd also blinged it up with Swarovski crystals, but that was just Eve. Always finding a fun use for the glue gun that nature never intended.

There were stairs going up and down. "Second floor," Shane said, and she nodded. They went up fast but quietly, and as they reached the landing of the second floor, Claire heard something that sounded like a distant gush of water through pipes, and then the lights just . . . failed. Then they struggled back on, flickering badly.

"Not good," Shane said. "Come on. This way."

The hallway was long, straight, and uncomplicated, except that the pipes running overhead had developed leaks . . . some slow drips, some silvery (or brown) streams of water that had created thick pools on the floor. The smell was stronger here. *Right*, Claire thought. *Avoid brown water at all costs.* Not that the apparently clear water would be safer; it was just less disgusting.

"Hang back," Shane said, and unhooked the nozzle from the pack on his back. He thumbed the ignition switch on the side, and the blue pilot flame wicked on, hissing slightly. "Fire in the hole!"

And he unleashed an incredibly dense stream of flame that rolled over the puddles, steaming them into a boil. When he took his finger off the trigger and the flames died, Claire blinked to bring her eyes back to pre-flamethrower focus, and looked for any sign of the draug.

Nothing. The way seemed clear.

"Go!" she said, and ran forward. Shane matched her. He had the nozzle still at the ready and the pilot light burning, but they didn't need it after all; apart from splashes, the pools of water didn't produce any evil beings, grab at their feet, or do anything at all. They raced breathless to the end of the hall, and Claire pointed at a panel of switches marked with red signs on their right. MANUAL VALVE SHUTOFF CONTROL, it read. USE ONLY IN AUTHORIZED EMERGENCY.

"I think this qualifies," Shane said. The valves were covered with glass panels, but there was a handy little hammer hanging from a chain, and he used it to shatter all of the panes, one after another. "You start from that end. I'll take this one."

That was an okay plan until Claire tried to *turn* the valve—it was big, heavy, and, most important, hadn't been moved (probably) since they'd stuck the glass over it in the 1950s. She tried, but it just wasn't happening. Shane was managing his first one, with difficulty, but Shane had about ten times her upper-body strength.

She threaded her shotgun through the spokes on the valve and used it as a lever, careful to keep her hands far away from the trigger mechanism. With a deep, metallic groan that vibrated up through the floor, the valve started to turn. As it spun, it got a little easier, and she tightened it off, took the shotgun out, and moved to the next one.

"Claire," Shane said.

"Almost got it!" She gritted her teeth and threw her shoulders into it, and the second valve squealed as rust flaked free.

"Claire!"

She looked up this time, and saw that he was facing away from her, down the hallway. The expression on his face . . . she didn't want to look.

But she had to.

The draug were approaching in utter silence, gliding through the metal halls like ghosts. Identical men, all gray and indistinguishable and yet so very wrong, rippling and boneless.

There must have been *twenty* of them coming their way.

"Get behind me," Shane said.

"I'm not done!" She threw herself into moving the valve again, the last one, and more rust flaked as the metal screamed and turned, inch by grudging inch. Her hands slipped, slick with sweat, and then Shane was shouldering her aside and grabbing the makeshift lever of the shotgun and applying his own strength to it. It turned another half circle, and jammed tight.

"That's it, we're boned," he said, and pulled the shotgun out to hand it to her. She almost dropped it, but got it under control and pointed it at the approaching draug. *Tight into her shoulder.* She was already badly bruised there, but a few more hematomas were a small price to pay. She looked silently at Shane, and he stepped *forward*, gripping the nozzle of the flamethrower. He pressed the ignition button, and when the blue flame leaped into life, he grinned fiercely.

"I love this job," he said, and he probably would have added something else to that, something witty and funny, but before he could, the draug closest to him flung out its hand, which stretched impossibly far and turned into water, clear and formless, and hit the nozzle with a wet, sizzling slap.

It drowned out the ignition flame.

Shane looked down, shocked, and hit the button again. Then again. He got a clicking sound, but no pilot light.

"Fuck," he whispered, but he didn't waste time on regrets; he just holstered the nozzle and grabbed the shotgun from the rig on his back. "Claire, stairs. Now."

She was already on it. Over her shoulder was the dim light of an exit sign, with the reassuring figure of a little stick man walking down steps. She backed up toward it and it looked clear . . . but the hallway had looked clear when they'd come that way, too. The draug were more than nasty—they were clever. Really clever.

She kicked the door open, and saw nothing. Again. No choice, really; the draug were steadily advancing toward them now, and Shane was saving his shotgun blasts to make them count. Between the two of them they could take out maybe half of the draug that were facing them. Retreat was the only option.

"Come on!" she shouted, and plunged down the first six steps. At the halfway point, where the stairs turned, she looked back. Shane had backed through the door, and now he unloaded one ear-shattering blast from his shotgun, jumped in, and slammed the door. Then he hit the quick-release button on the flamethrower. Its heavy weight clanged to the metal floor, and he grabbed the loose nozzle and jammed it through the door handle to hold it shut. It wouldn't stop the draug for long, if it stopped them at all, but he'd done what he could.

He was coming down toward her when she heard the sound . . . like water through pipes, but different this time. Closer. Echoing.

And she saw the wave flood down the steps from the next floor up, thick and murky.

It hit Shane in the back and knocked him off his feet. Then, instead of continuing to fall down the steps as gravity demanded, it just . . . stopped, formed a thick, trembling bubble, and consumed him.

He floated in the liquid, as if it had more density than real water. He was thrashing, but he couldn't get leverage.

"No!" Claire screamed, and lifted her shotgun, but there was nothing she could do; firing at it was firing at him, and she couldn't, *couldn't*.

More fluid rushed down the steps toward her, and she saw his face through the distorted lens of the liquid drowning him, saw the fear and the rage and the horror, and she saw him say something. Maybe it was her name.

Maybe it was just *run*.

She ran.

The liquid snaked after her, more like tentacles than a wave now, grabbing and reaching for her as she flung herself forward and around the corner of the stairwell. Shane wasn't in the way now, and she fired wildly up at the thing. The noise slammed her like a physical blow, and the hammer of the shotgun hit her shoulder with brutal force. She hardly felt it, because the real pain was inside, where she was screaming Shane's name.

I left him. I left him.

The force of the shotgun blast pushed her backward, off balance, and she fell the last few steps. The silver spread hit the draug's shape with awesome force, ripping it apart, but it only flowed *up* the stairs in retreat. It made a sound, a horrible, shrieking chorus.

She couldn't see Shane.

I left him.

The door opened behind her, and a hand grabbed her shoulder and yanked her backward. She fought it blindly, tried to get the shotgun turned around, but a cool, pale hand grabbed the barrel and held it away, and then she realized that it was Myrnin. He looked past her and saw the draug flowing down the steps toward them, and without a word, grabbed her around the waist, lifted her, and *ran.*

"No!" she screamed, and struggled to get free. She lost the shotgun in the process, but it didn't matter now; the only thing that mattered was she had to make him understand that they had to *go back.* She kept screaming as the walls flashed by at nightmare speed, and there was a sound around them that drowned out even her own anguished cries, something brutal and triumphant and terrible. There were draug, too. She could see them coming for them, but Myrnin fired his shotgun one-handed to clear the way and never stopped, never faltered. "No, go back!"

Then they were outside, and Michael and Eve were in the truck's driver and passenger seats. Claire saw them in a tear-streaked blur as Myrnin passed them, opened the back door, and flung her bodily inside. He entered, slammed the door shut, and shouted, "Go! Now!"

"Where's Shane?" Eve asked. She'd turned, staring, and the dawning horror in her eyes was nothing to the blackened fury and terror inside Claire. She grabbed for the door, but Myrnin held her still.

"He's gone," Myrnin said, never taking those dark eyes away from Claire's face. "Shane is gone."

Michael's face was grim and ashen. "We can't just—"

"He's *dead*," Myrnin said, and it was as cold and cutting a thing as she'd ever heard him say. "He's dead and you will kill us all if you don't *get us out, now.* Do you want to see what your pretty Eve will look like in their pools as they strip her down to the bones? Because I promise you, Magnus will make you watch."

Michael flinched, and hesitated, and then . . .

Then he put the truck in reverse and no matter how Claire tried to scream, fight, *stop him*, he drove away.

And left Shane behind.

CHAPTER SEVEN

SHANE

W hen the draug's liquid surrounded me, flowed over me like syrup, everything just . . . whited out for a few seconds. And then it went black.

And then I just . . . woke up.

It surprised me how easily I got away.

One second I was trapped in that sticky, thick, stinging liquid—death by drowning in jellyfish—and the next I was clawing my way free, *up*, and finding the edges of the bubble that held me prisoner. I got my hand out, then my elbow, and then my face broke the surface and I gasped for air as I slithered completely free. I was slimed and disgusting, and I was stung all over, but that didn't matter. I slipped in the thick draug residue and tried to follow Claire down—but part of it split off and came back for me.

I went up instead, taking the steps two and three at a time. Outpacing it.

I made it back to the second floor and then kept going, because the door I'd braced was shuddering and there was liquid flowing around the edges. The draug were very angry.

Top floor.

I hit the exit door hard and stumbled out onto the decking. This area was mostly offices, locked doors, and I needed to get to the main stairs in the center. I needed to find Claire and Michael and Eve and get the hell out of here, *now*, before the draug caught up to me again . . . but the thought did cross my mind that if they were after me, maybe that would give everybody else a chance to get clear of them.

That would be okay, if so. Not that I wouldn't rather live, if it came down to it.

There didn't seem to be any draug sliming their way toward me, which was a temporary blessing. My clothes were soaked, and the stinging just got worse, as if I was rolling in a million tiny shards of glass. I could see the pink wash of blood spreading through the damp fabric of my shirt. I needed to get clean and dry, fast; whatever bits of draug were still on me were trying to feed, and I had no idea what that would mean. What if they got inside me? I had a vision of chest-bursting alien parasites that made me want to puke up the taste of rotting slime.

For a fraction of a second, that felt so real it was terrifying. *They're eating me. Eating me alive.* And then a kind of strange calm settled in, because I was okay, I was alive, I was going to make it. I just knew it.

Because I was Shane Collins, and the fact that I was still alive was an ongoing miracle anyway.

But the clothes had to come off.

I kicked open an office door and found a locker that held extra coveralls. I stripped down to the skin, toweled off with a sports flag pinned to the wall (finally, a good use for a TPU souvenir), and put on the coveralls. They were a thick orange paper with reflective white strips on the sleeves, back and legs, and they just barely fit me. If I did a lot of bending, it was going to get interesting, but ripped pants were the least of my worries. The stinging died down to a dull, constant ache, and I found a pair of heavy work boots that were only a little small. I left them untied.

Then I tried for the main stairs.

No good. The draug were in the way. They had resumed their human disguises, and all of them were moving purposefully toward the front exit—where the truck was parked, probably still waiting for me because I knew Claire wasn't going to leave without me. Michael and Eve wouldn't want to, either, but Myrnin? That plasma-sucking asshat would dump me in a hot second, and I knew it.

"Over my dead body," I whispered, but very, very quietly, because that was all too likely right now. So I couldn't go down.

That left up, to the roof.

The stairs I'd taken to get here *had* no up, but there were things on the top of the building—air conditioners, at least—that people needed to repair, so there had to be access somewhere. I found an evacuation plan beside the silent, dead elevator, and it showed roof access on the other fire stairs. I headed that way, moving as quietly as I could. The draug didn't seem really interested in me now, but that could change at any time. I needed to get to Claire, to make sure she was okay. She'd run downstairs, and maybe she'd gotten away, but what if she'd run into another trap? What if they had her?

I found the roof door. No locks, but it was alarmed, according to the big red sign. Great; pushing it meant that I was giving the draug a big neon sign that said IDIOT ESCAPEE HERE. Not much I could do about it, though; it was either sound the alarm and hope to find an escape, or stay here and hope I could play keep-away with things that vampires found horrifying and wrong.

I pressed the exit latch on the door. The alarm sounded a shrill, monotonous drone that hit me like an ice pick through the ear, and I ran for it. The shoes felt weird on my feet, molded to some other guy's balance; the wintery chill and damp quickly soaked into the thick paper jumpsuit, and I had a mad second's worry that it was just going to dissolve around me, like tissue, leaving me running around naked in work boots on a roof while the draug pointed and laughed before eating me.

Something was eating me. For a white-hot second, I felt the sting, but that wasn't right. I'd changed clothes, I'd wiped down. There might be draug residue, but it wouldn't be enough to hurt me.

I was okay.

Overhead, thunder boomed and lightning danced in the clouds.

I made it to the edge of the roof and peered over. There was no railing; this wasn't some terrace or balcony—it was just tar, gravel, and a sharp drop for three floors, straight down to a parking lot.

And a big, square, gray armored truck that was still sitting right where we'd left it. Of course they were okay. I believed it, I *knew* it. Just like I knew they wouldn't leave me behind.

Stinging. A breathtaking wave of it, again, flashing over me and then fading into a wave of calm. *Everything is okay. Look, they're here. They're waiting for me. We're okay.*

I saw the driver's side door open and Michael step out on the running board. Even in all that gray, dim light, his fierce grin glowed right along with his blond hair. "What's with the prison-wear?" he shouted up.

"You know me. I've spent so much time behind bars I miss the fashions." I looked at the drop. It didn't get any better. "I'm cut off, man. Is Claire—"

"She's here, screaming her head off. She made us turn around for you. I think she's about to stake Myrnin, and me, and maybe Eve if we don't let her come find you, so save us, get your ass down here."

"Uh, I'd love to, but I'm not half superhero like you. And I left my Spider-Man costume at home."

Michael got serious. In one fluid move he was out of the van and leaping up on the roof like some big, dangerous cat.

He was staring up at me, and in a calm, clear voice, he said, "Jump."

"Dude, I am not *jumping*."

"I mean it."

"You mean you're going to catch me like some old-school damsel in distress? No way in hell, man."

He didn't say anything. I didn't say anything. We just looked at each other, and then I felt a damp breath of chill on the back of my neck, and I knew, *knew* the draug were there, they were rising up out of the puddles on the roof, dripping down out of the clouds, coming up in a liquid rush from the stairwell. . . .

Something was eating me. Part of my brain was screaming, but the thick wave of calm descended again, smothering it. *It's all okay. Everything's okay. Jump.*

I jumped.

It wasn't a hero kind of thing, I didn't do a swan dive or let out a warrior yell or anything. I probably looked stupid as hell, actually.

It seemed to take forever, but I was sure Claire could have told me exactly how long it took me to fall, simple math and all that, and then something cushioned me and bounced me up on my feet again with a solid thump, so smooth and fast that it was like Michael hadn't *actually* caught me at all.

Which he had, of course, but we pretended really hard that it had never happened.

"Get in the back," he told me, and swung himself down into the truck's cab. I jumped from the top of the truck to the ground—ouch, even that small distance was tough on the knees—and opened the back door.

Claire was fighting with Myrnin, and by God, she looked like she might just win. Well, probably not, but from the expression on her face she was never going to give up, *ever*. I kind of froze for a second, because I had never seen her look like that, so focused and burning with rage and just . . .

Beautiful.

And then she saw me, and the look changed, and it was something even more amazing. There's this word I always had trouble with in school: *transcendent*.

But that was it, right there.

Myrnin let her go without a word, and she flew into my arms so hard I almost tumbled out the back again. She was all soft skin and tensed, trembling muscle. I hugged her hard, just for a second, and then let go to slam the back door shut and lock it. "Go, Mikey!" I yelled, and then grabbed Claire again. I kissed her. I wanted to kiss her forever. No, that wasn't true—I wanted a hell of a lot more than that, but it wasn't going to happen in the back of an armored truck with a damn vampire leaning up against Amelie's velvet throne, watching us with an expression somewhere between distaste and longing.

Claire looked vague and dumbstruck for a second when I let go, but she grabbed a handhold—me—as the truck backed up. "Hey," she said, "what the heck are you wearing?"

"I went shopping," I said. "What do you think? Straight off the runway."

"Where, at the detention center?"

Banter was tiring, suddenly, so I resorted to the truth. "I had to ditch my clothes. They were full of draug."

She winced, and unsnapped the top of the jumpsuit to see the red marks on my skin. The bleeding had stopped, at least, though the worst bites had leaked into the paper, making it look either festive or horrific, depending on how your mood ran. Me, I was just happy to be alive and have my girl holding me. Today, that was one hell of a win. "Did you get hurt anywhere else?"

"We can explore that somewhere better than this, but I think I'm okay. Got away clean. I mean that like a metaphor, because I could really use a shower."

Then I felt the sting again, hot as acid rain. *I got away clean. . . . No, I couldn't have. I didn't get away. Nobody gets away. Something is eating me. I know it. I feel it. . . .* No. No, I was okay. Everything was okay. Claire was right here, holding on to me. It was all *fine.*

"Did you close the valves?" Myrnin asked.

"One was stuck," I said. "All the others are closed. You don't think they can open them?"

"Unlikely. Magnus can manifest enough physical strength to manage it, but he is about to have much more to worry about," Myrnin said. "I flushed the lines with silver nitrate. They can't use the pipes with any safety. We've slowed them down considerably, at the very least."

The truck did a three-point turn and accelerated, which was a relief. I'd been afraid the draug were going to do some end run around us and trap us all. But from the roaring of the engine, Mikey wasn't going to let anything at all stop us now, and if the draug wanted to splash the windshield I supposed they were welcome to try.

Myrnin sat down on the cushy throne that was decorated with the Founder's symbol on the top, and heaved a big sigh. He was *smiling.* Not the usual look for him, either—this had a certain gleeful cruelty to it that made me glad he wasn't directing it at me.

"Can you hear that?" he asked us. He had his eyes closed and his head tipped back against the heavy velvet padding.

"Is it the draug?" Claire asked anxiously. "Are they singing? Is it getting to you or—"

"Not singing," he said, and the smile grew wider. "Screaming. They're screaming. And it is *lovely.*"

There was something off about him, I thought with a weird, fleeting chill. The Myrnin I remembered was a crazy asshole, but he wasn't some kind of sadist. Then again, I supposed they'd been afraid of the draug for so long that maybe a little gruesome victory dance might not be so strange.

He opened his eyes and looked at me, and for a moment there was something *wrong* in him. Something not Myrnin at all.

It hurts. It shouldn't still hurt. Something's wrong. I need to . . . to wake up. . . .

No. There was no pain. I was fine. Everything was *fine.*

"We should definitely celebrate that we did not die," Myrnin said. "I believe you're all old enough for champagne, are you not?"

"Yes," I said, and heard Michael and Eve chorus from the front.

"No," Claire blurted, and her cheeks turned adorably pink. "Oh, come on, you already knew that. And by the way, *none* of us are legal drinkers yet."

"We're old enough to carry flamethrowers," I pointed out. "And shotguns."

"I know, and it's not that I would turn it down. I just wanted to be . . . on the record. That we're not old enough for *any* of this."

I kissed her forehead, because that was just . . . cute.

Something's eating me. Oh God, I can feel it. . . . The pain . . .

But that was wrong, because I'd escaped. We'd all escaped.

It was all just . . . fine.

By the time we reached Founder's Square, things were happening. We couldn't see them from the back of the truck, but Michael relayed a constant stream of information as he drove. Police cars were speeding out of the secured area instead of into it. Word there was that flushing nitrate through the lines had worked—worked lots better than we'd ever expected. The draug were trying to escape, but they'd been poisoned.

They were dying.

You're dying. Wake up. It felt like my own voice, screaming inside, but it made no sense, no sense at all. Everything was going perfectly.

We were taking back our town.

The next few hours were a confused blur. Oliver ignored us and ordered us back to the room where we'd slept, and that was okay, because after all the danger and adrenaline I was bone-tired, and I could tell Claire and Eve were asleep on their feet, too. I don't think any of us expected it to be quite that . . . fast.

Claire and I zipped our sleeping bags together and fell asleep spooned together. I thought I'd sleep soundly; I had good reason to, but instead I kept feeling the sharp, digging stings, needles burrowing and probing inside me, and even though I knew it was a dream, just a dream, *nothing*, it kept me awake.

Whimpering.

Afraid.

Something's eating you, Shane.

No. I was fine. Everything was fine.

I finally dozed, and woke up to find Amelie standing in the doorway. I'm not big on impressing the vamps, but there was something a little unfair about facing the Queen Bee with bed-head and morning breath. I guess the most important thing, though, was that she was awake, and standing up, and actually seemed better. Oliver was with her, looking like a scowling black crow, but I think that was mostly because he was still spoiling for a fight.

Evidently, he wasn't going to get it.

"Magnus is injured," Amelie told us. She sat, gracefully, on a chair and made it look as if it was her own idea instead of something to prevent herself from collapsing in a heap. She had her hair down, which made her look almost our age, though there's nothing about the Founder's eyes that reminds me of youth. "He hides now, and his draug thralls are dying quickly. Your actions may have turned the tide. I will not forget that."

"You," Oliver said, and pointed to me. "And you." Michael. "Come with me."

I traded a look with my best friend, and he shrugged, and we got up and followed the two vampires out of the hall. Claire wanted to come along, but I promised her I wouldn't do anything stupid—though she probably knew that was a nutty promise, coming from me.

The voice inside my head rose to a deafening shriek. *You're breaking all your promises. You're giving up, you asshole. Wake up!* It felt like being plunged into ice water, and for a breathtaking second I couldn't breathe, couldn't *live* with the stinging pain of it.

Michael grabbed my shoulder. "You okay, man?"

Yes. Of course I was. I was always okay, right? Everything was fine.

"I am leading a group to take Magnus," Oliver told me and Michael out in the hallway; he supported Amelie with an arm under hers, as if he were escorting her to some fancy dance, but it was obvious he was keeping her upright. "I want the two of you with us."

"Good," I said. I was always up for a good fight, even against the draug—maybe *especially* against the draug. I would never get the images of Claire lying so still and broken on the floor of the Glass House out of my head, even though she was okay now. It had been the lowest moment of my life, in a life with plenty of cellar-diving events. I tried hard not to relive how I'd felt, seeing her that way. "Where are we going?"

Oliver didn't bother to give info, but that was typical. He did arm us up, which was nice—shotguns, which felt solid and deadly in my hands. Then we fell into line with a bunch of vampires and even a dozen humans—surprisingly, the new leader of the human resistance (all the resistance leaders were named Captain Obvious) was one of them, sporting his I-hate-vamps stake tattoo but carrying a shotgun all the same. He nodded to me guardedly; I nodded back. That was like an entire conversation for somebody like him.

"How'd they talk you into this?" I asked him under my breath as we started moving toward the exit. Amelie was watching us go, like a queen sending her troops off to battle—back straight, hand raised, shining and pale and hard as diamond.

"Temporary," the captain said. His eyes kept darting around at the vampires, never trusting for a second; I knew that feeling—hell, I lived it. "Common enemy and all that crap, but it ain't like I'm signing up to be best friends. These vermin kill people, too. That's all I care about." He gave me a longer glance. "You?"

"The draug hurt somebody I care about," I said. "And they're going to answer for that."

It was an acceptable reply, and he jerked his chin in approval—but his eyes went flat and cold when he looked past me at Michael. For him, Michael was the Enemy. I wondered whether that was ever going to change. Probably not, not until the vampires themselves changed it. And let's face it, the chances of that were slim. Nobody likes giving up power, especially the kind that keeps them rich and safe and well fed.

Captain Obvious looked back, straight into my eyes, and said, "Something's eating you. Wake up."

Something's eating you! Listen!

I struggled against that wave again, this time hot and red instead of icy cold, and came out the other side of it, into calm, still waters. "I'm fine," I told him. "Everything's just fine. We're all okay."

"Sure we are," he said, and smiled. "Damn straight."

The vamps had appropriated more buses for troop transport; these happened to be Morganville school buses. Ah, the memories. The cheap, shiny leatherette seats smelled like melted crayons, piss, and fear; I'd gotten the snot beaten out of me a couple of times on a bus just like this, before I'd taken charge of that. It had been righteous, though; I'd jumped in when ninth-grade Sammy Jenkins was slapping sixth-grade Michael around. Good times.

The vampires obviously didn't care for the nostalgic ambience, because they slammed the windows down and let the cold, moist air roll through the bus. The rain had stopped, and the clouds were thinning and blowing away to reveal a clear blue sky. It might even warm up a little, burn off the thin puddles standing on the asphalt.

The desert was sluicing off the water as fast as it had fallen.

Within a day, rain would be a distant memory. That was why the vamps had moved here—because water wouldn't stand. It gave the draug fewer and fewer places to hide.

You're drowning, Shane. Wake up. Something's eating you. WAKE UP!

This time, I could almost ignore it. Almost. Except for the horrible, burning pain that wouldn't go away. Wouldn't let me *think*.

I could feel the tension and the anticipation in the vamps around me. For the first time in a long time, they were going to war—against an enemy who'd been hunting them, killing them, for ages. And they were *ready*. The violence in the air was thick, and every single one of them looked as hard as a bone knife. When Michael glanced at me, his eyes had gone bloodred. Usually that would have scared me, or at least disgusted me, but not now.

Right now, I wished mine could do the same, because what was burning inside me was just as bright, and just as crimson. I wanted to hurt the draug for what they'd done to Claire.

To all of us. To *me*.

This isn't right. . . .

Shut up, I told whatever it was in my head. *Nothing's wrong. Everything's fine.*

Nobody talked. Not even the other humans. Not even Michael. We just concentrated on what was ahead of us.

A fight, a real, genuine, straight-up fight. I was scared on some level, scared in a way I'd never been before, but I was part of something bigger now. Was this what it felt like to be in the army, to put on a uniform and all of a sudden be brothers (and yeah, sisters) with people you might not even like in private life? I imagined it was, because right now, in this moment, I would kill or die for anyone on this bus. Even the vamps. Somehow that felt wrong, but it also felt *right*. A better version of the life I'd been struggling to lead these past few years.

I would even fight and die for Myrnin, who was sitting up toward the front. He'd changed clothes. I liked him better when he
was dressed crazy, but he'd gone black leather now, and that
looked damn dangerous. I was glad Claire wasn't there to see it.
Some part of me was always going to worry about how she felt
about him, so it was best she didn't see him looking all tough.
That was *my* job.

As the clouds parted, the vamps snapped the windows back
up, and the tinting—why the hell was there vampire-quality tinting on a *school bus*, anyway? That made no sense . . .

Wake up, Shane!

The tinting cut off my view of where we were going. Not that
it mattered. I had my shotgun, and I was ready to rock. It was so
much easier to *do something* than to just . . . think.

Because when I stopped to think, everything fell apart. *Shattered. Melted.*

Wake up.

We pulled to a stop, and the vampires sitting behind me opened
the emergency door; those of us nearby piled out through it, and
the vampires moved in a blur to the shelter of the nearest shade
while the humans took their time sorting out where we were.

It was Morganville High.

The old pile hadn't improved from the last time I'd been walking the halls and ditching class. It had been ugly when it had been
built back in the 1950s, and hadn't gotten any prettier over the
years. Solid, square red brick, with patches where people (including me) had tagged it that had been covered over with white paint
(all the damage, none of the art). The sign outside had a picture of

the school mascot, the Viper; we'd all known how stupidly ironic that was, but right now I kind of liked how his faded plastic fangs flashed in the sunlight. The lettering on the sign itself read CLOSED FOR RENOVATIONS, but they weren't renovating. It was just closed, like everything else in Morganville.

With no students running around, it looked and felt eerily dead. Water dripped from the gutters on the roof, but slowly; the gushing rains were long gone now, and the puddles in the yard were dried to a thin crust of wet sand under the sparse, struggling grass. Behind the school was the football field, the single most important thing in any small Texas town, but we weren't headed there, of course.

The vamps shattered one of the big steel-wire-reinforced windows in the shadows, and began piling inside. I joined up with Michael and Captain Obvious. "Where the hell are we going?" Captain Obvious asked, which was—heh—a perfectly obvious question, really.

And I knew the answer, without even thinking about it. "The pool." MHS had its own indoor pool. I'd been on the swim team, so I knew all about that. It wasn't a great pool, and in retrospect I was surprised the vampires had been persuaded to allow one to be built at all, but I supposed they'd figured one more enclosed indoor pool wouldn't hurt.

No. They closed down the pool. Drained it. Filled it in. It's not there anymore. Wake up, idiot.

The voice in my head wouldn't shut up. Of course the pool was there. Now the surviving draug had withdrawn to this one spot, this place where I'd swum meets and won prizes. It was a personal place to me, and they'd violated it.

They were trapped.

So are you!

They were stranded, because of the closed valves on the pipes and the silver nitrate in the water.

Wake up, Shane!

I shot my first draug halfway through the hallway; he was hiding in a classroom and oozed out of the shadows to grab a vampire by the back of the neck. The vamp had twisted free, and as soon as she was out of range I yelled and fired, and the silver shotgun pellets ripped the draug apart in a splatter of colorless liquid that smoked on the floor. It tried to reform, but another vampire— Myrnin, in his black leather—took what looked like a salt shaker from his pocket and tapped out some metallic powder into the mess.

Silver. It set the scraps of the draug on fire, and when the blaze was done, there was nothing but a damp smear on the floor.

Myrnin bared his fangs in a fierce grin, and we went on.

Nothing had changed in the school since I'd last been inside— the same lockers, dented and scratched; the same classroom doors; the same trophies in the case. I'd won at least two of them.

They were still there, with my name shining on them.

You never won any trophies, Shane. Of course I had. I'd always wanted to win them, and I had. *This is a fantasy—don't you get that? Wake up!*

About a hundred draug later, we reached the pool, and we hadn't lost a single one of our party along the way. But the pool was a different story. Firing shotguns loaded with silver in a room full of vampires was pretty damn dangerous, so only the first and second ranks got to have the firepower; the rest of us had to wait until the first rank had to reload, and then we pushed forward, dropped to one knee, and fired steadily at the mass of draug—the identical faces, the bland and empty not-people with *things* shivering inside them—as they approached. A second rank fired over our heads. My ears went quickly numb from the pounding, shattering roars of the guns, but I didn't care. What I cared about was making every single shot count.

I wanted Magnus. I wanted the bastard who'd started this, who owned it, who had *killed Claire* and nearly killed me along with her, even though I'd gotten her back.

Magnus, of course, didn't risk himself.

Myrnin figured this out, because that was what Myrnin did; like Claire, he was a sideways thinker, and while the rest of us Joe Average idiots blasted away at the draug in front of us, he stepped away toward the edge of the pool and crouched down. He had a beaker in his hand, glittering and full to the brim with deadly silver and he set it down to pry the cap loose.

"He's in the water!" Myrnin shouted. "Keep them busy—"

But he didn't have time to finish whatever he was going to say, because Magnus reached up out of the water, grabbed him, and dragged him down.

I dropped my shotgun and ran for the beaker, pried the top off, and emptied it into the water.

The silver inside sluiced out into the water in a spreading, toxic stream. Myrnin had hold of something that had to be Magnus, the master draug, the *first* draug, and he was pulling him relentlessly toward the silver.

And into it.

I couldn't see Myrnin at all now, because the water went from murky to black, swirling with vivid veins of silver. And then *boiling*.

The vampires were just standing there, even Oliver, staring down into the water. Nobody was moving. Captain Obvious wasn't going to go racing to the rescue, either.

I'm not going to lie; I could have saved Myrnin. I was probably the only one who could have, who might have survived diving into that boiling, raging pool where the draug were dying.

But I didn't try.

I left him there to die.

Just like he left you. Remember? Left you to be eaten. You need to wake up. NOW.

Nobody had left me behind. I was fine. I was just fine.

It's you in there. You're being consumed, Shane. Eaten. Can't you feel it?

I did, for an agonizing second of utter horror. Felt it stripping me bare. Felt the invasion.

And then the calm settled over me, and it was all okay.

Everything was okay.

Always.

The clock ran faster after that.

The time between the pool and Claire's eighteenth birthday was a gauzy blur; I didn't remember much, but nothing much happened to remember, either. Amelie got better. Vampires came back. Morganville got rebuilt. Nothing ever changes, really—that's how Morganville is. It just . . . exists.

I was just happy. We were all . . . happy. Claire cried over Myrnin, but she was happy he had saved us, happy he had died a hero.

The hero of Morganville.

The martyr.

You're no martyr. You're a fighter. So fight. NOW. Stop this!

Everything was fine.

One year to the day from their not-so-successful engagement party, Michael and Eve finally tied the knot, in the church with Father Joe presiding. Amelie gave her blessing, and I had to wear a tuxedo and a tie. Eve wore bloodred. Of course she did. Claire was the one who looked like a bride, really; she was wearing some other color, but I didn't really notice except to see the light in her eyes and the smile on her lips as Michael and Eve kissed under the flower arch. Eve threw the bouquet, and as usual, her throwing arm sucked, especially backward, because somehow she managed to throw it to *me*. I tossed it back. On the second try she hit Monica Morrell, Bitch Queen, which was so not going to happen; no man in his right mind would go there.

At some point when we were passing around the champagne and cutting the cake and dancing, I remember Eve twirling in my arms, light and damp with sweat, and she looked me in the eye and said, "This is a lie, Shane. It's all a lie, and you know it deep down. Wake up. You have to wake up." But then she was gone, dancing away with Michael, and I forgot.

It was so much easier to just . . . forget. Let go. Drift.

I think it was around this time that I went to see Claire's family. Her mom and dad had moved out of Morganville, because of his health problems more than anything else, though she'd been happy to have them out of the fray; they sort of remembered Morganville, but not the vampires. I went by myself, with Amelie's permission, and ended up standing in front of Claire's parents—her dad looked a whole lot healthier, which was odd—to tell them what was on my mind.

"I want to marry your daughter," I said. Pretty much just like that . . . no hello, no buildup, nothing, because I was nervous and it just came out.

And Mr. Danvers smiled and said, "Of course you do." There was something great about that smile, and also, something . . . off. It was exactly what I'd hoped to see. And that was . . . weird.

No, there wasn't anything weird about getting what I wanted for a change. I deserved to be happy. I *needed* to be happy.

It's a lie, Shane. Wake up.

Mrs. Danvers said, "Shane, she couldn't have a better young man." And her husband nodded. I looked at them for a few seconds in silence. I was sitting in their living room, which looked a lot like the living room they'd had back in Morganville—but then, they would have kept the same furniture, wouldn't they? I even recognized all the pictures on the walls. They'd put them back in the same spots.

The last time I'd sat down with them like this, it hadn't gone nearly so well. Oh, no. Mr. Danvers had been angry, and I hadn't blamed him, because I'd never intended all this to go so fast with Claire, but I'd said I loved her and I meant it. I still did.

"You're not angry?" I finally asked. Mr. Danvers chuckled. He sounded just like one of those fathers on an old TV show, I forget which one.

"Of course not," he said. "Why would we be? You've always been there for her, Shane. You've always looked after her. And we know she loves you."

I found myself saying, "What about the stuff you said last time? That she had to wait until after college? About MIT and a career and everything?"

"Well," Mrs. Danvers said, with that warm, sweet smile that my own mother had never given me, although she'd done her best, "that's Claire's decision, of course, but we'll support whatever she feels is more important."

It's all so easy, isn't it? Like a dream. Exactly like a dream. Wake up.

I didn't want to wake up. I liked it here.

I found myself shaking Mr. Danvers's hand, and getting a hug from Claire's mom, and promising to work with her on the wedding, and all of a sudden I was in my car—when had I gotten the car? I couldn't remember, but it seemed like I'd had it all along, my own black, shiny, murdered-out car—and driving back to Morganville, with Claire's grandmother's wedding ring in my pocket. It was a diamond with rubies on both sides.

No, that was your mother's ring. Your dad pawned it, remember? To get the money to send you back to Morganville. You didn't want him to do it. You can't have it now, can you?

Of course I could.

I was getting married.

The only problem was, none of it seemed real as it sped forward. Not the days that passed in a haze, not when Michael and Eve moved out on their own and left me and Claire the Glass House (and why would they do that, it was Michael's house, why would he leave it to us?).

Newlyweds needed their own place, Eve told me, and winked. But she didn't seem like Eve anymore. She was almost . . . a shadow. Threadbare. A memory of someone I'd known once.

But Claire . . . Claire was still real. Wasn't she? I couldn't tell anymore. It was as if I was watching us, not *being* us. A voyeur in my own body.

Not that that was a bad thing, sometimes, but there were other times when time just seemed to slip sideways, and the walls seemed to sag, and everything flickered . . . but it was just the machines in Myrnin's lab, Claire said. They malfunctioned. She had to fix them. She was in charge of them now. Amelie said she was smarter than Myrnin had ever been. The savior of Morganville.

Wake up! Can't you see how wrong this is?

Claire and I were married in the church by Father Joe, and Eve and Michael were our maid of honor and best man. Eve wore red, and Michael had on the same tux, and we stood under the flower arch, the same flower arch they'd been married beneath, and when I turned around it seemed like it was the same people, sitting in the same places, wearing the same clothes, and everything was pale and patchwork for a moment and I felt panic tearing at me . . .

And then Claire took my hand. Her fingers felt cool and gentle, but they stung a little bit, too. She kissed me, and it tasted sweet and salty and it stung, too, like lemon on a cut, but this was *Claire* and I had to love it, because I loved her. The gold ring with its diamond and rubies winked on her hand, and she was my wife.

My mother's ring. I can't have my mother's ring—it's gone. . . .

WAKE UP.

Then the vampires left Morganville. One day they were just . . . *gone.* Amelie left a note, saying that she was leaving the town to us and that she trusted us to run it properly. Eve inherited the coffee shop where she'd worked so many years. Michael became a rock star overnight and went on tour, and I never thought to wonder how he was managing that, given the blood drinking and all, much less the sunlight. I was busy, you see. Busy being the new mayor of Morganville. The rule of the Morrell family was over, and Richard owned a used-car lot and Monica worked at a nail salon, until one day she got run over by a bus. Very sad.

You're making it up, Shane, in your head. You have to wake up now, or it's too late.

And Claire, my sweet and beautiful Claire, she got pregnant six months after we were married. I only remember parts of that, little parts where I listened to the baby's heartbeat and saw the sonograms and Claire in labor and crying with joy after all the screaming, and then the weight of my daughter in my arms and her eyes, water-blue eyes wide and staring up at me.

It had a threadbare beauty to it, like an old film, and it kept feeling less and less like my life and more like dreams, dreams that sagged around the edges at the corners of my eyes, dreams that melted and puddled and hid in the shadows.

Because it isn't real.

Then it was like a jump cut in a movie, no transition. I was walking, and it was raining, just a light, cold mist that beaded up in fine drops on my leather jacket. I was shivering, and I didn't know why I was out in the rain when the Glass House was right behind me, with its warm lights and Claire smiling from the window with our daughter in her arms. Where was I going? What was I doing? I felt a bubbling sense of panic, and then I turned the corner and stopped, because my father, Frank Collins, was standing there in front of me, and he said, "Hello, son. I've been trying to reach you."

It wasn't the Frank that had abused me and betrayed me and used me. It was the Frank I never knew, who never existed. A kind man with Frank's face, and a TV dad's smile, and eyes the relentless color of water on glass. "Dad," I said. I didn't feel all that surprised to see him, which was strange, because he was kind of dead. "How are you?"

"I'm fine, Shane. I heard you got married."

"Yeah."

"Are you happy?"

I was supposed to be happy. No, I *was* happy. I *was.* "Yes," I said. Pain sheeted through me, just as it did all the time now, red hot and icy cold, stinging and gnawing and grinding.

Something's eating you.

"I'm glad you're happy," he said. "You deserve to be. You've made me proud, Shane."

I was silent for a moment, struggling with that. He didn't blink. There were tears running down his cheeks, which was weird, because my dad didn't cry, had never cried, not even when my sister, Alyssa, died.

It was as if his face were melting.

"You're dead, Dad. And you were never like this."

"Like what?"

"A real human being," I said. "You were never proud of me, or at least you never said it. You always wanted more. I was never good enough for you, even before I killed Alyssa."

"You didn't kill her."

"I should have saved her. Same thing. Didn't you tell me that a million times?"

The tears were ice, and the ice was melting. "I'm sorry if I said that. I didn't mean it, Shane. I've always been proud of you."

Liar. Liar liar liar liar.

I pushed past that, because as much as I'd always wanted to hear it, always, there was something else bothering me. "But you're *dead.*" The Frank Collins that existed in Myrnin's lab was a cheat, a ghost, a two-dimensional image, a brain in a jar, not this flesh-and-blood person who didn't even look right. I reached out and shoved his shoulder. He rocked back, real to the touch. "This isn't you."

"It's what you want," the not-Frank said. "It's what you always wanted. A father to be proud of you."

"I want a real life!" It burst out of me in a shout, and I knew it was true, the only true thing in a long time. "Dad, help me."

"I've been trying to help you," he said. "Wake up, Shane. You can't get what you want. Isn't that what I would tell you? You can't be the hero. You can't wish the vampires away. You can't marry the perfect girl and have a perfect little baby and get your dad back alive, and reformed into the model you always wanted. But now you have all that. What would you call that?"

"A fantasy," I said.

"Is that what you want?"

"No."

"Then wake up before it's too late."

His eyes were water, they were *full of water,* and I felt a surge of blinding terror and nausea. I felt that tingling burn again, all over my skin. Even though I'd turned the corner and I remembered turning it, I could see the Glass House right in front of me. Someone had painted it, and it glowed neon white in the rain, and Claire was looking at me through the window, smiling, holding our baby.

What was our daughter's name? *I should know that.* But I didn't. I didn't.

Because she doesn't exist. Wake up!

"Dad—" I looked back. Frank was gone. There was just the sidewalk, and a gray fog, and the rain, rain beating down on my face, beading up on my skin. "If I wake up I'm going to lose them. I can lose everything but them. Dad—" I didn't want this, but I didn't want to let it go. I couldn't. I started to walk back to the house, to Claire, to the baby whose name I hadn't decided yet, to a future without vampires where I was respected and important and my dad loved me and . . .

And I knew I couldn't have that.

Because I'm Shane Collins, and I don't get those things.

Because that isn't how my world is.

WAKE UP!

I did.

There was a solid sheet of glass above me, and water beading up on it and dripping down on my face. I was submerged in the water, except for my face. And everything burned.

The water was thick, and turning pink from my blood.

I hadn't escaped the draug. I'd never escaped at all. Some people see their lives flash before their eyes; I'd flashed *forward*, to all the things I wouldn't see, wouldn't have. I'd escaped into dreams.

I was a prisoner of the draug.

And they were eating me alive.

CHAPTER EIGHT

CLAIRE

☽

"No!" She'd been screaming it until her throat felt bloody, but Myrnin wouldn't let go of her, and she couldn't get Eve or Michael to do anything. Eve was huddled in the front seat, crying; Michael was driving and not looking in the rearview mirror at her. From the glimpses she'd had of his reflection, his face was set like a mask, but there were tears glittering in his eyes. Tears and fury. "No, you can't leave him there, you can't!" But that wasn't what she was really saying. *I left him,* she was screaming to herself, inside. *I left him there. I abandoned Shane and I can't let that happen. I can't live with that. I should have stayed.*

Myrnin was muttering under his breath, a liquid flow of what she was sure were curse words in a language she couldn't recognize. Welsh, maybe. He broke off to say, sternly, "That's *enough.* You won't be helping him by all this, will you?"

"You're not helping him at all!"

He wrapped both arms around her, pinning her helplessly with her back against his chest, and it was like being held in an iron vise. "Hush," he said softly. "Hush, now. If we go back, we'll die. All of us. He's already gone."

"They have him, you know that, they have him, and they—they—maybe he's still alive, maybe—"

"He's dead. There's nothing to go back for. I'm sorry."

She screamed then, without words, just a tortured shriek that echoed around the metal box. It sounded like someone else's voice, someone else's pain, because no matter how tormented it was it couldn't even begin to approach how much she *hurt*.

Claire felt Myrnin's cold lips brush her cheek, and heard him murmur, "You will never thank me for this, *fy annwyl*." And then he moved a hand to her throat and pressed in a specific place, and in seconds, the world tunneled into gray, then black, and she was gone.

She came to again with her head in Eve's lap.

They were sitting in their makeshift bedroom, the big ballroom with their cast-off clothes and sleeping bags littering the floor, cups of drying coffee sitting on antique tables that had been pushed to the wall. Claire's head hurt, her throat hurt, and her eyes felt swollen, and for a moment she couldn't remember why. Eve was silently stroking her hair. Upside down, Eve looked strange. Her eyes were red, and she looked very shaken and sad.

She pulled in a deep breath as she realized Claire was awake. "Michael!"

He was there in a flash beside her, kneeling next to Claire. He took hold of her hands and pulled her up into a hug.

He didn't say anything. Not a thing.

She didn't want to remember. Her hands fisted behind his back, her whole body shook with the need *not to know*. Michael was shaking, too. After a moment, he let go and sat back, avoiding her eyes as he wiped his face with an impatient gesture, but not before she saw the tears.

"He's not dead," she said. "He's not. They took him. I saw them take him."

"Claire—" Michael slowly shook his head. He looked tired, angry, and . . . just broken. "Myrnin said he was dead."

"He's *not*."

It was Eve's turn to put her arms around her. Unlike Michael, she wasn't crying now. She'd finished, Claire supposed, and how was that fair, that anybody could *ever* finish crying? Ever?

"If I believed there was a chance, any chance, I'd already be going," Eve said. "But, sweetheart, he's gone."

Claire shoved her back with a burst of white rage. She jumped to her feet. "Myrnin knocked me out," she spat. "How long?" They didn't answer her until she kicked at the limp sleeping bag and yelled it again. *"How long?"*

"Five minutes, maybe," Eve whispered. "Claire, don't. We're not your enemies—don't do this. . . . We love him, too."

"Not fucking *enough*, you don't!" she snapped, and left them there. She was walking first, then running. Nobody tried to stop her. She flew through confusing hallways, reversed course, her heart hammering, and tried three different routes before she saw the room at the end with the vampire guards standing sentry.

They stepped out in front of her, right palms outstretched in a clear *no way* signal. Claire slowed, but she kept coming. "I need to see Oliver," she said. "Right now."

"He's not available."

"I need to see him!"

"Stop."

She didn't. She wasn't sure what her plan was, because right now there was nothing inside her but the burning, ripping need to *do something* . . . probably fifteen minutes had passed since she'd last seen Shane, and he was still alive, she was *sure* he was. Something had to be done. Someone had to *listen.* She locked gazes with the vampire on the right—she knew him, he was one of Amelie's regular crew, and sometimes she caught him looking, well, not human but approachable.

Not now. His expression had set like concrete, and his light brown eyes were cold. "Turn around," he said. "Now."

She couldn't. She couldn't give up, because Shane wouldn't have given up on her. He'd have fought like a wildcat, made them put him in a cage or let him go, and she couldn't do any less for him, could she?

It took about one second for the vampire to reach out, grab her, and carry her back down the hallway. She kicked and screamed but it didn't do any good, and the fast motion made her dizzy and sick, disoriented, so that when he dumped her off and slammed and locked the door on her she was still too woozy to stand and fight.

Claire screamed and kicked and battered the heavy wooden door with pure adrenalized fury until she collapsed in a gasping, shaking heap next to it.

Then a voice said, "You finished?"

She looked around, surprised, and found she wasn't the only occupant of this makeshift cell. It had a couple of camp beds in it, some bottled water, and half a box of energy bars sitting on the floor nearby . . . and a boy she recognized. He was skinny, and he had a mass of greasy dark hair that flopped over his face.

"Jason!" she blurted, and felt an immediate surge of fear. Eve's brother wasn't someone she could trust, not even at the best of times, and being locked in a room with him was definitely not the best of times.

He was sitting cross-legged on one of the beds, chewing an energy bar. "I hate being locked up, too," Jason said, "but screaming at the door won't get you anywhere, and you're giving me a headache. So, you got on the wrong side of the vamps, finally. Good for you."

"What are you doing here?"

He laughed dryly and held out his hands. They were cuffed. "Prison labor," he said. "They've got me loading up shotgun shells. It's my rest period, which you're screwing up with all your screaming."

Claire knelt down to examine the lock on the door (new, and good) and then the hinges (located on the outside of the door, not the inside). Then she started looking around the room. No windows, like most of the rooms in this vampire shrine. Nothing but four walls, carpet, paneling, and the few things provided for comfort.

Her gaze fixed on Jason. "What do you have?" she asked him. Myrnin, or someone, had searched her and there was nothing left now in her own jeans pockets but lint.

"Not a damn thing," Jason said. "Why, you gonna search me?" He laughed. "Shane's gonna get a real kink in his tail over that."

"Shane's in trouble," Claire said, "and I swear to *God* that if you don't help me, I'll break your finger off and use the bone to pick the lock."

Jason stopped laughing and gave her a long, odd look. "You're kind of serious," he said. "Huh. That's dark, for you."

"Shut up and *help*."

"Can't. I got my own ass to save here. I do anything off-limits, like touching that door, and I end up bags of blood in a refrigerator, if I'm lucky. Sentence of death, remember?" He rattled his handcuffs for effect. "I'm working out my appeal."

Claire ignored him. *Think. Think!* She tried, but there wasn't much to work with. Water. Plastic bottles. A box of energy bars that came in crinkly metallic wrappers . . .

She lunged for those, stripped the wrapper loose from a bar, and began folding it in careful, precise movements.

"I'm all for hobbies, but you think this is the time for origami? Whatcha making, a crane?"

Claire made a thin metallic probe. It was too flexible to serve as a lock pick, but she searched the baseboards. One good thing about modern life—you were never far from an electrical outlet.

She shoved one end of her probe into one of the flat sides of the plug, then bent it and jammed the other end of the U into the plug's other side, completing the circuit. Getting shocked was inevitable, and she gritted her teeth and took the pain; it wouldn't kill her. She'd been shocked plenty of times on things in Myrnin's lab.

She tore a piece from the cardboard box the energy bars had come in, and held it to the metallic strip. It started to smolder, then smoke, and then a thin edge of flame licked at the paper. Claire grinned without amusement and held the burning cardboard up to the rest of the box. Once that was burning, she dropped it on the carpet, which—flame-retardant or not—rapidly began smoking and melting.

The fire alarm went off.

"Holy shit," Jason said. "You are *crazy.*"

Vampires took fire seriously; it was something that would kill them, quickly, and every building in Founder's Square was equipped with massive fire detection systems.

The smoke was rising, and acrid, and Claire coughed involuntarily, then coughed again. The stench was bad. The plug sparked and a thin thread of fire ran up the wall.

"Put it out," Jason said, no longer even a little amused. When she didn't, he grabbed a blanket and flung it over the burning carpet, stamping hard just as the alarms went off with a fierce shrilling sound. Greasy smoke billowed up, sending them both into a hacking fit, and now the wall was on fire, *really*, and Claire felt an awful surge of destructive joy as the door rattled and a guard stepped in with a fire extinguisher. He assessed the situation instantly, disregarded the two of them, and went to the wall to spray it with foam.

Claire broke for the open door. She didn't realize until she'd gained the hall that Jason hadn't followed her; when she glanced back, he was standing right where he'd been, facing the open doorway.

He raised his cuffed hands and gave her a finger wave.

Fine. If he wanted to stay in prison, she had absolutely no objections.

There were alarms all over the place, summoning people to fight the fire. It wasn't a big one, and it'd be out in seconds, but she'd created chaos, and that was all she needed. She just had to get to the basement, find a car, and . . . she'd figure out the next part as she went along. She'd have to. If Michael and Eve weren't going to help . . .

She made it to the elevator and pushed the button for the parking garage. There had to be some car she could steal, *something*. She needed to get out of here and back to the treatment plant. Seconds counted. Shane was still alive; she *believed* it, despite what Myrnin said.

She refused to believe him.

The elevator doors opened, and Claire rushed out, then skidded to an immediate halt, because Hannah Moses, Morganville's police chief, was standing there, gun drawn, looking really damn serious. She wasn't aiming it, but it wouldn't have been much work to take that step, either. Standing a couple of paces away was Richard Morrell, the mayor. He was tall, good-looking, and young, not even ten years older than Claire, but he looked older, way older now. Stress, she guessed.

He was holding his sister, Monica, by both elbows as she twisted to get free in a storm of flying long, dark hair. She froze when she saw Claire. If Morganville had a queen bitch, it was Monica; she'd elected and crowned herself way before Claire had ever run afoul of her. It didn't help that she was *also* pretty and had a huge budget for clothes and shoes. Monica's lips parted, but she didn't say anything. She tried to stomp on her brother's foot with her high heels, but he was obviously used to handling her, and he must have been wearing steel-toed boots.

"Let's all just be calm," Hannah said. She was a scary figure, Claire thought; there was *presence* to her, a cool and competent sort of aura that made you instantly believe, in any situation, that she'd been there, done that, and written the how-to book. It was almost certainly not true some of the time, but it was impossible to tell that from her body language and expressions. She had her corn-rowed black hair tied back in a messy knot, and although she was wearing her police uniform, she'd lost the hat somewhere. The scar that jagged its way down her face looked fearsome in the dim light, and her dark eyes were very, very steady. "I'd ask where's the fire, but I'm guessing it's upstairs."

"It's out," Claire said. "Hannah, I have to go. Right now."

"Not alone, you're not."

"Why is Monica here? She left with the others." Morganville's privileged elite—mostly vampires, but a few well-connected humans—had fled before the draug had really attacked in force. Monica had cheerfully boarded the bus.

"God, let *go*, Richard. I'm not going anywhere!" Her brother released her, and Monica made a show of smoothing down her entirely-too-high-priced dress, which ended just below illegal. "My brother's all I have left, and *he* came running back here out of some misguided sense of loyalty to the little people. I couldn't let him face danger without me, could I?" She hesitated, then shrugged. "Besides, I ran out of money. And my credit cards were frozen."

"So you came back *here*?" Claire stared at her for a second, stunned by the magnitude of the void that was Monica.

Monica said, "Bite me, preschool. I don't care what alligators you're swimming with, anyway. I hope they eat all the best parts."

"Whatever. I don't have time. Shane's been taken by the draug, and I have to get him back. I *have* to."

Hannah's whole body language softened. "If he's been taken, you know how that ends, honey. I'm sorry about that, I truly am."

"No, he's strong. Shane is so *strong*. If anybody can survive, he can—I believe that. Hannah, *please*, you have to help me. . . ." She gulped back tears, because tears wouldn't help. "Please."

Even Monica had gone still now, and she'd lost some of her edge. Hannah considered all this in silence, and then slowly shook her head. "You've got no chance," she said. "You don't even know where he's being held—"

"The water treatment plant," Claire interrupted. "They haven't had time to move him anywhere, and they can't, because Myrnin closed off the pipes. They can't leave there, not easily."

"I'd never say *can't* when it comes to these bastards. They supposedly couldn't get here at all, but here they are." Hannah made a decision of some kind, and holstered her weapon, though she kept her eyes on Claire. "What's your plan?"

"Go get him."

"Honey, that is not a plan. That's what we in the military call an *objective*." Hannah said it compassionately but firmly. "You don't know he's even still alive."

"Actually," said a voice from the shadows by the stairs, "we do." Michael emerged, along with Eve.

He had Myrnin by the throat, and Myrnin was *not* looking good. In fact, he was looking like he'd gone ten rounds with Michael and lost.

He looked . . . beaten.

Michael shook him, his face tense and hard. "Tell them what you told me."

Myrnin made a choking sound. Michael let go, and the other vampire fell to his knees, coughing. "I meant no harm," he whispered. "I was trying to *save you*. All of you."

"Just tell her."

Myrnin's head was bowed, his dark hair hiding his expression. "He may yet be alive."

Hope wasn't a peaceful thing; it was painful, a jagged white-hot explosion that ripped through her and forced her heart into overdrive. Claire heard herself say, over that heavy hammering, "You lied."

"No. No, it's true, he's *gone*, Claire. When the draug take humans, without exception, they die. It's just—vampires last for a long time, humans for a much shorter one, and humans seem to . . . dream. They don't suffer as vampires do. It's easy for them. They slip into . . . visions." He looked up then, and she honestly couldn't figure out what was in his face, his eyes, because her own were shimmering with tears. "It's kinder to leave him in them. He's dying, Claire. Or dead. But either way—"

"He's alive right now," she said flatly.

"Yeah," Michael said. It sounded like a growl, and his eyes glowed dull red in the shadows. "He lied to us. And we're going to get Shane. Right now."

Myrnin looked down again. He didn't even try to speak this time. He just . . . shook his head.

Claire couldn't begin to think of how much it hurt her for him to do this, so she just . . . didn't. She turned to Hannah. "We're going."

"You still don't have a plan."

"Yeah, we do," Michael said. "They came after us because we were attacking weak points in the system. Attacking them directly. We're not doing that this time. We're just going in after him, and they don't really care about humans; they care about vampires. They hunt us." He let that fall into silence before he said, "They'll care about me. I'll *make* them care. I'll go a different way and lead them off. That lets everybody else get to Shane."

This plan was clearly news to Eve. "No!"

"Eve, I can do this. Trust me."

"No, Michael, they already had you once, and—"

"And I know what it's like," he said. "That's why I can't leave him there, and we don't have time to beg for help, which Oliver isn't going to give anyway. Claire was right about that."

Hannah glanced down at Myrnin. "What about him? Is he helping?"

"He's helped enough," Claire said. "He stays here." Myrnin looked up at that, but she just stared at him, hard, until he looked away. "We don't need another vampire right now. Agreed?"

"All right," Hannah said. "It's a decent rough plan, but you don't know exactly where he's being kept, and it's a large building. You need more boots on the ground—humans, not vampires. I'll go with you."

"Hannah," said the mayor. He sounded tense, and his expression mirrored that. "You can't. It's dangerous."

"Danger's what you pay me for, Richard," she said, and smiled at him. There was something a whole lot warmer in that smile, Claire thought, than just a mayor/police chief sort of friendship, and the look in Richard's eyes confirmed it. "You go on, take care of your sister. I'll be fine."

He closed his eyes for a second. "No," he said. "If you go, I go, too. I'm coming. Monica, just get inside and stay there."

"No way. I'm not letting you run off to get killed somewhere without me, jackass."

"Shut up," Eve said flatly. "We have zero time for you and your bullshit dramatics."

"Or what, you'll bleed on me, Emo Princess of Freakdomonia?"

Claire stepped forward and got Monica's attention. She didn't know how she looked, but Monica seemed to shift a little, as if she was considering taking a step *back*. "Fine. You come with us." At the very least, Monica was a rabbit to throw to the wolves, and she wouldn't hesitate to do it if it was the difference between life and death for Shane. "If you get in my way, I'll kill you." It was glaringly simple to her right now, and she meant it, every bit of it. Monica had never earned herself anything else, and despite all the breaks Claire had been willing to give, and how kind she was deep down, right now all that was gone. Just . . . gone.

And what was left was something Monica fully understood, all right, because she took a breath and tossed her hair back and nodded. "I'm not getting in your way," she said. "I'll help. I owe

Shane for something. Besides, who do you know who's more ruthless than me? *Them?*" She tilted her head at Michael and Eve, and Claire had to admit she had a point. "It's just once, and then it's all square. I'm not your friend. I'm never going to be your friend. But Shane doesn't deserve to die like that. If he dies, *I* get to kill him."

She was perfectly earnest about that, and Claire didn't have time to untangle the crazy, anyway. She just said, "Fine. Let's go," and headed for the armored truck. Michael was already unlocking it. "But you ride in the back, Monica."

Michael drove, because he was once again the only one with vampire vision; Eve and Claire shared the rest of the front seat, not very comfortably because of the shotguns he'd given them, and Monica, Richard, and Hannah were in the back.

Eve was watching Monica through the narrow window. "If she puts a foot wrong, I am seriously considering playing Shank the Skank," she said.

"What happened?" Claire asked. "You and Michael—you were convinced he was dead. I saw you. But then . . ."

"Then Michael overheard Myrnin fessing up to Lord High Inquisitor Oliver, and Oliver mentioned how Shane just *might* be alive. Which Myrnin already knew." Eve bared her teeth in a thing that was *so* not a grin. "Michael decided to have a chat with him. We went to the garage because we figured you'd end up there." The not-grin faded. "I'm all for having more hands with guns on this, but you sure we can trust Richard Morrell and Hannah Moses? Not to mention *Monica*?"

Claire shrugged, not really caring right now. "I think that once they're in it, it's pretty hard for them to back out," she said. "I'm not leaving without him, Eve. I can't. Not again. I don't care what happens, but I'm not letting him die like that."

Grief and terror threatened to spill out of the tightly locked container inside her, and Eve grabbed her hand and held on to it, hard. "I know," she said. "Trust me, I know." She did. Michael had been taken by the draug, anchored underwater. Fed on.

She knew.

Claire swam up out of her misery long enough to ask, "What about, you know, the two of you? Better?"

Eve cut a glance toward Michael, who was driving and pretending hard not to be hearing any of this. His acting needed work. "Sure," Eve said, but that wasn't so convincing, either. "We're good to go."

"I'm not asking if you're good to be working together. I mean—"

"I know what you mean," Eve interrupted. "Let's just . . . talk about it later."

Michael could not, Claire thought, have looked more tense, or more sad.

Richard and Hannah were having a fierce, whispered conversation in the corner of the truck as they braced themselves against the metal walls, and gripped the panic straps overhead. Monica had apparently decided that she had every right to sit on Amelie's plush throne, which wasn't at all a surprise. Claire really hoped that Amelie found out about it later.

That would be fun.

The drive back across town didn't take long, especially at the speed Michael was driving. Night had fallen hard because the clouds were still hanging heavy over the town, though the rain had stopped. The air still had that moist, unpleasant feel to it, and Claire felt as if she had mold growing on her skin in a sticky, invisible net.

The clock in her head was ticking, and it had been too long, way too long, for Shane already. She closed her eyes and concentrated on him, on somehow reaching him, giving him strength. *Stay with me. Please, stay with me.* He'd begged her for the same thing, not so long ago, when things had looked darkest. He'd had faith that she'd survived beyond any reasonable evidence to the contrary, and she couldn't do any less for him. She *couldn't*. She couldn't face the darkness without him by her side.

If she'd ever had any doubts that she loved him, really loved him, she knew now. It was easy to love somebody when love was happy, but when it was hard, when it meant facing things you feared . . . that was different. He'd done it for her, many times. And now she had to do it for him.

She opened her eyes, feeling calm and centered and focused, as Michael brought the truck to a halt. "Same drill," he said. "I get out and open the back. Claire, you keep the keys." He didn't say, *in case I don't make it back*, but that was what he meant. Eve let out a wordless little sound of despair; just for a moment, their gazes locked.

"I still love you," he said. "I mean it. All of it."

She didn't answer, not verbally, but she nodded.

And then he was a blur as he bailed out of the truck.

Tears rolled down Eve's cheeks, and she whispered, "God, I love you, too."

Maybe he heard it. Claire hoped so.

Claire climbed out, helped Eve, and by the time she'd made it around to the back, Hannah, Richard, and Monica were out. And Michael was gone. Claire locked the truck again with the remote and stuck the keys in her pants pocket.

Hannah clicked on a heavy flashlight. Eve had one, too. "Richard, I'm with you and Monica. Claire, the cell network should still be working for high-priority users. Call if you find Shane. I'll do the same. Either way, we're back here in fifteen minutes."

I'm not leaving without him, Claire thought, but she didn't say it. She just nodded and checked her phone. She had a signal. "Good," she said. "They'd have him in water, right?"

"Through the center entrance, staircase down. Then we split off, right and left. Check every pool and tank," Hannah said. "Girls, you watch your backs in there."

"Ay-firmative," Eve said, and tried for a smile. "Sorry. An *Aliens* reference always makes me feel better at times like this. Except I'm not sure I'm the one who lives through the movie."

They moved together in a group, in through the main entrance.

It was dark inside, and Eve's flashlight didn't light up too much. They took the stairs down, and Monica stumbled; Eve hissed at her, something about *what dumbass wears heels at a time like this?*, but Claire was focused straight ahead.

They reached the bottom of the stairs, and Hannah nodded. "You go right," she whispered. "Stay quiet. Fifteen minutes, Claire. I mean it."

Claire nodded. She didn't mean it at all.

She and Eve split off to the right. Eve's flashlight illuminated a hot circle that showed concrete, pipes, neon yellow signs and tags; there were some faint emergency lights down here, still functioning on battery, Claire guessed, so she asked Eve to switch her flashlight off. It took a few seconds for their eyes to adjust, but it meant better peripheral vision.

This bottom level of the building extended out into open-air pools, but they were farther away, on the other side of a large chain-link fence. Inside, there were regimented rows of closed and open tanks. Eve climbed the ladder to the first one and used her flashlight. She shook her head and jumped down.

The next, farther on, was a closed tank with a plastic curved lid over it and some kind of sliding port for taking samples. Claire's turn to climb, and she slid open the port, gagged on the smell that issued forth, but she couldn't see anything in the cloudy, foul water. If Shane was in there, he couldn't have made it.

She jumped down next to Eve. Eve didn't even ask; Claire guessed she didn't have to.

They kept going. Five more tanks, some closed, some open. Nothing.

The draug were nowhere to be seen, thankfully. Maybe Michael had been right. Maybe they'd ignore the humans in favor of Michael's wild-goose chase . . .

"Out there," Eve whispered. "Look."

Michael. He was outside by the pools, running over catwalks, and the pools were bending, twisting, shuddering, *reaching.*

The draug were after him, but he was giving them a game.

"We have to go faster," Claire said. "Come on." She swarmed up the next ladder and looked in the pool.

A dead face looked back at her, eyes pale and blind in the dim light.

She screamed, and her scream echoed and echoed and echoed through the dark, loud as an alarm, but she didn't care because oh *God*, she'd been wrong . . .

"Move!" Eve shouted in her ear. She'd climbed up next to her, and had her arm around Claire's waist. "Go on, get down! Now!"

"He's dead," Claire whispered. "Oh, God, Eve—"

Eve gulped, visibly gathered her courage, and turned her gaze on the dead face in the pool. And then she said, "That's not Shane."

"But—" A bubble of hope rose up, fragile as glass. "Are you sure—"

"I'm sure," Eve said. "That's not him. Come on. We have to move it. If they didn't hear that—"

They jumped down, landed with simultaneous thumps on the metal grating, and headed for the next tank.

But just ahead, the darkness *rippled*.

And then a white face emerged from that blackness, eyes that weren't eyes, a mouth that moved all the wrong ways, that wasn't human *at all* except when she looked at it straight on.

Magnus. There were others with him, but she could somehow tell when it was him; the others looked like bad photocopies. They didn't have the same . . . gravity.

Magnus said, "You. The girl with clear eyes."

"Yeah, me. You want me," Claire said. "Because I can tell who you are. I always could. I just didn't know it. So give Shane back, and you can have me."

"Child," he almost purred. "I can have you in any case." Magnus's whole face *distorted* into something so monstrous and evil that she screamed, couldn't help it, and all the others copied him like reflections, because that's all they were, shards and fragments of him.

They were *linked*, and somehow that was important, vital, but she didn't have the time to think about it.

She fired at him.

The shotgun kicked hard at her shoulder, and a stinging fog of gunpowder blew back over her, but she was too late; he'd read her intentions and melted back into the others, and the ones who were splattered weren't him, weren't the master.

And then he was gone, sinking through the grating.

"Time's up," Eve said. "We have to find Shane *now*."

CHAPTER NINE

SHANE

)

I was nearly gone. I could feel it now, how my body felt light and weirdly empty, how my muscles ached. My head pounded harder and faster—low blood pressure, less oxygen getting to where it counted. The water (*not really water*) around me was a dull crimson now, and it reminded me of terrible things, of opening a motel bathroom door and a tub and my mom's slack white face and the color of the watery blood around her. She'd had her clothes on, I remembered suddenly. And she hadn't filled the tub all the way, only about halfway.

I was thinking about it too much, because it started to become real, like those fantasies I'd already rejected. All of a sudden I *was* there, standing on cold tile, staring at my mother, and her papery eyelids opened, her eyes were the color of ice water as she said, "If you let go, it won't hurt so much, sweetheart.

Claire's not coming back for you. Nobody ever comes back for *you*."

"Mom—" I whispered. It was her voice, just like I remembered . . . sad and quiet and disappointed. Maybe a little scared. Mom had been scared most of the time. "Mom, I'm sorry, I can't just give up."

"You can't do a lot of things, Shane," she said. It sounded kind, that voice, but it wasn't. "You couldn't save me. You couldn't save your sister. And you can't save yourself, either. It's too late for you. You have to let go, because that's the only thing that will help stop the pain now. I'm your mother. I don't want to see you hurt."

"Claire's going to come back for me."

"Claire's a dream, too. She never loved you. Nobody ever really loved you, sweetie. You're just not built that way. Why would a smart, pretty girl like that want *you*? You made it up, the way you made up all that other nonsense, about getting married and having a little baby and being happy. Because that will never happen either, son."

That sounded like my dad, not my mom. He'd always been the one telling me I was hopeless, helpless, worthless. She'd quietly tried to make me feel better, not worse. Until the end.

But the terrible thing about what she was saying was that somewhere deep inside me, the black monster that lived there actually agreed with her. Good things didn't happen to me, because I didn't deserve them. All I was made for was fighting, right? For trying, and failing, to protect other people.

"Claire died," my mother said, and sat up in the tub. The red water swirled around her. "Claire is *dead*. All this is just you refusing to admit any of that. You've gone crazy—don't you understand that? It's very sad, but you can't hold on to fantasy any longer. You know I'm telling you the truth, don't you?"

"No," I said. It sounded faint, and lost. "No, that's wrong. We brought her back. She's alive."

"Of course you didn't bring her back. That's ridiculous. She died, and they took her body away. And you took your father's gun and you shot yourself, and you've been dying ever since. You want to know the truth? She never loved you. She loved that vampire. Myrnin."

"No." I was backing up now, and the tile felt sharp and wet under my shoes. No, not shoes. I was barefoot. It felt as if I was standing on broken glass, and the pain helped, somehow. Helped me remember that this room was wrong, that the walls of that bathroom in that cheap motel hadn't been dripping with water, that my mom hadn't opened her eyes and said these terrible things, that it was *him*.

All this was Magnus, talking through my dead mother's mouth.

"No." I said it again, louder. "Get out of my head, you freak."

"Son—"

I charged forward, grabbed the edge of the claw-footed tub and tipped it over on its side, away from me. There was a rush of bloody water around me, and then *I* was in the tub—no, in water, staring up at cloudy glass, and I was fighting it, banging my hands against the cover that held me in. I left bloody handprints on it, and the blows were weak, but it *meant something*.

So did the bobbing light that I could see coming from the side.

My face was out of the water, the *liquid*, and I pulled in a breath and yelled. It came out a weakened croak, but I tried again, shouted harder, and battered the glass again.

Claire. Claire came back. But wait, maybe that wasn't right, maybe I'd made her up, made it all up, maybe she'd never existed, or maybe she had died, or maybe she didn't love me at all . . .

But it wasn't Claire who found me.

The face was familiar, but not her. And it wasn't a girl. A larger, more squared-off face I recognized. *Dick,* I thought finally. Dick Morrell. To be fair, I guessed, I really ought to call him Richard now, if he was here to save my life. It *sucked* to be rescued by a Morrell, after all the energy I'd put into hating the whole family.

This *couldn't* be a fantasy, because no way in hell would I ever fantasize about a Morrell showing up to save me.

Richard wiped moisture from the glass and saw me, and from his expression what he saw must not have been pretty. He yelled something, and then Hannah Moses was there, too, and somebody else, God, was that *Monica*? Maybe I was hallucinating after all. The three of them shoved the glass away.

I tried to sit up, but I couldn't. The draug were swirling around me, devouring my blood fast now, trying to kill me before I could get away. They'd been holding back, I realized. Making me last. That was why they'd put me in shallow water, so I wouldn't drown before they sucked out the last drops.

I managed to hold up a hand. It was pale and trembling, but I got it in the air, and Hannah grabbed it and pulled, hard. Once my shoulders were up, Richard took hold, too, and pushed, and I rolled over the lip of—what was it? A pool? No, some kind of container, maybe part of the purification process for the water treatment—and I hit hard steel grating with enough force to bruise, except I probably didn't have much blood left to form any bruises. My skin was sunburn-red and stinging as if I'd rolled in broken glass, but I was alive.

Barely.

"Claire," I whispered. I tried to get up, but my arms were too weak to lift me up. "Where's Claire?"

Hannah crouched down next to me and took out her cell

phone. She hit a button, listened for a tense few seconds, and hung up. "We need to get him out of here. Monica. Take his other side."

"Me? Are you *kidding*? Blood is never coming out of this dress!"

I wasn't imagining *her*, that was for sure, because I would never, ever, imagine Monica, and even if I did, why would I make her so damn useless? "Shut up," I managed to say. She gave me a filthy look as she bent down and put her shoulder under mine. My right arm draped over her shoulder. I hoped I was bleeding on her.

"*You* shut up. I broke both heels off my shoes on these stupid grates of yours." She looked pale, and scared out of her mind, but she was still Monica.

Maybe that did mean there was still a Claire out there, some-where. It was hard to know. Hard to figure out what was real, what was false, what was just a dream.

This felt real. The pain felt very real.

Hannah and Monica muscled me up to a standing position, not that it did much good, because I couldn't do more than shuffle along with them. "Richard," Hannah said, and Richard Morrell turned to glance at her. "Watch our backs."

"Done," he said. He looked at me for a second, and nodded. "Glad you're okay, Shane."

I wasn't, of course. But it was nice of him to think so. "Thanks," I said. "For coming." Like it was some kind of party that I'd thrown. How polite I was, all of a sudden.

"Thank Hannah. She was the one who signed us up." He smiled, and all of a sudden he wasn't the Dick Morrell I'd dis-trusted all my life, the one who was the shining football star and class president and perfect student, the good son of the bad mayor. He was just Richard, a guy who'd come to get me.

A guy who'd saved my life. "Hey," I said, "sorry I've been such an asshole to you all your life."

"Can't really blame you," he said. "Everybody judges me by my little sister and my old man. It isn't unfair exactly."

"Hey!" Monica said, and aimed a halfhearted, off-balance kick at her brother. Which he avoided. "I am *so* not voting for you next election."

"I don't think there will be another election," he said, "or that I'd want to be mayor of this slow-motion disaster, anyway. I only did it because they said I had to." He was walking backward now, facing away from us and watching our tails as we inched along the walkway. I began to wake up enough to see that we were in the water treatment plant's lower levels, which *reeked* even though they were open to the air. There were tanks on all sides, and open pools on the other side of the chain link. Sewage was moving through there, or should have been, I guessed; it was no longer going anywhere, which was part of why it stank so badly.

I'd been locked in the last set of shallow tanks, where the recycled and treated water was given a final rinse before heading into the storage towers.

But it was worse than that, a whole lot worse. The pool we were passing now was large, and it was deep, and it had *bodies*. Just like the Civic Pool, but this water was a murky gray-green color, thick with draug and contaminants.

This was Magnus's new blood garden, and it teemed with the draug, although few of them had any kind of shape to them. They were ignoring us, because we were human, and they were ripping into their favorite snacks. I felt the droplets of draug that were still on me sliding down, drawn toward the main pool, and a trickle of water ran from my feet to the edge.

Hannah had paused, staring. Monica made a strangled noise and tried to pull me forward, but I stayed put. "What?" Monica demanded. "Okay, fine, drowned people, gross, but we have to *go*!"

"Not yet," Hannah said. "Hold on to him." She slipped out from under my arm, and Monica staggered on her heel-less shoes as I sagged against her.

"Hey, watch the hands, Collins!" she snapped. As if I had any control over them, or wanted to feel her up anyway. She was just scared, and she wanted nothing more than to dump me and run.

I guessed that it was kind of impressive that she didn't do that.

"Hannah?" Richard asked, backing toward her. "What are we doing?"

"We can't leave this. They're growing in numbers again. We have to take them down if we can."

"How?"

"I have silver powder," Hannah said. She grabbed the phone again and dialed. "I need to let them know to evac. Come on, come on . . ."

She finally got an answer.

I heard the screams coming out of the phone from four feet away.

CHAPTER TEN

MICHAEL

☽

Getting the attention of the draug wasn't a problem. From the moment I ran into the water treatment plant I knew they'd felt me, seen me, sensed my approach; they could detect me the way I could feel a heartbeat across the room. Predator senses. They were tuned to vampires, and I was young, vulnerable, blasting full volume *Come eat me. I'm easy.*

So far, my brilliant plan was working. Shane would have been pleased; in fact, he would have been right in there with me, I knew that. *Hang in there, bro,* I silently begged him. We'd had our good times and bad times, but when I thought of Shane what I mostly remembered was holding on to him the night Alyssa died. Holding him back from running into the burning house to die along with her. Then holding him back from attacking Monica Morrell, who'd been standing there flicking a lighter.

That crazy suicidal streak of his had always scared me, because I knew it was still inside him. But this time . . . this time I was hoping he'd be holding on with both hands. He had things to live for now. People who loved him.

Yeah, and one of them is you, and you left him here.

Shane wasn't the only one who could wallow in guilt. I was soaking in it, because I'd left him. I'd done it because at the time I'd thought Myrnin was right—that Shane couldn't have survived more than a few minutes. Myrnin had taken advantage of our shock and confusion. Mine especially. I had the keys. I could have said, *Hell no—screw you. I'm going back for my friend.* Instead, I'd mostly thought of getting the girls away from there, cutting our losses. And that had been Myrnin's focus. Claire wasn't ever willing to admit it, but we all knew that Myrnin put her safety ahead of anyone else's. Even his own.

Just as I had put Eve's first, in the heat of the moment. Shane wouldn't even blame me for that, the jackass. He'd have done exactly the same thing. And he'd be right here, right now, moving with the shadows, luring the enemy away from those we needed to protect and taking the worst of it on ourselves.

I sometimes thought he'd had a little too much influence on me. I never *used* to be suicidal.

I spotted a still pool of dirty water ahead, near the corner of the building, and slowed; there was no way to be sure if it was safe or infected with the draug, but I couldn't take the chance. Avoiding its slippery edges took me under a drain spout, which I missed until the liquid gushed out and landed on me with a wet *slap.*

The draug formed out of it, clinging to my back, clawing at me. They weren't strong, but everywhere they touched skin it felt like acid burning off layers. The clothes stopped it for only a few seconds. If the draug couldn't soak through it, they flowed around and under, seeking prey.

Junkies seeking their particular brand of crack.

I had a shotgun loaded with silver, but there was no way to get it into position to hurt the one on my back without doing damage to myself. My strength didn't work well against the draug, because they were mush in this form, and when something has a blob of a body, it's difficult to get anything like a real grip.

I scraped it off against the rough brick side of the building, and my shirt got torn in the process. The skin beneath felt burned and raw, and already I seemed noticeably weaker.

Worse: the noise cancellation device that I'd been wearing clipped to my belt was shattered. I held my breath and tried not to listen . . . and then realized that I didn't need to worry. The draug weren't singing here. Not at all. Not even a *hum*. If they'd been able to make that sound, I'd have lost my focus, gotten confused, been overtaken . . . but something had happened to them, something to impair their ability to generate that call. When they'd first arrived in Morganville, they hadn't been able to sing, either. Magnus had gone after vampires one by one, and only when he had a certain number of draug under his command could he start that eerie, beautiful call that drew us in against our will.

We must have killed enough, at least for now, to rob him of that power. Eve would have, at this point, said, "Go us!" but I wasn't feeling especially victorious. I was feeling weak. *Got to keep moving.* The whole point of this was to draw Magnus's attention and get the rest of the draug to come after me; they needed all the hot, tasty vampire they could get, and I was right here, waiting. But if I waited too long, I could draw them right into my friends instead, especially if I stuck too close to the building itself.

I avoided the puddle, which looked *too* still, and moved on.

On the side of the plant was a long chain-link fence, posted with warning signs. These made handy grips as I scaled up and over and dropped on the other side ... then saw the treatment pools. The water was also treated in the pipes, but there was some kind of system I didn't fully understand to take it from gray to clean, and each of the pools looked different—a progression of treatments. There were also covered sections and containers on the other side of the fences, probably for taking samples. All in all, it was pretty much Draug Heaven ... as long as they didn't mind questionable water quality.

And I was in trouble, because I almost immediately realized that the pool nearest to me had waves in it. Thin, small waves at the far end, building into large tidal surges as they approached the edges of the ponds.

They were coming for me, and I was already weak. If another one got hold of me, I'd end up at the bottom of that pond, helpless and hopeless this time.

There were walkways over all the pools—rusted metal grates that were elevated about five feet over the surface. I got a running start and leaped over the onrushing waves, landed with a solid *thump* of feet on metal, and started running *against* the tide, heading for the far end of the body of water.

The waves collapsed and churned in confusion, as if a school of piranha had turned on itself, and then reversed course to race after me. I felt the shuddering slap as the liquid hit the metal. Smaller waves were trying to leap up and grab hold ahead of me, but they didn't have momentum and I was hauling ass; the best any of them did was to throw droplets on my shoes, and I kicked those off as I ran. I made it to the end of the walkway. There were two choices here—off onto the ground on the other side, and from there over the fence, or a switchback that ran another, identical walkway at an angle across the next pond.

This one wasn't quite as murky, and it was smaller; the water was an eerie bluish jade color, completely opaque. It was as still as stone, too, as I vaulted onto the catwalk that angled over it. The draug weren't slopping over into this pond. I thought they'd chase me . . . but they stopped at the concrete barrier. Even the waves curled back on themselves rather than fall into these still waters.

I slowed, and stopped. *It couldn't be.* I looked ahead; at the next angled intersection between catwalks was another divider, another pool. The water there was clearer, and it almost boiled with activity just like the last pool.

But here, in between . . . there was nothing. I took a breath, and immediately wished I hadn't; this whole area reeked of human waste and something else, something sweetly rotten that might have been the draug. No way I could pick out one individual component from the general stench.

I needed a sample of the water the draug seemed to avoid . . . and I had something to put it in. Eve's latest gift to me, which I wore on a chain around my neck . . . a blood vial. Some Goths were into it, keeping each other's blood as either mementos or trophies, but she'd gotten it mainly because it was, as she put it, my "break glass in case of emergency" supply. It was Eve's blood. I'd never really planned on drinking it, because it was just a taste, really, but this was a true emergency, after all.

I uncorked it and drained it in one small gulp. The taste of her essence exploded on my tongue in a rush, and I felt my pupils contract and my fangs come down in response. It's hard to describe what it feels like, except that it's a whole lot like wanting something you know isn't good for you. Craving, lust, hunger, fear, all balled up inside a sense of wonder, because you can actually *feel* the person the blood came from, at least a little. The fresher the blood, the sharper that sensation.

I held that taste in my mouth for a long second that seemed to stretch toward eternity, and then finally swallowed. The blood trickled in warm drops down toward my stomach, and I felt a spurt of energy run through me. Not much, because it wasn't much blood, but it helped.

I knelt down and stretched out as far as I could; I had to hang at a precarious angle, but I finally got a scoop of the turquoise water into the vial and corked it. Even in the bottle, the liquid looked opaque with whatever was suspended in it. I looped the chain back around my neck and rolled to my feet.

Ahead of me, more turbulence in the next pool. Behind me, the draug were definitely ready to welcome me back.

"The things I do for you, bro," I said, and ran straight ahead, top speed. The railing flew by in a blur, and as I approached the sharp V-shaped turn that angled across the next pool, also dangerously active, I calculated the distance, propelled myself up and onto the railing, and leaped across. I hit the other catwalk still running, but this time the draug had anticipated me, and the waves were heading *toward* me, building fast.

They were going to build high enough to swamp the catwalk, and once they were on it, they could pull me off balance and down into the depths.

I snarled, fangs out, and timed it carefully. Wait . . . wait . . . I kept running, faster and faster, building up momentum as the wave broke through the catwalk's grating and raced toward me, and then I slammed both feet down, hard. It was a risk. The catwalk was old, and rusty, and if my feet had broken through I'd have been done, but the hard old bridge held, and I arced up, up and over. The wave reached up for me, and I pulled my knees up in midair.

The draug's murky liquid form slapped at the soles of my shoes, and then dissolved and fell back into the pool. My jump carried me forward, and I landed hard, rolling with it to shed momentum, then bouncing back to my feet before they could react.

I made it to the end and leaped the railing into the tall winter-scorched weeds.

They didn't come after me. The waves subsided back into the pool. I stared at them for a second, wondering what the *hell* it was going to take to really make them come out of their hiding place after me, and finally thought to look back at the *other* pools.

The one that I'd just crossed was agitating just enough to keep my attention, but the ones on the ends were suspiciously quiet.

Ah. The draug were crawling out from my right and left, silently circling toward me. *That* was better. As long as they were focused on me, they weren't going to be going after Claire and Eve and the others . . .

Except that there weren't enough of them. A few, sure—five, six on each side. There had to be a lot more of them that were strong enough to leave the pool. We'd killed many of them, but not *that* many; they'd been all over us inside when we'd come earlier. That meant that they were likely still inside.

With Eve.

I needed to draw them out, and to do that I had to present either a genuine opportunity . . . or a genuine threat. Preferably both.

I did two things.

First, I extended my fangs and ripped open my own wrist, and let the dark red blood—loaded with those delicious vampire pheromones the draug loved—spray out all over the ground around me. "Soup's on, guys. Come get some."

Next, as the draug charged me, I backed up against the fence, pumped the shotgun, and began to methodically kill them all. I'd never been one for killing things, but I'd had plenty of video game practice.

Turns out all that first-person shooter stuff is actually good for something. Especially in Morganville.

I was killing the last one—or at least, turning it back into splatters of liquid that crawled away to the safety of a pool—when my cell phone rang. Eve had changed my ringtone, again. She'd sampled one of my concerts. Weird, to hear my own music coming out of the speaker.

I grabbed the phone and thumbed it on. "Kind of busy right now!" I said, before the novelty of my cell phone actually working dawned on me. "Who is this?"

"Moses," came the breathless reply. "We've got Shane. Heading for the truck. Claire and Eve are pinned down on the main stairs. Go get them."

I was about to confirm all that when I heard the draug start shrieking. I wasn't prepared for it; the noise went through me like an arrow through the head, and I almost dropped the phone, but I managed to hang it up and get it back in my pocket. I didn't know what had happened to hurt them that badly, but even though the screaming hurt, it made me savagely happy, too.

It would damn sure keep them busy.

I raced back over the catwalk that led through the safe pool, and broke the lock on a door to the inside of the building. There were more pools in here, just a couple, with more catwalks, and I saw that one of the pools was a thrashing, shrieking mess of silver and black that, even as I watched, quieted into stillness.

There were open canisters of silver nitrate discarded nearby. And blood. Lots of fresh human blood.

Shane's.

The blood trail went off to the left, but I plunged straight ahead, for the stairs that went up a floor into the main lobby. I caught sight of the truck outside the doors, and figures moving around it—Hannah's distinctive form was standing guard, so they were all safe, for now.

I ran upstairs, toward the smell of burned gunpowder, rot, and fear.

I met Claire and Eve coming down. Claire was supporting Eve; she seemed to be limping and cursing a lot. Claire still had her shotgun, but Eve's hands were empty. Unarmed.

I didn't think, I just took Eve in my arms and lifted her. The scent and warmth of her wrapped around me, and she leaned her head wearily against my chest. "Hannah found him," she said. "Shane's okay. He's alive."

I kissed her forehead. "I know. You're safe now." She wasn't bleeding, which was a relief; the limping must have been from a twisted ankle. Tenderness flowed through me, relaxing muscles I hadn't even known were tense; her fingers crept around my neck, and even though she didn't lift her lips to mine, she didn't flinch. "I swear, you're safe, Eve."

"They had us," Claire told me. "The draug had us cornered. But they ran."

"Yeah. Looks like Hannah threw a bomb in their party pool," I said.

"Shane—"

"I know, she's got him. You were right. He's okay." I knew, but didn't say, that he'd lost a lot of blood; she could probably figure that out on her own. The important thing was that Shane had come out of this alive.

We all had, as far as I could tell.

Win.

Claire took a deep breath, racked her shotgun like a professional, and said, "I've got your back. You just take care of her."

I escorted her, or she escorted me and Eve, to the truck. I opened the back to find Shane sitting in the cushy throne chair, covered in painful draug stings, his whole body seeping blood all over the upholstery. He looked paper-pale and shaky, but he raised his hand and said, "Hey, bro."

"Hey," I said. It was all I could manage. I realized, looking at him, that we'd been maybe a minute or two away from all this being utterly useless. He couldn't have held out much longer.

It scared me.

Richard and Monica were standing, though Monica looked mutinous; her expensive shoes were broken, and her dress was smeared with blood. She glared at me as if daring me to make some kind of comment.

"Thanks," I said to her, and I meant it. "Both of you."

Richard nodded. Monica frowned, as if she'd never had anyone thank her before and didn't know exactly how to handle it. That seemed likely.

Claire shoved past me, jumped in, and headed straight for Shane. He put his arms around her when she hugged him, but there was something odd in his face, something . . . tentative. As if he wasn't sure all this was real. If *she* was real.

No time to sort it out. I slammed the back door and jumped in the front with Eve and Hannah, and we got the hell out.

Fast.

CHAPTER ELEVEN

CLAIRE

🌙

The entire ride back to Founder's Square, Claire kept telling herself that Shane was all right. His skin was slick with blood from the bites, and he was pale and weak, but he was *alive*. And anything else could be fixed. Had to be fixed.

It had been only twenty minutes, maybe twenty-five, that he'd been in the draug's power. Michael had survived a whole lot longer than that, and he was just fine.

He's going to be all right.

But the way he was holding her felt . . . strange. Tentative. It was more than the weakness.

"Hey," she said to him, resting her head against his chest. His heart was beating fast, but it sounded strong and regular. "What happened in there?"

"Where?" he asked. He was with her, but he sounded . . . empty. Or at least, very far away.

"Where you were." *Still are.*

"I'm fine," he said, which didn't answer her question at all. "You smell like gunpowder."

"New perfume," she said, straight-faced. "Do you like it?"

"Edgy," he said, which was almost his old self, but phoned in, again, from a long way off.

"Shane—"

"I can't," he said, very softly. "I can't talk about it right now, okay? Just—leave it."

She didn't want to, because the look in his eyes, the way he was holding her . . . It made her anxious all over again. It felt, some-how, as if they hadn't found him, or at least not in time. As if part of him was still trapped.

She just curled closer to him, willing him to be all right, and said nothing else all the way back. His body was there, solid and liv-ing, but there was something else that just wasn't there, and when she looked up into his eyes, she didn't see . . . didn't see *Shane*. Not completely.

"He okay?" Of all things, it was *Monica* asking that question, crouched awkwardly on her broken heels with her brother stand-ing silently behind her. She looked as if she was actually, momen-tarily, interested. "I mean, Jesus, that's a lot of blood."

"He's okay," Claire answered, when Shane didn't. His eyes were closed, but he wasn't unconscious; he was holding on to her tightly and shivering. "Just—he needs to heal, that's all." Her voice shook when she said it, and Monica shot her a swift, merci-lessly piercing look. There was blood in her hair, *Shane's* blood, drying in a stiffened patch.

"News flash, preschool, nobody's *okay* right now, and most of us didn't have that happen." She stood up suddenly, her expression hardening, and tugged at her dress. "I came back here to *get* help, not to get dragged off to rescue your lame, limp ass, Collins. So you could be a little grateful."

Shane slowly raised one hand, and . . . flipped her off. It was weak, but it was so very him that Claire almost cried.

Monica almost smiled. Almost. "Yeah," she said. "That's what I thought. Truce over, asshole. Next time I see you bleeding on the side of the road, I back up and run you over again."

"Monica," Richard said, in a tone that said he'd had enough. More than enough. She shut up and pressed herself against the wall of the armored truck as it bumped and shuddered along. "Claire, is he still bleeding?"

"Some," she said. She could feel the slow trickle of it soaking through her clothes. "But not as bad." That might have been wishful thinking, which was the *only* kind of thinking she could do right now. "Thank you. If you hadn't come with us . . ." *I'd be dead. And Eve. And Shane. Maybe Michael, too, because he'd have tried to get us all back.*

Richard nodded, not refusing the thanks but not making a big deal out of it, either; he just let it roll off him without really registering. "He's strong, Claire," he said. "He held on. That means a lot."

"I never should have left him," she said. "Oh God, this is my fault, *my fault.*" She started crying, heavy, aching tears that pushed up from the core of her body. They tasted as salty as Shane's blood when she kissed his cheek and buried her face in the hollow of his neck.

She felt Richard's gentle touch on her back. "Sometimes things just happen," he said. "It's not right. It's not fair. But it's nobody's fault, Claire. So don't do that. Don't take it all on yourself. I promise you, it's the last thing he wants you to do."

She nodded, but she didn't really feel it.

"About my sister," he said. "She was a sweet kid, you know. When she was little. Used to come home crying every day in first grade. Everybody hated her, because her dad was the mayor. So by second grade, she gave it right back. She started fighting back when nobody was coming at her."

"Why are you telling me this?"

He shrugged. "I thought you should know she wasn't always . . . what she is. She was made that way. Not born. She can change. I'm hoping she will."

"Yeah," Claire said. "Me too."

Richard patted her on the shoulder again, and withdrew over to the wall of the truck.

Shane held on to her with desperate strength, all the way to Founder's Square.

Shane needed a transfusion.

When Theo told her, Claire burst into tears again, frantic ones. Eve hugged her from one side, Michael from the other, until she calmed down enough to listen to what Dr. Goldman had to say.

"He did lose a lot of blood," Theo said very gently, and captured her bloodstained right hand in both of his as he stood in front of her. She, Eve, and Michael were sitting in some antique white chairs in the anteroom of what had become Theo's make-shift hospital; as waiting rooms went, it was fancy, but cold. "The transfusion will help replace that volume quickly, and it will take about four hours; I doubt there will be any ill effects, though he may continue to have some weakness as his body recovers. I tested him, since the draug carry diseases at times, but it appears he is clear of that, which is a lucky thing. All he needs is blood for now, and rest. He should be better very soon, I promise you." He was quiet for a moment, then said, "Has anyone told you how much of a miracle that is? That he, a human, survived?"

"He's strong," Claire whispered. She'd been saying it from the beginning, and had been confident, so blindly confident. But seeing him so pale and weak and shaking . . . that had terrified her.

"Yes, strong indeed," Theo said, and patted her hand before he let it go. "A fighter, as he always has been. Today that served him very well, but you must understand that he will require more than physical strength. Michael can tell you that, to a point, but there may be . . . other factors, for Shane. What little we know of draug encounters with humans tells us the humans are forced into a dream world . . . or nightmares. I do not know which Shane experienced. So be patient with him, and watch for signs of any . . . odd behavior. All of you."

They all nodded. Eve's grip on Claire's hand was almost painfully tight, but she took a deep breath and eased up as Theo rose and walked away. "That's good news," she said, with forced cheer. "See? Transfusion fixes him right up. He's going to be fine, CB. Honestly."

Eve was saying that as much to cheer herself up as to hearten Claire. Claire looked, instead, toward Michael. "How bad is it?" she asked. "Really."

He didn't flinch from the question, but she'd seen his nightmares, and he knew it. "Bad," he said. "But vampires don't react the same way to the chemicals the draug secrete; we don't get the dream state that Theo was talking about. So we're awake, and aware, the whole time. Humans . . . I don't know what he was dreaming about, Claire. It could have been good. I hope it was good."

"Have you talked about what it was like? To anyone?" She glanced at Eve, who looked away, lips compressed. Of course he hadn't. Eve would have been his listener, but there was a gap between them now that they had to shout across. Maybe it was smaller than it had been, but it was still there. "You should, Michael. It must have been horrible."

"It's over," he said. "And I'm dealing. Shane will, too." *Because that's the guy code,* Claire thought in mild disgust. *Deal until you break into a million little pieces.* "Come on. Let's go see him."

She was almost . . . reluctant, somehow. Not to see Shane, but to see him so weak. But she was relieved to see, as they entered Theo's ward room with its neat camp beds and sheets hung between, that Shane was one of two patients, and he looked . . . better. Theo, or someone, had cleaned him up, so he didn't look like he'd bathed in his own blood anymore. Even his hair was clean, though still damp.

There was a needle in his arm, and an IV stand with blood bags. Claire winced. She knew how much he hated needles.

She held his hand as she sank down in the chair next to him. "Hey," she said, and leaned over to brush his messy hair off his forehead. His skin was still ivory pale beneath the tan, but no longer that scary paper white. "Are you feeling better?"

"Yes." He didn't open his eyes, but he smiled, a little. His hand squeezed hers a little. "You're here, aren't you?" That sounded like a blow-off question, but it wasn't, she realized. There was something else behind it.

"Yes, I'm here, I'm right here," she said, and kissed his cheek. His face didn't have the pinprick stings of the draug on it, but she'd seen them on his neck and chest—they'd suspended him in the water with his face up, the better to keep him alive while they . . . No, she really couldn't think about it. Not now. "Michael said you—you might have felt what they were doing to you. Did you? Feel it?"

He took a little too long to answer. It might have been weariness, or it might have been a lie. Very hard to tell. "Not so much," he said. "It was more like I was . . . dreaming. Or they were making me dream."

"What kind of dreams?"

"I don't think—" He opened his eyes and looked at her, just for a second, then closed them again. "Claire, I don't think I can talk about it right now."

That . . . hurt. It hurt a lot. She had a sudden dread that he was going to tell her something awful, like *I dreamed I was in love with Monica Morrell and I liked that better.* Or maybe . . . maybe just that he'd had some happy dream that didn't include her at all. Because she knew, oh yes, that Shane could do better than her; there were taller girls, prettier girls, girls who knew how to flirt and tease and dress for maximum success. She didn't fool herself about that. She didn't know why Shane loved her, really.

What if the dream had shown him that he really didn't *need* her, after all?

Michael leaned over to her and whispered, "We're going to leave you two alone, Claire. If you need us, you know we'll be close."

She nodded and watched them go; Eve seemed reluctant, and she made a little *call me* gesture on her way out the door. Claire swallowed through a suddenly desert-dry throat and asked, "Why don't you want to tell me about it, Shane?"

"It might scare you," he said. His voice sounded thin, and a little shaky. "Scares the hell out of me." After a short hesitation, he continued, "Some of it was good. The two of us, we were good, Claire."

"Us," she repeated. The fist around her heart let up, just a little. "The two of us?"

"Yeah," he whispered, and she realized that there were tears forming at the corners of his tight-shut eyes. *Tears.* She caught her breath and felt a stab of real pain. "I just—it was good, Claire, it was really good, and I didn't want to—I don't want to—I don't know what I—"

He stopped and turned his head away from her, then rolled over on his side.

Hiding from her.

If it was really good, she wanted to ask, *why are you crying?* But she didn't, because she couldn't stand to see him hurt like this. She was overflowing with questions, all kinds of questions, because she couldn't understand how if something had been *good* it could do so much harm.

But he wasn't going to tell her; she knew that.

And maybe, just maybe, he was right that she shouldn't even ask. Not right now, when it was so fresh and raw, an open wound.

In the end, she snuggled in next to him, her warmth easing his shakes. Just before she drifted off to sleep, she heard him whisper, "Please tell me you're really here."

"I'm here," she whispered back. Her heart ached for him, and she tightened her arms around him. "I'm right here, Shane. Honestly, I am."

He didn't answer.

In the morning, Shane seemed . . . better. Quiet, and with a wary look in his eyes that scared her a little, but he looked good. The red marks on his skin were healing up, and the transfusion seemed to have done a good job of restoring his healthy coloring. Theo had insisted on adding glucose in the last hour, even though Shane had begun griping about having the needle in.

Claire had finally left him, but not alone; Eve had shown up bright and early, coffees in hand and balancing a small tray of baked goods. Shane had accepted the coffee, and had been eyeing the cookies as Claire finally left to visit the incredibly awkward chemical toilets and do what sponge bath she could with shower gel and a bottle of water. She felt better, too, for having done it. She'd slept unbelievably deeply, not moving all night; that had been the deadening effects of the adrenaline draining away, she guessed.

Shane hadn't said a lot to her this morning, but then, he'd just woken up. *He will,* she thought. *He'll be himself again today.*

She was on her way back to the room when Myrnin stepped out of one of the hallways, saw her, and stopped dead in his tracks. His eyes were wide and black, and his expression tense and cautious. "Claire," he said. "I hear he is better." No question who the *he* was that Myrnin referred to, either.

"No thanks to you at all," she snapped, and started to bypass him. He got in front of her.

"Claire, I didn't—you must believe me, I never meant him harm. I thought . . ."

"You thought wrong, didn't you? You were willing to let *my boyfriend* die out there. Now get out of my way."

"I can't," he said softly. "Not until you understand that I *did not* want him dead. In no way is that true. I believed he was dead already, and I tried to spare you the pain of—"

"Shut up. Just *shut up* and get out of my way."

"No!" In a shockingly fast move, he backed her against the wall, hands braced on either side of her head as he leaned in on her. "You know me, Claire. Do you believe me so petty, so . . .

pathetic that I would do this for selfish personal reasons? The draug are *not to be played with.* You've taken huge and violent risks, going back there, and you must understand that I am a *vampire.* It is not in my nature to be so . . . careless with my own safety. Not for a single human."

She stared at him for a long few seconds, and then said, very quietly, "Including me?"

There was a flicker in his expression, a bit of agony, and he pushed off and walked away from her. She'd hurt him. Good. She'd meant to. "Yes," he finally said, sharply, and rounded on her from a few feet away. "Yes, even you. Stop thinking of me as some . . . personal tame tiger! I am *not,* Claire."

"And I'm not your puppet," she said. "Or your assistant anymore. I quit."

"It would not be the first time, would it?" Oh, he was angry now, eyes flashing with strobes of red. "If you are not adult enough to understand why I tried to minimize our losses, then I have no use for you, girl. Cling to your friends and your follies. I am done coddling you."

She laughed. "Wait—*you* coddle *me*? Are you *kidding*? I'm the one who follows you around and picks up the pieces of crazy you drop all over the place, Myrnin. *Me.* You don't take care of me. I take care of *you.* And the least you could have done for me was to *go back for Shane.* But you didn't."

The strobing faded away, leaving his eyes black and a little cold. "No," he said. "I didn't. And I didn't because in my experience, there's never been anything left to rescue. I couldn't allow you to see him like that, Claire, reduced to bones and blood. That was a *kindness.*"

She started to fire back at him, but couldn't find the words. He was serious about that. Very serious.

"Furthermore," he said, "I realized why they'd taken him. You didn't."

"Myrnin, just—I don't know what you're talking about, but just—"

"They were using him to get to *you*, Claire." He let her think about that in silence for a long moment, and then continued, "You are perfectly right to hate me. Feel free. But I am glad he is all right, all the same. They were using him to lure you back, and it worked. Magnus wants *you*. You might give some consideration to that, because I think it is quite important."

Magnus. Standing there, watching her. Waiting not for Shane, not for Michael, but for *her.*

Claire felt cold creep up her spine, and chill bumps shivered over her arms.

"Hey," Shane said. He was leaning against the doorway, looking almost back to his old self again; he had color back in his face, and he'd changed into fresh clothes—his own, brought back by Eve. She'd managed to grab his favorite ironic saying T-shirt; this one read ZOMBIE BAIT. "Are you two crazy kids fighting about me?" There was no amusement in his expression, Claire thought. "Because don't. Myrnin was right. You should have left me and called it good."

"Shane—"

"You're mad because he did something smart, not because it was stupid. You came back, yeah, but you got help, and that was important. If you'd tried it alone, you wouldn't have made it, and you know that's true. He was right to run." He sucked in a deep breath and met Myrnin's eyes squarely. "Thanks for making her be smart, too. Even if it didn't take."

"Oh," Myrnin said, clearly taken aback. "Well, yes, all right."

Claire stared at Shane. How could he say leaving him was *smart*?

And yes, okay, she'd gotten reinforcements, and maybe *that* had been smart, but she'd have come back all alone, and he knew it.

"Hey," she said. "You'd have done exactly the same thing if it was me."

"Yeah," he said, and shrugged. There was even an attempt at a smile. "But I never said I was smart, did I?" The smile—not convincing—didn't last long. "We can't afford to fight like this. Not right now. He's on Team Us. Don't kick him off. We don't have enough players on the field as it is."

"You're seriously going to go with a sports analogy right now?"

"Yep," he said, and sipped his coffee. "Just like normal." But there was a shadow in his eyes, a flash that made her wonder just how deep the fractures went inside him. "Theo cut me loose. I'm topped up and ready to go."

Myrnin was watching him with a guarded expression, and then he finally said, "I suppose you need rest, then."

"Not really. I slept, and I got a transfusion. I feel . . . pretty good, actually." Physically, that might be true, but Claire doubted he felt at all good inside. She remembered that whisper in the dark. *Are you really there?*

Always, she thought. *I'll always be here.*

"Did you have some kind of mission you wanted to send us on?" Shane asked. "Seeing as how brilliantly the last one turned out?"

"The last mission killed enough draug to prevent their singing," Myrnin countered, "and we lost no one."

"No thanks to you," Claire muttered. She saw his back stiffen.

"Oliver would like us to consider more . . . scientific approaches. I will need your assistance for that, Claire. I will expect you in the laboratory in—" He darted a glance from her to Shane and back again. "In your own good time. Good day."

He clasped his hands behind his back and walked away. For the first time, Claire realized what he was wearing: crazy lab coat. Cargo pants. And his vampire bunny slippers, bedraggled but still flapping their red mouths with every step. She wondered if he'd just thrown it on, or if this time he'd dressed to make her think of him as . . . helpless. Inoffensive.

There was a lot more to Myrnin than just the pleasantly crazy mayhem; underneath it, there was calculation, and a cold, still monster that he kept mostly caged.

She didn't realize that she'd shivered, again, until Shane put his arm around her. He was warm now, and she turned and put her arms around him. She rested her head on his chest and listened to the slow, steady beat of his heart. *Alive, alive, alive.*

"Hey," he said, and tipped her chin up. "I didn't get to say hello properly last night. Sorry. Mind if I—"

She lunged upward and captured his lips in midsentence, and the kiss was fierce and sweet and hot. His mouth felt soft and hard at the same time, and he sank into a chair and pulled her onto his lap, which was a relief from standing on tiptoe to reach him. It was a long, needy, almost desperate kiss, and when she finally broke it, it was to gasp for air.

He combed through her hair with his fingers, gentle with the snags, and searched her face with a dark, intense stare. She didn't know what he was looking for.

"What is it?" she asked him, and put her hands on either side of his face. His beard was a little rough beneath her skin. He needed a shave. "Shane?"

"You seem so . . ." He paused, as if he couldn't really think of the word. A little line formed above his eyebrows, and she wanted to kiss it away. "Different," he finally said. "Are you? Different?"

"No," she said, startled. "No, I don't think so. How?"

"More . . ." He shook his head then, and kissed the palm of her hand without taking his gaze away from her face. "More real."

That should have seemed romantic, but instead she felt another chill, a strong one. There was confusion deep in that stare, uncertainty.

Fear.

"Shane, I'm me," she said, and kissed him again, frantic with the need to prove it. "Of course I'm real. *You're* real. *We're* real."

"I know," he said, but he was lying. She could feel it in the tremble of his fingertips, and the pressure of his lips when he kissed her back. "I know."

She would have asked him right then what had happened to him, what those dreams had been, but a voice over her shoulder said, "I guess this means you're feeling better, bro."

Michael was walking in, yawning, drinking a cup of something that Claire sincerely hoped was coffee. She'd seen enough blood in the past twenty-four hours to last a lifetime.

"Yeah," Shane said, and gave her a quick glance of apology as he moved her off his lap. "Better." He offered a fist, and Michael bumped it. "Thanks for coming to get me."

"Couldn't do anything else." Michael shrugged. "Claire's the one to thank. She got us all together. Hannah deserves it, too; she didn't have to jump in, but she did. And I hate to say it, but you might want to thank Team Morrell."

"Already did," Shane said, and frowned a little. "Uh, I think I did. Did I?"

"You did," Claire said. "It's okay." But that worried her, too. Still, shock could make people lose memories, right? Not everything was suspicious. She couldn't think this way or she'd drive herself crazy. "Don't downplay it, Michael. You used yourself as bait for the draug. That's major."

"Bait?" Shane repeated, and blinked. "What?"

Michael shrugged again and sipped his coffee. "Somebody had to," he said. "I'm their favorite flavor, and I'm fast. Made sense."

"Makes zero sense for you all to risk your lives coming after me. How did you know I wasn't dead?"

"Even if you were," Michael said, suddenly completely serious, "we'd come back for you. I mean that. And it's my fault we left you to begin with. Claire didn't want to go. I had the keys, and I used them to drive off and leave you there. My fault. Nobody else's."

"All of a sudden, everybody wants to take the blame," Shane said. "Thought that was my gig, man."

"We can share. Many hands, lighter loads, all that crap." Michael took another drink and changed the subject. "Eve brought my guitar. I was thinking of playing a little later if you want to chill. New songs rattling around in my head. I'd like an opinion."

Shane flashed him one of those surfer gestures, middle three fingers curled in, thumb and pinkie out. "Shaka, brudda."

Michael flashed it back and grinned. "Claire. Got something for you." He pulled a chain over his head and threw her a necklace; she caught it and saw some kind of glass bottle, sealed, full of opaque liquid. "While I was playing my bait act, I scooped up some water from one of the pools."

She almost dropped it. "Draug?"

"Nope. No draug in that pool. It was empty. Only one that was." He shrugged. "Thought it might be important. Do your science-y stuff on it. Might be something that could help."

She shook the bottle, studying the contents, but it didn't tell her anything. It wasn't a big sample, maybe an eyedropper full. Enough, though. "Thanks."

"Sure," he said. "Later." He started walking.

"Wait," she said, and caught up with him. She lowered her

voice. "Would you—would you kind of keep an eye on him the rest of the day? Make sure he's really okay?"

Michael studied her for a second, then nodded. "I know what he's been through," he said. "Well, some of it. So yeah. I'll hang close. You go do what you need to do."

"Thanks." She kissed him on the cheek. "And do me a favor. Make up with Eve, okay? I can't stand this. I can't stand seeing the two of you . . ."

"It's not up to me," he said, "but I'm trying."

She went back to Shane and settled in on his lap again, arms around his neck. His circled her waist. "I thought you had to go," he said. "And don't think I didn't see you kissing on my best friend."

"He deserved it."

"Yeah. Maybe I ought to kiss him, too."

Michael, on his way out, didn't even bother to turn around for that one. "Oh sure, you always *promise*."

"Bite me!" Shane called after him. He was smiling, and it looked like a genuine one this time. That was good. He even turned to Claire and held on to it, though a bit of that shadow crept back into his eyes. That . . . uncertainty. "Not you. You, I was thinking more like *kiss me*. If that's okay."

"Always," she said, and proved it.

Going into Myrnin's lab was a very weird and awkward thing; she'd normally felt okay around him, even when he was strange or psycho . . . on some deep, fundamental level, there had been some trust.

Not now. Not at this moment.

He looked up as she entered, and the hopeful look on his face smoothed out as he read her expression. "Ah," he said, in a neutral tone. "Good. Thank you for giving me your time." That was way too polite for him, normally; it was as awkward as a schoolboy trying to remember his manners. "How is Shane?"

She skipped right over that, because the fact that he even said Shane's *name* made her angry. "Michael gave me this," she said, and showed him the vial full of liquid. "It's from one of the holding pools at the treatment plant. The draug were avoiding the water."

Myrnin focused in on the vial, and as what she'd said filtered through whatever he had going on in his head, he snatched the chain away from her to hold it up to a bright, shadeless incandescent bulb. "Interesting," he said. "Thoughtful of him to retrieve us a sample."

"Dangerous," she said. "He's lucky he didn't get killed out there."

"Aren't we all." Myrnin grabbed a test tube and carefully poured the contents of the vial in it. It was a meager amount, but he seemed happy enough. "Excellent. *Excellent.* A good start to our inquisition today." He paused, then picked up a slender glass pipette and drew off a sample of the water to add to a slide, which he covered with a second glass plate and put under a microscope. "I've been thinking about binding agents. Alchemically speaking, our goal was transforming an object from one state to another— lead to gold, obviously, but many different—"

"We don't have time for alchemy," Claire said flatly. "Alchemy doesn't *work*, Myrnin."

"Ah, yes, but I read—wait, I have it here somewhere—ah!" He shoved books around and came up with a piece of paper that looked as if it had been printed off a computer. "Alchemists believed it was possible to change the essential nature of a thing, and look, we were *right*. According to the *Journal of Physical Chemistry*, a very high-voltage charge conducted through water can actually bring about a phase transition, freezing diffusional motion and forming a single, stable crystal that—"

"I read it," Claire said. It freaked her out that *he'd* read it. Off the computer, not paper? Myrnin wasn't exactly the surf-the-Internet type. "It's interesting, but it takes a lot of power, and it doesn't last; plus, it's not a permanent phase change. As soon as you remove the current, water reverts to its liquid state." But it was impressive that he'd found that, she thought; she'd considered it herself, because the idea of turning water into a solid was . . . exactly what they needed, actually. Just not with so much crazy power consumption.

"But it's a start, is it not?" Myrnin said. He bent over the microscope and clucked his tongue. "I am honestly mystified by how you humans get anything done with the primitive equipment at hand. This is useless." He took the slide off and, before she could stop him, removed the glass top and *licked the sample.*

She fought the urge to gag. He didn't seem at all bothered. He stood quite still, closing his eyes, and then said, "Hmmm. A bit salty, bitter aftertaste . . . iron . . . hydroxide." He smiled then, and looked at her as if he was quite proud of himself. "Definitely iron hydroxide. That is a binding agent, is it not?"

"You are insane," she said. "You can't go around . . . licking things that come out of a *water treatment plant.* That's just . . . unsanitary."

"Life is unsanitary," he said. "Death more so, as it turns out. I don't believe that iron hydroxide has any effect upon me, but of course I should try larger doses. If it in fact has an effect upon the draug, that is quite an advance. . . ." He turned and rummaged around in drawers. "Bother. You can create iron hydroxide, can't you? Make some. I think we have all we need in supplies."

She found goggles, gloves, and an extra lab coat three sizes too big—she had to fold the sleeves back—before laying out the chemicals she needed, and the tools. "It'll take a while," she said. "Try not to lick anything else."

"Cross my heart," he said solemnly, and did so.

"I don't think that really works as a promise when your heart's no longer beating." That was snarkier than she probably needed to be, but it shut him up, for a while. She concentrated on her work. It was like being back at school again, with a chemistry problem laid out in front of her—something soothing and simple, steps to follow, and a stable and well-documented outcome. She liked science because it was neat. It followed rules.

And it never broke her heart.

Even with distilled water, it took almost three hours for the chemical reaction of iron wire, water, and electric current to create the thick green gel and scummy surface; she mixed it, then boiled it in water over a Bunsen burner until it was reduced to powder. The entire process produced only a couple of teaspoons of iron hydroxide. She'd lost track of what Myrnin was doing, but by the time she was finished, he took part of her output, mixed it into a glass of water, and drank it down.

No reaction. She wasn't sure whether she was happy or sad about that.

"On to the next phase." He picked up a sealed flask of murky liquid and set it on the counter in front of her. "Don't spill any."

The water in the container was moving and swirling on its own. Claire put her hand out for it, then drew back, because it *reacted* to her. "Is that the *draug?*"

"A sample," he said. "You do *not* want to know what I had to do to get it, and I will not be doing it again, so please, small sample sizes, there's a girl. Our goal is to come up with something that will immobilize them, or better yet, poison them without affecting a captive vampire."

"Isn't it dangerous, having this here?"

"Not really. It's too small to form any kind of cohesive entity. If it tries to organize itself . . ." He handed her a small saltshaker, which she peered at with a frown. "Silver flakes. A shake or two will destroy the sample, but use it only in an emergency. Now. *Work.*"

Claire shook her head, picked up a dropper, and began to experiment with the iron hydroxide.

After another long few hours, they had an outcome. It wasn't what they'd hoped—and it was just in time to report to Oliver, who swept in like the world's most intimidating CEO. "Well?" he demanded. "What results have you?"

"Science is not speedy," Myrnin snapped back. "Perhaps you're deluded by those ridiculous television shows where one waves a magic eyedropper and crimes are solved. But what we *have* discovered is that although they show promise, binding agents will not be enough. Not in the strength we currently have available."

"What the devil is a *binding agent?*"

"Iron hydroxide, for one," Claire said. "Basically, it binds chemically with contaminants in water and weighs them down. It does hurt the draug; it might eventually even kill them, but it's not fast. There are other agents like it, though. We can work through each of them."

"How quickly?"

"Not quickly enough," Myrnin said. "And frankly, most are far more esoteric than we can manufacture here in our crude little lab. It was a fantastic idea. Just not as practical as I had hoped."

"Still, it's more progress than the vampires have ever made before on their own," Claire said. Her head hurt, and so did her back, and she was badly craving a sandwich. And Shane. "It's something."

"I wouldn't say vampires never made progress. *I* provided the shotguns," Myrnin said.

"Humans invented shotguns. And flamethrowers."

"Don't try to claim you invented silver!"

"We learned how to mine it, smelt it, and work it," Claire said. "Sorry, but apart from you, Myrnin, vampires are not really big on the *invent* part of *inventing.* You just . . . steal."

"Adaptation is the key to survival," he said. "I believe Darwin pointed that out, quite brilliantly. Still, we need more time, Oliver. Much more. And I have no other ideas as yet."

"I do," Claire said. Myrnin turned to look at her, and she shrugged. "You didn't ask. But I do."

"Such as?"

"There are a lot of other uses for binding agents besides cleaning water. They are also used in cleaning up toxic spills, for instance. There are a lot that we might be able to find in Morganville, or make. But we'll need a bigger selection of chemicals."

"Which we will find where, exactly? Morganville is not exactly a hotbed of scientific—" Myrnin stopped in midsentence as the light dawned. "Ah. Yes. Of course."

Oliver was not looking pleased. Or indulgent. "I have much to do. Can you provide us with a weapon we can use that is not toxic to vampires, or not? I need an answer. Now."

"Maybe," Claire said. Oliver growled, and she saw how close he was to just letting go and being full-on vampire. Once, that would have scared her. Now it hardly raised her pulse rate at all. "I can't tell you until we get the chemicals, make batches, and test them on vampires. Some may be toxic. Some probably won't be. The question is, what's effective on the draug? And that's going to take time to figure out. Myrnin's right. It's not a magic wand."

"Then I have no use for it," Oliver snapped. "We will proceed without your assistance. If what's been reported is correct, we have cut off the draug's major method of advancement. They are pinned in two spots: this end of town"—he slapped the map with a pale, strong hand—"and here, at the treatment plant." Another hard slap. "It's time to launch attacks. We'll use the weapons we have if we must, but we can't delay."

"Why not? Magnus already has all the vampires he can get for his blood gardens; if he draws unfortunate humans, they won't last, and it's the equivalent to animal blood for us. It can't sustain him long. They can't raise the call. They can't reproduce now. Let them wait until we are ready," Myrnin said. He sounded smug. Too smug, Claire thought, and Oliver must have thought so, too, because he reached out, grabbed the lapels of Myrnin's lab coat, and dragged him very close.

"I. Do not. Take orders. From *you*," Oliver hissed. "You take orders from *me*, witch. And for as long as I find you useful, you'll enjoy your privileged status. Once you're a liability, we'll revise the terms of your . . . employment. Are we understood?"

"Amelie—"

"Is dying," Oliver said. His face looked hard as a bone knife. "Sentiment aside, we cannot leave a vacuum of power, and you know that. Without leadership, the vampires will battle each other in bloodline conflicts, run wild, attract attention. She has been a strong, fair leader. I hope I can be half as much."

"Which half?" Myrnin asked. "Not fair, surely."

Oliver's fangs extended to their full, terrifying length, and he hissed like a cobra. Myrnin didn't flinch. And didn't fight.

Oliver shoved him away. "Do as you like," he said. "But don't get in my way. Any of you."

He stalked out, throwing the door open and leaving it that way, and Claire pulled in a long, slightly shaky breath. Myrnin straightened the lapels on his lab coat with an irritated snap of fabric.

And another figure stepped into the doorway.

Shane. Carrying a glass of what looked like sweet, delicious, life-giving Coke, and a sandwich. Michael was with him, carrying another plate. On it was . . . a bag of type O, it looked like.

"Hey," Shane said. "Hope we're not interrupting. He's in a mood."

"You are a Greek god," Claire said, and grabbed the Coke and sandwich. She hesitated then, mortified, and said, "Uh, these are for me?"

"Thought you might be hungry," he said. Michael silently handed the plate to Myrnin, who bit into the bag without even the pretense of politeness. "Okay, that's disturbing."

"Sorry," Myrnin mumbled, and kept sucking. Claire turned her back. Funny; a year ago, seeing something like that would totally have put her off her meal, but nothing was going to separate her from a turkey sandwich now. She took a giant, delicious bite, chewed, and washed it down with tingling soda.

So much better.

"What's the drama?" Shane asked, and pointed to the door. "With Lord High Cranky, I mean?" He sounded like his old self, Claire thought. Maybe a day of hanging around Michael had been really good for him. Maybe it was . . . all okay.

"He wants faster action," Claire said. "I said we need chemicals from the university lab."

"You never actually got that far," Myrnin said, "but I did

know what you meant. And you're correct. They would have a far more elegant and extensive selection of things there. We shall go."

Shane said, "You're kidding. You actually think she's going anywhere with you. Ever." He gave Myrnin a humorless little smile. "Much less me, of course. But I promise you, she is *not* going without me." He watched as Claire crammed more sandwich into her mouth, moaning a little from the deliciousness of actual *food*, and then said, "So what exactly is it that you're making with your chemicals again?"

"Binding agents," she said, but it came out sounding a little like a foreign language. Maybe Klingon. She swallowed and drank more soda. "Sorry. Binding agents."

"Which are . . . ?"

"Chemicals that bind to contaminants in water. Or chemicals that can change the composition of water itself—something that causes a reaction or a state change."

"From liquid to solid?"

"Exactly."

"Like . . . Jell-O," Shane said. He sounded thoughtful. Claire blinked, suddenly taken by the idea of a dump truck full of gelatin being backed up to a pool. Some kind of world record in that, she was pretty sure. But not extremely useful.

Myrnin slowly straightened up, put down the empty blood bag, and licked type O from his lips. "Unless I'm very much mistaken, you have something to say, Mr. Collins. Please tell me it isn't about snack foods."

"Not exactly," Shane said. "But I think I know exactly the chemicals you're looking for. And you won't find them at the university. But I know where you *will* find them."

"Where?"

"Morganville High School."

CHAPTER TWELVE

EVE

)

My brother, Jason, was out of prison, again, which I found out because I walked into a room off of the Armory and saw him holding a shotgun.

It was like falling into a nightmare. I was younger, he was younger, it was four years ago, and he was facing me with my dad's pistol and telling me that he was going to kill me. I still remember the *way* he said it. An eerily calm voice, and empty eyes.

See, my brother's not someone you should trust with a gun. Or a sharp knife. Or empty hands, and it terrified me, a bolt of utter and paralyzing fear, to see him *armed* like that. And loose.

Jason's my *brother*, and some of his screwed-up-ness is my fault, but he's not the first guy I'd pick to hand any kind of weapon to, even in a crisis. Sure, he could fight. Sure, he could do damage. But he was the proverbial loose cannon, rolling around crushing everything in his path, friend or foe.

And some nitwit vampire had him on reloading duty. He was taking empty cartridges, filling them up, and sealing them using a reloader press. Oh, and he was cooking silver into shot, too, or rather coating regular shot with the stuff. Probably not as effective as solid pellets, but I wasn't surprised we were running short of precious metals to toss randomly at the enemy. The vampires stored surprising amounts of things that would hurt each other, but even their paranoia had limits, and we were bumping up against them.

He cranked out another shell on the press, then slotted it home into the shotgun, snapped the breech shut, and put the weapon aside on a rack. Then he saw me, and stopped for a second.

Neither of us said a word.

My brother was a little shorter than me, not really muscular, kinda weedy and angular. He wore his hair longer than Shane's, and most of it flopped down and hid his dark eyes. That was for the best. He had cold eyes, my brother. Really cold.

There was a scar on his forehead, angling from left to right. It looked pretty fresh. There was also a bruise on his jaw.

"Sis," he said. It was a nothing kind of voice, waiting for me to make a move. I didn't, because I didn't dare; I'd walked in here alone, and as far as I knew nobody knew where I was. Not Michael, who was hanging out with Shane today; not Claire, who was locked in the lab with Myrnin. I was dreadfully and irrationally afraid that he would somehow know that, know I was alone and vulnerable.

Deep down inside, he was a sociopath, and I'd helped make him into that by walking away from him when he needed me. By locking my doors and covering my ears and not doing what a big sister was supposed to do: protect him.

So I couldn't hate him. I could only fear what he'd become.

"I didn't know—" *Didn't know they let you out of jail.* "They put you to work here."

"You know vamps. Practical," he said, and shrugged. "No point in having prisoners if you can't get some kind of value out of them. They don't believe in rehab. It's all racks and iron maidens with them."

He was only joking a little, and darkly. The vampires weren't into torture these days, but they also weren't forgiving. And Jason had tested their mercy, a lot. He was lucky to be alive, and he knew it. My brother had a lot of sins on his conscience. He'd helped me sometimes, but he'd quit trying to be a better person some time ago, and I'd quit trying to help him.

So there was that between us, too.

"How are you doing?" It was an inane question, really, and I almost winced when I heard how it sounded. He tossed his hair back and smiled. Not a sane sort of smile, but it might have been for effect. I hoped it was.

"Peachy," he said. "Solitary confinement with vampire supervision is really healthy. You know, exercise, good diet, self-improvement. It's like a spa, but with teeth."

I glanced involuntarily at the guns, and when I moved my gaze back he was still smiling, but differently. It looked like someone had moved his lips and stuck them in that position, not that he found any real humor in things. "Ironic," he said. "Yeah? Me and the gun duty? But somebody's got to be making the shells, and vamps can't handle the silver very well. I can do it twice as fast, without burns. Like I said, they're practical." He poured some more silver shot into a shell casing, and jammed it in the press. "So. I heard you two are getting married. I think my invitation got lost in the jailhouse mail."

He was different, yet again, from the last time I'd seen him. He'd been trying, for a while—trying to be a better guy, a real person. And he'd been winning at it, until . . . well, I didn't really know what had happened. Drugs, probably. Jason was always looking for a new high, mostly to avoid facing his own crappy past. He'd blown past alcohol by eleven; by thirteen, he'd been dealing to classmates and staying high most of the time. It hadn't made him nicer. By the time I'd turned eighteen he'd already gotten too comfortable with weapons. Shane had a scar to prove it. I was lucky I didn't, since I'd been the one he was really after.

"I didn't think you'd want to come," I said. "Or, you know, be out of jail."

"Surprise. And why wouldn't I want to come? You need somebody to give you away, sis. I always wanted to do that." There was that creepy, empty smile again. Something had broken inside my brother. It had always been cracked, deeply, but now it was just . . . shattered. And I didn't know why, or what had happened to him, but whatever it was, it had left him feral and angry. "Guess that makes me a Glass by marriage. I always wanted a brother."

"Let's not get all Cain and Abel about it," I said. "You really don't want to go there, Jase."

"Cain was the killer," Jason said. "Which one of us gets to play the victim?"

Oh, Jason. I felt a tiny shiver ladder up my spine. My sweet, kind, rocker boyfriend had swallowed more darkness than my brother, and even though he kept it pushed way, way down, it was there when he needed it. He didn't let it rule him, but he could put it on a leash and make it work for him. It was pretty obvious to me, in that moment, who'd win that fight, whatever Jason might think. "Let it go," I said. "Trust me."

He laughed. "Yeah," he said. "That'll happen soon. You

pimped me out, and then you sold me out. Not exactly a rock-solid basis for trust."

"I thought—I thought we were getting over all that."

"Easy for you. You ended up getting exactly what you wanted. Freedom. A hottie boyfriend who has full vamp status. Oh, and even though you said you were never a fang-banger, you've got a bandage on your neck the size of Nebraska. Guess you're coming to terms with a lot of things these days." He lifted a pan full of silver-coated shot and dumped it into a tub half full of water; the shot sizzled and cooled, and he scooped it out with a strainer as he readied another empty cartridge casing.

As he did, his shirt collar moved a little, and I saw red bite marks on his neck, over his jugular.

Just like before, when he was little. When he hadn't had a choice.

I took an involuntary step forward, eyes fixed on the bite. "Jason," I said. "*Jase.* Who did that to you?"

He twitched the collar of his shirt back into place and kept working without a reply.

"Jason!"

"Why the hell do you care?" he asked sullenly, and pressed a cartridge closed. "Thought you were all into the recreational biting now. You want to hear all about my sex life? Kinky, sis."

"You're letting someone bite you," I said. "God, Jase, why would you *do* that?" Because I knew what he'd been through in his childhood. My parents had known and hadn't stopped it—hadn't even tried.

I had, once. Just once. But I was scared out of my mind, and I failed him. And I still, always, owed him for that.

"I'm not stupid." He glanced up then, and the shine of his eyes was bitter-bright. "I'm not going to be on the wrong side of the fang for long," he said. "And when I'm one of them, you better believe that I'm going to be taking my fair share. Money, sex, blood. Whatever I want."

Jason and Shane were two sides of the same coin. Both had come from abuse, both had felt vulnerable and frightened and alone, abandoned by everybody who was supposed to protect and care for them. But Shane had come out of it forged into something strong, something that wanted to fight to protect others.

My brother was just a carbon copy of his own abuser, ready to pay his pain forward. And I couldn't stop him, couldn't help him. Couldn't do anything except what I'd done for him my whole life.

Walk away.

"Who is it?" I asked him. "Who's biting you?"

"Why?"

"Because I want to know."

"She's really pretty," he said. "Blond. I think you already know her. I've seen her with you."

Not Amelie, obviously; the whole idea she'd stoop to this was . . . just no. "What's her name?"

He bared his teeth. "Why should I tell you? What are you going to do, *report it*? That'd be a first for you."

"Jason, you never wanted to be a vampire. Neither of us did."

"Why not? You think I'm not *worthy* or something?"

Worthy didn't enter into it. The idea of my brother on a permanent vampire power trip was a *really* bad one. I felt sick, and anxious, and afraid; whoever was biting him *had* to be feeding him a line of bullshit. The vamps didn't like to turn new recruits. It was some kind of a risk to them, and a burden. Michael had been the first one turned in a very long time, though there had been some complications to that. Nobody had been made a vampire since.

Why *Jason*, of all people?

"I know you don't believe this," I said, "but I do care about you. I always have. You scare the shit out of me, but I think deep down you know this is wrong. You still want to be . . . better. I know you can do it, I've seen it. You helped people. You even saved our lives. Why do you want to—to become *this*?" Not a vampire, but something worse.

Something truly without a soul.

He stared at me for a long second, then picked up the shotgun he'd laid aside and began slotting cartridges in with solid, even *thunks*. "Because it doesn't hurt as much," he said, and racked the shotgun with one hand. "Time to go, sis. Reunion's over."

He meant it, and I was acutely aware of what that shotgun he held could do to me, to fragile human flesh and bone. I didn't think he'd do it, but I didn't know. I didn't really know him at all anymore.

"Who is she?" I whispered. "God, just tell me."

I didn't think he would. Maybe he didn't think he would, either. But finally, as I was leaving, he said, "Naomi."

I forced myself to keep going.

But walking out of that room, leaving my vampire-to-be brother making weapons of vampire mass destruction, made me feel sick and helpless and—worst of all—guilty.

Again.

I found that blond vamp-bitch talking to Oliver, in his office. And it was *on*.

They both heard me coming, of course, and whatever serious conversation was under way was cut off before I heard a word; I didn't care, at all, because bloodsucking politics was the least of my concerns or interests at the moment. Oliver had guards, and one of them stepped into my path. He was big.

I didn't care.

"You!" I yelled, and pointed around him at Naomi. "Blondie. Get your room-temperature ass out here!"

"Well," Oliver said, "this is an interesting development. By all means, Naomi. Go. I assure you, we're quite done with our conversation."

She glared at him. I was used to seeing the nice, mannered Naomi, the one who seemed so sweet and buttery-soft; this one looked almost dangerous. "You're a fool," she told him. "We're far from done. You can pretend to the throne all you like, but you're nothing but a usurper, and always were even in your breathing days. You're no *king*."

"And I assure you, I know your origins as well. Amelie was generous with you, and kind, but rest assured that I will not be so well mannered." He smiled the thinnest smile I've ever seen, and maybe the most dangerous. "Come near her again and I will end you. See to your noisy little . . . guest."

The guard stared down at me impassively as he held me off; he must have been almost seven feet tall, and his shirt was big enough to make three dresses, and not cocktail-length, either: formal wear. I tried to give him my war face. "Better step off, Tiny," I told him. "Me and the princess have business."

"Do we?" Naomi laid a gentle hand on his arm, and Tiny moved for her. She gave him an absent smile and took his place in front of me as Oliver slammed his office door behind her. She winced a little at the noise. "Oliver might have been nobly born, but he has the manners of a pig farmer."

I didn't waste any time. She was turning on the charm, and I couldn't afford to let her defuse the ticking bomb of anger inside me. "It's about Jason——"

The kind glow in her eyes died instantly and turned into something about as warm as an iceberg. Her hand flashed out and fastened around my arm in an unbreakable grip, and she turned to Tiny with a sudden, brilliant smile. "There's no need to disturb others with this nonsense. I'll take her to my quarters."

"Ma'am," he said.

"Hey! *Not agreeing!*" I tried to pull free, but of course that didn't do any good at all. "Let go, bitch!"

"I stand corrected," she said smoothly, with another apologetic look at Tiny. "Oliver's hardly the only one with the manners of peasants. You should respect your betters." I tried to drag my feet, but she pulled me effortlessly down the hallway, opened another unmarked door, and pushed me inside.

Then she locked the door behind herself and leaned against it as she let me go. I backed off, holding my sore arm, watching her with wary intensity. It was really hard to see her as a threat. She had a certain ... delicacy that made her seem vulnerable and breakable.

That probably worked really well for her.

"You're biting my brother," I said. "And he says you're going to turn him vamp. Are you?"

She said nothing. It was as if I hadn't spoken at all. She swept a gaze over me, head to toe, then back up again. "Of all the clothing you could have chosen." She sighed. "Why is everything you wear either cast off by some ridiculous mummers' show, or filled with sharp edges? You could be attractive, in your way. It pains me to see Michael wasting his potential on you."

"Hey!" I'd expected a lot of comebacks, but not ... fashion

critique. "Excuse me, Project Runway, but I asked you a question! Are you biting my brother?"

"Jason," Naomi said thoughtfully, as if she was running the name over in her mind. That could take a while. She was about a gajillion years old. She walked away from the door and over to a beautiful old sofa, something in bone white wood and pale silk that matched the rest of the antiques in the room. The whole place looked like it had been ripped out of some French palace before the guillotine had gotten started—and so did she. I could actually imagine her with those high powdered wigs and giant sideways skirts from the movies. "Jason—ah, the felon." She shrugged and settled herself on the sofa, gracefully, of course. "He's of no concern to you."

"Did you hear the part where he's my *brother*?"

"According to Jason, you've rarely acted the part of family," she said, and shook her head a little, sadly. "Abandoning him in his hour of need. Turning your back. Hardly the actions of a devoted older sister."

I'd been a child, too. Terrified. And Jason had always been the strong, aggressive one, even then, but there was no sense in telling her anything like that. Trying to justify myself made me feel sick. "I'm not talking about the past, I'm talking about what's going on right now. You're biting him. Feeding off him. And you're telling him you're going to turn him. Are you?"

"Perhaps." She fussed with the corner of a small crystal vase on the table next to her, and seemed completely fascinated with the sparkle. "One needs allies, and of course servants. Jason has unique qualities that would make him an excellent vampire."

I laughed a little crazily. "You admit it. Oh my God, you actually think it's a good idea to give my brother fangs? He is a sociopath, lady. Look it up."

"I hardly need to," she said. "One doesn't survive the centuries by preying on the blood of others if one is vegetarian. Or overly empathetic." A dimple formed near her mouth; on anybody else, at any other time, it would have been charming and cute. "I assure you, I take no sexual advantage of him. He is, as you would say, not of interest to me."

"Yeah, yeah, vampire lesbian chic, I get it."

"Actually," she said, and now I got her full attention, "I have no interest in either sex, beyond what use they may be. Romantic love is an illusion, invented by poets and purchased by fools. I told you, and Michael, what was necessary at the time to make you understand that my goal was not to seduce him, only to . . . help."

"Help." My voice had gone flat and hard now, and I was starting to calculate my chances of getting out of this room alive. She was explaining too much. That meant she wanted me to know how clever she was. Never a good sign for the long-term survival of the listener. "Why the hell did you want to help us at all? Considering how Michael was wasting his potential and everything."

"Because it opposed my sister's wishes, of course. It showed me in a reasonable light. And I gained some supporters that I would not have otherwise had. None of this is about your great love affair, foolish girl. Marriages never are. They are alliances, politics, power. They are the politest form of war. If Michael chooses to squander his own power, then I will at least take advantage of the situation." Naomi smiled. It still looked lovely and tentative and charming, but I was starting to realize that she just had much better camouflage than the others. Underneath, she was still all teeth and hunger and cold, cold ambition. "Now. Your brother. He does have some wild tendencies, but those can be controlled with a firm hand. I've had a niais with spirit before."

"A *what*?"

"Niais? The vulgar call it an eyas. A young hawk. A fledgling." She rolled her eyes at my incomprehension this time. "A newborn vampire. Do they teach you nothing of your betters here?"

The insult to Morganville's educational system didn't faze me, but the implication that she was my superior did. "You keep your fangs off him from now on," I told her. "Nobody's allowed to turn a human without authorization. There are laws against it."

"Oh, yes, laws." Naomi dismissed that with a graceful wave of her hand. "Old and outdated, these laws of Amelie's. My sister always tried to put leashes on us, but we are not dogs, dear one, we are wolves. And Amelie is hardly in a position to enforce her laws now. Oliver won't care; he'll be busy turning his own small army. It will come to battle eventually. He's no king, as I just told him. He has no God-given right to rule."

"And you do?" I crossed my arms. "The Magic 8 Ball says doubtful."

She gave me a blank look, which proved she was *not* as cool as Oliver; that was tragic. He at least knew what a Magic 8 Ball was. But her confusion didn't last long. Not long enough, for sure. "You want your brother? Very well. I can trade him back to you, Eve. He would be a formidable ally, but I am prepared to sacrifice, provided you help me in something most critical."

I didn't trust her. Not at all. But Jason deserved the attempt from me, didn't he? "What exactly would I be helping with?"

"Research," she said. "Only research. And I promise you, it is research that Oliver needs as well. Your friend Claire means something to Magnus; the draug target her, and I wish to know why, and how it can be of use to us. You must help me discover it."

"But—" That felt uncomfortably like betraying Claire, somehow, and yet it was also something I knew Claire was wondering about herself. She could see the head draug, Magnus; nobody else seemed to be able to unless he wanted it. It *was* a good question, and even Claire wanted the answers. Win/win.

Unless there were traps I couldn't see. And there probably were. "Okay," I finally said, reluctantly. "I help you find out why Claire can see Magnus, and you back off my brother and promise not to turn him. Agreed?"

"Agreed," she said, and smiled. There was that dimple again. "May I send for tea?"

CHAPTER THIRTEEN

CLAIRE

"Just tell me," Claire said to Shane. She was getting annoyed with him just now; he'd been silent ever since they'd settled the matter of examining the map, determining safe routes, and discussing transportation for the latest mission to Morganville High School.

And, of course, going anywhere with Myrnin, which had been a lively, interesting discussion that had ended with Michael saying that he was coming along and if Myrnin tried anything he'd stake him with silver.

There was absolutely no question that Michael meant it. Even Myrnin figured that out.

"Tell you what?" Shane asked. They were sitting in the backseat of the car, and Michael was driving, which was a huge improvement over the prospect of Myrnin doing it; his modern-vehicle-piloting skills were—to put it mildly—tremendously bad. They were driving a standard-issue black vampire sedan, with tinted windows, although as best she could tell, it was gloomy and cloudy outside. Myrnin was in the shotgun seat in front, which left just the two of them in the back. It felt private, even though it really wasn't.

Why you still sit so stiffly. Why you touch me as if you can't believe I'm really there. Why, when nobody's paying attention, you look so . . . lost. She couldn't ask him those things yet. He was supposed to be better; he insisted he was. Michael, when she'd pulled him aside on the way to the car, had said he seemed okay.

But she knew he wasn't. No idea how she knew, but she just . . . did. He wasn't right, though he was faking it really well. It wasn't the kind of discussion they should have in front of Myrnin. Or maybe even Michael. There was something way too personal, private, intimate about those questions.

So instead she said, "Tell me what we're supposed to be out at Morganville High School looking for, because I *know* it's not their amazing chem lab."

"You'd be right about that," Shane said. "Although to be fair, chem class did turn out some would-be meth cookers—right, Michael?"

"*Would-be* is right. They blew themselves up in a trailer at the edge of town," Michael said. "Not exactly an endorsement of our fine public school system."

"Which way?"

"Either way."

"Good point."

God, Shane *sounded* fine, but when she touched his fingers she felt him shiver, then grab hold tight, as if he was clinging to a life raft in a stormy ocean. The question he'd asked last night kept haunting her. *Are you really here?*

Was *he?*

"You didn't answer my question," Claire said. "What are we *looking for?*"

"Let me have my moment," he said. There was something weird in his voice now. "Always dreamed of being the one to come up with the answer."

She suddenly didn't want to push him anymore. Instead, she just held his hand and scooted over close. He put his arm around her, holding her closer.

As if she might just . . . fade away.

Michael rolled the car to a stop and said, "We're here, guys. Shane, gonna need a plan now, please."

"Wait," Myrnin said, staring intently through the window. He had brought along his giant boom box thing, and now he clicked the switch on it and turned it off, and Claire heard the faint, whispery sound of the draug singing. It wasn't much, but it was there. Myrnin hastily flipped the machine on again. "We're too close to the infected side of town; they still have enough numbers to call, at least for now. We should be quick about this. Shane, I do hope you know where we are going . . . ?"

"Sure," Shane said. "It's a shed at the back, near the field house. Michael, you know where it is. You can drive around there. Just go around the building and park right there in front of it. I think it has a storage sign on it."

"Locked?" Myrnin asked, as Michael put the car in gear again.

"Yep," Shane said. "Big chain with a padlock. But I'm pretty sure you strong vampire types can take care of that, right?"

Michael maneuvered the car through some twists and turns, then hit the brakes and brought them to a movie-worthy skidding stop, throwing gravel in a wave ahead. "Stay in the car until I open the doors," he told Shane and Claire. "Myrnin, you get the lock and open the shed. Anything else?"

"Open the trunk," Shane said. "What we're looking for is pretty big. We'll need vamp muscle to move it."

He'd never asked for that, as far as Claire could remember. . . . *Shane*, saying he needed more muscle for something? Sometimes he accepted help, but he rarely *asked*. Even Myrnin seemed to recognize that. He didn't make any quips or taunts, just leveled a sober look at her boyfriend, nodded, grabbed the boom box, and left the car, fast, on the passenger side. As Michael swung open the car door beside Shane, Claire heard the snap of metal breaking, which must have been Myrnin snapping the chain, the lock, or the door itself; there was a dry, high-pitched squeal of hinges as her own car door popped open. Claire stepped out, and saw that Michael had also opened the trunk, as Shane had asked.

The shed they were facing was really that—a shed, sheet metal, nothing fancy. The ancient cigarette butts littering the gravel around the side showed it was the smokers' hangout. Probably the stoners' as well; those groups usually shared space away from everybody else, since both things were illegal. She headed for the open, gaping metal door, and stopped, because *Shane* had stopped.

He was staring at the school.

Morganville High was a not-so-big brick building that had that early-sixties uncomfortable architecture to it—boxy, intimidating, more like a prison than anything else. Even the fence around the perimeter was high enough to qualify as escape-proof. The faded sign towered over the school, with a really quite scary rendering of the high school mascot. Of *course* Morganville High's team symbol would be a viper, showing fangs.

"Shane?" Michael was at the shed door, looking back at them. "Faster is better, man."

"I know," Shane said softly, but he kept staring at the brick bulk of the main MHS building. "Hey. Is there still a pool inside?"

"A pool?" Michael frowned, and for a second he looked . . . worried. "No. You remember, there was some kind of accident and they closed it down, drained it, filled it in right before you left town. It's a gym now."

"I was thinking that the draug . . ." Shane's voice died out. It was too quiet out here, and Claire felt clumsy and awkward as she moved toward him. "I thought there was a pool."

"Hey," she said, and took his hand. "Stay with us, okay? I don't know what's wrong, but just . . . stay focused. We need you."

He took a deep breath and let it out. There was a dark, damp chill in the air, and overhead the clouds rumbled. "Right. I'm here. You're here. We're okay." He turned a smile on her, and it almost felt right.

But not quite.

"Come on," Michael said, more urgently. "Let's go, guys, *now*. We're in neutral territory, but it's too close to them for comfort. Move."

Claire led Shane across the gravel and into the shed, where Michael clicked a light switch that threw a bright, industrial glow over the contents. It smelled of chemicals and rust and oil in here, and there were industrial-sized drums, boxes, cans, all kinds of things that looked like they might be used by janitorial or grounds-keeping staff.

"Claire, you're not going to be of any help with this," Myrnin said. "Get shotguns from the trunk, please. One each for you and Shane, I think. I assume Michael and I will be lifting and carrying. And what exactly is it we are to be carrying, if you would be so kind . . . ?"

Shane looked around, and pointed to a big industrial drum painted shiny black. It was covered with labels, but Claire didn't recognize any of them; none seemed to have to do with flammability or toxicity, at least. She wasn't actually sure *what* it was, other than big and very bulky.

She ducked out and ran to the car. The trunk was mostly empty, but there were three shotguns stored in the wheel well area; she grabbed two, then added a third, because . . . well, because. Besides, they were going to need the space, it seemed.

She heard a grinding metallic noise, then a hollow boom—the drum tipping over on its side, she guessed. In another second or two, she saw Shane leading the way out as Michael and Myrnin rolled it over the gravel to the open trunk of the car, and then each grabbed an end, lifted, and dumped it into the space.

Vampire sedans had *incredibly* large trunks. They doubled, Claire guessed, as sunlight protection for the younger vamps who might be caught outside in the sun. This one could have fit four or five, at least.

Of course, there were other, less generous interpretations that she didn't really want to consider.

The drum settled the car down on the back tires, and slightly lifted the front. Myrnin slammed the trunk lid. He was carrying his boom box in one hand, and now he zipped around to the driver's side, loaded it into the car, and said, "Quickly now. I think we're safe enough, but there's no reason to—"

He didn't have time to finish, because the sprinkler system went off. It happened with a click, as the metal heads pushed up through the grass, and then a cough and hiss as water started spraying out in all directions. A *lot* of water. Much more, and more pressurized, than a normal sort of system. Fat drops hit the windshield of the car, and Claire felt them slap against her skin as well—*not* water, or not completely, because it had a different, thicker consistency.

And it burned.

Shane reacted fast. He grabbed a shotgun from her and pushed her toward the car; she dived in, and he got in after, rolled down the window and put the barrel out as he tried to pick out targets through the artificial rain. It was the draug; it had to be. Michael took the third shotgun and mirrored him on the other side of the car. The downpour of sprinklers—mixed with actual rain now—sounded like hail as it hit the roof and hood of the car, and Myrnin cranked up a dial on the boom box. Claire heard it as a thick mist of static.

"Get us out of here," Myrnin said grimly. "Quickly."

Michael tried. He put the shotgun in his lap, rolled up the window, and started the car.

It caught, roared, sputtered, and died with a rattle of broken metal.

There was a second of silence, with only the static and rain to fill it, and then Myrnin said, with soft viciousness, "Damn."

"So? What are we doing?" Shane asked, without taking his eyes off the constant artificial rain pouring down outside the car, running in rivulets, dripping down the paint. It was splashing in on him, and when he wiped the drops off, Claire could see the red welts that were left. "This is not the time to freeze, man. I'll take any kind of plan."

Myrnin hesitated, then . . . grabbed at Claire. He was fumbling at her, and she was so stunned that she started hitting him—with no result, of course—as he patted down her pockets and shirt, quick light touches as he muttered, "Sorry, sorry, beg pardon, sorry . . ." And then he pulled back with her cell phone in his hand. He squinted at the screen, awkward still with the technology.

There was a shadow forming in the rain outside, dark and ominous. A human-shaped shadow that took on form and substance.

It smiled at them.

"Yeah, happy to see you too," Shane said, as he aimed. The stunning smash of the shotgun's roar whited out Claire's hearing for a moment, and she missed what Myrnin was doing until the keening noise in her ears began to subside again.

"—School," he was saying, or at least she thought he was. "What? Yes, Shane is target shooting, and we are *going to die*. I just thought you should know." He listened for a moment, then said, "That is not comforting, you know." Then he hung up the call and handed the phone back to her.

Shane, and now Michael, were still focused on the shapes forming outside. More than one this time. Shane had exploded the first one, but they'd responded by making more.

"Why are the sprinklers on?" she asked. "We shut off the water! The cutoff valves!"

"Except one," Shane pointed out. "That's right, isn't it? We left one open."

"You *what?*" Myrnin whipped around in the seat to look at him with a wide-eyed stare.

"Partly open," Shane clarified. "At least, I think—" He looked uncertainly at Claire. She nodded. "Yeah. Partly open." Why didn't he remember that clearly? She saw growing panic in his eyes. "There's no pool in the building, is there?"

Michael exchanged a long, significant look with Claire. *Something's wrong*, it said. No kidding. "No, bro," he said gently. "No pool."

"Because they could be coming out of the pool."

"Shane. There's no pool."

Shane huffed in a deep breath, and nodded, visibly getting a grip. "Right. They filled it in. I know. It just seems—doesn't that seem convenient for us right now? That they filled it in?"

He wasn't making any sense, and this was the worst possible time. Claire swallowed and switched her focus to Myrnin. "Who were you calling?" she asked.

"Oliver," Myrnin said. "He's sent some of his forces out to attack the draug in the heavily infected area. No rescue will be forthcoming from Founder's Square at the moment. We're quite on our own."

Claire watched as other figures appeared beyond the heavy drops slamming down on their car and smearing the windshield.

All Magnus. All *not* Magnus. She could tell the difference. He'd sent his creatures, but he hadn't come himself.

Yet.

"What are we going to do?" she asked. Shane had no answer for her. Neither did Myrnin, or Michael. "Guys, we need *something!*"

Shane pulled his shotgun back in and rolled up the window, sealing out most of the sound of the pounding drops hitting glass, metal, ground. "We're going to have to run for the shed, or stay here sealed up."

"They will find a way inside here," Myrnin said. "Look." He pointed to the air-conditioning vents, and Claire saw there was now a thin, silvery stream of liquid pouring down from each of them. Not a lot, but enough. It was starting to pool on the floor mats.

She pulled her feet up with a sound of raw disgust.

"So we run," Michael said. "The shed must be built watertight, because of the chemicals stored inside. We should be okay there for a while."

A while. Not permanently. But there was no such thing as *safe* now, only . . . not yet caught. This cat-and-mouse game could end only one way: the cat's way.

But the mice had a trick or two left yet, and even a cat could get hurt if the mice bit hard enough.

"Did you bring the iron hydroxide?" Claire asked Myrnin; he nodded, gaze fixed outside the car windows. His face looked still, pale and empty, but his eyes were full of shadows. And fear. "Don't use it until you have to. They adapt."

"I know," he said. "But we have another secret weapon we should use first." Michael looked pleased with that . . . until Myrnin handed him an umbrella and said, "Don't open it in the car. It's terribly unlucky." He passed out more to Shane and Claire.

"I told you," Claire said as she threw open the passenger door on the roaring downpour. "Humans are more ingenious than vampires. We invented umbrellas."

And, for once, she got the last word.

They probably should have died running for the shed, and likely they would have if Shane and Michael hadn't been so fast and so good with their weapons. She gave her gun to Myrnin and held the umbrellas for them, which left her half uncovered and drenched in draug-infected water by the time they gained the shelter of the shed. She dumped the dripping umbrellas outside, and Shane pulled her inside as Myrnin slammed the door and bent the steel frame to lock it firmly closed.

"Crap, Michael, she's soaked," Shane said, pulling his hand back from her wet skin. She was trying not to scream in horror from the tingle—rapidly turning to pinprick bites—all over her body. "Stay calm, baby, just stay calm—" He stripped off his jacket and tossed it to Myrnin, who caught it out of the air, frowning.

"Hold that up in front of your face. If I see you drop it even half an inch, I'm blowing you in half."

"What?"

"Just do it. Michael—"

"Yeah," Michael said, and turned his back. "Got it."

Shane grabbed Claire's shirt from the hem and stripped it up over her head. She squeaked in protest, but it was too late. Myrnin had done as asked; his face was hidden behind the upheld leather jacket. Shane skinned off his own shirt, beaded with drops of water but far less compromised, and wiped her down with it to dry her off. Then he walked her over to stand behind a pile of boxes and went back to retrieve his jacket.

She stood there half-naked and shivering, feeling utterly exposed, until he came back and settled his jacket around her, then zipped it up. "There," he said. He spread their shirts over a box to let them dry. "All better?"

It was. The warmth of Shane's skin settled around her along with the fabric, and she hugged it close, breathing him in. "Yes," she said, finally getting her head back together. "You're cold, though."

"Not that cold," he said. "I'll be okay."

"No, you won't," Michael said, and stripped off his own jacket to toss it to Shane as he turned around. "Put that on. I won't exactly catch my death." The sound of the water droplets slamming down on the tin roof and walls was relentless, like a hail of marbles, and he had to raise his voice to be heard over the roar. "Myrnin! Do we have any leaks in here?"

"Yes," Myrnin said. He seemed quite calm. "Several. Substandard construction, unquestionably. I believe there might be cause for a lawsuit."

That should have put them all on edge, and it certainly raised shivers on Claire's nerves, but Shane shook his head. "Trust me. We're okay."

"Shane—we're *not* okay!"

"Want to see a magic trick?" he asked her, and kissed her, quick and light. For the moment at least, he was almost himself. "Come with me."

Myrnin was standing well back from the door, frowning at the silvery trickles that had wormed their way through cracks and were blending together into a shallow little pool. Some of it was watershed that had come off the umbrellas, and their clothing; the rest was liquid forcing its way past the gaps. It wasn't fast, but it didn't have to be. It was relentless. Anyone who'd ever seen a flood understood how terrifying that could be.

"If you have more brilliant ideas, this would be an excellent time to divulge them," Myrnin said. "Otherwise, I will do you the kindness of snapping your necks before Michael and I take silver." He was very matter-of-fact about it, but when Claire looked closely she saw the wild, trapped, horrified look in his eyes, the rigid set of his body. This was, very literally, his worst nightmare. How long had he been fighting and fleeing the draug? Ages.

And Michael. Michael had been trapped by them before. She looked at him now, and saw how sharp and focused his expression was, how tense the muscles cording his arms and chest. He was struggling to control his own fear.

The sprinklers were firing off everywhere around the building; running would just send them straight into the arms of their enemies, but hiding wouldn't do, either. Not for long.

"Move," Shane said. Myrnin did, backing up a few more feet, which allowed Shane to push past him to another barrel sitting on a pallet behind him. It had the same paint scheme as the barrel the two of them had rolled out to the car. Claire watched as Shane hunted around and came up with a small crowbar, which he used to lever open the seals on the top of the barrel. The top was hinged in the middle, Claire realized, and he flipped that part over. "Score," he said, and raised the crowbar in triumph. "Who's your daddy?"

Myrnin stared at him as if he'd gone completely mental. *"Excuse me?"*

"Figure of speech," Claire said hastily, and rushed over to join Shane. Michael beat her there, but he'd stopped, frowning, looking down into the barrel.

"Sorry, but what the hell?" He'd found a plastic scoop in a holder, and was poking around in the barrel. "What is this stuff?"

Shane took the scoop away and dug it into what looked like . . . soap flakes. "You remember in junior high when there was, oh, I don't know, maybe some incident where a boy threw a giant firecracker down in the toilet and blew it up and *maybe* there was a big flood?"

Michael blinked. "I remember the toilet blew up and the bathroom flooded half the hallway."

"And what happened then?"

"You got detention."

"Before that. The janitor had to clean it up, and I had to help him." He slapped the side of the drum. "Super Slurper. Developed by NASA. Absorbs about two hundred times its weight in water. Sprinkle it on, wait a minute, and scoop it up like powder. Watch."

He walked past Myrnin to the pooling liquid, gave it a little bye-bye wave, and dumped the scoop of powder on top of it.

A high, thin tone ripped through Claire's ears—a tiny bit of the draug scream. And then the powder darkened, and the liquid drew into it, pulled against its will.

Bound up in a chemical matrix and completely, utterly, trapped.

"Oh my God," she whispered, and felt her whole body heat up as the realization spread through her. "Oh my *God*, Shane!"

Myrnin came a hesitant step closer, staring. His eyes were very wide, fixed on the powder as it absorbed the water. He dropped to his knees to watch, then leaned over it.

Then he *poked* the remains.

The powder had turned darker, but it was still powdery—a little mealy, maybe. He picked up a sample and rubbed it between his fingers.

Then he sat back and looked up at Shane with an absolutely unreadable expression.

"You," he said, "are a genius."

"Nope," Shane said. "But it turns out my no-good past is good for something after all."

Michael threw his arm around Shane's neck and ruffled his hair. "Good job, bro."

"Dessicants," Myrnin said wonderingly. "A mostly modern invention. We used them before, with very limited success, because they took so long to work; silica was tried, and other minerals, but this . . . this is *astonishing*. How much can a scoop of it absorb?"

"One hell of a lot," Shane said. "Use enough and it turns into a solid, like jelly, and you can just pick it up and toss it out." He had a dark flush in his cheeks, but his eyes were gleaming. He was proud of himself.

Good. He deserved to be.

Myrnin did an absolutely crazy little dance, one that left Claire openmouthed and wishing she'd taken video, because that was something she was sure she'd never see again in her lifetime.

Michael took the rest of the scoop and made a little powdery line across the threshold. The incoming water ran into it and just . . . disappeared. "I'll check the perimeter," he said. "Hope you guys brought a deck of cards. We're going to have time to kill in here." He grinned at Shane. "Seriously, man. You're my hero."

Shane still looked happy, but then . . . then something happened. His smile faltered, fell away. He stood very still, watching Michael.

"What? What did I say?" Michael asked him. "You okay?"

Shane had just . . . shut down. Michael glanced aside at Claire, and she took Shane's hand. No response. "Shane? What's wrong?"

"Hero," he whispered. "Michael said I was his hero."

"Well, you're mine, too."

"Always wanted to be . . . but it isn't right, that can't be right. Isn't there a pool inside? We have to get to the pool, put the silver in the pool. . . ." He squeezed his eyes shut, and he was trembling now. "This is wrong. I can't be the hero. I can't be. That's how I know . . . know it's wrong."

"Shane!"

He just . . . folded up, suddenly, and collapsed with a hollow boom of his back against the metal wall of the shed as he sat down. His eyes opened, and they were haunted, dark, *empty*. "This isn't right," he said. He looked at her, but it was as if he didn't really *see* her. "You can't be here. You *weren't* here. You were safe. I'd never let you get hurt, Claire. Not again. It was just us, not you . . ."

"What in heaven is he talking about?" Myrnin snapped. "We don't have time for this—"

"He's remembering the dreams," Michael said softly. "The draug make humans dream. I don't think he can tell the difference anymore between then and now."

Myrnin considered that for about, oh, a second, and then shook it off. "Irrelevant," he said. "This substance he found changes *everything*. With this chemical, we can make weapons that will not just weaken but kill them, destroy them utterly, and do no harm to those vampires trapped inside the pools. Thousands of years of terror, death, running—all of it can *end*. We need to find a way to leave here and kill Magnus. He is the only one who matters now."

Claire watched as Michael's eyes narrowed and turned dangerously red. "Maybe you weren't paying attention, but we're surrounded by entire fountains full of draug. This stuff is awesome, but it's not a magic shield or anything, and the car is dead. We need transportation to get out of here."

"Well, that isn't forthcoming at the moment, now, is it? Perhaps there are other vehicles close by. The boy's fluent in stealing them, isn't he?" Myrnin frowned at Shane. "I understood he had such skills."

"Leave him alone," Michael said, and his fists clenched. "We wait."

"We *cannot* wait!"

"Hell we can't!"

The argument didn't seem to be going anywhere, and Claire found herself staring at something dimly glimpsed in the shadows. Something pale. For a heart-stopping moment, it resolved into a human shape, and all she could think was that somehow, the draug had found a way inside. Her heart slammed hard in instinctive alarm and shock, and she gasped out loud, but then she realized that it wasn't the draug, or even some weird lurker . . . it was a white jumpsuit on a hanger.

A *plastic* jumpsuit. Suitable, she guessed, for rooting around in mucky landscaping crises or blown-up toilets or whatever.

She dashed for it, grabbed it off the wall, and yelled, "Turn around!" as she unzipped Shane's jacket. She tossed it over her shoulder to Michael, then stepped into the legs of the jumpsuit, careful not to tear it; it was pretty thin stuff, but it ought to be waterproof. Basically, a form-fitting raincoat. It fastened with a plastic zipper up the front, and she hastily finished that and looked around for something for her hands.

Nitrile gloves, a whole box of them. She grabbed two and slid them on.

"Here," Michael said, and handed her a battered, oily cowboy hat. "I think the janitor left it. It should keep the rain off your face and neck." When she put it on, it dropped all the way to her nose. "Or maybe a lot more of you. Wait a second." He scooped a plastic bag full of Super Slurper and handed it to her. "Use it if you have to."

Myrnin shoved in between them and handed her a . . . wrench. A big, heavy thing. "There should be an emergency stop for the sprinkler system outside this building," he said. "Shut it down, and we can all get out. If you can't find it, run for help."

For the first time, Claire realized that she was going to run away and leave them all here, trapped. Shane was almost catatonic, shivering, paralyzed by something she didn't fully understand.

She had to do it. For *him*, if nothing else. She needed to get him out of here.

"Wait," Michael said. "Maybe I should do this."

"Run out into the draug? Are you *crazy*? If I do it, I'm just a puny little human, right? I get more time than you do. They'd be on you from the first second you step out the door."

Myrnin said, "She's right, boy. But Claire—Magnus will be looking for you. Be careful. You're at risk, too."

Claire held up the brim of the stupidly large cowboy hat and nodded to Michael and Myrnin both. "I'll be back," she said. "And I'm getting you out of here."

Michael didn't look happy, but he nodded. "I know. Just take care of yourself."

Claire crouched down next to Shane and stared into his blank eyes for a long moment. "Can you hear me?" she asked, and put her hands on his face. He still needed a shave. "Sweetie, please, talk to me. Can you?"

"Claire," he said, and a long, agonizing shudder went through him. "Are you really here?" He reached up and touched her fingers. Held them. "Are you?"

"Always," she said. She kissed him, and felt something in him responding, urgent and desperate for reassurance. "You have to stay with me, Shane. I need you." She dropped her voice to a bare whisper, lips right at his ear. "You promised me something, and you'd better not be backing out now."

When she pulled back, though, the panic was worse, not better, and he said, "What's her name? Claire, what's her *name?*"

He wasn't making any sense at all. She felt tears threaten, but she didn't have time. *Get him safe, then get him back.* That was all she could do. "I'll be back," she said.

Michael said, "Claire. I'll look after him."

He always does, Claire thought. For all that Shane hated the vampire side of Michael, Michael never let them down. She never doubted that he would protect them, not for a second. She never doubted *any* of them, really. Eve, Michael, Shane . . . they were her family.

Looking at him right now, she felt a surge of breathtaking love, for Michael, and for what the four of them were, together.

"What?" Michael asked, raising his eyebrows.

"I just want to hug you right now," Claire said. "You're the most fantastic—" She couldn't finish that, suddenly, because her throat closed up on her, and her vision dissolved into sparkles, refracted by tears. She cleared her throat, blinked, and said, "Never mind."

He understood. She could see it in his eyes. "Nobody's dying today," he said. "Go."

She ran.

It reminded Claire, stupidly, of running through the sprinklers when she was a little kid, squealing with delight as cold water slapped against her skin; she'd had a sunshine-yellow swimsuit when she was six, she remembered, with a big pink sun on it.

This was not nearly as fun.

The second she'd stepped outside the shed door, she'd had to revise her plan, because the umbrellas she'd left by the entrance were gone—carried off, she assumed, by the draug. She'd been hoping for the extra protection, but that was clearly not happening.

So she gripped the heavy, gritty weight of the wrench in her hand and took off running.

The draug were around her; she could see them in flickers, hidden in the falling streams of water. They weren't quite manifesting in human form; that must take energy, and a lot of it, and they weren't quite as strong now as they'd been before. They weren't singing. *We've hurt them*, she thought, and felt a fierce surge of pride along with the adrenaline.

And then her running foot hung up on a sprinkler head hidden in a tuft of wet grass, and she lost her balance. Her arms grabbed for some kind of support, and the fall seemed to occur in slow motion, each sticky droplet of liquid shimmering in front of her eyes as she lurched forward, and then she had a close-up, almost microscopic view of the moisture-dewed dead grass and mud.

She hit hard and rolled, and felt the sprinkler head catch the leg of her plastic jumpsuit. It would tear, of course, that wasn't even a question. She'd probably ripped a hole the size of Kansas in it. But she couldn't stop, because there was a shadow in the falling drops, man-sized, forming into hands, pale and grubby and boneless, and they reached out for her. There were puddles in the lowlying areas of grass, muddy but filled with shimmering silvery movement as they heaved toward her.

The hands—they felt like cold jelly through the plastic—closed around her ankle, and she felt herself sliding backward, toward the shallow puddle. *It can't be that deep.* But she knew it didn't matter; they could drown her in an inch of water if they held her down. It wouldn't take long, but worse than that, Michael and Myrnin and Shane wouldn't be able to stand by and watch her die; they'd come out to the rescue, and that would be the end of it. Nobody to tell the others what they'd discovered.

How they could *win.*

As she clawed at the wet grass, ripping up fibrous chunks and leaving muddy finger trenches, she saw Michael standing in the open door of the shed. He was tense, staring at her with fierce, angry, horrified focus. About to bolt outside.

"No! Stay there! Don't let Myrnin come out, either!" she yelled. The draug's liquid was pounding down on her back, and it felt like fists now, small but growing larger, the blows stinging with force. The pull on her ankle was as irresistible as being caught in a flood tide; she couldn't kick free of it.

Wait. Wait for it.

She twisted around and saw that the hand was pulling her foot down into the muddy water of the pool.

Now.

Claire pulled out the plastic bag, opened it, and plunged her hand inside to grab up a handful of the flaky white powder. It felt gritty and dry, like bone dust. She flipped over, sat up, and threw the powder into the shallow pool of water.

All hell exploded.

It wasn't just the puddle that reacted, it was *everything*, as if it was all one creature, connected. The puddle tried to crawl away, literally flowing out of the hollow and over the grass, but it didn't have the chance. It was like watching something freeze solid in super fast-forward. The muddy water turned into a muddy, rubbery gelatin, turned *solid*, and stopped moving.

She watched it turn black, and crumble into black flakes. There was nothing living in that.

The water coming out of the sprinklers stopped acting like water; it rose *up*, straight up, arrowing directly into the clouds.

Escaping.

The sprinklers kept spinning, hissing out pressure, but only a little water made it out, and it seemed like natural stuff.

Claire yanked her foot free of the gelatinous substance with a squishing, squelching noise, and realized that a lot of the grass had dried off around her—the draug had taken most of the water with them. There was still some moisture, but it was just that. No draug.

They were running away from what she'd used.

She picked up a handy stick and poked at the rubbery mass that had been the draug. . . . It was heavy, solid, flaking into bits, and it smelled dead and rotten.

She stood up, sealed the bag, and gave Michael a big thumbs-up as she settled the hat at a better angle on her head. "I think that's proof of concept," she said. "Now we just have to get the stuff out of here."

"Turn off the sprinklers!" Myrnin said, elbowing Michael out of the doorway. "Go on, shoo!"

"The draug took off, Myrnin, didn't you see it? How often do you see drops go *straight up?*"

"I'm not coming out until you shut the valve."

Chicken, she thought, but didn't say. He was right, of course. Maybe they were lying in the pipes, waiting for a delicious bite of vampire. She would have been only a snack, but Michael and Myrnin would be a sixteen-course meal.

"Stay there," she said, and jogged on around the side of the shed. Finding the valve was surprisingly easy; turning it off wasn't so much, since she didn't have vampire strength, but she managed to twist the wrench a couple of times until the valve snugged tight.

Overhead, thunder rumbled.

Claire looked up; the clouds looked dark and heavily loaded now with rain. The draug, back in their transportation, she supposed. They could come down again, anytime.

But what about Magnus? Could he travel that way, or was he different? She felt like he was, somehow . . . he could transform to liquid but he had more mass to him. He was more *there*, more *real* than the others. They were like pieces split off of him, but connected to him. That was how it felt, anyway.

A shadow blocked out her view of the clouds, and she pushed back the awkward cowboy hat to look up. It was Myrnin. He offered her a hand up, and she accepted it. Her gloved hand still felt gritty from the powder. There wasn't a single speck of moisture on it. Even when she swiped it over the still-moist ground, nothing stayed on the plastic without being absorbed.

"It works," she said. Somehow she sounded surprised, as if she'd been standing in the doorway watching instead of actually *doing* it. "Myrnin—it really works."

"Yes," he said. There was a look on his face that she couldn't understand at all. "Take that hat off. It ill becomes you."

She took that to mean it was stupid, which she agreed with, and tipped it off. It dripped a stream of water off the brim—clean rainwater, not the draug contamination. The cool air hit her damp hair—damp with sweat, she realized—and she shivered.

Michael wasn't far away. Shane was with him, *almost* there; she could see the struggle in him when he smiled. "Nice moves," he said.

"Thanks," she said. "It was my very best muddy crawl." Her heart ached to see how pale he seemed, how shaky.

Michael seemed to know it, too, because he cut in with the usual banter to take the focus away from Shane. "I agree. You threw that powder like a girl, though."

She channeled her inner Eve. "Which means what? Awesomely? Because you'd better not mean it any other way, or I might get offended."

Michael was smiling, but he still looked strained. There was a trace of fright somewhere in it. "Don't make us do that again," he said. "Don't make us stand there while you—take those kinds of risks."

"I'm okay," she said. "And we're going to be all right. Didn't you say we were, before I came out here?"

"Yeah," Michael said. "But I was kinda lying."

"I know, stupid."

Myrnin cleared his throat. "The draug may be gone, but they can return at any time." He cast an uneasy glance up at the clouds. "We need transportation. I can perhaps fix the car, but—"

"Won't have to," Michael said, and nodded toward the corner of the high school, where another car was slowly pulling around the corner. It was a police cruiser, sleek and dangerous, and there were two figures in it. One had a shotgun barrel pointed out the open window. Claire was surprised to realize that it was Richard Morrell.

Hannah Moses was driving.

She stopped the car and stepped out, frowning at them. "What the hell are you fools doing out here?" she asked.

"What brought *you?*" Shane asked.

Richard answered that one. "All vampire sedans are equipped with GPS and an automatic signal when there's engine trouble," he said. "We got an alert over her radio that one was out of service here. There wasn't any reason for it to be here, so Hannah wanted to check it out." He stepped out of the car, and seemed to lose his balance for a moment. Hannah gave him a sharp, concerned look, and he caught himself with a hand on the cruiser's roof. "Damn. Low blood sugar."

"And no sleep," Hannah said. "And pushing yourself too hard. Richard—"

"I'm okay, Hannah." Not, Claire noticed, *Chief*, or *Chief Moses*, which confirmed her intuition that there was more going on between the two of them than just professional courtesy. He even threw her a smile, and it was a sweet one. Hannah didn't smile back. She continued to look concerned. "Everything okay, folks?"

"The car's trashed," Michael said, "but then again, I think it was worth it. We found a way to kill the draug." He said it casually, but the gleam in his eyes gave it away.

Both Richard and Hannah looked at him with identical expressions of *What did you just say?* "Well," Hannah said, "I know we can hurt them with silver, but—"

"Not silver," Myrnin said. "Silver only wounds them, and it can't kill Magnus, though it can certainly make him very unhappy. No indeed. The boy's right. We can *kill* them." He dashed

off, and came back with his hands full of the blackened mass—
well, not his hands, because even Myrnin wasn't nuts enough to
actually pick up the draug with his bare skin. It was actually
dumped into Claire's abandoned cowboy hat. He shook it, and it
jiggled like gelatin.

Lifelessly. Bits of it flaked away.

"What the . . . ?" Hannah bent forward over the hat, then
reeled back, hand to her nose. "Oh, man. That smells like a week-
long floater."

Claire looked at Shane. "What's a floater?"

"Dead body," he said. "You don't want to know, trust me." His
gaze lingered on her, as if he was still in doubt that she was okay.

Or there.

She stripped off the nitrile gloves and gripped his hand tight
and fast. He sent her a fast, unsteady smile.

"What is it?" Richard asked. He was staying well back from
what was in the hat, but he took a pen from his pocket and poked
it into the mass. No reaction. "I mean, what caused this?"

"Chemicals. Janitorial chemicals, to be precise. Young Shane
here thought of it." That was generous of Myrnin to say so, Claire
thought; Shane seemed surprised, too. "It's led me to think of a
few other things that might work as well, but this is surprisingly
effective."

Shane's pride, however cautious and concealed, was catching;
Claire caught the gleam of it in Hannah's face, and Richard's, too.
No, not pride. *Hope.* A rare commodity in Morganville.

"There's a full barrel of it in the trunk of the sedan," Myrnin
said. "We'll need to get it in yours, quickly." As if to emphasize
that, the clouds overhead gave another ominous rumble; he
flinched, moved vampire-speed to the black sedan, and popped
the trunk open by breaking the lock with a sharp pull of his fin-

gers. He and Michael wrestled the barrel out, but allowed Shane and Hannah to help him roll it over to the police car.

Richard stayed with Claire. He glanced at her, raised his eyebrows, and said, "What's with the biohazard suit?"

Oh. She'd forgotten about it, actually. "The sprinklers were on," she said. "The draug were waiting out here for us. I had to have some kind of protection."

"Good thinking." Richard wasn't really listening to her, though; he was watching Hannah as she helped Myrnin and Michael muscle the drum into the trunk of the police car. It didn't fit quite as well as it had in the vampmobile. There was something kind of sad about the way he was looking at Hannah . . . as if he wanted something he knew he could never really have. Though he did have her, didn't he? Maybe?

People were complicated. Claire couldn't figure out what was in her *own* head most of the time, much less her friends'. Or Shane's. And she hardly even knew Monica's brother.

"So," she said, "you and Chief Moses—"

"What?" he asked, and suddenly his gaze was focused on her, laser-sharp. "Me and Chief Moses what?"

"Uh . . ." *Are dating,* she was going to say, but she was afraid suddenly that she'd misread all of that. Awkward. " . . . Make a good team, I guess." Lame. "She's pretty fantastic."

"She is that," he said. Crisis over. He let his attention wander back to focus on Hannah; Claire wondered if he even knew he was doing it. "Did she ever tell you how she got that scar?"

"No." The dark, seamed scar across Hannah's face was dramatic, but somehow it only made her look . . . regal. Scarily more beautiful, as if it were a really exotic tattoo.

"She pulled three people out of a burning truck in Afghanistan, under heavy enemy fire," he said. "She was going back for the fourth when the munitions exploded. She got hit by shrapnel. She was a hero. Got decorated for it and everything. And then she came back here." He shook his head. "Why the hell would she come back here?"

Good question. Claire wasn't sure she had any rational answer, either, but she tried. "It's her home. Maybe there was somebody here she wanted to come back for, too. Is that . . . you know, possible?"

That startled him, and he was thinking how to answer that when Hannah finally thumped the trunk closed and said, "Right. We're going to get cozy in here. Claire, in the back with Myrnin and Shane. Probably in the middle, knowing how they get along. Richard, Michael, up front with me."

Conversation over. Claire scrambled into the back and was breathlessly jammed between Shane's solid, warm heat, and Myrnin's oddly cool, angular body. *Manwich,* she could almost hear Eve say, only Eve would never actually count Myrnin as a man, exactly.

"Get us back to Founder's Square," Myrnin ordered. "I have quite a bit of work to do, you know. *Quite* a bit. This is a very promising beginning, but there is much left to discover. We will need better delivery systems, the ability to distribute the chemicals widely, and——"

"Yeah, we get it," Hannah interrupted. "Faster is better. No problem, we're going right now, just keep your fangs folded."

"That's very rude," Myrnin said. "I haven't brought my fangs out for some time. Not in mixed company, anyway."

Hannah gave him a long look in the rearview mirror, then put the car into reverse and began an expert, smooth job of backing up. Once in the parking lot, she did a wide circle and made for the exit. The boxy shape of the high school, with its faded cartoon snake mascot sign, quickly receded in the distance, and Claire breathed deeply in relief.

Almost there, she thought. *We're almost to the end of this.*

And then the rain fell. Softly at first, a few fat, pattering drops on the windshield . . . then more of them, a bucket being emptied, then a roaring flood. It came shockingly fast. It wasn't like rain at all, really, more like water with a few bubbles of air trapped inside. As if they'd suddenly been plunged into the deep, dark sea.

"Faster," Shane shouted across to Hannah. A flash of lightning from the dark clouds above turned his face into blue-white stone, except for the panic Claire saw in his eyes. "C'mon, *drive*, lady! We're going to get caught out here!"

She tried, she really did, but the water was rising so fast in the streets that driving faster built up a wave—first in front of the tires, and then at the bumper of the car. It took only a few short minutes for the narrow roads to flood up to the curbs. The drainage wasn't working—no, Claire realized, it *was* working, just in reverse. Muddy, tainted water was flowing *up* out of the drains, adding to the rain that was falling.

The draug were trying to drown them fast and hard.

Hannah had to slow the car as it approached the next intersection. There was a dip in the pavement there, a deep one, and there was no telling what would happen if she drove into it. No, there was—Claire remembered what had happened to Eve's hearse, with its burned-out motor.

The draug could disable the car.

"Turning around!" Hannah shouted, and executed a fast, sliding turn that pushed Claire hard against Myrnin. She grabbed for the back of the seat and wished she'd had time to hunt for a seat belt, but there was no room between them to fasten one now.

"Going for a side road. Richard, keep your eyes open. You see anything coming, shoot it."

She drove at a probably-too-fast speed down the side road, as closed and lightless buildings flashed past; gutters gushed water in thick, silvery streams, from what Claire could make out. The rain was coming down at a breathless pace, and it sounded like a hail of dropped ball bearings on the roof of the cruiser. *They're supposed to be getting weaker, not stronger. Or is this their desperation effort, since they know we can hurt them?*

Something hit that was harder than just a raindrop, with a sharp *crack*, and Claire twisted around to look behind them. There was a draug crouched on the trunk lid, leering in at them, its face smearing and running in the rain. It had a thick chunk of brick in its hand, and slammed it against the back window a second time.

Claire saw the spiderweb fracture form in the safety glass.

"Brake!" she yelled. Hannah didn't hesitate; she hit them hard, sending the front end of the car diving down and the heavily loaded back up, and the draug lost its balance. It rolled forward over the roof, over the front windshield, onto the hood, and suddenly turned liquid and re-formed facing back toward them, snarling.

Hannah hit reverse. It tumbled off into the roiling water in the road with a splash, sank, and was gone. She quickly put the car into drive again, but the next intersection was as bad as the one they'd tried to avoid. There was no telling how deep the water was, but from the current down the middle that Claire could see rippling, it was dangerous.

So was staying in one place. There were more of the draug, and they'd be here soon.

"Got to chance it," Hannah muttered. "It'll be no better on

the other streets. This dip runs right through town." It had been part of the original urban planning, Claire thought; they never got much rain. It was supposed to be clever.

Not so much, now.

She grabbed for Shane's hand and held it tight as Hannah eased the cruiser into the intersection. The front tires rolled downward. The muddy, fast-moving water rippled around the bumper as it submerged. Then it rose along the sides of the car.

"It's too deep," Shane said.

"It's too late. We're committed," Hannah said. She kept the accelerator pressed down, neither accelerating nor braking, and the brown water splashed up onto the hood.

Over it.

It was leaking into the door next to Shane. Just a little, but enough to freak Claire out. *It can't be this deep,* she thought. *It can't drown us.* But it didn't have to. All it needed to do was drown out the engine. Improbably enough, it hadn't yet. The cruiser was still running, still rolling relentlessly forward through the draug-infested water. Maybe cop cars were built tougher than hearses and vampmobiles.

They hit the bottom of the dip with a little jolt that sent waves of ripples out, and the water sloshed up on the windshield, leaving a thin, silver, unclean film behind it . . . and then Claire felt a strong rush of water against Shane's side of the car, and the car began to slip sideways.

"No, no, no," Hannah chanted under her breath. She pushed the gas, just a little, and the tires caught pavement and began to climb up. The water seemed to hold it back, not just in terms of mass but *really* holding on, clinging. Claire's breath felt hot and ragged in her chest, and she felt utterly terrified and helpless.

Nothing she could do. Nothing any of them could do, except

Hannah, and if she made one wrong move, the car would go spinning into the current, carried away.

But she kept hold of it, nudging the gas in careful increments
and pushing the cruiser up. The water level fell. The hood broke
the surface, and then the bumper, and then they were up and
through and moving fast.

Behind them, the current kept roaring, getting stronger. No
other cars were going to make it through there. Not right now,
anyway.

Richard reached over, took Hannah's free hand in his, and
raised it to his lips. "That," he said, "was world-class calm."

"That was luck," she corrected, but flashed him a brilliant and
very personal smile, just the same. "And I was freaking the hell
out inside."

"Cold as ice, that's my girl."

"Shut up," she said, but she sounded pleased. And then she remembered they weren't alone in the car, and cleared her throat.

Myrnin said, in a weary tone, "I could sincerely *not* care less
who in this town is carrying on secret affairs just now, so please,
declare your impassioned desires or be quiet. All of you."

It was a very quiet drive.

Six blocks later, it all changed. They were within sight of
Founder's Square's lights, even though they were difficult to see
through the smear of pouring rain; the constant hammering of
drops on the roof had made Claire wonder if she was going deaf.
But there was just barely enough visibility to see the open-bed
pickup truck that charged through the intersection, heading at
right angles to Founder's Square. It missed hitting the front
bumper of the police cruiser by a couple of feet, maybe, and
skidded out of control on the wet pavement, going way too fast.

And then it hit the curb, and flipped over twice, shedding

metal and glass and making a shrieking noise that was clear even over the roar of the rain.

Hannah didn't hesitate. She turned the patrol car toward the wreck, pulled as close as she could, and yelled, "Stay inside, all of you!" Then she grabbed a yellow rain slicker with a hood, put it on, and plunged out into the storm.

Richard found another raincoat and joined her.

Claire and Shane and Myrnin were locked into the back, like criminals, and Michael sensibly decided to stay where he was, since there wasn't another rain slicker available. Shane tried his door handle, but not in a way that meant he was seriously trying to jump out.

Myrnin didn't bother. He sat in cold silence for a while, and then said, "This is taking too long. We can't afford the distraction."

"People are hurt," Claire said. "It's Hannah's job to help them."

"It's foolish," he said flatly. "More will die every second we delay. If we allow the draug to play this game, we'll lose. Horribly. Get her back inside."

"Great idea!" Shane muttered. "Why don't you go take a dip in the pool, man?"

"I am not your *man*," Myrnin hissed back. "What pool are you talking about?"

"Hey!" Claire held out both palms, symbolically shoving them apart. "Enclosed space. Let's all get along."

"It's taking too long," Myrnin said.

And he was right.

CHAPTER FOURTEEN

HANNAH

I told them not to get out of the car. I was reasonably certain that the three in the backseat would obey; Shane, strong as he was, didn't have the leverage or the insanity to break out, and Claire, regardless of any intentions, didn't stand any chance. Myrnin wouldn't want to. I could see it in his face.

But Michael . . . Michael worried me. I could only hope that he wouldn't play the hero.

I knew Richard probably would.

I kept my attention focused on them, at least part of the time, as I raced across to the wrecked truck.

There were men down, four or five of them. Two were dead. I could tell that at a glance; they'd been thrown clear of the rolling truck, and the damage was done. I left them and went for the others who were still moving, however weakly.

One had a badly broken arm, and a gushing scalp wound, but he was awake and more or less focused. He reached up and caught a fistful of my yellow raincoat. "Get them out of here," he said. "Goddamn water vampires were on us. Couldn't get anywhere safe. Get my men out of here."

I blinked. It was the human resistance leader of Morganville, Captain Obvious. He'd taken over the role of vampire-hating rebel leader when the last Captain Obvious had been killed, and he was good at it because he'd served his country sometime, somewhere, in some branch. Not a Marine, I thought; a Marine would have been a better driver, and a Marine wouldn't be lying there with a busted arm and expecting someone else to save his men.

"Wait one," I said, and left him to move to the next man. Broken legs, two of them. His face was in the water, and I propped him up against the wreckage to make sure he continued to breathe. He was coughing and starting to scream as I moved on.

Richard and I got to the third one at the same time. I wasn't surprised to see him, but I was annoyed. "I told you to stay in the—"

"And I don't listen," he interrupted me. "Technically, I'm your boss, and don't give me chain-of-command crap right now. This man has serious injuries."

"They all do," I said. "And there's no room for them in the car. Take the cruiser and go. Send back adequate transportation."

"You really think I'm going to leave you out here, alone? You really believe that? Hannah?"

I looked up, and found him watching me with that strange mix of vulnerability and frustration that I'd come to know over the past few months. We'd been at this relationship a while. It had started in a frenzy of frustration and need, not love maybe but something close. It could have been love, in time, but there was just something not quite clicking between us. Some hidden switch that didn't trip.

I wished it was different. I *wanted* to be in love. He was worth it. Hell, *I* was worth it, too.

But it just wasn't the way it was going to be, and deep down I think we both knew it.

"Richard," I said, in my best commanding officer voice, "we do *not* have time for this. Take the cruiser and get us help, *now*. Go."

He wasn't used to taking orders, particularly; that's what happens when you grow up in the richest, most powerful human family in Morganville. He still thought of me as a girl from the wrong side of town, not somebody who'd been to hell, kicked ass, and come home alive.

That was a mistake. He was starting to realize it, finally. And revise his attitude.

"Okay," he said at last. "I'll go. But you stay safe."

I gave him a little smile, but it was my battle smile, without humor. "Always," I said. I was a survivor. Hell, I'd survived worse than this. Supernatural horrors were bad, but they were nothing to the burning hatred and viciousness that humans could visit on each other. I hadn't lived through segregation, but my dear, sweet, tough old Gramma Day had; she'd been born in the days when *colored* couldn't eat in the same restaurants, dance in the same clubs, drink from the same fountains, or pee in the same toilets as whites. Humans were capable of a whole lot worse than vampires, in my experience.

Maybe they just inherited their viciousness from us.

The rain was letting up, but where it hit bare skin it burned like stings, or bites. Cannibal rain. I'd seen a lot of crap, but this was weird even for Morganville. As Richard headed for the cruiser,

I resisted the urge to tell him to be careful. He was a Morganville native; he understood the rules. He was tough, deep down, too. He'd be all right.

I had a split second to wish I'd said it.

A sudden gush of water came off the top of the looming roof of the building, splatting down over Richard and in front of him, and in the next second it was forming arms that weren't arms, a body that was more boneless worm than human form, and my brain refused to process what that was, that *face*—

I yelled and brought the shotgun up but Richard was right in front of it, held as a shield. It knew. *It knew what it was doing.*

It grinned at me, some horrible and incredibly wrong configuration of teeth and tongue and lips, and its eyes were melting and forming and bulging and I felt an utterly strange impulse to scream and hide my eyes, like a child, as if that would stop what was about to happen.

Then it *enveloped* Richard. Dragged him into its own body. The thick, heaving mass closed around him, and I heard him scream. Just once, before his mouth disappeared.

If I fired, I'd hurt the draug, but I'd kill Richard.

"Shoot it!" Captain Obvious was screaming at me. I recognized the voice, heard the buzz of the words, but I was completely focused on what was in front of me. "God, shoot it *now!*"

It won't hurt him much, I told myself. *They had Shane for hours, submerged in that tank. It can't hurt him so much; it's just trying to force me to shoot and kill Richard.*

He was struggling inside it, like a bug caught in molasses.

The watery, sticky form of the draug was taking on a pinkish tint.

Do something!

I left Captain Obvious and his yelling, raced to the cruiser, and pulled open the back door. Claire was pounding on the window, reaching across Shane to do it. She was holding out a bag of white powder, and for an insane second I thought *drugs*, which was always a problem in any small town, but as I hesitated she screamed, "Throw it at the draug!"

I emptied the whole bag, flinging the contents at the creature.

The scream drilled into my head like a laser, and I dropped the shotgun and fell down, stunned, instinctively pulling into a fetal position and covering my ears, but that shriek plunged deeper and deeper into my head, whiting out every thought, every instinct except the purest, to *hide*.

And then it started to fade.

The rain stopped, as suddenly as the cutoff of a faucet. The puddles underneath me seemed to actually *crawl*, as if they were trying to get away, and I thought I was going insane, again, as I flopped over on my back and saw the silvery streams of drops going up into the air against the law of gravity, shimmering and weirdly, horribly beautiful in their sinuous curves.

The clouds were smaller overhead, I realized. They'd risked a lot to do this, and it had cost them. This was dry country, arid and unforgiving, and water got trapped quickly in the loose, sandy soil. Not all the draug's—cells? whatever it was—could survive this process of rain and reclamation.

I was just getting to my feet when I caught sight of Captain Obvious, staggering to his feet. He was cradling his badly broken arm close to him, but he'd picked up a rifle from the wreckage of the truck.

I looked where he was aiming.

The draug was—I didn't know what to call it. Misshapen, because it had tried to flee back into liquid form, but frozen into something that was misty, gelatinous, and shot through with thick black lines like veins. It was horrifying, and inside it, Richard was still trapped.

"No!" I screamed, and grabbed for my shotgun.

I wasn't fast enough.

Captain Obvious fired twice, directly into the dead, rubbery body of the draug. His eyes were wild and crazy, driven insane by the shriek and the utter *wrongness* of what we'd seen, and I understood that, I understood the impulse to smash that evil, horrific shape into bits.

But Richard was inside it.

I somehow managed not to shoot Captain Obvious. I don't remember moving, but suddenly I was standing over him, and I dimly remember clubbing him with the heavy stock of the shotgun in my hands. He was down again, senseless. I resisted the urge to kick him in the broken arm.

Michael Glass had gotten out of his side of the cruiser and was standing there, pale and still. He was staring at me as if he'd never seen me before. Well, he hadn't. Not like this. Not on full auto.

I tossed him my shotgun on the run, and he caught it, and then I was plunging both hands deep into that awful, cold, thick substance that had been the draug.

Elbow-deep.

I got hold of one of Richard's arms and pulled him out. It was like hauling someone out of deep, heavy mud; it took every ounce of my strength and leverage to wrestle his hand free, then his elbow, then his shoulder—and then the draug's dead, solidified form slumped away from him as gravity dragged its boneless body down, and he came completely loose.

He was covered in wet, stinking clumps of black matter. Whatever the powder had done to the draug, it had certainly killed it, because that was the smell of dead things rotting on beaches.

Richard pulled in a deep, bubbling gasp and opened his eyes. His skin was sunburn-red, stung all over from the draug's grip, and there were red flecks of hemorrhage in the whites of his eyes. He'd almost suffocated.

One of the bullets Captain Obvious had fired had hit him in the side, probably in the liver; that was bad, but the one that had hit him square in the chest was worse. The wound in front was pumping out bright red arterial blood, and the second I saw it a queer sense of calm settled over me. I knew that sensation. It was my emotions shutting down to protect me from what was coming.

I lowered Richard to the damp pavement and tried putting pressure on the wound, but it was useless. That was a major arterial tear, too close to his heart. I packed the hole with wadded-up ripped pieces of his shirt, but that couldn't stop it. I was only keeping the blood inside, where it would fill up his chest cavity and kill him from suffocation if his heart didn't stop first.

"Hannah?" Michael's uncertain voice from behind me. "We can put him in the back . . ."

"No," I said. Richard's eyes were open, fixed on mine. I could see the stark terror in them, and the knowledge. "No, we can't move him." I wouldn't say, *It wouldn't do any good, he won't last long*, but I could see Richard already knew it. I could feel it in the crushing strength of his grip on my hand. He was trying by sheer will to hold himself here, with me.

He was a good man. A very good man. Brave and kind, and better than Morganville had ever deserved out of the Morrell family.

I should have been able to truly love him. In this moment, at least, I finally did. Completely.

I bent forward and kissed him, very lightly, and whispered,

"I'm sorry I wasn't what you needed me to be. I love you, Richard. You hear me? *I love you.* I'm sorry I never said it."

He heard me. I saw his pale, already blueing lips shape the words back. His hand on mine was shaking—a little at first, and then more violently. But he wouldn't blink, wouldn't look away from me, until the very last second when he squeezed his eyelids shut, and the last warm blood flowed from the wound in his chest, covering my right hand as my left caressed his forehead, pushing the matted hair from his face.

"I love you," I said again. "And I'm so, so sorry."

And then he was still, and gone.

Michael was still standing there. I was dimly aware of him, until he finally moved to crouch next to me. "Is he—"

"Yes," I said. My voice sounded oddly matter-of-fact about it. I couldn't feel much, not yet. Not here. "Yes, he's gone." There was a lot of blood. A lot of it was on my hands, bright and red, still warm. There was a puddle of shallow water in a depression in the pavement near me, and without thinking I rinsed myself off in it; no burning, after. The draug weren't hiding there, not that I'd have cared in this moment. "We need to get you all back to Founder's Square now. I'll come back for him."

I'd never seen a vampire look so young, and so uncertain. I was completely freaking him out, I realized, and this was a kid who'd grown up with a fair amount of insanity and violence, and had inherited a great deal more when he'd crossed to the other side. I wondered what it was he saw in me that made him look so . . . tentative. "What about them?" he asked, and nodded toward the wounded by the truck.

I didn't so much as glance that way again. "They can wait," I said. "I'll send help." Maybe.

I knew that wasn't logical, or reasonable, or even *human*, to leave three broken men out there to suffer, or to die, if the draug came back, but I wasn't feeling logical, or reasonable, or human. Captain Obvious had shot Richard, and he hadn't needed to do that. I'd already saved him. Ten more seconds, and we'd all have left here alive.

I understood why he'd done it; I'd had to fight not to do the same exact thing.

But I couldn't forgive.

Michael didn't argue with me. Maybe he, too, realized that I was in a very dangerous place—dangerous for Captain Obvious, for his men, for me, even for him if he tried to get in my way. He bowed his head, stood up, and went to the car. The sound of the door slamming was as final as the lid on a coffin.

I made sure Richard's eyes were closed. I straightened him as best I could.

As I stood, suddenly and achingly aware of how very tired I was, how *weary*, the clouds parted, just a little, and a warm beam of wintry sunlight lanced through to bathe us both. I raised my face to it and closed my eyes for a few seconds. A better person might have thought that God was touching us to remind me that it wasn't all darkness, that clouds passed, and storms ended.

But for now, it was just sun, and warmth, and it soon was gone as the clouds shifted again. Because just now, I wasn't a person who believed in the future.

Only in what was right in front of me.

I kicked pieces of jellyfied draug out of my way to the driver's side door of the cruiser. As I got inside, I heard Claire say, in a choked and very shaky voice, "There he is."

I looked up and around. I started to ask, not that I was really curious, but Shane did it for me. "Who?" He had his arm around Claire, and she was huddled against him, quietly wiping tears from her face.

She pointed.

Myrnin—who to this point I had honestly forgotten about, because he'd done nothing, said nothing, reacted to nothing—leaned suddenly forward. "Where?"

"Right *there*," Claire said. She pointed again, straight over my shoulder through the front window. "Standing on top of that building. Can't you see him?"

"Who are you talking about?" I asked her. There was nothing on the roof where she was pointing. No—there was a passing shadow, something that shifted when I tried to fix my focus on it. Like fog, disappearing. "There's nobody."

"Magnus. That's *him*. I swear, he's right there. Watching us."

Michael and Shane were both eyeing her oddly. "Claire, there's nobody there. Nobody," Michael said. Myrnin said nothing. His dark eyes were intent, staring at the spot where she pointed. After a moment, he silently sat back and folded his arms.

"You think you can see Magnus," I repeated. "The leader of the draug. But I promise you, there's nobody there."

"And I promise you, he *is* there. I—I can see him." Claire bit her lip and took a deep breath. "I could always see him. I don't know why. When he was taking the vampires in the beginning, I saw him a couple of times and tried to follow him. I think that's why he came for me, in the house. Because I could see him."

Thoughts began sparking in my head, igniting into a fuse that burned directly to a very dangerous conclusion. "You can tell him from the others? The ones *we* can see?"

"The rest of the draug? Yeah. They're copies of him, but they're not as . . . as *present*, if that makes any sense. They're just reflections. Pieces of him that have split off. I think somehow they're all . . . connected."

"She's correct," Myrnin said. "I tell you now what only Amelie and I know about the draug. . . . The master draug is the seed from which all others spring, and they are his thralls. Not mindless, but close to it. He is the thinker. The planner. He is the one we have to stop. We have to find a way to trap and kill him. Once we do, the others will fall. They cannot exist long without a master."

He met my eyes, and that was when I realized that Myrnin was thinking *exactly* the same thing that I was. That as pathologically cold as I was right now, he was there ahead of me.

Vampires ain't like most of us, I heard my grandmother whisper in the back of my mind. *Cold ones. Cold at heart. Selfish. They don't survive all this time otherwise.*

I wondered what she'd say about me, now.

I exchanged a look in the rearview mirror with the vampire, and held it. Then I said, "We'll talk about this later."

He blinked, and inclined his head.

And just like that, we were partners in something that was going to have catastrophic consequences if it went wrong. Funny. I should have worried about that. But all I felt was a sense of savage relief, because I had an objective. Something to do. Something to *plan*.

And I could see, from the red sparks gathering in Myrnin's eyes, that he felt exactly the same way.

Michael shifted uncomfortably next to me. "I'm sorry, but we can't wait here. We really need to get to Founder's Square. This stuff in the trunk——"

"Yes," I said. "Absolutely."

And I drove them back, as I thought about traps, and the draug, and revenge.

It was the only thing I *could* think of now.

CHAPTER FIFTEEN

EVE

The vampire library was not my thing. It was maybe Claire's thing, but I like current novels. Freaky ones, preferably, with black covers and red type on the front. My idea of research is looking at take-out menus.

So it was kind of ironic that Naomi's concept of how to discover why Claire could see Magnus was . . . searching the library. The idea of me, sitting at a table, leafing through books that had been old before Columbus sailed was so very not right. Also, probably not very useful. But I didn't much mind. Letter of the agreement, and all that. The worst that could happen was a paper cut—of course, any blood drawn around a hungry vampire was, by definition, a worst-case scenario in the making.

"Honestly," I said as Naomi dropped another armload on the table, which was already overloaded with big, leather-bound selections, "*I can't read this.* And I'm not even sure that this is written in English, anyway."

"It is English. Middle English," she said. "Don't they teach Chaucer these days?"

"Well, they *teach* him," I said. "I didn't exactly *learn* him. Or, you know, translating. Isn't there software for this or something? Don't you digitize?"

Naomi had always struck me as calm. That had been her first characteristic: calm, then pretty. She was still pretty, but that was mostly an involuntary thing; she looked as tired as any vampire I'd ever seen. The calm was completely missing. She seemed just . . . *focused.* And annoyed.

"All you need do is look for one word," she said. "If you find it, I will read the section. Or do you want me to reconsider our agreement? Your choice." She pulled up a chair on the other side of the table and began scanning another book. Somehow she made it look effortless and graceful.

For me, it was very heavy lifting. We'd already been at it for an hour, and my eyes ached. So did my back. I went back to the stiff pages of the book I'd been examining—I wouldn't say *reading,* really. The words were strangely formed, much more vertical than I was used to seeing. It wasn't even typeset. Someone had actually written this out by hand. A *copy* of a book back in those days was just that: *copied.* By hand. With a pen.

Talk about carpal tunnel.

And then, to my shock, I focused in on a word.

The word. "Uh, I think I have something."

"Good," Naomi said, and was around the table in a flash, reading where I pointed. "That is not what I am looking for, but it does pertain to the draug. Keep searching."

Draug, draug, draug. I was honestly sick of thinking about

them. I wanted a day without a crisis. Just one. As I leafed through the book in front of me and watched the dust swirl in the air, I wondered if maybe there was some evil dormant virus in the pages that would infect me, like the mummy dust that used to kill archaeologists. Death by research. That was not a glorious end.

It was another hour and a half before I got another hit. A spiky splash of letters on the page caught my eye just as I turned another leaf, and I flipped back. Yeah, that said *draug*, again. I held up my hand. Naomi glanced at what it was, then leaned forward and smoothed her fingers over the old ink.

She took the book from me and sank down in the chair beside mine. Even tired, even rumpled, she was beautiful, and I had a revival of the Jealousy Parade for a second or two, even though I knew Michael wasn't interested in her . . . and even if he had been, Naomi was an iceberg. I knew that now.

"Yes," she whispered. Her eyes had grown wider, and a bit of color bled into her ivory-pale cheeks. *"Yes!"* She stood up, pacing with the book held in both hands as she read aloud: " 'The draug are creatures of the hive. The workers die, but the master draug survives to found his hive anew.' "

"Yeah, we kind of knew that already," I said. "He's here. The hive's breeding, it's awful, et cetera. What does it say about stopping him?"

"That he cannot be killed," she said softly. "Silver will not destroy him." She put the book down and closed it, then rested her head on the palm of her hand as if she had a pounding headache. A really human gesture, for really human distress. Around us, the library was silent—deep carpets, big shelves, solid books. The dry smell of ancient paper. Books that the vampires had spent thousands of years gathering . . . I'm not Claire—I don't get overwhelmed by that kind of stuff, but all of a sudden it seemed like I was standing in a tomb, or a museum, a building that was nothing but a memory of something long gone by.

The vampires were fighting their last fight here. The very last one, out of too many to ever count.

And Naomi, I realized, thought they were going to lose, big time, for all her talk of politics and future games.

"What about Claire?" I asked. "She can see him. How does that matter? Why does he care, if he can't be killed?"

"That is what I have you here to learn. So keep reading. It may be our only real hope."

Naomi threw the book in her hands violently. It hit a shelf and rocked the shelf back and forth in an arc that slowly settled back into stillness. The book flopped down onto the carpet, broken and dejected.

Like Naomi herself.

"Keep looking," she ordered, and stalked off into the shelves again. "I don't care how long it takes. Just find something I can use. If you don't, I'll have your brother for breakfast and make him mine. I promise you that."

"I can't find something that isn't here!" I shouted after her. I felt short of breath, ready to cry. This was *such* a bad deal. And honestly, what did it matter? Some part of me wondered that. My brother wanted it, right? He endured the bites because he wanted to have the power. He wanted to make himself into something else. Something new, and probably terrifying.

No. It mattered not just for him, but for all the people he would hurt if he grew fangs and had virtual immunity from justice. I was doing it for *them* as much as him.

So I kept working. My eyes felt as if they were bleeding, and my back ached so badly I was sure it was broken in a few places. Naomi only appeared to harass me and dismiss the few things I located that might be of use. I had no idea what she was doing now, but it couldn't be good.

And then . . . Then I found it. This time, since Naomi wasn't there, I tried to puzzle out what it said myself. This wasn't even Middle English. I had no idea whether it was High or Low or just plain bizarre, but it took me half an hour to make sense of it enough to realize what I held in my hands.

The answer. And an answer I couldn't give Naomi. No way in hell. I shivered, staring at the paper, at the dry, ancient words.

"Well?" I raised my head with a startled gasp, and found Naomi leaning over the table, inches away. She smiled slowly. "I heard your heart rate increase. You've found something."

"No," I said, and turned the page. "I didn't. False alarm."

I didn't expect that would work. It didn't. Naomi grabbed the book from me and flipped the leaf, found the passage, and began to read. Her brow furrowed, and she sent me a dark look. "What is this?" She put the book down and spun it toward me, tapping the image inked on the fragile page. "Does the girl have *this*?"

"Not anymore," I said, very reluctantly. "But she used to." The drawing on the page of that book was of a gold filigree bracelet. Amelie had given it to Claire as part of her Protection agreement. She'd taken it back later, but Claire *had* worn it for a while. And she hadn't been able to remove it. Not at all. "It's not like it was *magic* or anything." Except that it wouldn't come off, which would kind of argue . . . magic. Oops.

Naomi read the paragraph below the image again. "Amelie hasn't given a human a Protection agreement since she founded Morganville," she said, "save those she put in Founder Houses. Each had to be made *for* the person, and could not be used again. They were made with . . ." Her eyes widened. "With a drop of draug blood in the metal. And when the last of it was used up, she could make no more. Claire's was the last."

"But she doesn't *have* it!" I protested. "Really! Claire hasn't worn it for—for almost a year!"

"And yet she can see Magnus, separate him out from his reflections and shadows." Naomi's smile took on sharp edges. And teeth. "The bracelet infected her with just a tiny inoculation of draug blood, as it had all of those in the Founder Houses who wore them when the vampires first came here. They were Amelie's eyes. Amelie's early warning. And that is why Claire continues to see him, and why Magnus wants her dead, very badly."

"Then why didn't Amelie use her to find him?"

"Because she didn't realize the charm still worked, of course. Not until it was too late. The girl no longer wore the bracelet; it was reasonable to assume that she no longer had the ability."

Oh, I didn't like this. I didn't like it at all. "You're not going to hurt Claire."

"Of course not. Good work, Eve. Very satisfactory work indeed. Your brother's agreement has been canceled. I won't touch him again. I make you that solemn pledge."

I didn't believe that first part at all. I stood up in a rush, hands in fists. *"What are you going to do to Claire?"*

"Nothing," she said. "Nothing at all. She's a good pet to keep, for the future. I'm sure we can make great use of her, Eve." She gave me that sweet, charming smile again, the expression of a marble angel. "And of you, of course. All will be well. You must trust me. When I am queen, you will do very well indeed."

"Queen of *what?*"

"Morganville. Of course." Naomi seemed *way* too complacent now. "Now that you've found this volume, we can construct more of these bracelets, whether Myrnin cooperates or not. And draug blood will surely not be in short supply when Oliver is finished. He will win, of course. I have every confidence in him as a military leader. Just not as a ruler."

I was in over my head. Way, way over, and I knew it. "Amelie's the ruler of Morganville," I said. "And I have the feeling she'll never let you near that title."

"My sister is dying," Naomi said. For a moment there was a flash of sadness in her eyes—almost real. Almost. "Come with me."

"Where?"

That earned me a look that was back to cool, calm remoteness. "I don't answer your questions," she said. "You haven't yet earned those rights from me. Careful how you address your queen, Eve. You are not married to Michael just yet. Now *come.*"

I didn't know where she was taking me, but I had the sinking feeling that it wasn't anyplace I wanted to go.

I had made a mental map of this place by this time, and it was basically a maze—four central hubs, each with spoke hallways filled with doors. Nothing was labeled, and there were no signs, but if you stare at identical things long enough, you can start to pick out little differences. The hub where we made our first turn was the one I'd nicknamed Scratchy, because in all the moving of furniture someone had nicked the far wall in three places, at about knee level. The hallway we took had a slightly lighter strip of paint at one corner, where some old damage had been repaired and not precisely color-matched. At the next hub there was a particularly memorable portrait of some crusty old dude in a curly wig who'd been painted with his fangs showing. Charming.

There were more guards here. Amelie's guards.

Naomi walked up to them and got blocked—bodies in the way, palms outstretched.

"I wish to see my sister," she said. "Surely you will allow me to pass." It was one step short of *Don't you know who I am?*—but not quite over the line.

"Sorry, my lady. Orders from Lord Oliver," he said. Oh, God, it was *Lord* Oliver now? Better and better. "I'll pass the information on to him, if you wish. . . ." His voice trailed off. He was looking at someone behind us who was approaching, I guessed, and when I turned my head I saw Theo Goldman coming down the hallway into the hub. He had his black leather bag in one hand, and he smiled and nodded politely when he saw us.

For a vampire, he was one of the *nicest* I'd ever met. Or at least, he had the best manners. I never had the feeling he looked at humans any differently from vamps; we were all just potential patients to him. "Hello," he said pleasantly, and then nodded again to the guards. "If you'll excuse me."

They stepped aside for him immediately.

Naomi quickly seized the opportunity. "Theo," she said, "may I visit my sister? I only wish to give her my love before—" She looked so sweet and pretty and vulnerable it made my stomach turn. "Please?"

He shook his head. "I think it would not be wise," he said. "She's not . . . herself just now. It's dangerous enough for me. . . . And you, my dear, with your history together—no. I'm afraid that would be very dangerous to you."

He started to turn away, but Naomi put a hand on his shoulder, and Theo turned toward her. And something weirdly extraordinary happened. She leaned forward, put her lips close to his ear, standing on tiptoe to do it. I didn't hear what she whispered, but I saw the expression smooth out on Theo's face.

It turned . . . oddly blank.

"Yes," he said. "Yes, perhaps you're right. It would be good for her to see family."

"Ah," Naomi said. "And may I bring Eve?"

Theo should *not* have said yes to that, of course; no way. But he just nodded as if it was the Best Idea Ever. He turned to the guards and said, in a warm and perfectly self-assured voice, "Yes, I think they should both come with me. My responsibility, gentlemen."

The guards looked doubtful, and they *must* have known something weird was up, but they didn't stop us. I guess Naomi really did outrank most vampires. We walked with Theo down the hall.

He opened the locked door to a room there, and we went inside, and my hand instinctively flew to cover my nose and mouth, because this place *smelled*. It looked fine, but . . . it was a horrible, wet, nasty stench.

Theo didn't seem at all surprised.

"She's in the other room?" Naomi asked.

Theo turned to face her. "Naomi, perhaps now would be a good time to mention to you that I am quite immune to your powers of persuasion. You'd do well to not try that on someone less . . . forgiving. Oliver would have crushed you if you'd tried it."

"Oh." Naomi was, I thought, honestly taken aback. "But you—"

"Allowed you to come with me? Yes. Because I want to talk to you without prying ears. That's why I didn't crush you myself. I can, you know. One doesn't survive as long as I have without knowing how to do these things, even if they don't come naturally." For a moment Theo actually looked *dangerous*. "What do you really intend here, Naomi?"

"I *intend* to save our lives," she said. "As I expect you secretly want, Theo. My sister cannot be saved, can she?" At a slow shake of his head, she sighed. "Then there's nothing for it. Oliver's a fool if he lets the transformation become complete. I know my sister. I know her powers. If she transforms into a master draug, as Magnus intends, she will be able to force any of us to her will; it's a power that only a few have, as you know, but my sister has it in full strength. Combined with the will and hunger of a draug . . . she would end us all."

Theo, I realized, wasn't surprised. Just wary. "And you propose?"

"You know what I propose. You're no fool."

They stared at each other for a long moment, and then he said, "No. I don't accept defeat so easily, and you shouldn't either. We are *vampire*, whether we ever wanted it or not, and vampires survive. It is the core of what we are. We fought for life when life wasn't ours to keep. And she is *still* fighting. She has not lost the battle yet."

"We can't wait until she does!" Naomi hissed, and shoved herself away from him. She wrapped her arms around herself and paced like an agitated tiger. "What remains is not my sister. That *thing* is a virus grown inside her body, stealing her soul—"

"People have said the same of vampires, time out of mind," Theo said. "Are they right? Did you lose your soul when you lost your human life? I believe, I *must* believe, that I still cling to mine."

"The draug are *different!*"

I couldn't disagree with that, really. Everything that I'd seen about the draug made me think that Naomi had something there. None of the draug seemed to have the least bit of human feeling in them; they were monsters, predators, pure and simple. The vampires at least hung on to *something*—even the worst of them you could understand, even if you hated it, and them.

But there was nothing inside the draug *to* understand. It was like trying to reason with a hungry shark.

Theo sighed. "She's my patient," he said. "If the worst comes, then it's mine to do, not yours. And I won't do it without Oliver's consent. He is the leader now. Unless you plan to dispute that."

"Of *course* I plan to dispute it! He's nothing but a jumped-up pretender!"

"I am not involved in the politics of kings and queens," he said. "Or even those of pretenders. Go back, Naomi. Let me see to your sister."

She bowed her head and curtsied, just a little. "Of course, Doctor. Thank you. I'm sorry."

He turned his back on her to open the door. That was a mistake.

I didn't have time to react at all when she pulled a wooden stake from the side of her boot and stabbed him in the back with it—between the ribs, and angling up to his heart. Theo made a little gasping sound, hardly loud enough for me to hear, and then she caught him as he fell and eased him to the carpet. She reached past him to turn the dead bolt lock on the door. Then she snapped it off, leaving the metal tongue in place.

I wasn't getting out of there. Not easily.

"What are you *doing*?" I cried. "Guards! Get in here!"

"Yell all you like," Naomi said placidly. She opened up Theo's doctor bag and searched through it, calm as an ice sculpture. "Amelie is quite particular about her soundproofing. There's a hidden alarm, if you can find it, but I should not waste my time if I were you. Stay here until I return."

Theo was lying totally still, facedown on the floor. A wooden stake wouldn't kill him immediately, I knew; it would pin him down, paralyze him, leave him helpless for whatever might come next.

I let Naomi think I was paralyzed, too, with fear; it wasn't a tough job of acting. This was going too fast, and too crazy, and I had no idea what the right thing to do was, except that Theo had never hurt anyone, ever.

Naomi took something out of his bag, walked across to the other door, and closed it quietly behind her.

I dropped to my knees beside Theo, took hold of the stake, and yanked, hard. It was embedded between the ribs, and it took all my strength and three tries to pull it free.

He pulled in a tortured, gagging breath but didn't move. I rolled him over, and he blinked and slowly focused on my face. "Naomi," he whispered. "Of course." He held out his hand, and I stood and helped haul him up, too. It must have been very hard; he leaned on me, and I could feel his whole body trembling. "Must stop her." He pointed to his doctor bag, and I grabbed it and held it open while Theo sorted through with shaking hands. He finally pulled out a small aerosol can. "She's taken the knife."

Knife. Oh, God. I looked at the bedroom door. We might already be too late.

The door was locked, but not with a dead bolt, just the standard kind; I braced myself and kicked just above the knob with my heavy combat boot, putting all my leg strength into it. Wow, I was getting an unexpected upper- *and* lower-body workout. Inappropriate cheery aerobics music wandered through my head, but was quickly whited out by the pain from my knee.

It worked, though. The door flew open, and Theo staggered past me into the room.

Naomi was standing over the figure lying prone on the bed, with a silver knife held in both hands. She was trying to bring it down, clearly putting all her strength into it, but the figure had hold of her wrists and was keeping them suspended in midstab.

That was Amelie she was trying to kill. But not Amelie at all.

I recognized her, but it was the kind of horrified, shocked recognition that you'd expect from seeing a dead body, or someone severely injured ... and I knew something about both those things, big time. It was the same delayed jolt of adrenaline that hammered through my body—because Amelie wasn't Amelie anymore.

I wasn't sure *what* she was.

She looked ... wet. Covered in damp slime, gray strands of it over her skin like fungus, hair loose and matted with the same stuff. Her eyes had turned a different color of gray—not ice now, more like fog, grayish white and completely opaque. The bed around her was soaked with the same horrible damp *stuff.*

"Stop," Theo said sharply, and when Naomi didn't pay attention he lurched over, grabbed her from behind and levered her wrists and the knife upward, away from Amelie. It wasn't easy. Naomi didn't give up, and Amelie didn't let go, either ... it was as if she *couldn't* let go, really. I finally lunged over and pried her wet, slimy fingers off, one by one.

Where they'd fastened on Naomi's thin wrists, they left red welts that overflowed with blood, as if whole patches of skin had been melted away.

"Let me go," Naomi said, and twisted violently in Theo's hold. She almost got loose, but he held on with grim determination. *"Let me go.* You know this is the only way. We can't allow her to turn— we *can't."*

Theo took the knife from her hand, and shoved her away from Amelie's bedside. She screamed in sheer frustration, but she didn't try to steal it back. His expression was thoughtful, and his eyes were cool and distant.

He held that knife like someone who really knew how to wield it like an expert. That was what held her in place.

"You stabbed me in the back," Theo said. "I suppose I should be appropriately grateful that you thought enough of me to only use wood, and little enough of Eve to leave her behind to free me. But then, you never intended for her to leave here alive, did you? A silver knife, a human at the scene—conveniently dead, killed by you in outrage. You wished me to believe that Eve staked me, over-powered you somehow, and killed Amelie in some pro-human rampage. It won't wash, my dear. It simply won't wash."

I hadn't thought about it, but now that I could catch my breath, fury burned up inside me like acid. That *bitch*. She'd set me up. Even if she hadn't killed me, she could have blamed the whole thing on me, especially if she burned herself with a little silver. Me and my friends were well known to walk around armed with anti-vamp weaponry.

And the sentence for killing Amelie would, of course, be immediate, violent, and gruesome death.

"What are you going to do?" Naomi flung back at him. "Let her live? Let her become draug? A *master* draug, capable of destroying us all? Don't be a fool, Theo! You know what I was doing is necessary!"

"And Eve?"

She glanced at me, then back to him. "A human, determined to marry a vampire? How long do you expect she would last, in any case?"

I risked another look at Amelie. She was as still as a statue now, hands folded across her chest. But as I watched, I felt her attention . . . shift. Toward me.

And I heard her, in my head. There was a clear, silvery sound to it, like bells and singing, sweet singing.

Go, Eve. Go and don't come back.

I didn't wait. My nerve just . . . broke, and I ran into the other room. Theo must have known where the alarm button was, because a few seconds later I heard the thumping of violent but muffled blows on the door, and it crashed open to admit Amelie's two guards. I held up my hands. They disregarded me and ran into the other room.

And I got the hell out before anybody could ask me any questions. I didn't know what Theo was going to say, but if I hung around, there was no way I wouldn't end up somehow coming out of it badly.

I wished I'd never seen Amelie like that, because it was awful, and terrifying. If she was fighting, I couldn't see any sign of it; she looked like she was slowly drowning in that slime, and the awful gray color of her skin and eyes made her look like something washed up on a beach.

We were losing the Founder of Morganville, and once we lost her . . .

. . . We lost everything.

I dashed down the hallway, blind with tears and anguish, and ran headlong into Michael. I stopped, trembling, and stared at him for a few long, horrible seconds. What I'd just seen . . . what I'd just escaped . . .

He didn't ask. He just opened his arms, and I fell into them, sobbing my heart out as he stroked my hair.

"It's okay," he whispered to me.

But it wasn't. It really, really wasn't.

CHAPTER SIXTEEN

SHANE

☾

Michael had his arms around Eve, and that was going well for a change; Myrnin had already taken his goodies off to the lab, leaving the three of us behind. Hannah had ditched us, too, locked in her eerie calm. None of us had dared say anything to her.

Claire was looking at me with dull, tragic need, and I just couldn't . . . I couldn't give her what she needed. Not yet. I couldn't *feel* it. But there was something I could feel, after all.

I said, "I need to tell Monica about her brother."

I heard Claire suck in a deep breath, as if she hadn't even thought that far ahead. "Oh," she said in a choked voice. "Should I go——?"

"No. Better if I do it alone." Because if I could feel anything real, it would be now, looking into Monica's eyes. It was karma. She deserved to hear about her brother from me; while my sister died, caught in our burning house, Monica had stood there and smiled and flicked a lighter. Mocking me. Mocking how helpless I was.

I'd always believed she'd set the fire, from that moment on; Richard had always insisted she hadn't, that she'd just been a troll and hadn't even known Alyssa was trapped inside. I didn't really believe him. Maybe he didn't even believe it himself.

I found Monica in what I guessed was some kind of vampire entertainment room. There was a TV, tuned now silently to static, and a leather couch. She was lying on the couch, wrapped in a blanket, and she was asleep.

I didn't think I'd ever seen Monica asleep, and the surprise was that when she wasn't actively being herself, she seemed . . . normal. She looked tired, too; her hair was mussed, and she'd taken her makeup off. Without it, she looked her actual age, which was Michael's—no, she was still human. She was older than Michael now.

All of a sudden, real or not, the pain I was about to inflict didn't seem right—but she needed to know, and I'd volunteered.

Isn't it perfect, how you get to tell her about her brother? More wish fulfillment, Shane. You really think all this is the truth?

That damn stupid voice in my head wouldn't shut up. It was a constant, grinding monologue, a headache that wouldn't go away. And the worst thing was, I wasn't sure it was imagination. *Wake up, Shane.*

But I was awake. Wasn't I?

I crossed the room toward the couch. The lights had been turned down low, but on the coffee table there was a remote to turn them up, so I pressed the button. As the artificial sun came up, Monica moaned a little, mumbled, and tried to bury her face in the pillow.

Then, as I sat down on the edge of the table, staring at her, she suddenly sat bolt upright, and the fear that raced over her expression surprised me. I hadn't thought she was capable of that kind of vulnerability . . . but then, she'd been born here, just as I'd been, and having strangers walk in on you asleep was rarely good.

Monica stared at me blankly, without recognition, for about two seconds, and then awareness overtook alarm, and she just looked annoyed. And angry. "Collins," she said, and ran her fingers through her hair, as if getting it settled was her first priority. "God, there's a new thing called *knocking*—look into it. If you're going to get all stalkery over me saving your life today, please don't. It wasn't my idea in the first place. Though if you want to dump your Playskool girlfriend, I might be persuaded to throw you a boner." She smiled at me, suddenly all inappropriate hormones and insanity.

I didn't know how to do this. The responsibility felt heavy and harsh, because I was about to totally destroy her world. I knew how it felt, and yeah, there was a certain justice to it, not denying that, but I found that I couldn't take any real joy, either. I just waited her out, until she was silent, frowning at me, clearly made uneasy by my lack of reaction.

And then I said, very quietly, "Monica, I have to tell you something. It's bad."

She wasn't stupid, and about one second after I said it, I saw the awful light start to dawn. "What happened?" she asked, and folded her arms together over her stomach. I remembered how that felt, the drop off the edge of the earth. "Is—is it my mom?" Because, I realized, news that her mother was dead, even a mother who no longer even spoke to or recognized her own kids, was the best-case scenario she could think of now.

"No," I said. Maybe I should have been taunting her, I don't know; maybe I'd have been fully within my rights to do it. But suddenly all I wanted out of this was to be kind, and to be quick, and to be *out*. I wanted to hold Claire, and forget how fragile we all were, just for a moment. "No, it's not your mom. I'm sorry. It's Richard."

"He's hurt," she said, and threw the blanket back. She was wearing sweatpants and a tank top, like a normal girl, and she reached for a pair of flat shoes. Her hands were trembling. "Is he here? Can I see him? He's going to be okay, right? God, these shoes don't even match, but I couldn't bring everything. . . ."

"No," I said, "he's not going to be okay." She stopped in the act of sliding one shoe on, but she didn't look up. After that hesitation, she finished, and donned the other shoe, and stood up. I stood too, not sure what to do now.

"What do you know, dumbass?" she said, and shoved past me, heading for the door. "When did *you* go to med school? You couldn't even pass bio, for God's sake. I'm sure he's fine."

"Monica," I said. Maybe it was the fact that I didn't insult her back, or raise my voice, or grab her; maybe it was just that she already knew. I don't have any idea what happened inside her head. But she stopped as if she'd run into an invisible wall, and waited. "I saw it. I'm sorry. Hannah was with him. They're going to bring him in soon. I thought you ought to know before—" *Before you saw his body.*

She whirled on me then, and the rage in her face took me by surprise. "You lying son of a bitch!" she screamed, and picked up the first thing she could reach—the TV's remote control—and flung it at me as hard as she could, which was pretty hard, actually. I batted it out of the way and didn't respond. She went for something heavier, a big marble bust of somebody I supposed I should have recognized, but she couldn't throw that nearly as well. It hit the carpet three feet from me and rolled.

And then she stumbled and fell on her knees. All the anger drained out of her, just as if someone had pulled a plug, leaving her pale and empty. Her eyes were open wide, pupils contracted to pinpoints, and she stared at me with her lips parted.

"I'm sorry," I said again. Seemed like all I *could* say. Had I thought this was a dream, a perfect revenge? Wish fulfillment? It wasn't. It was just . . . sad. "He was okay, your brother. He always tried to be fair. And he cared about you."

It wasn't much, as eulogies go, but it was all I had. Whatever entertainment I'd thought I would get out of this had been pure fantasy, and all I felt now was sickness, and bone-deep discomfort. I should have let Michael do it. Michael would have been good at it; he was all sensitive and crap, knew what to say and when . . .

Monica just *stared at me.* As if she was waiting for me to tell her it was all just a really nasty joke.

This should have been Oliver's job, I thought. Oliver was her vampire godfather Protector, wasn't he? Where was *he*?

Monica finally said, in a voice I would never have recognized as belonging to her, "You're a liar. He's not dead. He can't be *dead*. He's hurt, that's all, he got hurt and you're just a fucking *liar*. You're messing with me, you asshole. Because of your sister."

"I wish I was," I said. I shook my head and started for the door, because there was nothing else I could do here. Nothing but hurt and get hurt.

"Wait," she said. Her voice was shaking now, as her world fell apart inside. "Shane, *wait*. I didn't do it—I didn't start that fire. You don't have to be a jerk about this. This isn't *funny. . . ."*

"I know," I said. I wasn't sure which part of that I was acknowledging. Maybe all of it, with a sad kind of acceptance. "Sorry."

She'd always had her friends with her. Gina, Jennifer, any of a dozen other hangers-on circling the orbit of Monica, Center of the Universe. She'd always been invulnerable, armored up in attitude and trendy clothing and makeup and gloss. Always the one doing the damage.

Maybe I should have taken some satisfaction at having brought her to this, alone, on her knees.

I didn't.

"I'll—send somebody," I said. I didn't know who I could possibly send, but it didn't matter; she didn't hear me. I looked back to see her pitch forward in slow motion, catch herself on one arm, and then roll over on her side on the carpet. Her legs slowly pulled up toward her stomach.

She started to cry in hopeless, gulping whoops.

Jesus.

I pulled in a deep, resigned breath, and went back to the couch, where I retrieved the blanket. I settled it over her, found a box of tissues and brought them to her. Then I poured her a stiff drink from an open bottle of Scotch on the counter at the back of the room—vampires liked their alcohol as much as humans, but they had a much better class of the stuff. This was single malt, and it smelled like smoke.

"Come on," I said, and hauled her upright to lean against the sofa's corner. I pressed the Scotch into one hand, pulled a couple of tissues out and stuffed them in the other hand. "Drink."

She did, obeying like a child; she choked on the first sip, but got it down, and then took a second, between gasps and shudders. A little awareness came back into her eyes, and a flash of something like shame. She used the tissues to wipe her nose, then got another to blot at her eyes. The tears were still coming, and her eyes were red and swollen. Never mind what the movies say—girls don't get prettier when they cry. That made her more . . . human.

"Why'd you come?" she asked, finally, when the whiskey was down to a thin amber line at the bottom of the glass. Calmer now, maybe artificially, but at least she wasn't shaking like she was about to come apart. "Why not *Claire*? She's the nice one." She tried to make it sound like an insult, but her heart wasn't in it.

"I figured maybe—"

"Maybe this would make you feel better about your sister?" she asked, and drained the last of the alcohol. "How's that going for you?" Her hand was trembling.

I didn't answer. I was seriously considering getting myself a shot, which was all kinds of wrong. Monica held out the empty glass to me, and I put it aside.

"I was hoping for a refill," she said.

"You don't need one. Last thing you need is to be drunk right now."

"Speaking from experience?"

"Yes," I said. I met her gaze solidly. "You're an evil bitch, and a bully, and I can't count the number of times I've wanted to break your neck. But I kind of liked your brother. That's why I came."

She took in a deep, fluttering breath, but she didn't break out in tears again. That was done, at least for now. I waited for the snappy comeback. It didn't make an appearance. Finally she said, "He always said that he hoped he was adopted." She made a weird little attempt at a laugh. "Most kids think that, but I think he was right. He deserved better." She swiped at her eyes again. "Shit. I can't believe I let you see me like this. You're never going to let me forget it, are you?"

I let that pass into silence, and then asked, "You going to be okay?"

This time the laugh was a little more recognizable, but hollow, as if she was empty inside. "No," she said. "But thanks anyway. For not—"

For not standing there smiling while she suffered, the way she'd done to me. She couldn't say that, but I figured it was what she meant.

"Is this where we hug and say we're BFFs?" I said. "Because I'd rather skip that part."

"Ugh. Absolutely." She blew her nose, threw the tissue at the coffee table, and pulled another from the box. "I guess I should— get dressed or something." She didn't know what to do, I could tell, but getting dressed was Monica's go-to coping mechanism. "So get out already."

I nodded and stood up. I put the glass on the coffee table, then said, "Richard wanted you to be less of a bitch. You might want to look into that, if you really loved him."

She said nothing, and finally I was able to escape.

The door shut behind me, and I leaned against the wall, eyes shut, breathing in deep, cool gasps. I felt weirdly feverish, and a little sick. No satisfaction at all.

In a strange sort of way, that was *good*.

CHAPTER SEVENTEEN

CLAIRE

Richard was *dead.*

Claire had seen it, and somehow, she just couldn't . . . believe it. At the last second, she'd realized what was going to happen when Captain Obvious had fired his rifle; she'd just . . . known. So she'd turned and hidden her eyes.

She was sorry about that now, as if she'd somehow let Richard down. As if she'd owed him that much.

Shane had left her standing there in the rotunda while Michael and Eve hugged out their differences, and she felt . . . useless. Alone.

And so, so exhausted. It just all seemed overwhelming. She was so tired of being uncertain. Isolated. Scared.

She walked back to the room where their beds were, alone. Someone had neatened it up since they'd left; there were beds now, foldaway cots instead of the camping kind. The sleeping bags were neatly rolled and stowed against the wall. There were sheets, blankets, pillows.

She sat down on her cot and just . . . stared. *What is happening to us?* she thought. *He went to talk to Monica instead of coming with me. Monica.* Okay, that was probably mean and cruel to even think it; he'd gone to break the news of Richard's death, and that had taken guts. She really hadn't wanted to do it, though she'd offered. *I just wish he'd come back. I need . . .*

She needed to know he was okay. Because he'd seriously lost it out there at the MHS shed. Whatever was happening in his head was strange and disconnected, and she was afraid, deeply afraid, that it would never get better.

It's a miracle he survived, Theo had told her. But what if he hadn't, all the way? What could she do to help?

Her brain kept whirling around, desperate to find answers, and she wasn't even aware of the time passing until she heard the door open and close.

It was Shane. He looked . . . tired. And, for a moment, pretty sad.

"How'd she take it?" Claire asked, and sat up.

He shook his head. "Not well." He rubbed his forehead as if it hurt, and there was that distance in his eyes, that distraction.

"We need to talk," she said.

"I can't. Not right now, okay?"

"No, you know what? Really not okay," Claire said. "What *happened* to you?" She wasn't going to let it go, let *him* go. Not this time. There was nobody here, nobody to worry about overhearing whatever he had to tell her. Just the two of them. "You haven't been the same since—"

"Since you got me back," Shane said. "I know." He looked around at the room. "Somebody redecorated, didn't they?"

"*Shane!*"

"You should get some sleep, Claire."

"No! I will *not* get some sleep, because you are going to *tell me what's going on with you, right now!*"

He sat down on the edge of the cot where his old camp bed had been. "That's not how it works," he said. "Trust me. It's just not. Because I don't know how to explain it. It's all . . ." He lifted a hand, and let it fall. "Mist."

She tried to guess, out of wild desperation. "Was it—Michael said they made you dream. Bad dreams? Was it—was it about your sister?" Because he'd been haunted by Alyssa's death for a long time now, and about his failure to save her in the fire. Never mind that he couldn't have done anything. "Your mom?"

He let out a frayed sound she only recognized a second later as a laugh. "I wish they'd stuck to that," he said. "I can deal with nightmares, I really can. But not dreams. Not . . ." All of a sudden his eyes just filled up with tears, and spilled over, and he ducked his chin and grabbed the frame of the cot as if it were moving around him. "Not seeing what I can't have."

"What can't you have?" She sank down on her knees, looking up into his face, watching the tears roll silently down his cheeks. He wasn't sobbing. It was as if he didn't even know it was happening. "Shane, *please*. Help me understand. You're not making any sense. What happened?"

"The dreams. They gave me what I wanted," he said. "Everything right. Everything . . . perfect." He sucked in a sudden, damp breath and blinked. "I can't explain it. It doesn't matter. I'll be okay."

"Stop *saying* that! You're not okay, Shane, there's something— just tell me. You know you can tell me, right?"

"No," he said. "I can't." He lunged forward and kissed her,

hard and fast, clumsy, desperate, and she made a surprised sound deep in her throat but didn't try to pull away. Instead, she moved closer, wrapping her arms around him as if she never intended to let him go—never. The warmth of his tears soaked the collar of her shirt, made damp spots against her neck. He spread his knees to let her in closer, and then he collapsed back on the mattress, taking her with him.

Then he just . . . shut down.

She felt his muscles go tense and still, as if he was fighting against himself, and his breathing sped up to a frantic pace, as if he was running a sprint.

"Shane, *please*. Let me *help*."

He squeezed his eyes shut. "Tell me you're here."

"God, Shane—" She bent forward and pressed her lips to his, and tasted tears. "I'm here, I swear I am. What do I have to do to prove it?"

"Tell me her name," he said. "Please tell me her *name*."

"*Whose* name?"

He was breathing so fast she was afraid he would hyperventilate now. "She was so real, Claire, she was so real and I held her in my arms and she was so *tiny*, she had blue eyes and I don't know her name, I don't know. . . ." His eyes flew open, blind and almost crazy as his gaze locked on hers. "It was so perfect. Do you understand? *Perfect*. And I had to let it go. But what if I was wrong? What if this is . . . what if I never . . ."

"What if you never left that place?" she guessed, and cupped his face in her hands. "You did leave. We got you out." All of a sudden, what he'd been saying made sense to her. Crazy, wicked, awful sense. "A baby. You—you dreamed about a baby. *Our* baby?"

His nod was more of a shudder. "I don't know her name."

She collapsed on top of him, trying to hold every bit of him close. "I'm so sorry. It wasn't real. You know that, don't you? You know it couldn't be real?"

"I need to know. I just—I just do, Claire. I'll go crazy if I don't *know*." His warm breath stirred her hair, and his arms went around her, pressing her as close as his own skin. "Tell me what you'd name her. Just . . . please."

It was crazy. *Crazy.* But if he needed to hear it—it wasn't that she hadn't secretly dreamed about all of that, about what it would be like to marry him, to have babies with him. That fantasy life she'd gone through about a million times already, all the details vivid and bright in her imagination.

But somehow, saying it felt like giving something up. Something precious and fragile and private.

"Carrie," she whispered. "Carrie Alyssa Collins. That's what I'd name her."

Shane shuddered hard, as if she'd punched him someplace vulnerable. "But it won't happen," he said. His voice sounded so raw now. "That's what hurts. I don't get the things I want. I never have. That's why they showed it to me, because it's not true."

"You have to trust me. You have to *believe* in yourself. In me. In us." She raised her head and looked at him, kissing-close, but their lips didn't touch. Seeing him like this, broken open . . . it didn't happen often, and it scared her. Shane was the strong one, the one with the quips and the ferocious delight in the fight. She'd thought she understood what had happened to him, that he'd been through nightmares, but this . . . this was terrifying.

The draug had taken away his reality, twisted it, made him afraid to believe in anything.

They'd taken away his hopes and dreams and made them something punishing.

And she *hated* them for that.

"You said it was perfect," she said. He nodded. "I was perfect, too?" Another nod. "But I'm not. We're not. Remember the first time we—remember how scared we were? How it all felt crazy and awkward and honest and real? That's us. You. Me. Together."

He was watching her now, and actually seeing her. The Shane she knew was in there, struggling. Fighting to get to her.

"Real life isn't perfect," she said. "Perfect is boring." They'd taken away perfect, made it death and dreams and the draug. He had to understand that. He had to *reject* that.

"Watch my lips," she said. "I love you. And you're *not* perfect."

He laughed. It still sounded raw, and painful, but more *him*, somehow. Then he kissed her, but this time it wasn't a fast and furious kind of thing. . . . If anything, he seemed tentative in the way he touched her, as if she might vanish if he pushed too fast, too hard. She stretched out next to him and let the kisses carry them away into that thoughtless, warm, golden place where nothing else mattered, nothing beyond the need to touch and be touched.

He didn't say it back to her, not yet, but she felt it with every kiss, every slow and gentle caress. He was holding himself back, and it was some sort of test, a goal he'd set himself. Mostly, she thought he just needed to . . . feel. To get real sensations in his head again.

To know the difference.

"You know what?" she said after a long, sweet few moments. "You seriously stink, Shane."

This time, she got a *real* laugh from him, and the look in his eyes was utterly surprised, and totally in the moment with her. "You really know how to turn a guy on, Claire."

"Not perfect, is it?"

His smile faded, and what was left in his face, his eyes, the tension in his body—it was very different. She knew that look. That hunger. "Not perfect at all," he said. "Then help me out here. No showers. What am I supposed to do about this problem?"

"Lie still," she said. She went across the room, locked the door, and picked up a bottle of water, a basin, and a cloth. "No fair tickling me, because I *will* spill this all over you." She straddled him and helped him pull the shirt off over his head. He collapsed back to the mattress and watched as she wet the cloth, then pressed it to his chest.

He twitched and yelped. "Cold!"

This time, she grinned. "Any doubts about reality *now*?"

"Not so much," he said, but kept his gaze fastened on hers, wide and hungry, as she moved the washcloth over his skin, gliding it under his arms, down his sides. Over his stomach. "You're not asking me to strip all the way, are you?"

"Maybe not yet," she said. "My turn."

She hadn't had a chance to take off the stupid plastic jumpsuit, which was *so* not sexy; she reached for the zipper, but in one of those startlingly fast, strong moves that always took her breath away, he flipped her over so her back was against the mattress, and he was the one straddling her. He considered the zipper.

Then he took hold of the thin plastic and ripped it all the way down. She had on her bra underneath, but somehow it felt like she was naked to his eyes.

And . . . crazily hot.

"Oh," she breathed, and shut her eyes as the cool air hit her skin. "So, this is getting a little on the adult channel side and that's not exactly what I—"

"Shh," he said, and pressed his lips to hers before he straightened again. "I'm working here."

He reached out, as if in a dream, and the cool cloth touched her skin and glided damply over it. She shivered from both the delicious chill and the feel of his fingers following it, warming her up again. He turned her over and stripped the rest of the jumpsuit away, washed her back, skipping past her bra strap, then moving down the line of her spine, all the way down to the waistband of her jeans. Next, her arms—left, then right.

And then she turned to face him, and he looked into her eyes and put the washcloth on the floor.

"Not fair," she said softly. "Stopping in the middle."

He leaned forward and kissed her again—not as urgently this time, more sweetness, turning stronger and more passionate as he leaned into her. This time he was the one in charge. It took a sweet, breathless eternity for him to slide her jeans off, and reach for the clasp of her bra, and then . . .

Creepy organ music played, muffled by her fallen pants.

Her cell phone.

"No," she moaned, and beat uselessly at the pillow. It wasn't *quite* the worst possible moment, but it was close. Really, really close. "No, no, *no!*"

"You'd better answer it," Shane said. He sank down on the other side of the bed, and his skin was lightly flushed and damp with sweat. His voice was half an octave lower than normal, and his pupils wide and dark, and she knew, *knew* it was unfair to him to do it . . .

. . . But she answered the phone after all.

"Put your clothes on," Myrnin said, clipped and cold. "We have work to do. Now."

He hung up on her. She screamed inarticulately at the phone and thought about flinging it at the wall, but it wouldn't help, not at all, and besides, he was right. That was part of why she was so *angry.*

Because it wasn't the time. Not here. Not now.

"Claire," Shane said. He was still lying down, watching her, and there was a small, quiet smile on his lips. "Hey. Thank you."

"For what?"

"For making it . . . not perfect."

She laughed. "What a romantic."

"Trust me," he said. "I am. That was the whole reason they could get to me, Claire. Because of how much I wanted . . . all that perfection. That life I never got to have when I was . . . growing up."

She kissed him again, slow and warm and sweet. "I know. But don't worry. We're in Morganville. Nothing's ever going to be perfect."

The stroke of his tongue over her lips made her want to throw the phone away and crawl back into bed. "Hmm. Imperfection tastes pretty fantastic, actually. I'm getting really fond of it."

Her phone rang again. "What?" she snapped as she answered it.

Myrnin, of course. "Are you on your way?"

"No!"

"Claire, there are *things to do*."

"Here, too," she said. "And I'm staying here, believe me."

Myrnin was silent for a beat, and then he said, "Bob would be very disappointed in you."

"Bob the spider?"

"He looks at you like a mother, you know. I'm surprised at your lack of work ethic. Think of the example you set for—"

She hung up on him and turned the phone on vibrate and relaxed in Shane's arms.

"You're not leaving," he said. He sounded surprised. "You always leave when he calls."

"Not now," she said. And kissed him again, sweetly and gently. Because they had all the time in the world.

Shane fell asleep, peacefully, spooned against her in the bed; they hadn't actually *done* anything, after all. It had been enough to just lie there together, skin to skin, feeling safe, and relaxed and . . . quiet.

It might have been almost a normal day. Almost.

Just before he drifted off, he'd sighed on the back of her neck, and whispered, "You're here." That had been enough to make tears form in her eyes, and they spilled over when he said, after a few more seconds, "I love you, Claire."

She'd been lying still now for half an hour, probably, just . . . savoring that. The relief. The feeling of having him back, real, alive.

Present.

Reality wasn't something she could lock out for long, though; the phone continued to buzz, and buzz. Myrnin, the idiot, was going to run down the battery soon. She considered breaking it, but finally picked it up, thumbed it on, and whispered, *"What?"*

"Claire," Myrnin said. "Claire, please. It's important, very important. Oliver wants to talk to you as soon as possible. I'm sorry if I upset you, but—"

Oh, great. *Oliver.* He probably wanted a full report of everything; Claire twisted a little to look at Shane, but he was deeply asleep, completely relaxed. So vulnerable.

"Be there in a minute," she whispered.

"Just you," he said. "Please."

"No problem." She shut the phone off and carefully, slowly, slid out of bed. Shane moved a little, groaned, and rolled over, burying his face in the pillow. But he didn't wake up.

Dressing didn't take long; she found her jeans, a T-shirt, and her kicks easily enough, and she'd never actually taken off the underwear. She paused to look in a mirror on the way out of the room; there was a happy flush in her cheeks, and even though there hadn't been anything she couldn't have told her mom about, it still *felt* intimate. Very. And she looked like someone with a secret.

Screw it. Myrnin and Oliver were just going to have to get over it. She ran fingers through her hair and ordered it as best she could, unlocked the door, and slipped out.

Her phone buzzed again. She answered it as she walked. "Okay, fine, I'm heading out. Where are you?"

"In the garage," Myrnin said. "Hurry." He hung up. Well, *that* was odd. Extremely odd, actually. Why was Oliver, of all people, hanging out in the garage, waiting for her report? Not that it was any weirder than many things going on today. Or actually, ever.

She made it to the hub room, where Eve usually kept the coffee going, without incident. Eve and Michael were nowhere to be seen, and she hoped they'd found some privacy of their own by now. They needed it. Michael had been trying to put on a good face, but it had been pretty clear how much he worried about Eve, and how much he wanted things to work. At least, it had been clear to Claire.

Maybe not so much to Eve.

There were lots of strange vampires around, but they ignored her, hustling to do their own business. Humans were no longer important, she thought; now that the vampires could fight the draug with an edge, the last thing they wanted was their blood bank underfoot. It was all business now.

She liked being ignored.

"Hey," said a quiet voice from behind her. She turned and saw a door open just a crack, and through it peered a slice of a narrow face. Someone shorter than she was, and probably not a vamp. "Don't go, Claire."

The door opened wider, and Claire saw that it was, of all people, Miranda—Morganville's town psychic/lost girl. If she had any real family, Claire had never met them; most often, the girl looked as if she'd dressed out of one of those donated clothing bins, and she never quite looked . . . *there.* Until suddenly she focused on you. Then things really got interesting. Claire hadn't been a true believer in psychic predictions when she'd come to Morganville—she was too scientific for that. But a few encounters with Miranda, and she was prepared to at least entertain the idea of some very esoteric physics that nobody could quite explain yet.

"Don't go where, Mir? And what are *you* doing here? I thought you left town!"

"I tried, but I couldn't go," Miranda said, and swung the door all the way open. It was a storeroom of some kind, piled with boxes. "I've been hiding in here."

"You don't need to do that. We'd let you stay with us . . ."

"That's not a good idea," she said, with confidence that was far too firm for her age. "You know that things happen when I'm around. I try to stay on my own as much as I can."

"Miranda—"

"I only wanted to tell you not to go. That's all." Her blue eyes studied Claire with eerie focus. There was something sad about the girl's expression that didn't make Claire feel any better. "You should go back to Shane. He's okay now. I don't think he's going to be all crazy anymore."

"Was he going crazy?" Claire asked.

Miranda shrugged. "Maybe," she said. "It's not exactly easy to tell with him. I think that's because I don't understand boys very well." She said that with utter seriousness, and Claire had to fight not to laugh.

"Who does? Anyway. Where is it I'm not supposed to go?" Because Miranda's warnings, while usually on the nose, rarely occurred in a logical fashion. It was always beforehand, but how *long* before it would happen was an open question. Once Claire had tried graphing the intervals. It was as random as the value of pi, and made her head hurt in Myrnin-like ways.

"Home," Miranda said immediately. "Don't go home."

"I'm not likely to be going home before the situation outside gets better," Claire said gently. "So it's probably not an issue, right?"

"Maybe," Miranda agreed, but she still looked troubled. "I just—it keeps moving. I don't understand. Maybe you should just stay here with me and not go anywhere. It might be safer here."

"I can't stay here, sweetie. Listen, do you have any food? Water?"

"I took some from the other closets. Power bars and water and those energy drink things. Do you ever read the labels? It's a little scary. And they don't taste very good. Next time Eve makes cookies I'll get some." Claire couldn't tell if that was a promise or a prediction. She decided to let it go.

"Mir, thank you, but I really need to go now. Are you going to be okay here?"

"Here?" Miranda nodded. "I'll be okay *here*. But you really shouldn't go home."

"I won't," Claire promised. "Not soon."

"Don't tell anybody I'm here."

"I won't," she repeated, and backed out the door. "Stay safe."

Miranda caught the closing door and locked gazes with her. "I mean it," she said. "Claire, *don't go home. Bad things happen if you go home.*"

That sent a little shiver over the back of Claire's neck. "Promise," she said. "Not going home."

Miranda nodded and closed the door, then locked it.

That is one screwed-up kid, Claire thought, though Miranda wasn't a child anymore, not really. Maybe she had never been. But she was more than fifteen now, probably sixteen—the age Claire herself had been when she'd arrived in Morganville. Wow. It didn't seem so long ago, but at the same time, it seemed like ... forever. Like there was no world out there beyond the borders of the town.

One day, I'll get out of here, she thought. *I can leave anytime I want.*

That sounded uncomfortably like what addicts told themselves, now that she thought about it.

The ride down in the elevator was uneventful, but when she stepped off, she didn't see Myrnin, or Oliver, or ... well, anyone. Not right off.

Then she saw a Myrnin-shaped shadow over on the left side of the garage, standing next to a Morganville police cruiser. He was talking to someone.

Claire walked over, and Myrnin spun in place toward her. "Ah!" he said. "You're here. Good." He had that manic, frantic edge to him this time; she always dreaded when that happened. It made her very tired, and it was bound to be a sackful of crazy, whatever he wanted.

"Where's Oliver?" Claire asked. Because he wasn't here, although this had allegedly been all about the scary boss man. Hannah Moses was, standing next to the driver's side door of the cruiser; she looked ... *remote* was probably the best way to describe it. Closed off. "Don't tell me he left. I didn't take *that* long."

"Yes, yes, Oliver," Myrnin said. He seemed nervous to her. Oddly off balance, whereas Hannah just seemed—cold. Nobody was acting quite like they ought to, and for some reason, it rang an alarm bell, deep inside. "Oliver is over here. Come, he's right over here."

Claire took a step back instead of toward him.

She was too late.

Myrnin lunged forward, grabbed her with one hand over her mouth to trap her scream of surprise and the other around her waist to lift her, kicking, off the ground. "Shhh," he whispered. "Claire, don't. I promise, this is necessary. Trust me. Please."

Hannah was opening the back of the cruiser. "In there," Claire heard her say, over her own muffled shrieks. Myrnin slid in with her, keeping a tight hold so she couldn't scream or struggle much. Panic was racing through her veins now, because this was *wrong.* Myrnin—there was a lot of crazy in Myrnin, but violence? Abduction? Not right. Not right at all.

And Hannah? Why was *Hannah* helping? Claire trusted her, absolutely trusted her. This . . . shook the world right out from under her feet.

Hannah slammed the back door and got in the front. "Keep her quiet," she said. "I need to get us past the front lines. Once we're out of here, it won't matter."

"I don't prefer to do it this way," Myrnin said. "I can make her understand. Truly."

"In time, maybe, but we're committed now. We don't have time to sort out her questions. Oliver has the timeline?"

"Yes," Myrnin said. "And I suppose you're right. We can't wait." He looked down at Claire, who was staring up at him with horror and betrayal. And trying desperately to bite his hand. "I'm sorry, my dear. Just . . . relax."

She didn't. Couldn't. She fought and fought, kicked the seats, shrieked, scratched, until finally, with a growl of frustration, Myrnin put his fingers to the side of her neck and pressed.

And she . . .

. . . Went dark.

CHAPTER EIGHTEEN

OLIVER

I had been waiting for this moment, and finally it had come. Our enemies, vulnerable. Our future, finally visible, if only we could reach out and take it. On that far horizon was freedom from the fear vampires had carried in their bones since before I'd been made immortal.

Freedom to rule unchallenged, again.

Whatever magic Myrnin had worked, there was no doubt that if he said such drab stuff as this powder would work against the draug, it *would* work; he was insane, and of doubtful loyalty to me, but on one front he had always been unshakable, and that was his commitment to destroying our enemies. Even when it had been advisable to run, perhaps necessary, he had been one to argue for the fight.

We had that in common, unlikely as it seemed.

His message over the radio had been simple: *The powder in the drum in the lab will kill the draug. You will find them at the locations marked on the map. Dispatch your teams. Destroy them all.* Myrnin was capable of surprising ruthlessness when pushed. We had that in common, too.

But it was the other part of the message that had startled me. Myrnin had, I realized, known all along how this would end. It was a measure of him that he had not given me any indication of that—or, as far as I understood it, *anyone.* Not even his pet, Claire.

No. *Surprising* did not, in fact, quite cover things, I found. *Shocking* might come close.

Before following his instructions, however, I had a problem to address. Amelie's sister was a danger to her rule and a potential usurper, but by definition that made her a competent enough leader, and I needed all our resources now. I had the guards summon her as I put on my battle clothing; I missed armor, but it had never done us any good against the draug. It had only weighed us down, and that was never an advantage when fighting something that thrived in water. Leathers would do.

Naomi must have thought the same, because when she appeared in the anteroom of the Founder's apartments, she, too, had donned thick leathers. The black made her stark as bone by contrast, a pale, sharp face and blond hair pulled back in a simple style for battle. She looked a great deal like Amelie—but there was no tug of connection between us at all. She eyed me coldly and said, "I will not be summoned like a servant by you, Oliver. This had best be important."

"I have need of your skills," I said. "You heard the call to battle, I assume."

"Of course."

"Then I need not tell you that this is the time to strike, hard and fast." I smiled thinly, allowing my fangs to show. She responded with the same, measure for measure. "I shall entrust you with command of this mission."

That set her back a step. "*Me?* You won't be leading it?"

"No," I said. "I have another duty to perform. A more difficult one."

She understood, then, or thought she did, and bent her head to me, just a little. "You have my respect, Oliver. And my sympathy. It is a terrible thing to do."

At that point Theo stepped out of the shadows near the door. "You seemed ready enough," he observed. When she sent him a murdering look, he shrugged. "I told you I don't play politics. I don't. But you, my dear, stabbed me in the back. Quite literally."

"I wanted to spare my sister the agony to come," she said. "As you do now, Oliver. I think we understand each other well enough. Whatever this heretic liar has said . . ."

"We are all heretics together, now," I said. "Theo's beliefs are between him and God above."

She laughed at that and crossed her arms. "Quite a change from *you*, the warrior of God."

She was right. I had changed. Vampirism does that—carves away all the arrogance of your place in the world and forces you to accept new, starker realities. It builds a far different kind of arrogance, which both Naomi and I had in full, violent, dark portions.

"I task you with the attack, Naomi, but be certain you understand: you are not Amelie, nor will you ever be Amelie. You will not rule Morganville, now or ever, while I survive. I am her successor. Not you. We can dance around it until you try to stick your stake into *my* back, but I can promise you, I won't be as forgiving or as just as Dr. Goldman. Are we clearly understood?"

That earned me a full, cool stare. Full of steel, this one, underneath all the fine manners and kind graces. I wondered if the humans who liked her really understood her depths. Likely not. Amelie had been the same, capable of things no one would have ever guessed, and she had possessed more of a human conscience than Naomi ever had. There were many bodies in this one's past, and that was well before she'd taken the path of immortality.

Politics was a game of murder, and always had been.

That was why she believed me now. And why she bent her head, very slightly this time, to acknowledge my sovereignty. For now. She knew it was not the time to challenge me.

But the time would never come. Not for her.

I accompanied her out into the area where the vampires were gathering. Eve and Michael were there, parsing out bags from the ridiculous barrel that—so Myrnin said—held the final victory of the vampire nation; I supposed I should not feel so disappointed that the fight would not be won with steel and silver, but with something so . . . humanly mundane. It was not my affair any longer. Naomi quickly took charge, once I showed the flag and acknowledged that I made her commander; she tried to appropriate Michael and shut out Eve, a tactic I knew to be doomed from the start. I didn't bother to enlighten her.

"But there is no place for a human in this fight!" Naomi said, trying for her usual innocent charm. "Michael, you must understand that I am only trying keep her from danger. There will be no mortals at risk in this fight."

"I'm not leaving him," Eve said. "You take him, you take me. Or you leave us both. We're a package deal."

"But—"

"No," he said, and stared Naomi down. "We stay together. Eve's told me about your little plots. You don't get to have either of our backs." He looked past Naomi to me. "You can punish me if you want, but I don't trust her. Not with Eve."

The boy was right. He had matured considerably, I thought, from the unsure, tragically trusting young man I had so nearly murdered on my first night in Morganville. I'd meant to turn him, make him one of my vassals, but instead the outcome had been ... less ideal. He had not fully trusted me since, of course. I couldn't blame him for that.

It was a little amusing that he trusted Naomi *less.*

"Remain here," I told him. "You won't be needed in this, in any case. Not if this chemical Myrnin so loves is truly effective."

"Oh, it is," Michael said. "I've seen it."

"Then you won't require his assistance," I told Naomi.

"I thought you said I was to lead this attack."

"You are," I said. "*Delegated* to lead. Don't confuse it with commanding." I nodded to Michael and Eve, who nodded back and kept filling plastic bags with the chemical to hand to my ... what were they to me, precisely? Vassals? No, they owed their allegiance, such as it was, to Amelie. Kinsmen? Some I might claim, but no.

They were my army, though. *Mine.* And a fierce and angry one that had finally seen the chance to strike back at an enemy that had haunted us since the earliest memories of vampires.

I did not see them off on their mission. There was no need; Naomi would not thank me for taking the focus from her moment of glory, and there was nothing I could add. Michael and Eve would stay or not, as they pleased; I had given them my blessing to do so. There was no sign of Shane, which was a very good thing. I did not need the complication of his involvement just now.

I returned to Amelie's apartments, now unguarded; her loyal men and women had gone to fight the draug, of course. I opened the door to her bedroom and stopped there, because the sight was . . . grim.

Amelie was hardly recognizable now. Still fighting, because there was still a human form to be seen beneath that . . . growth, but she was losing, slowly and grimly. I pulled the soft silk comforter from beneath her to wrap around her body. I needed the full thickness to cover her. Once I had cocooned her so, I tied it off with ripped curtain cords, and took her slight weight over my shoulder. The smell of the draug settled around me, rotting fish and flesh, and I fought the urge to gag. *She is not one of them. Not yet.* I stopped breathing. A convenience of vampire physiology, but not always effective; our senses are too acute.

Smells pervade.

Amelie didn't move. She could well have been an inconvenient corpse I was removing for disposal; that would not be unique in my lifetime, either in my human days or in my new life. She felt heavier than she should have, but that might have been the burden of what I was about to do. I did not waste time; I was well aware there was little left. I carried her through the halls, now mostly deserted. I heard a buzz of human conversation from one room, and identified voices I knew. The Morrell girl, mourning her lost brother; she was right to do so, because he would be a grave loss to the town. A smart, fair man, unlikely as one was to arise from such low beginnings. The girl had no such . . . quality.

I could sense that only humans were left in the building now, save for Michael. It allowed me to easily avoid them all.

My car was parked below, silently waiting, and I put Amelie in the trunk, not so much for her protection as for mine, should she finish her transformation before I was ready. Driving out into the cloudy night, I saw signs everywhere of decay and destruction. The draug accelerated such things, turning creaking structures in need of paint and repair into crumbling, sagging ruins. They would destroy Morganville and rot it into the desert in a few months if left unchecked.

There were more than a few humans remaining in town; some had come against us in force a few nights ago, hoping to wrest control from the vampires. Those had scuttled back to their hiding places to await the end, whatever it might be, of our fight. I did not blame them. When giants fought, ants were crushed.

I navigated the streets without encountering a single draug, though I sensed their heavy presence. The lack of singing from them was an important and blissful indication of their wariness, their fear. *Yes,* I thought. *You are right to be afraid. This time, we will end you.* I imagined Magnus had felt the same exultation in discovering Morganville, the last bolt-hole of a doomed species. He'd gloried in the chance to finally, completely, eradicate us, even if it meant the end of his own—or would it? Without vampires to destroy, the draug would turn more toward less nutritious but more plentiful prey. Shane's captivity was proof enough of that. They could make do with humans.

In a way, as we saved ourselves, we saved those who served us as well.

I parked at the mouth of the darkened alley, opened the car door and checked around the area. There were shadows, ominous ones, but those were quite normal for this place. No sign or smell of the draug, save what was coming from the trunk. I reeked of it myself, I realized. A filthy business, and heartrending.

I carried Amelie down the narrowing alleyway to the shack set at the end of it. Myrnin's hovel, which contained only a stairway leading down to his laboratory and nothing else but the flickering glances and scuttles of nighttime lower-form intruders. It was dark there, all lights extinguished, but as I descended lamps flickered on in response to the motion. Claire's improvement, I should imagine. Myrnin would hardly have cared much.

The lab was a shambles, but that also was normal; Myrnin was, to put it mildly, not concerned with appearances. The girl had made attempts to clear it, but they never lasted long. I navigated around broken glassware, fallen chairs, scattered loose books and papers, and stopped in front of a large, locked cabinet marked DANGER, with many different dire-looking symbols and icons stickered on the face of it.

As I reached out for it, I felt a flicker of energy behind me, and glanced back to see a shape forming in mist and static. Not the draug.

Myrnin's creation.

It was unnatural, this thing, this *apparition*; he had used the brain of a vampire to power it, and the spirit of the man remained. A reluctant vampire, to be sure; Bishop's little joke, making our bitterest enemy into one of our own. Punishment for both the father and the son. I wondered how Shane Collins felt, knowing his father survived—if it could be called that—in this pathetic, impotent form.

Frank Collins was an image, nothing more. He existed as flat as a photograph, and with about as much power. He was indefinably degraded since last I'd seen him; then, he'd worn a certain cockiness, but now he seemed . . . faded. And old. The power in the lab flickered unsteadily, and so did his image.

He said nothing to me, and I said nothing to him. There was no point in bantering with the dead.

As I rolled the cabinet aside on its concealed track, he finally spoke up. "Is my son still alive?" he asked.

"I am much surprised you care," I responded. "But yes, so far as I am aware."

"Tell him——" Frank hesitated, and I had the curious sense that he was struggling to remember how to form words. "Tell him I said I was sorry."

"I doubt that will matter very much," I said, "given your history together. But if I survive the day, I will do so."

"I'm dying," he said. "My brain, I mean. The power keeps going out. Maybe that's . . . that's good."

"Maybe it is," I said. I was not without sympathy, but I chose where to give it, and Frank Collins was not my choice. I opened the door to the portal that led from Myrnin's lab, and beyond it was thick, black, empty space. "Are the portals still functioning?"

"I don't know," he said. "Sometimes. Yes. Maybe. I don't know . . ." And his image flickered and faded, and didn't return.

Not reassuring, perhaps. The portals were Myrnin's creation as well—magical doorways (though he assured me they were based on his blend of alchemy and science) that tunnel through space, linking places together as if adjacent rooms in a single house. One could cross town in only a few moments, theoretically, if one knew the secrets of the portals and their locations. I knew a few. Myrnin never shared the full extent of his invention with anyone save Amelie.

I faced the portal and concentrated hard. There was a whisper of color through the dark, dim but definite. I traced the outlines of the place I wished to see in my mind—the brightly colored stained-glass lamps, the red velvet sofa with its lion's-head arms, the thick, dusty carpeting. There was a small Monet painting that Amelie had favored, hanging just there . . .

I felt another force suddenly add itself to mine in one intense surge, and color exploded out of the dark, showing me the room in shining, perfect focus.

No time.

I plunged through, into freezing cold, then heat, and then I was stepping/falling through the dark and into the light.

The portal snapped shut behind me with an almost metallic shriek, and I sensed that it wouldn't be opening again, not without repairs. Morganville was shattering all around us. Soon there'd be nothing left to save.

That power. It hadn't been Frank; he'd had little or nothing left to give. No, this had been power with a familiar sort of feel. Amelie was, at least on some level, still awake. Aware.

Alive.

Perhaps because of this place. This room, this house, still held a sense of eternity, peace, and a measure of her own power. Here, of all places, Amelie could find strength. In many ways, the Glass House was the unbeating heart of the town—the first of her Founder Houses to be completed, the first of her homes. When the structure had been built, it had been the first of thirteen identical buildings, all linked, connected, strengthened by blood and bone and magic and science.

Here, in this place of power, I hoped she could maintain a little longer. And if not . . . it was a fitting place for it to end.

I put her down as gently as possible on the red velvet sofa, and unwrapped the silken covers from around her body. They pulled away wet and sticky, and beneath she was a melting wax sculpture with pale, blind eyes.

I left the hidden attic room and went to the second floor. The young people who lived here—Claire, Eve, Michael, Shane—were indifferent housekeepers, but the bathroom held clean towels. No water, of course, but in the kitchen I found a sealed, safe bottle of water, and a not-yet-curdled supply of blood that

Michael Glass must have stored against emergencies. Prudent. I would have stored more than that, but I am by nature cautious and paranoid.

The house had a curiously empty feel. I had been here many times, but always there had been a sense of *presence* to it, of something living within it that was not just the occupants, but the spirit of the house itself. Myrnin's creations had odd effects, and the oddest had been the awakening of these immobile, unliving buildings made of brick, wood, mortar, and nails. But the spirit that had dwelt here seemed as dead as Morganville itself.

When I knelt beside Amelie with the dampened towel and began to sponge her face clean, her eyes suddenly shifted to fix on me. For the first time in hours, I saw a spark of recognition in them. She didn't move otherwise; I continued my work, wiping the damp residue of the draug from her pale cheeks, her parted lips.

Her hand moved in a flash, and caught my wrist to hold it in an iron grip.

"I can't," she whispered. "I can't hold, Oliver. You know what to do. You can't allow me to lose myself. Naomi was right. Unkind, but right."

"We still have time," I told her, and put my other hand over hers—not to pull it free, but to hold it close, even if it hurt me. "If Magnus can be killed, this will stop. It will all stop." Because that was the secret of the draug, the one that Magnus had sought to keep so close. That was why he had targeted Claire, who could see through his disguises and defenses. He was the most powerful of the draug, and the most vulnerable. Kill him, and his vassals died. They were nothing but reflections, shells, drones serving a hive.

But Amelie was shaking her head, just a little. As much as she could. "The master draug *cannot* be killed. Not by steel or silver,

bullets or blades. The most we can do is force him to flee and re-
group. You *must* kill me before the transformation is complete, do
you understand? I thought perhaps, this time—but we are not so
lucky, you and I." Her smile was terrible, but beneath the alien
taking her body, I could still see the ghost of Amelie. She had been
my bitter enemy, my gadfly, my bane—we had hundreds of years
of bile and ambition between us, but here, at the end, I saw her for
what she was: a queen, as she had always been. In my mortal life I
had brought down kings, laid low monarchs, but never her. There
was something in her stronger than my ambition. "Do me the
kindness, my old enemy. It's fitting."

"In a while," I promised her. "Bide with me."

"I will," she said, and closed her eyes. This time, the smile was
utterly her own. "I will try."

CHAPTER NINETEEN

NAOMI

☽

Finally, *finally*, I was taking my rightful place. Thirty vampires, all at my unquestioned command. It rankled me that Oliver had been the one to grant it to me, but I would see to him soon enough. I was royalty. He was nothing but a jumped-up king-killer and fanatic who'd once stolen a throne, and there would be a reckoning. It had been foolish of him to give me his vassals to command.

I would use them to do more than finish the draug. I would do it for my sister's sake. Amelie was queen, true, but when a queen can no longer rule, her heir must act, swiftly, to ensure that no chaos erupts.

I was the heir. *Not* Oliver.

The only vehicle large enough to carry us all was a yellow-painted bus; it stank of human children, and other less pleasant things, and I ordered the windows put down. The clouds were rolling away on the winds, leaving the skies over Morganville finally clear and ice-cold, with stars glittering in spills of diamond. So many stars here. My sister had chosen her defensive ground well, and if the weapon Oliver had given us worked as he claimed, this would be the final, triumphant victory.

And I would lead it.

I was already planning for what would occur after this battle. First, I would ensure that Amelie did not rise a draug; next, I would bind her people close to me by right of blood. Oliver could be exiled, or dispatched if he refused to go. And Morganville, such kingdom as it was, would be mine. Once the draug were finished, we would rebuild this town in the right and proper way . . . and the nonsense that Amelie had allowed, this equality between humans and vampires, that would stop.

It would stop with her niais, Michael. As her direct blood descendent, he would have to set an example for the others. I would ask him to put aside his human girl and behave as a vampire ought; this confusion of servants and masters was maddening. Courtesy toward them was proper, to be sure, and if he chose to keep her as a personal sort of pet, I could look the other way. But marriage was an alliance by law and custom that could not be allowed.

It gave the humans incontestable rights.

"My lady," said one of Amelie's favorites, bowing to me as he stood in the aisle next to my seat. He had adopted modern dress, but I remembered him in armor, from earlier times. A good man. Good warrior.

"Your name is Rickon," I said. "I remember you."

"You have a long memory, lady. Rickon it is." He watched me with pale green eyes that were a little too sly, a bit too knowing. How *well* had I known him? Out of so many ages, it was difficult to remember. I scarce knew how Amelie kept such things straight. She even remembered the names of humans. I'd had to memorize the three she allowed to live as company for Michael, and that had been a struggle. "We're approaching the treatment plant. The other bus signals that they have arrived at the university and are prepared to work their way through to the edge of town."

"Then it begins." I gave him a warm smile. "Do well, today, Lord Rickon, and there will be rewards. Significant ones."

He lifted an eyebrow and said, "I am no lord now, my lady. Only a shopkeeper, and a happy one. And I require no rewards; this is my home. I don't take pay to defend my own land."

I had mistaken him. He was, it seemed, one of those sad vampires who had believed Amelie's strange philosophy that required us to give up our rights to status, and become . . . ordinary. Well, I was not ordinary. I'd not allow her to make me into some . . . *shopkeeper*. Lords and ladies we were, and would remain.

I gave him a nod, as if I agreed with him, and he withdrew without another word. At least the man was capable of a proper exit, with a deep bow from the waist before turning his back. Manners had not faded quite so far among the old ones.

The gravekeeper, Ransom, sat behind me in the bus. He was a dusty old thing, ancient in appearance; I had always wondered why anyone had bothered to make him vampire. It hardly seemed worth the trouble. Turning someone so old was useful only when they had considerable gifts; this one hardly seemed to remember his own name most days, though he was, I will admit, fully capable of fast action when needed. I glanced at him, and he nodded and gave me a smile, and vampire or not, royal or not, I shivered. Some of Amelie's followers were . . . unpleasant.

"Highness," murmured my next visitor, the tall Pennyfeather—one of Oliver's favorites, another fanatic who had, in breathing days, administered tortures for the church. I did not trust him, but he had a useful streak of coldness, and proper respect. He bowed over my hand without being so vulgar as to brush his lips over it. "When this is over, I will be happy to follow you wherever you may lead."

I accepted him with a regal nod and smile. We were understood, the two of us. And there were more here, dissatisfied with the disorderly state of Morganville, who would gladly follow a banner when I raised it. Even Ransom might, though Lord Rickon was, I feared, a lost cause.

I felt the speed of the bus slow, and then stop. We were here. It was my moment, *mine*, to draw their love and loyalty, and I stood and made myself the queen I knew I was.

Ransom shoved past me as I drew breath to speak. "We know what to do," he said. "Get out of the way, girl."

The green-eyed shopkeeper smirked as he followed Ransom. Others fell in behind him, ignoring me. Rejecting me.

Pennyfeather said, "Ignore the rude peasants, Highness. Once you have won the day, they will fall in." He had a soothing tone to his whisper, and I allowed it to calm my rage. I would use it against the draug.

For now.

Instead of being in the vanguard, I was solidly in the middle of the group who descended from the bus. I was forced to fight my way through to the front, where I *finally* took command. "You've all been armed with this," I said, holding up the bag of powder. "I have been told that the draug cannot resist it. You must be prepared for anything; each of you has been armed with silver as well, but be cautious in its use—"

Someone made a muttered comment, a rude one, and I fixed him with a stare. It didn't seem to have the same effect that my sister's stare would have. "Pennyfeather will lead one team. I will lead another. We approach from either end. The draug cannot sing; do not let them touch you if you can avoid it. Use the chemical powder on the pools. Do not waste it."

More muttering, and one isolated, quiet laugh, but I ignored it, for all the fury it ignited inside me. I *would* rule these people. It was my right by blood and history. Surely Amelie would agree it was so, if she was able.

I led my force into the complex.

None of us breathed, and for that I was profoundly thankful; this was a foul place, even without the threat of the draug. Full of shadows, but that mattered little to our eyes. All was still, quiet, watchful within.

When the draug came for us, they came in a rush, and the battle was on.

I slashed my way through their assault, using silver where it was necessary; a few vampires were overcome and dragged into the pools, but by then Pennyfeather had reached their watery sanctuaries, and I heard the eerie, piercing screech of terror as he dumped his chemicals in. I began the same on my end, dumping my bag of powder into the murky, dark waters, and I watched black threads spread fast and toxic through their blood garden. There were vampires in there, anchored fast; as the draug died, I shouted at others to enter the waters and retrieve the victims. We saved most.

And the draug died. They died hard, and they died fighting, struggling to pull us into their own realm, but we poisoned that home against them, down to the last refuge. Those who emerged we killed with silver.

It was an unqualified triumph. We saved almost twenty vampires from their horrible fate, but most important, my command, my *battle* had been won, and I would return covered in glory.

No one would question my right to rule after this, after Oliver had abandoned his duties and left it to me to wage this war—and I had succeeded.

"We've won," I said. I was already thinking of the future, of my rule. Though I greatly preferred the company of women, I would deign to take Michael Glass as consort, I decided; he was young, but he came of pure bloodlines and would satisfy those who wished a token thrown to our human servants. As to his human girl . . . Well, if he would not give her up, it would be simple enough to get rid of her.

"No," Rickon said. "There's no sign of the master draug. Unless he's put down, there is no victory."

"Surely we've killed him in the pools," I said. "There's no question."

He gave me a cold, impudent look from those green eyes. "We must have proof."

"*My queen*," I told him, and showed my fangs. "I would prefer if you gave me my title, Lord Rickon."

He ignored me. *Ignored me.* He turned away to deal with one of the last of the draug.

I found the very last of them, clinging to its filthy life, crouching in the shadows. I flung a bit of the magic powder over it, and watched as its legs turned black, solid, rotten. It was dying before my eyes. "Magnus," I said. "Where is Magnus? Tell me!"

"Not here," it whispered, and it *laughed* at me.

I needed to kill *Magnus.* Once I had done that, there would be no question of my superiority, my rights. Magnus was *mine.*

Pennyfeather was standing behind me; I sensed his cold, angular presence. Oliver's man, but mine now. He knew which knee to bend, and when. "Send out search parties," I commanded without turning from the sight of the last of the thralls dying. "Find

Magnus at any cost, and bring him to me. And Oliver. I will require his head, of course. We must settle the question of who rules immediately."

Pennyfeather didn't move.

I became aware of a great stillness around me. The shrieking was done, the draug finished here, and the vampires, *my* vampires, were watching me.

Like Pennyfeather, unmoving.

"You heard me," I said, and whirled on Pennyfeather . . .

. . . Just as he buried his slender silver knife in my heart.

I grabbed for it, wrapping my cold hands over his, and saw nothing in his face but my own death. "No," I whispered. "No, I am your queen——"

"You'll never rule here," he said. "You should have remembered that."

The silver coursed through my body, poisoning me. He left the dagger in me. It paralyzed me, and I could only watch as the vampires of Morganville left this place, and left me to die among the blackened corpses of our greatest enemies.

Not over, I thought. I wanted to shriek it at him, at all of them. *This is not over!*

But all I could do was watch them go. Amelie's creatures. Oliver's. Never mine.

I will have you, I promised them, in a burst of terror and fury. *You should have made sure of me, Pennyfeather.*

Because I would find a way to survive. To take this town, and our future, from them.

Somehow.

The draug I had poisoned was still alive, though blackened and crippled. Dying fast now. But it dragged itself to me and stared down into my open eyes.

And it pulled the silver dagger out of my heart.

For a long moment, I still was unable to move; the silver had weakened me, blackened me within. The draug dropped the dagger.

"Why?" I asked it.

And Magnus's voice answered me, echoing through his own creature. "Waste not," he said, "want not."

And then he laughed, and the draug finished dying.

I retched up silver and stumbled to hands and knees, then upright.

The war was still on.

Magnus first.

But after that, those who'd betrayed me.

Amelie, my sister. And Oliver, whose creature Pennyfeather was.

Mine.

CHAPTER TWENTY

EVE

I stood on the sidelines, with Michael, and watched the vampires go to war.

It wasn't much of a seeing-off parade, really . . . just the two of us, standing together, holding hands. But I'd always thought of myself as the cocky sidekick type, and cocky sidekicks don't have to go to war, right? They get to cheer from the sidelines and . . . be cocky.

I didn't feel particularly cocky anymore. I felt terrified, and even with Michael holding my hand, I'd never been more aware of how much was at stake, how much was bound to go wrong. "What if it doesn't work?" I asked him. "What if—what if none of them come back?" I could just see the nightmare of being trapped in Zombieland Morganville, the draug haunting every source of water we had.

"Then we grab everybody who's left, steal a school bus, and head out," Michael said. "I don't like running, but sometimes it's about all you can do."

School buses. The last time I'd sat on these cold green fake-leather seats, I'd been the outcast praying for graduation and Michael had been in the back with the cool kids. He'd always been able to move between cliques—hottie, music nerd, closet *Star Trek* enthusiast. Fitting in was his superpower, and my deadly weakness. "Speaking of school buses, remember when Jamie Montgomery punched out what's-her-name, the red-head . . . ?"

"Carly," I said. "Carly Fox."

"Carly the Fox, right. I think she broke her nose."

"Good times." I remembered it vividly; it was one of the high-lights of senior year, a hair-pulling, full-on hot girl catfight. Carly's nose had never been the same. Neither had Jamie Montgomery, because she'd disappeared without a trace about two weeks later—escaped from town, rumor said, but I knew most of those rumors were bull. She'd probably gotten drained by Carly's vamp Protector out of sheer annoyance that he had to mediate high school girls. These things happened. "Hey, whatever happened to Jamie, anyway?" Because Michael was on the other side now. He'd know.

"She left town," Michael said.

"Is that code for . . ." I mimed fangs in the neck. He raised his eyebrows and said nothing. So that was a yes, then. "Damn."

"You already knew."

I had, kinda. But still. Thinking back on our class, I wondered how many of them had survived; most, sure, but a few would have fallen off the radar, gotten bitten, tried to run, or just had the pro-verbial fatal accident. Morganville's rate of missing was pretty high, and most of them weren't missing at all.

"So," I said, and turned to Michael. "Enough reminiscing. I guess it's just us around here."

"Private," he replied.

"As much as we ever get. And . . . there's not a lot to do right now."

"No." He was playing along with me, waiting for me to get to the point.

So I did. "We need to talk about things."

That was *not* where he had expected the next turn to go. I knew that, but it was his fault for letting me drive the metaphorical conversation bus. But to his credit, I caught only a small flash of impatience and disappointment, quickly submerged. "Okay," he said. Not as if he really wanted to have the heart-to-not-beating-heart, but as if he knew there was no getting around it. "You want to do it here?"

I shrugged. "Shane's in our room with Claire, I think. They've been tense since he got back. Better let them have some time." I led Michael over to a set of chairs and pulled two of them together.

And then I felt oddly weird about starting the conversation. There had been a moment, when I'd run away from Naomi and into his arms, when all that had happened between us had vanished, but now . . . now here it was again, big and bad and getting bigger with every moment we didn't deal with it. Or rather, *I* didn't. He was trying.

So I looked up and said what was in my heart. "I love you."

He met my eyes squarely, and my God, he was beautiful. It always surprised me, a bit, how everything just *worked* with him— his eyes, and his hair, and his cheekbones, and his mouth, and . . . everything. Living art, so gorgeous that sometimes, like now, it hurt. But if his looks burned a little, the expression on his face soothed it; he was intent on me, as if I was the only thing in the world. Nothing in his eyes but open, honest feeling.

"I love you, too," he said. "What are we going to do about this?"

"I don't know," I admitted. "I thought I did, but . . . it's a little like being in a relationship with Superman. You sometimes don't know your own strength."

He smiled, and it made his dimples come out. "I think I'm more Batman," he said. "You know, what with all the bats and nighttime activities. And Batman is much cooler."

"Geek."

His smile widened. "You say the nicest things. Haven't you heard? Geeks run the world now."

"Yeah, what Goths allow them to run." This felt so good . . . so much like the old days, when we were friends, and before everything got so complicated. So dangerous. "You're avoiding the conversation."

He looked down at his hands, then back up as if willing himself to do it. "Yeah, I guess I am. I hurt you. I could do it again, if the conditions were right; I don't really know *what* could trigger me to do it, Eve. Wish to hell I did. I just . . . lost myself. And I can't promise you it won't happen again." There was something tentative about the way he was watching me now. Afraid, I realized. Afraid I was going to reject him, and knowing it would hurt, but just . . . holding still for it all the same.

"That makes jumping into getting married sound a little crazy," I said. "Doesn't it?"

He nodded. This time, when he looked down, he didn't try to meet my eyes again.

"Michael."

"I'm sorry," he said. It came out half a whisper, and a little unsteady. "It's not your fault, it's mine . . ."

"*Michael.* Look at me." He did, finally, bracing himself for impact. "I said getting married sounds crazy. I do crazy for a living."

For a blank few seconds, he didn't seem to understand me; I think he must have run that through his head at high speed a dozen times before he finally got the translation. "You mean you're okay. We're okay."

"Yes, Michael, you fool, we're very okay. But what I said before still stands. You'd better not think of me as a victim, even if something does happen. I'm no weak little flower, and if I need to defend myself, I will. Just—try not to make that happen. I really don't want to have to hurt you. Okay?"

His smile was bright and sweet and hot enough to melt solid steel. "Is this the part where I kiss you?"

"If you like."

"Oh," he said, "I like." And he leaned forward, gripping the arms of my chair, and slowly, slowly, sweetly brought that mouth to me. It was a long, lovely kiss, the kind that melts your spine and fills you with sunlight and steals your breath away. The kind that, as far as I knew, only Michael Glass could give me, because he knew, he just *knew* that kissing me with those gentle little butterfly-soft presses would make my toes curl, and the way that the teasing sank into something deeper, darker, more intensely *needy.* His tongue stroked my lips, and I let them part, hungry for him, for the taste of him.

I had missed him so, so, so much. Missed this.

Missed *us.*

"Eve?" He kept his lips close, punctuating his words with small little electric brushes of our skin. My own mouth felt swollen, tingling, intensely and darkly *aware.* "I think . . . we should . . . find some . . . privacy. Right now."

I was one hundred and ten percent in favor of this idea. In fact, parts of me were redlining at one-twenty. "Yes, please," I said. I kept my mouth just as close, teasing him right back. "Does this mean we actually have to stop kissing?"

"I'm afraid it might."

"Wait . . . not sure about that, then . . ."

He pulled me up to my feet and put his arms around me, pressed his lips to mine and began guiding me around the chairs. I giggled into his mouth as we bumped awkwardly into walls, tables, a large vase . . . and then suddenly he let go of me and turned away, just as I heard Shane say, "Where's Claire?"

"What?" Michael sounded blank, and just a little bit frustrated. I could understand that, because I was struggling to tamp down the furnace he'd ignited inside me and reconnect with the rest of the world. "What are you talking about? I thought she was with you."

"Was," Shane said. He was pulling a shirt over his head, and looked better and more focused than he had before. I was glad to see that. I'd have just been happier to see it in say, an hour. Or two. "She got a call from Myrnin."

Of course. Nothing strange about that, although I was a little surprised she'd gone. He must have made it seem important. Well, with all that was going on, it probably *was* important. I made sure my clothes were on relatively straight, and stepped out from behind Michael. "I didn't see Myrnin earlier," I said. "Did you?"

Michael shook his head. "He wasn't with Naomi's crew."

"Maybe he's with Oliver, then."

"Oliver wasn't letting anyone near Amelie. No reason to take Claire in there, even if Myrnin got pulled in." Michael bumped fists with Shane. "You look better, man."

"I feel better," Shane said. "Or I would if I could figure out where Batty McCrackula took my girlfriend."

"Oooh, good one. I'm writing that down. Lab?" I suggested. "I mean, the one he set up here?"

The boys thought it was a good idea, too, so we tried it. There was trial and error involved, what with all the hallways and doors; the more rooms we opened, the more it seemed obvious that this place was deserted. We found Theo in the infirmary; he had a couple of human patients in the beds, and his hulking friend Harold as his nurse.

"Myrnin?" Theo repeated when we asked, and straightened up from where he sat staring into a microscope. "I'm afraid he's not been here. I haven't seen him for some time. Have you tried the lab?"

"Can't find it," Shane said. He sounded like he was ready to break something, and I couldn't really blame him.

"Ah. Second hall, turn left, then three doors down on the right. Tell the madman I said hello." Theo went back to his microscope as if it was vitally important, which maybe it was, and Harold waved to Shane. Shane waved back, looking a little confused about it, and we backed out of the mini-hospital and into the hall.

Theo's directions took us straight to Myrnin's makeshift lab, but although it was full of glass and books and tables, there was absolutely no one there.

"Hang on," Michael said, and took out his phone. He dialed, and listened. I watched his expression grow set and a little worried. "She's not answering."

"Try Myrnin," Shane said. He was as tense as a guitar string, and about as likely to break at the wrong pressure. Michael dialed, listened, and shook his head. "I can't help it, I have a bad feeling about this . . ."

"You should."

We all turned, in varying degrees of fast, and I don't know about the guys, but I was really surprised to see my uncomfortable little friend Miranda standing in the lab doorway. She looked as mismatched and odd as ever, and her eyes had that looking-through-us focus that made me shudder.

"What are you talking about?" Shane asked, and walked toward her. He probably didn't mean it to be threatening, but he was agitated, and an agitated Shane was an intimidating thing. Miranda backed up. He stopped and held up both hands in frustrated surrender. "I'm not going to hurt you, kid. Just tell me. Where is Claire?"

"Home," she said. "I told her not to go. *I told her.*" She looked . . . distressed, which was weird to me. I'd seen Miranda go through a car wreck and the loss of a sister without *that* much of a reaction. "It's all going wrong. It wasn't supposed to be like this."

"Mir." I pushed past Shane and took the girl's hand. She was all soft skin over thin bird bones, and I made a mental note to make the poor kid a sandwich sometime; she desperately needed it. "Miranda, you know me, right?"

That knocked her out of the psychic trance state, and she gave me a wary, annoyed look. "Of course," she said. "You're Eve. Why wouldn't I?"

Excellent question, but I let it go. "Take a deep breath and explain what's going on. You're not making any sense."

"It doesn't make any sense. That's what I'm trying to tell you," Miranda shot back, and sighed. "Claire's at the Glass House. And she shouldn't be there. I *told* her that before she went to see Myrnin."

I looked over at Shane. "Did she say anything about—"

"The last thing I knew, she was going to meet Myrnin, but I

don't know where." He was staring at Miranda with a fiercely still expression, as if he was throttling the impulse to shake something out of her. "He must have taken her home is all I can figure. But why would he do that?"

"Murky," Miranda said. "I can't see what's going on. It's scary, Eve. I don't like it. But I know we have to help her. We *have to*." Her hand was shaking, and her small fingers wrapped tight around mine. She lowered her voice to a whisper. "Except if we do, we won't all make it."

I swallowed hard and suppressed the Shane-like impulse to shake her. She was making as much sense as she could, I knew that. The kid was half-autistic, half-psychic; it was a miracle she got out as much as she did. And it always made sense, later. "Who won't make it?"

"Unclear," she said, as if she was one of those Magic 8 Balls I liked so much.

"Screw this," Shane said. "I'm going to get Claire."

"We," Michael said. "We're going to get her."

Miranda nodded. "But there's someone else we need." She pulled free of my grip and darted away, running surprisingly fast; I ran after her, and heard the boys pounding in my wake. The girl ran like she had an absolutely accurate map of where she wanted to go, and I quickly lost count of the turns and blurred doorways until she skidded to a stop in front of one that looked identical to all the others. "It's locked," she said, and looked at Michael. "Break it."

He shrugged and took hold of the knob. It was vampire-reinforced, but he was determined, and a few sharp sideways tugs snapped it off in his hand. He reached into the hole and pulled the metal tongue back, then swung the door open.

Inside, my brother, Jason, was sitting cross-legged on a rumpled bunk in a bright orange prison-style jumpsuit with numbers over where a breast pocket would have been. He looked up, tossed lank hair back from his face, and stared at Michael, then past him at me. "Family reunion," he said. "Cool." He raised one hand, and I saw he was handcuffed to a length of chain that was fastened to the wall—enough slack for him to get to the bathroom, but not much more. "No need to be afraid. I'm safe."

Shane cast a sidelong look at Miranda, and said, "Seriously?"

She nodded. "We need him."

"Okay, then," Michael said. "Just so we're clear, Jason: I love your sister, but that doesn't extend to you. You step out of line, you do anything that isn't in your sister's best interests, and I'll carry out your sentence. We clear?"

"Michael!" I blurted. I wasn't sure what appalled me more—that he was thinking about letting Jason go, or that he was thinking of killing him. Maybe both.

"Clear," Jason said. "Look, man, you let me go and I promise you, I'll do whatever you want. Once that's done, I'm out of Morganville and out of your lives. All right?"

"Deal," Michael said. "I'll be watching you."

For an answer, Jason held up his pinned wrist. Michael took hold of the chain and bent one of the links, and just like that, my brother was . . . free.

"Are you *totally* sure about this?" I asked Miranda under my breath. She nodded placidly. "Because I know him. And he's not—"

"I know," she said. "He's not trustworthy. But that's okay. This time he's what we need."

Jason stood up, moved his arm as if reveling in the freedom, and said, "So, what are we doing?"

"Getting guns," Miranda said. "Lots of guns."

That drew a scary smile from my brother. "I like this plan," he said, and followed Miranda out. Michael went after, dogging him with a worried frown.

I exchanged a look with Shane.

"I know," he said. "We are into the This Is a Bad Idea neighborhood, and heading down I Have a Bad Feeling Street. But either we believe her or we don't. Maybe she's gone completely over the edge. You considered that?"

"I consider it every time I talk to her," I said, "but do you want to risk it? With Claire's life on the line?"

He shook his head. "Let's go," he said. "But keep an eye on your brother."

Both eyes. Absolutely.

CHAPTER TWENTY-ONE

CLAIRE

☽

She had *never* seen it coming.

The first moments of waking up were spent wondering what the hell had happened. She remembered getting the call. Dressing. Going down in the elevator. Meeting Myrnin and Hannah in the garage.

And then ... and then he'd turned on her. Grabbed her. *Abducted her.* She'd fought, too. Fought until he'd put her out.

And now she was here, and her head ached miserably. But where was *here*? And what the hell had *happened*? *Why?*

The next thing that came to her, after the panic, was the realization that she wasn't submerged in water. It wasn't the draug, at least. The relief of that was intense, until she tried to move, and discovered that she was tied to a chair. A heavy one, thick wood, plush fabric. A smell of old dust.

The room was dim, but after a few blinking seconds of confusion she realized that she knew it.

She was *home.* In the Glass House.

Don't go home, Miranda had said. Oh God.

This was the parlor room, the one they rarely used; it was mostly a place to dump backpacks, coats, purses, *stuff* on the way into the living room, where they actually gathered. She tried to remember when she'd been home last. Days blurred together— God, had it only been *yesterday?* No, that had to be wrong. It felt like at least a week. Maybe it was somewhere in the middle.

Her head hurt in pounding waves, but she couldn't feel any bruises. When she tugged at the ropes holding her in the chair, they were firm. Whoever had tied her up had been nice about it; there was soft padding between the ropes and her wrists and ankles.

That consideration didn't make her feel any better about being restrained.

"Easy," said a voice from behind her, and she felt someone tug on the ropes, probably checking the knots. Hannah Moses. She immediately knew it even before Hannah came around to look at her. The police chief looked eerily the same as she always had— competent, calm, a little hard around the edges. But still, always, honest and fair. That was creepy, considering their relative situations. "Easy. I don't want you to hurt yourself. You're fine, Claire. You're perfectly safe."

"Safe?" Claire echoed. "What are you *talking about?* I'm tied up!"

"For your protection," Myrnin said. She hadn't spotted him, but he was standing stock-still next to the front window, looking out through a crack in the blinds. "To keep you out of the way."

"The way of *what?*" she demanded. Myrnin turned and exchanged a look with Hannah, and Claire didn't like that, didn't like it at all. "Where's Shane?"

"Hopefully he is with the others," Myrnin said. "Safety in numbers and all that."

"The others—I have no idea what you are talking about!" She yanked at the ropes, unsuccessfully. "Let me *go!*"

"Where do you think you would go? The vampires' ragtag army is, even now, taking your chemicals to the water treatment plant and the other targets I marked out for Oliver on my map," Myrnin said. "They will almost certainly succeed in their attempts. You and Shane have given us an advantage the draug could not have planned for, and the draug will die, trapped where they are. Those in the clouds cannot stay; their safety there is shrinking and will soon be gone. They will have to fall to earth. The desert will consume what's left."

"Excuse me, but then why am I *tied up?*"

"Because those are the spawn," he said. He still *sounded* like the old Myrnin, the one she mostly trusted, the one who always seemed to have a point, however weird and twisty it might be. "The spawn are nothing, they are the bees industriously gathering pollen for the hive. The queen—king, in this case—is vital to the survival of all. Magnus thought he could hide himself among his spawn, but he cannot. You can see him, whether he chooses it or no. He cannot afford that. Once his spawn are dead, there is nothing left to hide him. So he must count them lost, and find *you*. Kill *you*."

He seemed to think that explained everything. Claire gritted her teeth and forced herself not to scream at him; it wouldn't do any good. Neither Hannah nor Myrnin was looking like they had any doubts about what they were doing. "I don't even know how I do it!"

"Myrnin explained that," Hannah said. "The bracelet Amelie gave you to wear. It's a kind of draug early warning system. It inoculates the wearer to be able to see them clearly. You wore it long enough for the effects to still be in your system. Myrnin's right, Claire. Wherever you've gone since Magnus realized you could see him, he's sent his creepers after you. Or even come himself."

"He must come himself. With his spawn dead, he cannot hide in numbers," Myrnin said. He was speaking to her directly now, and earnestly, as if he really wanted Claire to understand why he was doing all this. "You can see him, and he *cannot* hide. Nor, in Morganville, can he easily flee. This is the first time that we have ever had this advantage over him. We've never been able to destroy his thralls without damage to ourselves; we've never been able to hunt *him*. It equals the contest, you see. He won't have it."

"And *this* is why you tied me up. For *bait?*"

"Well," Myrnin said, very apologetically, "it does keep you in place. I believe he sees you as a genuine threat. He *killed you*, and yet you are here, taking action against him. That makes you very nearly a master draug yourself. I suppose it's a bit of an honor, if you look at it that way."

The urge to scream was coming back, fast. Claire yanked against the ropes convulsively. She just couldn't help it. "You're using me as *bait!* It's not an *honor!*"

"Well, not if you equate yourself to a worm. That's a terrible self-image, Claire."

Nobody knew she was here, she realized with an awful sinking feeling. Amelie probably wouldn't have ever allowed this; even Oliver might not have. But Myrnin and Hannah were acting on their own. Myrnin was always—well, crazy; Hannah wasn't thinking straight. She'd just had Richard die in her arms, and—

"Oh God," Claire said softly, looking at the woman. "You think it was my fault. My fault that Richard died."

"They were coming for you," Hannah said. "They didn't go for the wounded men on the street, they didn't go for me. They went for the *car*. Where you were."

"Myrnin was in the car! They were going for the *vampire*, not me!"

"Think," Myrnin said quietly. "You know it's true, Claire. Magnus has sought you out for a reason. And now we must use it to bring him here."

"You think you can kill him."

"Well," he said, "I certainly think this is our best and only chance. Once his spawn are dead, he will have to run—for the first time in their history, the draug will have failed to conquer vampires. We cannot afford to let him leave Morganville alive. Or find a hole in which to hide and hibernate and rebuild his hive."

"You're wrong," she said. "He's not going to come here. Not for me."

"Then there's nothing risked," Myrnin said. "And I chose you a very comfortable chair."

This time Claire *did* scream, in pure frustration, and struggled so much that the chair rocked over on two legs. Hannah simply put a hand on the back of it and thumped it down to the carpet again. She didn't say anything. Neither did Myrnin.

They just waited, hunters at the water hole, with the stupid goat tied down for the lion.

I am not the goat, Claire told herself. *I am not.*

All her struggling had loosened the joints on the wood of the chair enough to make it creak, just a little. She had a moment's fantasy of somehow supercharging her strength, ripping the chair apart, whacking Myrnin over the head with a piece of it (more for satisfaction than damage), and grabbing Hannah's gun from its holster to hold her at bay.

That wasn't going to happen, obviously, but it was a nice fantasy.

Something sharp scraped against her wrist as she uselessly twisted it back and forth. Claire froze, and carefully moved her wrist again, pressing.

A nail. It had popped loose from the old wood when she'd twisted around. It wasn't much, but it was something. By pulling her wrists apart, she could get the tough nylon rope in a position to scrape it over the nail, back and forth, until her shoulders were trembling with strain. Nobody spoke. Hannah and Myrnin were just going to let her struggle uselessly, she supposed, except that now it wasn't useless. She could feel the rope fraying—slow, but steady.

Fifteen minutes passed, by the tick of the old clock in the corner. Outside, Morganville continued to be silent. No lights flared against the windows. It was like being on the moon.

And just as she felt she was really making progress, Myrnin turned his head and said, "Hannah, I believe she may be fraying her ropes. Please check them."

No, no, *no!*

Claire yanked hard, frantic with frustration, and felt her right wrist slip loose as the rope gave, just a little. As Hannah bent over to check, Claire risked everything on one awkward lunge.

And grabbed Hannah's gun.

Hannah straightened up, fast, and Claire held the pistol in a shaking hand, aimed at her. "Cut the other ropes," she said. "Now. You can't want this, Hannah. This isn't you. You wouldn't just let me die like this, tied down."

"We'll protect you," Hannah said.

"You *can't* protect me! At least let me try to protect myself!"

"Hannah," Myrnin said, "stand aside."

If she did that, Claire knew Myrnin would take the gun away.

It'd be easy for him. Even if she shot him, she couldn't stop him. He'd probably gripe about the hole in his shirt; that would be about the worst damage she could inflict on him.

Hannah didn't move, though. She was blocking Myrnin's path. Her dark eyes were on Claire's, and for a moment Claire saw just a bit of doubt on her face.

"You couldn't do this, either," Claire said to her. "Sit helpless, waiting. Could you? Look, if you want me to play bait, I will. But not tied up."

Hannah reached behind her back and took out a carbon-black combat knife. It must have been razor-sharp; it sliced through the ropes in three quick jerks, freeing her other hand and her ankles.

Hannah turned to Myrnin. "The kid's right. She deserves to be on her feet, at least."

Claire got up, rubbing her numbed hands, and glanced toward the parlor door.

And found that Magnus was standing *right there*.

She froze, unable to move or speak from sheer surprise. He was just as he had been the last time she'd seen him here in the Glass House—average, forgettable, a man without a face of any note until you concentrated a little, and things *moved* behind that shell, things that were wrong and utterly sickening. He was a bag full of grave worms, wriggling. He was rot and ruin and destruction, mouths and teeth and madness.

And Hannah glanced at him, then away, as if she couldn't see him at all.

Myrnin didn't even turn toward him.

"He's here," Claire said through a suddenly bone-dry throat. She could feel the ache in it, where his hands had grabbed and twisted and shattered. "He's in the doorway. Right now."

Myrnin turned and stared in that direction, but it was very

clear that all he saw was an empty space. Hannah, too. Claire clutched Hannah's handgun in both hands, raised it, and fired.

It had a kick, but not as bad as the shotgun; the noise was sharper, like a slap to the ears that left hers ringing. Her eyes stung a little, and her nose hurt with the sharp smell of burning cordite . . . and she hit Magnus, square in the chest.

It didn't matter at all. The bullet passed right through him and buried itself in the far wall. *Well*, she thought, *that wallpaper's toast.* Michael was going to be so mad.

Hannah grabbed the gun from her, holstered it, and tossed Claire a shotgun loaded with silver—but it was too late.

Because Magnus had moved, in a sickeningly liquid, boneless rush, and now he had Myrnin pressed against him as a shield.

Claire brought the shotgun up, but she couldn't fire.

"Kill him!" Myrnin shouted at her. "Claire, I don't matter. *Kill him!*"

She couldn't. She angled around for a better shot, but Magnus turned with her, his teeth gleaming silver-sharp over Myrnin's shoulder. If Magnus bit, he would infect Myrnin just as he had Amelie. The threat was very clear.

"I don't want this one," Magnus said. His voice was pale and whispery, and Claire had the eerie feeling that she was the only one who could hear him. "His blood is tainted. But I will kill him if you don't put down your weapon."

Hannah had backed away, into the far corner of the room, and Claire pretty much forgot her immediately. The world narrowed to the shotgun barrel, Magnus's multiple rows of gleaming teeth, Myrnin's pale, exposed neck and the horrified look on his face.

"Kill him," Myrnin said again. His voice was soft and gentle and very steady. "I don't matter so long as he is stopped, Claire. There are things that are more important than a single life."

"Like I didn't matter when you stuck me here as bait?" she asked. "I'm not you. And you *do* matter." Claire felt the pressure of Hannah's stare, suddenly, from the corner, as if Hannah was trying to tell her something. Something silent, yet important.

All of a sudden Claire realized what it was. This hadn't been quite so stupid an idea after all.

If they could pull it off.

She took a step back, toward the hall. Magnus pushed Myrnin ahead of him, following her. "Drop the weapon," he said again. "Submit. It will be quick."

"Like last time?" Claire said. "Didn't really enjoy that. And I'm not doing it again." She felt giddily like she was channeling Shane now, or maybe Eve. God, she wished they were here. Wished she had people she could trust at her back. "No second dates for you." She took another step back. Another.

Magnus followed, and showed Hannah his back.

And Hannah pulled out a plastic bag full of white powder, opened it, and flung the contents straight at him.

Magnus dived away at the last second, but part of the powder hit him. He let go of Myrnin and shrieked as the stuff settled on his shoulder and turned gray, leaching away his vital moisture. It was the same scream his spawn had given, but deeper, longer, and louder. Claire yelled herself and tried not to drop the shotgun; the urge to stop up her ears was almost overwhelming. Myrnin lunged away, toward Claire, grabbed the shotgun from her hands as he spun gracefully around her.

"Surprise," he said, and gave Magnus a savage grin. "You're not as invisible when you're hurt."

The silver pellets hit Magnus squarely in the chest and tore through him, splintering wood and fabric and wall, breaking the window.

But it didn't work. The shotgun didn't *work*.

The powder didn't take him down. Neither did the silver pellets.

Magnus was still coming.

"God help us all. Go," Myrnin said softly and shoved Claire into the hall. "Run!"

She ran.

CHAPTER TWENTY-TWO

OLIVER

☽

I felt Amelie's hand tighten on mine, and looked up to see her watching me. Her eyes were no longer her own—still gray, but a muddy, watery gray, not the shining steel that they had always been.

She was drowning just as surely as the draug's other victims, but this was somehow even worse than what I had expected. She was trapped within the prison of her own body, drowning in her own extracted and infected fluids. Nothing I could do for her would save her.

"You need more blood," I said, and bared my wrist, but she shook her head.

"It only feeds the other side now. Oliver, I can't. I can't hold."

"You must," I said.

"Kill me or go. You have whatever's left of my city to protect.

My people." For a moment, the queen was there, gazing at me, her vassal. "You *will* save them, Oliver. You must. No matter the cost. Do you understand?"

I smiled thinly. "It has always been my goal. We have simply had differences of opinion about what it meant to save them."

"Humans, too. Don't betray my dreams. My promises." Her eyes slowly closed. "I am very tired now. So tired. It has been a long fight, has it not?"

"Ages," I said. "Against Bishop. Against me. Against a thousand foes, all laid at your feet."

That got me a dry rustle of a laugh. "I never laid you at my feet, Oliver. Never you."

She was wrong in that, and had been for some time, but there was no point in telling her. And I was still proud enough to want to conceal that . . . weakness. "If I am not defeated, then you cannot order me to leave you, can you?"

She released her hold on my wrist, but I kept my hold on her hand. She didn't open her eyes, but I saw the faintest lift at the corners of her mouth. I had won a smile, at least.

But she said nothing else.

Not even good-bye.

I had no warning before she lost the battle. The draug rose in a glistening, heaving surge, coating her, *consuming* her. I fell backward in momentary shock; I could see Amelie's form within it, trapped, but the thick, gelatinous coating on her skin grew in size, multiplying rapidly to cover her. She was only a shadow within it in seconds.

Gone.

I had known it could happen, *would* happen, but I had hoped . . . hoped for more time. For, perhaps, a miracle. I used to place such trust in miracles, in my breathing days when I was right with God.

I had not felt such an impulse to pray in many years, but this . . . this was the face of evil, overtaking us. *God helps those who help themselves,* I thought, and shook myself out of that dark hollow of fear. The draug were enemies, yes, but I had fought enemies all my life, and beyond. Some were well deserved; some I had created through my own actions, and those, I regretted.

But this was pure, a battle against something more evil than I could ever be, vampire or no.

And I had to win.

I drew the silver knife from my belt, the one that Naomi had urged me to plunge into Amelie's chest, and I began to fight for my life.

Where the silver tugged through the draug's gelatinous, rippling, changing form, it burned, blackened, and shriveled the thing; like us, they were vulnerable to it, but unlike us, the silver did not significantly slow it down. A master draug was strong, dangerous, fast, and cunning; a master draug fueled by *Amelie* was far worse. It was still fighting to absorb her power, still vulnerable in at least a small degree, but that would be done soon.

And this room was very small. Our plans were crumbling before my very eyes.

A sound drifted up through the house, shuddering it to its very bones, and I recognized the shriek of pain of a master draug.

Magnus was below, and something—someone—had hurt him. Badly. *Yes. Yes, at last.*

As if fueled by that scream, the draug came for me, and as it did, the form finally solidified, pulled into human-seeming flesh, and it was Amelie striding toward me, pale and strong, but with rot and foulness writhing behind those shining silver eyes.

I took a firmer hold on my dagger, and prayed.

And then I stabbed straight at her chest. *Forgive me.* I didn't mean to kill her, but I had to get her back, the Amelie within. The Amelie who understood what was at stake.

Her hand caught my arm and paused the silvery point just as it touched the writhing slime that covered her body. I felt the stinging agony of the draug's tiny mouths drawing away my blood, even through the protective leathers. "Amelie, you know the plan, you *know what you must do.* Hold on. *Hold!*"

"No," the master draug that had been Amelie said, in a voice like rotten silk. "No more plans. No more scheming. Now you are mine."

And I realized that the draug was in control. And this draug had Amelie's power—the power to compel. The power to force a vampire to her will.

And I sank slowly to my knees under that cold silver stare, screaming inside, as the draug's slime crept up my hand and under the leathers, and began to feed.

CHAPTER TWENTY-THREE

CLAIRE

)

The only place she knew to run, the place she'd be safest, was Amelie's hidden room upstairs. Claire didn't hesitate. She knew the darkened house by memory, and dodged around chairs and tables on her way to the stairs. She didn't dare look back. She could hear furniture crashing, the shotgun going off.

It was so unreal, suddenly. On the sofa Shane's game controllers would be right where they'd dropped them, and the blanket crooked on the back of the cushions; she couldn't remember if they'd washed the dishes or not, or just dumped the last things they'd used in the sink.

This was their *home*. She ought to be safe here.

She was used to the Glass House feeling *alive*, and she still felt it, a little—a pulse, beating slowly beneath her awareness like a big, sleeping beast. There had been a spirit trapped here of the original owner, but he hadn't been the part that had really bonded with her, Eve, Shane, and Michael. That had been the house itself, alive on some level she didn't truly understand.

It couldn't help her now, even if it wanted to. It didn't have the strength, or the will.

She reached the steps, slipped, and almost fell. As she grabbed the banister for balance, she heard the front door smash open, and heard a wild war-cry yell.

She knew that voice. *Shane!* She reversed course and ran for the hallway, then skidded to an off-balance halt. Shane had just come in, holding a shotgun. "Claire!" He locked eyes with her, just for a moment, then started forward . . .

Only to stop as Myrnin backed out of the parlor room firing his shotgun. Shane spun that way, too, aimed, and fired. Claire heard a high-pitched, angry screech. They'd hit Magnus again. Shane muttered a curse and fired twice in rapid succession, then shoved Myrnin up the hallway toward the living room. Toward her.

"Okay?" he shouted at her.

She managed a shaky smile and made an OK symbol with her thumb and forefinger.

Magnus slid/slithered/lurched into the hallway behind him.

Claire gasped and screamed, "Behind you!" Shane lunged forward, landed on his stomach, rolled, and fired upward at Magnus as he came toward him. From the doorway Claire saw more people entering the hall—Michael, Eve, *Jason*? And even, improbably, Miranda.

They all had shotguns. Even the kid.

Michael's shot hit Magnus dead-on from behind as Myrnin and Shane rolled out of the line of fire, and Claire ducked behind the wall. Eve's shot came a second later.

Magnus pitched forward to the wood floor, oozing blackened fluids.

He didn't move.

"We got him," Michael said. "Claire? Shane? You okay? We got him!"

"No," Myrnin called, and kept crawling, well away from Magnus's body. "Not so easily. Careful!"

It was good he said it, because it forced Michael to slow down—and when Magnus reared up, reaching for him with pale, strong hands, he had time to skip backward and fire again, point-blank.

Magnus made a horribly liquid gurgling sound, but it wasn't pain; it was amusement.

Michael backed up fast, pulling Eve with him. They ran into Jason, who was staring at the whole thing as if he couldn't quite believe what he was seeing. "What the hell is it?" he asked. "That's not a vamp. That's—"

"Watch out!" Claire cried, and so did Miranda, almost in chorus, as Magnus's vaguely man-shaped form rippled, changed, and rolled forward. Michael, vamp-fast, pulled Eve out of the way.

But Jason just . . . stood there.

Out of nowhere, Miranda stepped ahead of him and pushed him aside, looked straight at Claire, and said, "It has to be like this. It's okay."

And Magnus then rolled over her.

Miranda disappeared into him, absorbed the way Shane had been at the water treatment plant—trapped inside the bubble of draug fluid. But unlike that time, where they'd been trying to keep Shane alive, Magnus had no interest in Miranda at all.

Claire saw her . . . dissolve. Like flesh dropped in acid. Miranda disappeared in a cloudy mist of red, and in a matter of seconds, what was left of her oozed out to clatter on the floor.

Bones.

Eve screamed, and Michael grabbed her and held her close. Jason had gone milky pale, but he raised his shotgun and fired, three times, straight into Magnus's body.

Magnus ignored it.

Myrnin scrambled up and jammed more shotgun shells into the weapon, then racked it. "None of this will work," he said. "There's only one thing that can kill him."

Shane was up, too, and he was breathing hard, fighting, Claire thought, not to be sick after what they'd just seen happen. "What?" he demanded. "Because this son of a bitch *has* to die."

"Upstairs," Myrnin said. "Lead him upstairs. Claire, *go.* He needs to destroy you, not us. *Go now.*"

After a breathless look at Shane, Claire turned and ran. She scrambled up the steps, only half balanced now, and made it to the top with a surge of relief. The hallway was so familiar, this was *home*, she loved it here, and there was Eve's room with the door open on its crazy, dark chaos; Shane's door was closed. Her own was open, her bed unmade. It hadn't been long; the place still smelled of cinnamon and Eve's perfumes, of chili, of the normal life that had been taken away from them.

We'll get it back. We have to get it back.

Shane and Michael and Eve were down there, fighting for their lives. For their home. *Please, God, please let them be okay.* She could hear the sound of the shotguns going off, but then . . . then suddenly they went silent.

She felt for the hidden controls in the paneling. For a heart-stopping moment she couldn't find them, and then it seemed that they wouldn't work; she glanced back down the hall and there he was, Magnus, standing motionless next to Michael's closed door.

Watching with those terrible, monstrous eyes.

"What did you do?" she asked, and panic smothered her—not for herself but for *them*. For Shane. For her friends.

"They're unimportant," he said. "You have a power the others do not. You must not survive to lead them to me again."

His whole body rippled in a sickening, *wrong* way, and she knew that she had seconds to live. *No. Not again.*

She slapped frantically at the controls to the hidden door, and it popped open in the paneling. She charged in and slammed it shut. It was inky in the shadows down here, but at the top of the steps she saw the warm, colorful glow of the Tiffany lamps. Safe up there. It had always felt like another world. If there was any-place Magnus couldn't reach her, it would be here.

Deep down, Claire knew it wouldn't be enough. But there was a portal up here, and maybe, just maybe, she could get through, get out that way . . .

She reached the top of the stairs and saw . . . Amelie. But not the Amelie she knew. This was only the shell of her, glossy and hard, and underneath was the same rot and writhing awful foul-ness that was inside Magnus.

Amelie was a draug, a *master draug.*

The creature—*like* Amelie, but *not* her—was holding Oliver by both wrists. He was on his knees in front of her, face upturned and marble white, and Claire could see the horror in his eyes.

The loss.

There was a silver knife on the carpet next to Amelie, and Claire, not even thinking now, threw herself at it, grabbed it, and plunged it to the hilt into Amelie's back.

The shrieking knocked her backward into the wall, then into a shuddering, fetal ball with her hands over her ears.

Amelie let go of Oliver and turned toward Claire, just as the wooden panel opened below with a sudden cold rush of damp air.

The smell of dead things doubled.

Oliver toppled over heavily to the floor, facing away from Claire. She tried to get up, tried *hard*, but nothing was working in her body. It was like receiving a violent electrical shock. She couldn't stop shaking.

Something wet slithered over her outstretched foot, and she pulled it in closer, whimpering. That touch felt like worms and mold, filthy water, dead flesh. She was grateful it lasted for only a second, and then was past her as Magnus flowed up into his human form, facing Amelie—or at least the draug that had once been Amelie.

She pulled the silver knife out of her back and stopped screaming, and for a second neither of them moved.

Magnus said, "Your transformation is almost complete. You will be a beautiful and terrifying thing, my queen."

She said nothing. Her silvery, shimmering eyes looked empty as a moonlit lake.

Oliver made a raw sound, and it took Claire a moment to realize that he was laughing. "You've lost, Magnus," he said. "Your thralls are dead."

"You were passing clever in using human science. I will have to find a new defense to counter it." Magnus didn't seem overly concerned about it. "No matter. I will create a new generation. They will have resistance to your poisons. And after all of you are dead, they will learn to feed on lesser fare. I have heard there are seven billion humans on the earth now. Enough for us to feed for thousands of years."

Oliver pushed himself up to a sitting position. He looked awful, but there was fire in his eyes, bright and furious. "No," he said. "You won't. Because you're not leaving this place alive."

"I am a master draug. You, fool, can't kill me. But you'll make a fine addition to my blood gardens." The draug reached down for him, and Oliver batted the hand—the misshapen thing that passed for one—away.

"You're not the only master draug here," he said.

"You mean my lovely creation?" Magnus laughed, a sound like saws rubbing together, and Claire flinched and fought the urge to cover her ears. "Your former queen? She has no thralls. No hive. She is no master draug yet. She will make her own kingdom, yes, but not here. This town is mine. You and the last of the vampires are my meat. She can feed her spawn on the thin blood of humans, far from here, when I allow her to go."

The draug that had once been Amelie was watching him with blank concentration, and something eerily like hunger. She took a step toward him, and Magnus watched her without any sign of alarm.

"You forget something," Oliver said. "Legend says a master draug cannot die by the hands of *vampires*. But it says nothing about dying at the hands of another *draug*."

Amelie continued to advance with steady, relentless steps. And this time Magnus backed up. Just a little. "I am her maker," he said. "And she must obey my commands."

"Think you so?" Oliver sounded viciously amused. "Try."

Claire pulled herself into a tighter ball. *This is bad,* she thought. *Really bad. I need to get out of here.* Being in the middle of this was like being caught in a swarm of hornets, but despite the panic tearing at her, she knew that if she tried to get up, tried to run, Magnus would kill her instantly.

Or Amelie would.

Magnus had forgotten all about her, his focus now on the new master draug before him. "Stop," he said. "I am your maker. I command you to *stop*."

Something happened, deep inside that *thing* . . . the inner dark shadow seemed to thrash, come into focus, and then that was *Amelie*, looking out of the draug. The real Amelie. *Her* eyes. *Her* anger. She wasn't gone after all. Not completely.

She said, "I am a queen. I take no *orders*." She plunged the silver knife deep into Magnus, punching through the slimy shell. He gave a horrible metallic screech as Amelie dropped the knife and reached into his broken shell with her bare, pale hands.

"No one," she said, almost in a whisper, "commands me in Morganville. I command *you*. I command you to *be still*."

His mouth stayed open, but the sound just . . . stopped. He wasn't fighting her. It was as if he couldn't. This, Claire remembered, was Amelie's terrifying gift. She could compel vampires.

And now she could compel draug.

In that awful ringing silence, Claire heard the queasy squishing sound of Amelie's hands pulling out of Magnus's body. Something thrashed in her hands, alive and covered in suckers, mouths, teeth, something horrible dragged up out of the depths of the ocean where monsters lived.

The real form of a master draug, stripped of all its defenses.

Amelie crushed it. It made a wet sound, like a sponge being wrung out, and then there was a sudden, glassy *snap*.

Magnus's shell collapsed, and the thick, murky fluid that inhabited it flooded out in a sticky, stinking rush to the thick old carpets. Claire scrambled up to a sitting position and crawled away from the mess, retching.

Amelie turned to Oliver and gave him that awful draug smile, full of death. "Now," she said, "now it is mine. All of Morganville. All of *you*."

"Not quite," he said. He sounded far too calm, Claire thought, for someone who was about to be horribly killed by something as beautiful and terrible as Amelie was now. "Your transformation isn't complete. You never made a thrall. Never made a hive. And now your maker is dead." He smiled as she reached down for him. "And you will never be a master draug."

She paused, and just for a flicker of a second Claire saw terror in her face. "I rule here."

"You are wrong," he said. "The woman inside you has never surrendered to you, never fully allowed the draug control." He held out his hand, and in it was the leather-wrapped handle of a silver knife. "And never will. Remember who you are, Amelie. Reject this. You have the power to kill her. Do it now."

She took the knife. And then she plunged it into her own body, and with her own hands tore out a small, weaker version of the creature that had existed within Magnus's shell. It shrieked in high, thin tones that made Claire's ears ring, and then Amelie's cold white fingers closed around it and squeezed with remorseless strength.

It died.

Silence.

Amelie's shell cracked like glass, and the liquid flooded out of her, too, in a black gush . . . and underneath lay her vampire body. Horribly shrunken, covered in black spots like mold, but still there. Unconsumed.

The real Amelie, the Founder of Morganville, looked a thousand years old, and she collapsed in a heap like a skeleton held together by nothing but string.

Oliver grabbed her, pulled her away from the blackening spot of the decaying draug, and held her in his arms as he sank down in the far corner of the room. Her eyes were open, but filmed and blind. He fumbled for the sleeve of his leather jacket and yanked it apart with one sharp move, baring a pale, muscular forearm covered with red marks that Claire recognized. Draug stings, in the shape of hands. Amelie had been feeding on him.

And now he was ripping open his wrist with his teeth and forcing her lips apart, giving it to her freely.

It seemed to take ages for her to move, but she finally did, raising her gray hands and taking hold of his arm. Claire had seen vampires feed when they were starving; they wouldn't let go. Couldn't.

But it wasn't like that. Amelie's touch stayed light on his arm, and after a moment she pushed his wrist away. She still looked awful, but the film was off her eyes, and there was a little more of her, as if the blood had inflated her dehydrated tissues. Still a mummy, but able to blink, move, and speak.

She said, "Let me die, Oliver."

"No," he said. There was no real emotion behind it, just a straightforward denial, as if she had asked to borrow a dollar. "You've won. You killed him before your transition was complete. You'll heal."

"I won't," she whispered. "I can't. There is part of me—"

"You'll heal," he repeated. "I'll hear no more of this. You are the Founder, you will heal, and everything else can be dealt with. Your subjects need you, my queen."

"I have no subjects. I am no queen."

Oliver smiled. It wasn't a good thing. "You have been, and will be again. There's nothing to fear. You've won, Amelie. Your enemies, at your feet."

She smiled back a little. "You were my enemy once. I never laid you at my feet."

"Not yet," he agreed. "But for just now, there will be a truce. It's a new age. A bright new age for vampires."

Claire moved, and both of them immediately focused on her, and she wished she hadn't. There was something shining and predatory about their eyes.

"Claire," Amelie whispered, "come here."

She backed away slowly. There wasn't any real chance of her escaping, not from the two of them. She'd seen too much; she knew that. Heard too much they wanted to conceal.

And she'd served her purpose in luring Magnus there. They didn't need her anymore.

"No way in hell," she said, and broke for the stairs.

She didn't quite make it there before Amelie had her in those ice-cold wrinkled hands. She bent Claire's head to one side, brushed her hair aside with a calm, gentle gesture, and said, "You'll have a rare honor, Claire. You will become one of us. Few deserve it more. It is the highest compliment I can give. And it will please Myrnin, as well."

"No," Claire whispered. "No, don't—"

"No," echoed another voice, and it was punctuated by the thick metallic sound of a shotgun being pumped for the next round. "Not her. No way in hell."

She somehow thought she'd see Shane there, Shane defending her, but it wasn't him at all.

Eve's brother Jason was standing at the top of the stairs, a shotgun in his hands. He still looked pale and shaky, but determined. "No way in hell do you take her instead of me," he said. "Naomi promised. She *promised* I'd be turned. You're going to do it or I'll kill you all."

Oliver snarled, showing teeth, but Amelie held out a hand toward him. "No," she said as Jason aimed the shotgun. "He's quite serious. He will fire. He's too close for it not to do significant damage to at least one of us." She considered him for a moment, then gave him a slow, cool smile. "Very well."

"Very well *what?*" Jason didn't lower the shotgun. His eyes were wild behind it. "Swear. Swear as the Founder that you'll turn me."

"I swear as the Founder that you will be turned," Amelie said. "I need the blood, and we have lost significant numbers of our ranks in this war. You will be . . . useful."

Jason nodded, took a deep breath, and lowered his weapon. "Let Claire go first."

Amelie opened both hands and spread them wide, stepping away from Claire. She stumbled forward, not quite daring to come near Jason, either. He gave her a disinterested glance, then moved away from the stairs.

He walked straight toward Amelie.

She came up in one smooth, vicious motion, and all the restraint she'd shown with Oliver was suddenly, awfully gone. Her eyes flared bloodred, and she buried her fangs in Jason's neck. Claire couldn't look away, somehow; that could have been her, *should* have been her.

It didn't take long. Jason collapsed, and Amelie took his weight in her arms, drinking until finally she shuddered, pulled away, and let him fall limply to the carpet.

She looked at Oliver as she wiped the blood from her mouth. She seemed almost herself again. Almost. But there was something savage and bright in her eyes that Claire had never seen before.

"He's yours to finish and raise," she said to Oliver. "I'll not have him as my get. He's damaged."

He nudged Jason with a foot. "I'll find good use for him," he said. "We need new, strong blood in Morganville." Oliver's shining, alien gaze came up to rest on Claire. "You should go now if you want to survive."

For the first time in a long time, Claire turned and ran . . . from the Morganville vampires.

And straight into Shane's arms, as he came charging up the stairs to her rescue.

CHAPTER TWENTY-FOUR

SHANE

It hadn't been much of a fight, because it isn't a fight when your enemy just completely ignores you. I'd never seen anything like that.... Magnus was hard to see—he kept slipping in and out of shadow, blending into the background—but whenever I caught a glimpse of something, I nailed it with buckshot.

I might as well have been tossing rose petals at him, for all the good it did.

I'd tried to cover Claire's retreat, but the fact was, I couldn't stop him from going after her. None of us could. I was still in shock from seeing how fast, how easily he'd killed Miranda; it wasn't as if she was my friend, exactly, but nobody deserved that, and it was a terrible end to what must have been a pretty hellish life.

I'd tried. I'd jumped onto Michael's chair, swung onto the

banister, and then onto the stairs, halfway up. Shotgun ready. I hadn't wanted to die, especially not with the cold, stinging horror of the draug closing over me. But I'd known it would be better than living with knowing I'd let it get Claire.

I'd fired at Magnus, knowing it wasn't going to do any good, and closed my eyes.

And then something—not Magnus, not even one of my friends or allies—tossed me like a rag doll off the stairs into a windmilling, uncontrolled fall that ended in a bouncing landing on the sofa.

Saved my life.

And that was when I saw her. Miranda. Pale, flickering, translucent. Holding a hushing finger up to her lips, and giving me a sweet, crazy smile.

The Glass House had a brand-new resident ghost. Too late for me to stop Magnus, who'd already passed us by and gone upstairs; Jason, who'd been about as useful as snowshoes in the whole fight, had run up after him. I rolled off the couch and saw that Michael and Eve were standing together near Myrnin; Michael's arm was around Eve's shoulders, and she was crying a little.

Myrnin should have looked sick, or horrified, or *something*, but instead, he just looked . . . smug.

I wanted to break that grin in pieces, but when I lunged for him, Miranda was in my way again. Granted, she couldn't stop me, but she could chill me to the bone, and she did. *No*, I heard her say. *This has to happen.* She didn't sound especially happy about it.

"Claire will be all right," Myrnin said. He sounded unbearably happy with himself. "We planned this, Oliver and Amelie and I. We needed him here, in her place of strength, and Claire was the only bait tasty enough to lead him to the trap."

"Then you don't need her up *there!*" I said. "She's done her job. I'm going to get her."

"No, not yet," he said. He was looking up, as if he could see through the ceiling. We all instinctively looked up. Even Ghost-Miranda's glowing form, which was starting to gradually take on flesh and substance, like a real live girl. Drawing on the power of the house.

"We have to wait," Miranda said. "It's not done yet."

The *hell* with them. If Jason could go up, I could, too. I headed that way, but Myrnin's room-temperature hand shot out and locked me in place. "Not yet," he said. "You heard the girl."

I put my shotgun business end against his chest. "You're going to want to stop touching me now. And I'm getting Claire. You know, the one you're willing to let Magnus *eat.*"

"He won't," Miranda said, with that same eerie calm that she'd always had. "Wait. Please."

I should have pulled the trigger. Thought about it, real hard. But instead, I looked at Michael, who was always the one with the cooler head, and he said, "She's always right, isn't she?"

She always was. Damn her.

When Miranda finally said, "You can go now," Myrnin let go of my wrist, and I took the gun from him and ran for the stairs. I don't even remember pounding up them, just landing at the top, and seeing, in the murky shadows, Claire running toward me.

Into my arms.

I dropped the shotgun and hugged her close, but I kept watch down the hall, just in case. There was no sound. I saw a glow of electric light cut off as the hidden door to Amelie's upstairs room slid shut.

Whatever had just happened, it was over.

I picked up the gun one-handed, held on to Claire's waist with the other, and walked her downstairs. The others were gone, except for Miranda, who smiled at Claire. Claire, after a shocked second, smiled back. "You're—here."

"Yes," Miranda said. "I'm home. Right where I'm supposed to be. Don't be sad. It only hurt a little." She twirled a little, and vanished in a sparkling haze. I was pretty sure that when Michael had been a ghost, he hadn't been able to vanish at will. Or, for that matter, sparkle.

She popped back in, just her face hanging in midair. "They're in the parlor." Poof. Gone.

"We are really going to have to tell her to stop doing that," I said. "Because it's upsetting." I turned to Claire. "Are you okay? Really?" I couldn't stop touching her, smoothing my hands over her skin, her hair, her face. She had red marks on her wrists, and a nasty bump on the head. They'd tied her up, and she'd struggled. None of that surprised me, although I was going to take it out of Myrnin's hide.

"I'm fine," she said, and I sensed that it was half a lie, but considering how much I'd faked it since the water treatment plant, I could cut her some slack for now. "Hannah. She was in the front room . . ."

I hadn't seen Chief Moses anywhere, but then, I hadn't gone in the parlor. According to Miranda that was where we'd find the others, too, so I led her that way.

Hannah was the first one I saw. She was lying on the floor with her head in Eve's lap; she was alive, too, but just barely. She'd lost a lot of blood from a gash on her leg, and Michael was twisting a belt tourniquet around her thigh to slow the flow. He looked relieved to see us. "Hold this," he said. "How are you at field sutures?"

"Lot of practice," I said. Michael handed me a sewing kit—probably Eve's, since it was in black patent leather with a death's head sticker on the back—and went to wash his hands, or lick them clean, whichever. I tried not to think about it. I took his place at Hannah's side. "Is she awake?"

Hannah's eyes slowly opened, and she gave me a hard-edged smile. "Still here," she said. "Lost more plasma than this in the last blood drive."

"I think you've got a sliced vein," I said. "I don't know if I can fix it. Either way, it won't be pretty."

"Do your worst, kid." She shut her eyes again. "Scars are the least of my problems."

I gritted my teeth and pulled the wound open, and immediately saw the vein. It wasn't far beneath the surface, and it hadn't been sliced through, just nicked; if it had been an artery, though, she'd have expired already. I handed the sewing kit to Eve. "Fix me a needle," I said, and grabbed the vein. Claire was still next to me, hovering. "Towel. Clean one. I need something to mop up the blood so I can see." She dashed off.

Myrnin settled himself in the corner. He'd been to the kitchen, I saw, and come back with a blood pack, which he opened and chugged. I glared at him as Eve handed me back a threaded needle with a thick knot. "Thanks for your help," I said, as sarcastically as I could. Which was pretty damn sarcastic.

"If I had come near her in my present condition, I wouldn't have been able to swear to her safety," Myrnin said, and took another drink. "It's been a very long, trying day. Proceed."

I did. The vein was tough to hold on to and stitch, but I managed—it wasn't pretty, but it held when I let go. I started in on the cut itself, sewing the edges shut. "Hey, Hannah," I said, "Eve gave me yellow thread. Sorry about that."

Hannah dredged up a dry laugh. "Festive. I like it."

Eve watched me anxiously, bottom lip between her teeth, as I finished off the stitches. Claire came back with a towel and I cleaned up the mess as best I could. It wasn't leaking much now.

"Amelie and Oliver," Claire said. "They're upstairs. Someone should see—" She was staring at Eve, but looked away when Eve glanced her way. "See about Jason."

"What happened to Jason?" Eve asked. She sounded almost resigned, though. As if she already knew.

"I'll tell you later," Claire said.

"They made him a vamp," Eve said, and Claire looked up, fast. "I already knew he wanted it. It's not a good thing. Not for us, anyway."

"Definitely not," Michael agreed, from the doorway. "I checked upstairs. Nobody's there except a pile of rotting slime. Amelie doesn't clean up after herself."

"She doesn't have to," Claire said. "She's the founder. The queen." There was something about the way she said it that made me wonder what she'd seen. And what was coming.

Myrnin finished his blood pack and said, "They've gone to hunt."

I closed my mouth on the question of *Hunt what, exactly?*

Because I figured I already knew.

The draug were finished. All of the vampires' enemies, gone.

The rules of Morganville were changing, and I had the feeling that they wouldn't be in our favor.

EPILOGUE

CLAIRE

☽

"You're certain," Father Joe said. He stood across from Michael and Eve, lit only by the candles burning in the holders on either side of the altar and the sunlight bleeding through the stained glass. "I haven't seen any paperwork from Amelie allowing you to do this." Father Joe, Morganville's resident priest, looked exhausted. They all were exhausted, Claire thought. The lights still weren't functioning reliably; most of Morganville was in the dark at night, and deserted, though the first buses were scheduled to return today to bring those who'd evacuated back to town. Water was on, and the pipes had been flushed, tested, and declared clean.

Not that Claire was taking any chances yet. Bottled water was a must.

"Amelie's not the boss of me," Eve said flatly. She was, Claire thought, *very* angry about her brother, though she hadn't talked about it. At all. She looked at Michael. "Or him, either."

Father Joe gave him a long, considering look. "If Amelie is against this, there'll be trouble, Michael," he said. "What you're asking is binding not only for the church and by law, but in ways that I can't explain among the vampires. You'll be . . . elevating Eve to a new status. It could protect her, or it could make her even more of a target. You understand?"

Michael nodded. "I understand," he said.

"And you don't want to wait."

"No." Michael didn't say anything else, but, Claire thought, he didn't need to. He'd come ready for this. There weren't any tuxedos, or gowns; Michael had pulled out a dark suit, a gleaming white shirt, and a nice tie. He'd forced Shane to wear one, too, somehow; there must have been some arm-twisting that Claire hadn't been privy to, but then she'd been busy rooting through Eve's closet with her, trying to come up with something wedding-appropriate at a moment's notice.

Eve had her gown. It was red chiffon, and it fell in waves from a beaded bodice. Her arms were bare, and she hadn't gone with a veil at all. The dress, Claire thought, made her look about six feet tall, and incredibly graceful, but it was shockingly *not* wedding wear.

Which was what Eve had wanted, of course.

Claire was wearing her best dress—one with buckles, one that Eve had bought for her—and high heels that were higher than anything she'd ever tried before. She felt awkward, until Shane looked at her, and then the feeling changed into something hot and proud.

"You promised," she said to Father Joe. "You said that you'd do this if they wanted it. Well, they want it. We're here. Official witnesses."

He sighed and nodded. "I'm only warning you that what you're doing may make complications you haven't considered. For you all."

"Don't care," Eve said. "We're ready. And we're not letting them stop us again."

Michael was holding Eve's hand, and although he wasn't saying much, he was utterly still and solid and *there*. If he was scared, or worried, it didn't show at all. He glowed like marble and gold, and for the first time in the light of the candles Claire noticed there were threads of copper in his hair, like his grandfather's much redder hair. He even looked like Sam just now; Sam, the kindest and best of the vampires, who'd died at the hands of humans.

She hoped that wasn't some kind of omen.

"Then let's proceed," Father Joe said. "Are there rings?"

Shane dug in his pocket and held it up—not the traditional diamond, Claire saw. Eve must have insisted on a ruby. And a skull.

"Then I suppose there's no turning back. Let us pray," Father Joe said, and bowed his head.

The door at the back of the church opened, admitting a burst of pure white sunlight, and out of it came four figures. Two were holding umbrellas to shade the others in front, and as they shut the doors behind them Claire recognized the ones in the back as Amelie's security, dressed in their dark suits and glasses again.

Amelie was wearing white, a blinding white silk suit that tailored itself perfectly to her body. Her hair was up in a pale blond crown around her head, and she wore a ruby pendant in the hollow of her throat.

Oliver was next to her, wearing black leather.

"No," Eve whispered. "No, not *now*..."

The vampires walked down the aisle and came to a halt a few feet away. Amelie's eyes were wide and cool gray, no hints of red, at least. She was wearing white gloves to match her suit.

"What's this?" she asked in a very neutral tone. "Father?"

"They've come before the altar to be joined in marriage," he said, and for the first time Claire heard strength in his voice. Real strength. "They're in the presence of God now, Amelie. And not under your control."

She raised her pale eyebrows and fixed Michael with a stare. He met it without wavering. "And yet," she said softly, "they must leave this church, and live in Morganville, and I assure you, that is *utterly* under my control. I put out a call for all those in town to help us restore the town. Yet I find you here."

"We'll help," Eve said. "But first we're doing this. And you're not stopping us." She sounded brave. And very certain. "You can't."

There was a little sparkle of red in Amelie's eyes—or it might have been the candlelight. Claire hoped it was, anyway. "Can't I? That is . . . debatable. But I grant you this hour. Enjoy your . . . respite. Tomorrow begins the dawn of a brand-new Morganville. We will rebuild."

"Together," Claire said, and drew that cool, icy stare.

"Perhaps," Amelie said. "And perhaps that is one of many things that will change."

Oliver spoke up for the first time. "The next time you do something without permission," he said, "it'll be the last. New rules, children. Brand-new rules. Remember that."

And he escorted Amelie out, trailed by the guards. The doors boomed shut behind them.

Eve let out a shaking breath. "So, that's . . . not so great," she said. "Michael, maybe—"

He raised her hand to his lips and kissed it, looking straight into her eyes. "No," he said. "No more letting the world tell us what we ought to do. We know, Eve. *I* know."

For a moment she didn't move, and then she smiled, and it seemed to light up the whole church.

"Yes," she agreed, and turned to face Father Joe. "We're ready."

Are we? Claire wondered, but she quickly buried the thought as he began the prayer.

They had to be.

Because now there was no going back.

TRACK LIST

Music is important to my process of writing. It's the first thing I do before I start a new book . . . pick at least ten songs for this track list. Then, as I go along, I search for more music to fill it out and keep the soundtrack in my head going. I think I got some particularly juicy songs for this one! Hope you enjoy them . . . and *please*, remember that, like writers, musicians exist on the money you pay for their work. So please pay to play.

"Iron"	Woodkid
"Way Down in the Hole"	Blind Boys of Alabama
"Two Against One"	
(featuring Jack White)	Danger Mouse & Daniele Luppi
"Pumped Up Kicks"	Foster the People
"Stranger"	Katie Costello
"Me Me Me"	Kids in Glass Houses
"Death"	White Lies
"Vampires Will Never Hurt You"	My Chemical Romance

"With Light There Is Hope"	Princess One Point Five
"I Can See Clearly Now"	Screeching Weasel
"Heroes"	Shinedown
"Little Lover's So Polite"	Silversun Pickups
"We're Through"	Smile Empty Soul
"Back to You"	Thenewno2
"Beyond Here Lies Nothin'"	Bob Dylan
"Hero"	Scarlet Haze
"Preliator"	Globus
"Gypsy Woman"	Jonathan Tyler & The Northern Lights
"Static"	King's X
"Beating Heart Baby"	Head Automatica
"We Want War"	These New Puritans
"Bury Me with My Guns On"	Bobaflex
"Self Control"	Dukes
"Poster Child"	Lions
"Blood"	Band of Skulls
"Monster"	Paramore
"The Sound of Winter"	Bush
"Renegade"	Paramore